LIFELINES

LIFELINES

Heidi Diehl

Houghton Mifflin Harcourt
Boston   New York
2019

For information about permission to reproduce selections from this book, write
to trade.permissions@hmhco.com or to Permissions, Houghton Mifflin Harcourt
Publishing Company, 3 Park Avenue, 19th Floor, New York, New York 10016.

hmhco.com

Library of Congress Cataloging-in-Publication Data
Names: Diehl, Heidi, author.
Title: Lifelines / Heidi Diehl.
Description: Boston : Houghton Mifflin Harcourt, 2019.
Identifiers: LCCN 2018036017 (print) | LCCN 2018038739 (ebook) |
ISBN 9781328482792 (ebook) | ISBN 9781328483720 (hardback)
Subjects: | BISAC: FICTION / Family Life. | FICTION / Cultural Heritage. | FICTION /
Contemporary Women.
Classification: LCC PS3604.I3447 (ebook) | LCC PS3604.I3447 L54 2019 (print)|
DDC 813/.6 — dc23
LC record available at https://lccn.loc.gov/2018036017

Book design by Chloe Foster

Printed in the United States of America
DOC 10 9 8 7 6 5 4 3 2 1

For my mother, Margrit Meinel Diehl
and in memory of my father, John Dornfield Diehl

A walk expresses space and freedom and the knowledge of it can live in the imagination of anyone, and that is another space too.

—Richard Long

LIFELINES

LOUISE

2008

LOUISE WAS A PASSENGER in her own car. Richard, her husband, the inveterate cyclist, was driving her to the airport. When they got to Amazon Parkway, he turned left instead of making the right that led to the freeway, the fastest route there. They passed the rose gardens, then the pizza place run by second-wave hippies. Soon the streets were unfamiliar. Houses sank into hard yellow grass. Flowers, their stems bleached and brittle, offered no premonition of the rainy season ahead. Louise had lived in Eugene a long time; it was nearly impossible that this terrain could feel new. But Richard taught urban design, and he never took the same route twice. *That detour made us discover those donuts,* he liked to remind her. *We never would have found that park.* Life presented constant opportunities for research, he told his graduate students.

And maybe he wanted her to miss her flight.

It was October, and for the first time in many years, Louise was not shackled to the school calendar. At fifty-nine, she was newly retired, or perhaps just unemployed. Until a few months earlier, she'd taught art at a private school across town — the Cedar School, with its experimental curriculum and sliding-scale tuition — but in June, the principal had confirmed the swirling rumors: the strapped school would be closing for good.

Normally at this point in the fall, Louise would have been dreading the annual barbecue at the vice principal's house — a time for teachers to get together and moan about their seasonal panic, to swap verbal recipes for horrible dips made of sour cream. Now she longed for that familiar slump. The usual classroom anxieties had filled her recent dreams, and it took a few minutes in the middle of the night to remember that she wasn't going back.

This drive to the airport prompted similar feelings: she was urgently nostalgic for Eugene's hippie pizza and ordered green spaces, even though it was all still right there, the colors softened by fog.

Richard squeezed the wheel. "Remind me what I'm doing with the wood."

Louise had charged him with maintaining her project while she was gone, adding a piece to the cumulative sculpture she had been working on for almost twenty years on the land behind their house.

"The next piece is in the garage," she said. "With the drawings." She'd cut plywood into triangles and squares already, their sides four or five feet long, and painted them. Each new shape was added to a line in the yard that pushed forward and turned back as its tail end decomposed. The rules were simple: a new piece and two photos on the 18th of every month, documenting how the untreated wood had faded and settled into the earth. The wood's decay was the most interesting part — it gave her a way to measure time, to feel its pressure. An ongoing reminder, a clock. The *18th* project was at once a utopian vision — that plotted spectrum against the green grass — and a document of its failure. Fading and breakdown left in its wake. To see both the possibility and the aftermath offered a gratifying sense of control.

What will you do when you run out of space? people often asked. That wasn't the threat. Their two-acre yard cut into a patch of forest at the edge of the property. She could work on the project at the same rate for decades longer; the wood's decay cleared space for a return, and that promised room had always reassured her. Money was the real limitation. The question was whether she and Richard could afford to stay in the house now that Louise had lost her job and her pension.

"What about the camera?" Richard asked.

"One shot from the ladder, one from the roof," Louise said. "You know how to do it."

He'd done it before. Taken over for Louise when she was out of town. But it was unusual for her to go away without him. The two of them timed their trips around the project—camping on the coast, visiting their scraps of extended family. Some things were unavoidable, of course. Graduations, weddings, parents' weekends: occasionally they fell on the 18th. Louise would ask their younger daughter, Margot, to set the next piece, or else a friend, if the whole family was away.

"What if the pictures come out wrong?" Richard asked. Back when she'd first devised the project—an eroding line—Richard had been the one to suggest the photos in regular increments. She hadn't switched to digital photography, at least not for the strict confines of the project. Her simple rules made it easier to keep going.

"You've always done it right," Louise said.

Richard nodded. He knew exactly how to take the pictures, but knowing and wanting to be told were two different things.

Louise would be taking three flights that day. The first leg was from Eugene to Las Vegas, and then the second would go on to New York, a city she'd never visited. The place where artists were supposed to go, the center of the market she eschewed. She was happy to make her work far from that inflated scene, and she tended to say this out loud, so that Richard could hear her. Because New York was also where Louise's ex-husband, Dieter, lived.

But now Louise's daughter Elke was there, too. Elke, who was thirty-five, and the daughter of Dieter, not Richard, had moved to New York from the West Coast that year. Louise and Dieter had split up when Elke was a baby, and Louise had barely seen him since.

For the twenty-five years Louise and Richard had been married, they'd maintained a tacit agreement that Louise wouldn't see Dieter any more than necessary, an understanding that would have seemed absurd —paranoid, extreme—if ever spoken aloud. Instead this arrangement was enforced in the way they lived. Louise and Richard on the West

Coast, Dieter on the East. Elke the one to move between them. The envoy, the dual citizen, the constant reporter.

But today New York would only be a layover; Louise knew that her ultimate destination vexed Richard even more. Elke was going to meet Louise in the airport, and together they'd fly to Germany, where Dieter's family still lived. It was in Düsseldorf that Louise had met Dieter; Düsseldorf was where Elke had been born. But Louise had left Dieter and Germany and art school in 1974. She'd never been back.

Elke had called last week, though, asking her to return. "My grandmother died." The very first thing Elke had said, efficient in her delivery of this news. Her professional mode. Elke was a corporate recruiter, or rather she had been until a month ago, when she was laid off from her job, the one she'd relocated to New York for.

Sitting in the kitchen with the cordless, Louise had to study Elke's words. Her grandmother. Hannelore. Dieter's mother, in Bad Waldheim.

Louise fumbled with her condolences. She'd known that Hannelore had Alzheimer's; she'd been slipping away for years. This was not unexpected. Yet the news came with a swift punch. Hannelore, Louise's former mother-in-law, had, at one time, been both an ally and a burden. Sitting now at her own kitchen table in Oregon, Louise remembered how Hannelore had helped her care for infant Elke, how she'd cared for Louise, too. Louise could nearly taste the soured milk that Hannelore had poured for her, nutrition necessary, she'd said, while Louise was nursing.

"There'll be a funeral," Elke said. "At the end of next week."

"So you'll be going there." Elke had the time. She'd been looking for a new position—she had the job-hunting skills, obviously—but hadn't been lucky so far.

"That's the thing." Elke's voice had gone soft now. "I was wondering if you would go with me."

Louise thought of the half inch of sugar that was always left at the bottom of the milk's cool glass. Hannelore's advice gentle and insistent at once. But she was in her own kitchen now, not at Hannelore's flowered bench. She couldn't go back. Out of the question. Ridiculous, for everyone involved.

"Why," Louise asked carefully, "do you want me to go with you?"

"I don't want to go by myself."

"Dieter will be there. You won't be alone."

"I know that," Elke said. "I want you to be there, too."

"That's his family, not mine. Germany's not my place."

"I was born there. You've never been back."

The line was quiet. The sound of a siren from Elke's end.

"The funeral is on the twenty-first," Elke said. "So we could spend time in Düsseldorf. I'd like to see your old haunts, and it'd be good for your work. To see your art school again. We could go to Berlin, too, go to museums. You could look up your friend Ute. You have more time now. You should be focusing on your art."

"Does Dieter know about this?"

"Not yet," Elke said. "He's leaving for Germany tomorrow. I thought I'd run it by you first."

A sign that Elke knew she was being nuts. And yet there was something desperate and vulnerable in her daughter's voice that made Louise want to consider her request. And beyond that, Louise felt she owed it to Hannelore. When Louise left Düsseldorf with baby Elke, she hadn't gone to see Hannelore. She'd never said goodbye.

"I'll have to talk to Richard about it," Louise said.

And she did, that evening, though she already knew how he'd respond.

"It's not really the time for expensive trips," he'd said at the kitchen table. They needed to make more of a dent in the house payments, he argued — they'd remortgaged in order to send Margot to Reed, on top of the huge mortgage they'd started out with when they bought the house in '89 — and with Louise working less, that task would be harder.

"One flight is not going to cost us the house," Louise said.

"The economy is tanking," Richard said. "Our property value is pretty much guaranteed to drop. I don't want to be underwater on the house."

"She's only asking me to go for a week." Louise had to consider what was best for Elke, too.

"It's up to you," Richard said. "If you feel you should go." But his face made his misgivings clear.

Now, in the car, Richard was braking at a four-way stop. He squinted at the intersection. Four drivers, stridently cordial, waiting for the other cars to go. A distinctly Eugenian contest of patience and manners, or rather a contest for displaying those qualities. *No, you go, I insist.*

"I'll give you a full report on Margot's show," Louise said. Their daughter, Margot, was in an experimental band — Sky Mall, a name Louise wasn't supposed to laugh at — and somehow the ramshackle outfit was touring Europe. Funding for the arts, Margot had told Louise — Europe was so much more progressive than the States. Margot was twenty-three; she'd graduated from Reed last year and embarked on this foray into the avant-garde. Louise knew Richard was hoping Margot would get back to her plans for a PhD program in political geography, but she was proud of their daughter's imagination. Louise could understand Margot's creative ambitions. Elke's corporate career had always mystified her.

"I can't believe the coincidence," said Louise. She wanted to emphasize that she wouldn't be spending much time with her ex-husband and his family — she'd be going to Belgium, with Elke. They'd see Margot.

Richard nodded. "It's fated," he said. "A cosmic journey."

Elke had said something similar, without Richard's note of sarcasm. She'd called Louise the day after her sudden request, jazzed and confident. "I just talked to Margot," said Elke. "Her band's going to be playing in Belgium. It's actually not that far from where we'll be. We could go see them play. Or drone, or whatever it is they do."

Never mind that Margot lived in Portland, two hours from Eugene, that Louise could see her band perform much closer to home.

"It's serendipitous timing," Elke said.

Now Richard kept glancing over as they followed the long road into the airport. In his professional life, he solved problems with information that could be measured and qualified. An errant wife must have been like a dangerous intersection—study patterns of use, collect data, implement calming measures. A problem to be solved with staggered lights, a subtle gradation in the asphalt.

"Margot says their music is made entirely with microphones," Louise said. *We're improvising, Mom,* Margot had told her. *It's like this perfect fleeting world when we finally get it right.*

"They drone," Richard said.

"We'll have to go see them drone when she gets back to Portland."

"Psychedelic drone, she keeps saying," Richard said. "What does that even mean?"

At the terminal, he reached for the glove compartment and pulled out a little homemade sign to prop on the dashboard—*Clergy on Call.* Louise wasn't sure what Richard was pretending to be—a monk, a priest—but he used the sign in parking crunches in downtown Eugene or on campus, where, because he usually biked, he'd never bought a permit. He relied instead on the suggestion of spiritual emergency. The trick worked, most of the time.

Richard wheeled her suitcase into the terminal. The departure desks made an unbroken line. Louise could have brought her students here, instructed them to sketch. Lessons in perspective everywhere she looked, though she no longer had to think this way. There was something wonderful, selfish about that—everything she saw could feed her own work—but she was uneasy, too. If they had to sell the house, she'd lose her studio and the site of her project.

Richard stayed with her until the x-rays. "Imagine the plane is resting on a giant bowl of pudding," he said. Louise hated flying. "That's all the stratosphere is, anyway." It was his turn to soothe. The human joint, their friends called Richard. Something in his loose limbs, his easy expression. The way he asked questions. He could have been an investigative journalist. A therapist, probing gently, or a radio host, ready to expound.

"Hurtling through tapioca," said Louise. She promised she'd call, they'd Skype, and then he left her to go through.

On the other side of the terminal, moving sidewalks floated forward, carrying Louise through the airport's soft buzz. Outside the broad windows, there was tarmac and forest. And beyond that, a glimpse of the Cascades—another lesson. *Think about what happens when you look into the distance,* Louise used to tell her students. The things that were farther away were lighter; they were harder to see. How could you convey that distance? With texture, with shadow, with shade.

Later, as the plane lifted up, Louise thought of what she'd once read, that a crash was most likely to happen during takeoff or landing. The risk was strongest in that liminal space. Between things. So she found only temporary relief once the plane reached its cruise. With a complimentary half ounce of pretzels, she waited for the dangerous return to earth.

She'd be arriving in New York that evening. Louise pictured Elke at the baggage claim, where they'd planned to meet. At thirty-five, Elke still wore the same expression she'd had as a little girl: determined, making up for the shortcomings of those around her. She was taller than Louise, and wore shoes that exaggerated her vantage point further. Elke carried herself with an awareness of what she looked like, gorgeous and impeccable, a bit weary, as though her appearance was still another burden she had to bear.

And though Elke resembled her father, Louise couldn't picture what Dieter would look like now. A loser, she feared, though perhaps that could also be satisfying. She could recall his voice, the way he leaned on certain syllables. German words came swimming through her mind —those perfect, absurd names for things. Elke had told Louise that

Dieter had a dog. *Lebensabschnittsgefährtin,* Louise thought, a companion for old age. Together in the evening of life. As far as she knew, Dieter was otherwise alone.

When Louise thought of her time with Dieter in Düsseldorf, it was always Easter, invariably early spring. Everything was yellow, all flowers and rabbits and eggs. But she knew her memory was incomplete. There'd been autumns at the Kunstakademie, spent painting in her drafty studio, where she unraveled her professor's fierce, vague guidance. Summer at Hannelore's house in the country, with newborn Elke. Strange for Louise to realize that she was nearly the same age now as Hannelore had been then—Hannelore had seemed like an old lady, with her set hair and exacting rules. And Hannelore had lived through poverty and war. That must have aged her, too.

The summer came back to Louise in color. Washes of blue and green, and black coffee in the afternoons. The orange umbrella over the table, the berries in the *rote Grütze* that stained the bowl a purplish red. Hannelore's garden had been the site of Louise's closest moments with her mother-in-law, their confidences.

Hannelore was gone now, and though Louise's apology for taking Elke so far away could only be symbolic, she still felt it was important to pay her respects. But she wasn't sure if Dieter would want her to be there. She'd written to him last week, to ask him if he was comfortable with her coming to the funeral, though Elke had assured her that he was. It took her a long time to compose the message—she'd never emailed him before.

I have a deep appreciation for what your mother did for me, and I was very fond of her. But I want to be sure that my coming to the funeral is all right with you. I hope that if you weren't comfortable with my being there, or didn't think it was appropriate, that you would let me know.

She and Elke had their tickets by then. Dieter didn't write back. He was already in Germany. Maybe he had no internet access there. Maybe he didn't really use email. Only a few days had passed, and he'd had a lot to deal with, certainly. But she'd feel better now if he'd responded.

The plane would be landing in thirty-five minutes, the pilot announced. Louise had an hour layover before her connection to New
York. She couldn't help but think about it: what if she'd gone there
with Dieter when she had the chance? How might New York's constant
stream of inputs have affected her work?

She called herself a public artist now, and she mostly made site-specific installations. But as the plane's wing sliced through clouds, above
a distant grid, she was thinking about painting. She longed for the time
when she'd devoted entire days to that slow unfolding.

The plane's slow descent was registering in her ears. She prepared for
another lesson in perspective, one that seemed impossible—her tiny
daughter, enormous in front of her. Louise would be in New York soon,
where Elke would be waiting just beyond the gate.

LOUISE

1971

LOUISE SET COINS ON the counter, and the cashier, encased in a collared smock, used two fingers to pull them back. Then—with just one finger—she slid Louise a key. It was so quiet there. The lobby's floors and walls were tiled in the green of worn glass. A turnstile indicated the capacity for a crowd, but the lobby was empty except for the scrubbed promise of chlorine.

She didn't understand how it would work: she needed to bathe, rather urgently, she thought as she climbed the stairs. Her scalp itched; her hair was thick and woolly. But the cashier hadn't offered instruction. A high balcony framed a swimming pool. Roman columns cast an ancient silence over the water. Old women with hard, set hair drifted toward the deep end, their faces careful above the surface.

Louise wanted a more rigorous cleanse. The thermal baths, this place was called—how stupid that she'd expected a tub. Another door led to the sauna and, within, flowered curtains enclosed a bank of lockers. There was no separation based on gender, just one small space for everyone to change. She folded her clothes, wrapped her towel around her torso. She had to get to it. She'd only paid for an hour.

When Louise arrived in Düsseldorf for the start of the school year a week earlier, she'd moved into a room in the attic of a three-story house in Unterbilk, a working-class neighborhood not far from the center of town. The Kunstakademie had helped her find it. *Unterm Dach,* they told her—under the eaves. She had a bed in one sloped corner, a desk, a radio, a chair. Everything she needed was perfectly contained. Almost everything. The toilet was on the second floor of the house, and the landlady had told her that she'd have to bathe in the public bathhouse near the Hofgarten, an enormous, leafy park.

"You can go on Saturdays." Loose flesh wobbled from Frau Kerbel's arm as she pointed. "There you will have a nice bath."

Louise wrote down the directions. "There's no bathtub in the house?"

Frau Kerbel shook her head. "We've been through a lot here, you know." She was indignant, as though this absent plumbing resulted from something Louise herself had done wrong. It wasn't until later that Louise realized the older woman hadn't answered her question.

All week Louise had stooped at the sink, scrubbing her armpits and dusting talcum powder through her hair. But now it was Saturday, and she was going to bathe properly. Buying soap and shampoo required only basic phrases, the type she'd drilled in her German classes in high school and college. As an undergraduate in Eugene, she'd planned to become a language teacher — language represented escape from her parents' narrow world. Her parents had never left Oregon, and their life in small-town Cottage Grove was isolated and routine. When Louise was fifteen, her parents, only moderately religious before, had been born again; they joined a new church that preached in ecstatic, frightening terms about end times and the Second Coming. They wanted Louise to be baptized, too. She refused and left for college in Eugene, just twenty miles from their house in Cottage Grove. She bulked up on French and German in her first two years, before she declared her major as studio art. Now, freshly graduated, those endless verb conjugations had brought her to Düsseldorf, where she was on fellowship as a guest student at the Kunstakademie.

She'd set up her studio the day before, stretched canvas and purchased paint, but she hadn't started working yet. She'd learned since arriving that the Kunstakademie was the best art school in West Germany, which only added to her uncertainty. The students she'd seen so far were serious and assured, and the studio prompted the same feelings as the sauna: she'd wanted to hunch over, face the wall.

With her towel cinched, she joined two elderly women in the sauna. *"Morgen!"* the ladies cried, stretching the word to a melody. These women used their towels for bench covers rather than discretion. They chatted about grocery shopping; from what Louise could pick up, the butcher was their next stop.

Louise had been to hot springs in Oregon, where she'd dipped in naked, not so self-conscious. But in that setting, she'd had some padding. Usually a few joints were going around, a warm flirtatious buzz. Here in the sauna, she was sharply aware — the cedar dry in her nostrils, the raw light from the overhead bulb.

One of the women squinted at Louise's towel. "It's not hot enough, right?" The old lady's skin was deeply tanned, all of it — clearly this wasn't the only place she'd gone nude.

Louise was supposed to keep her eyes up, but she studied these elderly bodies, their skin limp and leathery. She wanted to draw.

When the heat got to be too much, she left the sauna and circled from an icy shower to a steam room with more blue tiles. The hall was lit by sun through frosted glass, and lined with shower heads, all of them offering only cold water. Louise saw one man among the shuffling old women. He was young, his hair wet against his neck. She didn't look at his body, just glanced quickly at his eyes.

A cold plunge, a hot float: Louise was aware of the man's orbit as she moved through each room. She went to the deck for fresh air and found a shriveled bather eating a meat sandwich, while others stood casually bare over the street below. When she came back in, she allowed herself a glimpse of the young man, now under the shower — his back both thin and solid, his neck bent to fit. He yelped beneath the spray, his deep voice an echoing surprise.

She made one more pass through the sauna, and after a few minutes, the man came in, too. There were three of them in the small space —

on the ledge above Louise, a recumbent shopper was breathing audibly, with long, gravelly exhales. The man sat on his towel, just a few feet away. Louise closed her eyes and listened to him breathe, softer, barely there. She hadn't touched anyone for a long time. Her last boyfriend, Ronny Dominick, had left Eugene after graduation—he'd wanted her to go with him to San Francisco, but that choice felt too easy, too prescribed. Ronny, with his political theater troupe that had never performed, his rambling ruminations about his acid trips, was just heading to California for more of the same.

Her towel was wet—from the repeated dips and showers, from her slow and trickling sweat. She kept it pinned around her body and perched so that the fabric covered the lip of the bench.

She drifted. When she opened her eyes, the man was leaning forward, hands clasped and head down. A pose of devotion. An athlete waiting for the score. She stood to leave, dizzy with the heat. Her hour was probably up—better to avoid the indignity of forced removal.

In the hall she used her soap and shampoo, the water a cold blast, and at the locker behind the flowered curtain, she assembled her fresh clothing. She sensed someone on the other side of the curtain, hovering, waiting, perhaps, until she was dressed. She pushed it aside and there he was, fully clothed. *"Wissen Sie, wo man den Schlüssel abgibt?"*

He'd asked something about the key, but in the sauna's lingering haze, she couldn't add up his words. He was looking right at her, expectation radiating from the points of his eyes and cheekbones and jaw. Blue eyes, with a worn quality that matched the tiles.

She told him that she didn't know—*"Ich weiss nicht"*—but her voice indicated something more to him. Recognition crossed his face. In English, he told her that his name was Dieter.

She introduced herself. Her hair was gathered over one shoulder, soaking her shirt. Dieter lifted his key. "I don't have certainty about where I am placing the key," he continued in English. He was nearly a foot taller than her, in a black shirt open at the collar, a dark line up to his hair, which was becoming wavy as it dried.

Louise switched back to German; her ability was on par, at least, with his ability for English. "Downstairs," she told him, and they walked together to the desk. Dieter nodded to the attendant, who lifted her chin as she accepted their keys. They went through the turnstile and out to the courtyard, where a long driveway led to the street.

"I notice that you're American," Dieter said. "So I'm guessing that you're new to Düsseldorf." He looked at her, a measuring she didn't mind.

"Was it my accent or my appearance?" It was hard to banter in German, difficult to be spontaneous as she ordered that slow string of beads. But Louise, newly clean, was emboldened. She'd spoken only to Frau Kerbel and the officials at the school, and those conversations required cordial obedience. This was something else.

"Your accent is impeccable." Dieter's smile was knowing, maybe sardonic. Her physical appearance allowed her to fit in—her brown hair and eyes indicated no overt nationality. She could have been German. But her hesitation prevented that passing.

She asked him if he was a student.

"No," he said. "But you probably are."

"I'm a painter." It was easier to make this declaration in another language. The word had burned her parents, the symbol of a life misdirected, of false idols and sinful behavior. Her parents had told her, vaguely and then exactly, that she should not go to Germany. They wanted Louise to stay within a thirty-mile radius and become a teacher or, better, a wife.

I'm praying you change your mind, Louise's mother had said when Louise announced her plan to study abroad in Düsseldorf; this was how Mary communicated, using God as a go-between to deliver her disapproval.

"Are you from Düsseldorf?" she asked Dieter. They were walking along wide Nordstrasse.

"I grew up in a small town in the country," he said. "It's not far from here."

"So did I," Louise said.

Dieter glanced over with a teasing smile. "You grew up in Bad Wald-heim?"

She shook her head, tried to match his long strides. "Cottage Grove." Shoppers hurried around them, confident and removed, holding flow-ers or bread in thin paper bags. The idea of Germany she'd carried with her from the U.S.—those pictures from her textbook, of red-faced farmers, of women in folk clothes spilling frothy beers—stood in con-trast to this muted elegance.

"Louise of Cottage Grove." Her details sounded different in his voice: the "eh" he added to the end of her name, the careful trip over the *t*'s.

"Oregon," she said. "The West Coast. But small towns are all the same." Over the summer she'd attended an advanced German immer-sion course during the day, reviewing grammar while she waitressed at night. She'd been ready and assured in the classroom—she'd mastered the *Dativ*, was reading Rilke and Mann. But now her sentences were halting and disordered.

"Small towns are similar," Dieter said. "But it's different here." A stern shadow passed over his joking tone.

"Of course," she said. "I meant in a larger sense." She waved her hand, trying to convey a feeling she couldn't find the right word for, the cramped judgment she'd been happy to leave behind.

They passed a fruit stand, heaped with apricots and peaches and plums. "I'd like to buy an apple," she said. Something to ground the sauna's high.

Dieter nodded. "Get one for me, too."

She picked up two green ones, and a man behind the produce, neat in a shirt and tie, stopped her, waggled the fingers of one hand.

Louise apologized. *"Es tut mir leid,"* she said. She sensed Dieter watching—he hadn't stopped her or told her how it worked.

"Would you like apples?" the fruit seller asked in hard English. "I will select the apples for you."

Fifteen minutes earlier, Louise had been naked with indifferent strangers. But picking up fruit was a social taboo. The man dropped her change into a little dish, and this, too, struck her as odd. Germans might have embraced public nudity, but the fruit seller wouldn't even touch her hand.

Louise and Dieter ate the apples as they continued down Nord-strasse. She wasn't sure what was happening. Dieter was flirting with her, but only slightly; he hadn't helped her with the fruit guy, wasn't offering anything now. Though she wasn't either—she was searching for something clever to say, and whatever it was, she'd have to say it in German. Distracting her, too, was the question of whether his behavior was unsettling—it was a little creepy, the way Dieter had picked her up in the bathhouse. The way he'd waited for her as she changed her clothes. She knew she'd be more disturbed by the creepiness if he weren't attractive—the straight line of his back, the haunted pitch of his features, his loose and confident gait.

He stopped on the corner, even though they had the light to cross. "This is where I turn," he said. With familiarity, as though she knew his routines.

"There's a concert happening tomorrow night," he said. "At eight o'clock in the *Mensa* at the Kunstakademie."

"That's my school." She wondered what the music scene was like here.

"Perfect," he said. "You'll like it. The band is really good."

As abruptly as he'd appeared, he was gone, and again she felt adrift. She didn't know the city yet, didn't recognize the place where they'd wound up. Later she would remember this corner by the Hofgarten, at the edge of the Altstadt—the old town. But it meant nothing to her then. She caught her breath and rehearsed her phrasing. She asked for the way back to Frau Kerbel's house.

In her studio the next morning, Louise sketched the view through the window—a rectangle of the glinting Rhein—and thought about

Dieter's invitation. Even if he hadn't been flirting with her, even if he turned out to be creepy, the show would give her a chance to meet people. In the studio down the hall, she found Gemma Warwick, a British painter she'd met at an international students' mixer a few days before. Gemma could be a buffer, an escape hatch.

"Brilliant," said Gemma. "Let's meet at eight and go together."

Armed with a plan, Louise returned to her sketchbook. Some combination of chance, nepotism, and actual talent had brought her to Düsseldorf—she wasn't sure of the ratio. In Eugene, her mentor had been a professor named Mitch Pringle, who drove down from the Museum School in Portland, whose humor was weighted with the cynical self-deprecation of missed opportunity, strayed ambition. Pringle had studied with Josef Albers at Yale, and he replicated Albers's color studies for Louise's class, pairing paper shapes. A red triangle next to a blue one made it appear more purple. *Change is a result of influence,* Pringle intoned. *Color is fooling us all the time.*

On a field trip to the Portland Museum of Art, she'd stood in front of a Rothko, bewitched. A deceptively simple canvas. The emotional power of the yellow and green fields surprised her—she felt a not-unpleasant loneliness, a sense of longing she wanted to explore. She circled back to that painting several times that afternoon. She hadn't considered until then how to look.

She won the U of O art department's undergraduate prizes for the still-lifes and landscapes she'd produced in class, but those exercises felt rote, and at Pringle's urging she'd experimented with abstraction. For her senior show, she'd made four large paintings that Pringle told her were strong enough to use in an application for a fellowship—a new exchange program attached to the School of the Art Institute of Chicago. Louise could earn a certificate, but really it was about the value of the experience. The European model of art education was different, Pringle told her, and with his recommendation she had a good chance of getting it. He happened to know the man in charge, and the fact that she knew German would help, too. Funding for three years, life in a foreign country. Good for the work, he said.

That evening, Louise went to the *Mensa* with Gemma, in the basement of the Kunstakademie, where she'd enjoyed potatoes and stringy meat during her first days at the school. Now the large room was jammed with people, the smells of soap and gravy the only indication of its usual function. In back beside the folded tables, she stood with Gemma and scanned the crowd.

In the front, a guy was tuning a guitar, and that's where she found Dieter, lit by conversation. All the way across the room, she felt sharp longing. Already jealous of his focus on something else. She kept looking until he noticed her. His smile deepened as he caught her gaze, a private flash in the anonymous crowd.

"A bit stuffy, isn't it," said Gemma, lifting her thin hair off her neck.

Dieter sat down behind the drum set. Of course—he'd invited her to see his own band; *the band is really good,* he'd told her yesterday. As arrogant as that was, she still wanted to see him play. The music started, and Louise, trailed by Gemma, pressed into the crowd. Along with the guitarist, a third guy hunched over a lofted keyboard, and their sound was immediately huge, roaring, distorted, blowing out through giant amps. A rock band, messy and pounding, but without a singer. Dieter was fast, consumed, and yet his arms bent and lingered with a dancer's athletic grace.

In Oregon, hippies dominated the music scene; Eugene was a frequent venue for the Grateful Dead. Louise had found herself caught between two extremes there: her parents' paranoid moralizing or the hippies' sloppy excess. Neither side was right for her.

Now she was paying attention. Her elbows bumped the people around her, even though no one was dancing: the crowd pulsed, radiated rapt energy, but they didn't actually move. The band played without stopping. The guitarist kept jamming on the same notes. And the beat—Dieter—was propulsive, transfixing. His playing was urgent and yet somehow leisurely. A drifting, assured control.

Gemma Warwick tapped Louise on the shoulder. She pressed her palms together, mimed sleep. Louise nodded, relieved. She wanted to listen on her own.

When the band finished, Louise moved through the crowd slowly. Dieter was packing his cymbals into a round leather bag, this neat effort contradicting the chaos she'd just witnessed.

"Louise of America," he said, approaching her, flushed and smiling.

"Dieter of the drum set," she said, staying in English because she couldn't think of the word for drums. It didn't matter; it was too loud to talk, and he motioned to her to follow the clumps of people heading up the stairs. "We'll move the equipment later," he said. "We're going to have a drink first."

As the group pushed through the narrow street, Dieter, keeping a brisk pace, told Louise that the band was called Astral Gruppe. He lived in their studio. The rest of the guys had real places to live, but Düsseldorf wasn't cheap.

"That's why you go to the bathhouse," Louise said.

"Right," Dieter said. "What's your excuse?"

"I just don't have a bathtub," she said. "Is that normal here?"

"Some of the older buildings don't have modern bathrooms," he said. "You must be living in one that survived the war."

She saw the briefest flash of his hesitation. That vulnerability intrigued her. He'd been so certain and direct, assuming she would follow along.

"A strong building," she said, immediately regretting her insensitivity. Too flippant. But it was hard to strike the right tone when she was grasping for words. They were speaking German again.

"Why did you ask me about the key?" Louise said. "If you go there every week."

"Amnesia," Dieter said in English. Smiling.

He stopped in front of a bar—*Ritterhof* in cursive on the sign—and pushed through its heavy door. Inside was all leather and dark wood, an open room rimmed with a ledge just wide enough for slender glasses of beer. The rest of the group pressed around them, and Louise kept her place beside Dieter as he negotiated for drinks.

He handed her a beer. "What music did you listen to in America?"

"The same stuff as everyone else." Music was texture for her, it was wallpaper, a rug, but it was not a consuming passion. "In Oregon people like the Grateful Dead."

He nodded. She hadn't expected him to know what she was talking about.

"You know their music?" she asked. "I thought it was just for hippies." The beer was bitter and rich and setting her loose.

"I love the sound of their guitars," Dieter said. "So you're a fan of the Grateful Dead?"

Louise shook her head. "It was just readily available."

"Surely there was something else."

"The Rolling Stones," she said, because someone had put "Under My Thumb" on the jukebox.

"You like that better."

He was teasing her, but Louise wanted him to know that she wasn't square. "I liked what your band was doing," she said. "Even better than the Rolling Stones. I guess I want to learn more about German music."

He shook his head. "German music is all *Schlager* pop songs—it's boring, completely empty." He leaned closer to be heard over the noise of the bar. "And anyway, we don't really want to make German music."

"Why not?"

"It's not an identity we want to grab on to. The German one, I mean." He signaled for more from the bartender. "They didn't tell us anything in school about the war," he said. "Not our parents either. No one talks about it. They pretend it didn't happen." Caution clouded his face again, and she wanted to tease it out, explore that side of him.

"How did you find out?"

"Other kids," Dieter said. "Listening. Watching. It's in the air. You'll see."

Louise thought of herself as political; in Eugene, she'd gone to demonstrations and drawn up signs. She'd railed about Vietnam to her parents; she and her friends had spent hours dissecting the war, the pointlessness of it, their anger and fear when the draft lottery started. She knew her experience wasn't the same as Dieter's, but she wanted to convey to him that she was trying to understand.

"American history is shameful, too," she said. "We had slavery and Jim Crow. Segregation isn't over, not on the ground."

Dieter was frowning. "You can't compare terrible with terrible. It's different. It's easier to be an American."

"Maybe," she said. "It's all I know."

"And being German is all I know. We have to pretend we don't have any history, when actually we have too much history." He looked at her. "That's the difference from America," he continued. "Here it's as if we don't have fathers."

He stood there looking at her, evaluating, as though she could tell him what he wanted to say next. "I mean it literally," he continued. "My father was killed in the war. I didn't know him."

Louise tried to calculate his age. "How old are you?" The wrong way to follow up, but she wanted to learn whatever she could about him.

"I was born in forty-five." He stood right beside her, sipped from his empty glass. "I was an infant when he died. And I'm twenty-six now. So I've spent my entire life with no father."

Another turn, leading her in. *"Es tut mir leid,"* Louise said. But her apology wasn't quite right—she wanted to convey sympathy, not to suggest she'd done something wrong.

"It's not a happy story." He was stern and yet lit up by what he was telling her. Hardly the usual stuff of flirtation, and yet he was offering intimacy, his head tipped into her ear.

"You'll hear the denial in the way people talk," Dieter continued. "They say, *after what happened,* or *before it ended.* They can't even say the real words."

His speech was slow and deliberate, and whether that stemmed from his thoughtfulness or a desire to help Louise understand, she wasn't sure. But his deep voice was magnetic, giving her rich pleasure as she leaned in to make sense of his words.

Louise saw two of the guys from the band pushing through the crowd. "So do you want to make American music?" Louise asked. "If you can't make German music?"

"I'm not American," Dieter said.

"I noticed." Louise was rewarded with a smile — his eyes looked green in this light.

"We want to make a different sound," Dieter said. "Something new." The guys from the band had joined them, and they ordered more drinks. Dieter moved closer to Louise to make room against the bar. He introduced them: Gerd, the guitarist, whose soft face reminded Louise of a cat. And Klaus-Peter, who'd stood over the keyboard, whose disheveled enthusiasm made him immediately familiar, like the boys she'd known in Eugene.

Louise told them that she'd enjoyed the music. And they responded with a string of jokes and asides that changed the conversation's tone. She learned that Gerd, who'd studied architecture at the Kunstakademie, was teaching there now, and Klaus-Peter was a sculpture student. Dieter kept Louise in the circle, touched her shoulder and her arm. She felt that the night could continue indefinitely, but at the end of the round, the men set their empty glasses on the bar.

"We have to move the equipment back to the studio," Dieter said. "I'll see you again soon." He kissed her cheek, a gesture disappointing in its formality, and left her holding the details of their earlier conversation, the weight of which she wasn't sure. As she watched him wind through the crowd with a series of elaborate goodbyes, she realized he hadn't asked how to reach her. He disappeared; she felt herself lurch after him.

In her attic room the next morning, Louise wrote a letter to her parents. She crammed the thin blue airmail paper, detailing Frau Kerbel's house but omitting the bathing details. For her father, a mechanic, she described the tiny, spare German cars; for her mother, who tended sprawling flower beds in the yard, she wrote about the Hofgarten. How funny, how strict, that this public park had cordoned-off lawns and signs warning visitors to stay on the path. But the gardens and court-yards were beautiful, the blossoms set in straight lines.

She finished the letter and mailed it on her way to the Kunstakad-emie. She could feel the pulse of the previous night's music, her steps propelled by the unexpected pitch of her conversation with Dieter. She wanted to produce something worthy of that intensity.

Louise shared her studio with two guys, Ulf and Joachim, who os-cillated between quiet focus and easy joking. They were in her class, which would be led by Hartmut Knecht, a color field painter who'd been prominent in the early '60s, who met with students only sporadi-cally for group critiques. As a guest student, Louise had been allowed to skip the first-year foundation courses, but now this isolation unnerved her.

The students around her were chic, confident, driven, and the school's physical space was dignified, too. The arched ceilings, the sweeping stairs, and marble columns seemed to demand her seriousness. Before the start of the first all-school meeting in the Assembly Hall, the room rattled with competitive gossip. But Louise sensed camaraderie, too, the ease of shared humor, and she longed to be part of it.

She spent her time shuttling between the school and Frau Kerbel's house. Her rental agreement included a cold supper, with sliced meat and cheese and bread left out in the kitchen. Louise would come back late from school and quietly assemble sandwiches. She could hear Frau Kerbel's TV, the upbeat music and emphatic laughter of variety shows, but she rarely saw anyone. She woke early, had breakfast in her sloped room with the percolator and *Brötchen,* though she had no milk for the coffee, no butter for the rolls. There was no place for cold things in her room, and Frau Kerbel hadn't offered morning access to her kitchen.

Louise thought about Dieter and wondered how to find him. She remembered his intensity, the feeling of his breath on her ear. His lanky frame, the shifting shade of his light eyes — she looked for him in the narrow streets of the Altstadt, looked for his bandmates in the *Mensa.* But he found her first, appearing at the door of her studio less than a week after the concert.

It was evening, just beginning to get dark, and she was alone in the studio.

"I was visiting Klaus-Peter," Dieter said. "I thought I'd see what you're painting." His nervousness excited her. The hesitation was in his body, not his face — his hands pushed into his pockets, his stiff slouch against the door frame.

She brought him in even though there was nothing to see. "It's genius work," she said, sweeping her arm over the waiting canvas, a dispiriting white expanse.

"Clearly," Dieter said. "The minimalist approach." A helpful cognate — *minimalistisch.* He invited her to another concert, not his own this time. "But if we're going, we have to go now."

She was wearing the clothes she'd put on to paint — jeans and a T-shirt stained by work done long ago in Eugene, as though the memory of inspiration might coax it out of her now. She changed in the bathroom, ran her fingers through her hair.

The club was a few blocks away. In the half-empty room, they set up with beers from the bar, and while the band played, they stood in the back and talked.

"I'm working in a carpentry shop," Dieter said. "Making furniture." On the low stage, a drummer punctuated a bleating saxophone, and Dieter cupped his hand over her ear, his body bending into hers. He'd done an apprenticeship as a carpenter, he said, a path he'd chosen when

he was eleven. In West Germany, kids were tracked into their profes-
sions early.

"Did you make the right choice?" Louise asked. "I can't imagine
what I would have picked at that age."

A skinny shirtless man, face shrouded by his long hair, was murmuring into a microphone, his words, even the language he was speaking,
indecipherable.

"It's impossible to know what else could have happened," Dieter
said. "But I don't mind the work. And I'm saving money by living
in the studio. Money for a move. I'm not going to stay in Düsseldorf
much longer."

A quick jolt of panic: though she barely knew him, already she was
drawn to him, and she couldn't help thinking about separation, about
losing him if he left.

He wanted to go to America, he told her, smiling.

"To become an American musician," Louise said.

"In New York." He had a cousin who'd moved there, another carpenter, who'd offered to sponsor Dieter's immigration, who could help
him line up a job.

They got more drinks at the bar. Flashing red lights threw shadows over the panes of Dieter's face. Those cheekbones. She wanted to
draw. The next act was all keyboards, mellow and dreamy. Synthesizers,
Dieter corrected her, telling her the word in English, and then he was
saying something else, his mouth was close to her ear, his hand on her
shoulder, now pushing back her hair.

"I'll show you Klaus-Peter's synthesizer," Dieter said. "It wasn't
cheap."

Klaus-Peter came from a prominent family, people with money on
the other side of the Rhein, Dieter told her as they walked past the
Haubtbahnhof, the central station, closed for the night, and through
the shuttered streets. He led her through an interior courtyard and up
flights of stairs. The music studio was a large room with white walls and
the faint suggestion of mold. The equipment took up most of the space

—the drum kit and the guitars in their cases. The vaunted synthesizer, a heavy box on a stand. She thought the promise of the synthesizer was just an excuse to get her back here, but Dieter really wanted to tell her about it, pointing out a series of names and functions.

"It's hard to use," he said. "It has to be plugged in for hours to get warmed up. So Klaus-Peter has rigged all this other stuff to play."

He pointed at a table laid with wires and smaller boxes, but Louise was looking elsewhere, at the traces of Dieter's domestic life: the stack of records, the clothes folded on a shelf with rolled cords. The mattress standing vertical in the corner. He was putting a record on the turntable now, and she wanted to get him closer. She sat on the low couch against the wall.

The sound from the turntable was sprightly, wordless. Dieter turned up the volume. "I love being loud here. It's an industrial space. There's no one around at night."

The blasting music was public, declaring their presence to an empty building that seemed to belong only to them. He knelt in front of the records, flipped through the stack. "What did you think of the show?"

"No one was dancing," Louise said. "But the music was so groovy."

"They were probably waiting for instruction." He was joking, agile. "From you, the American audience."

"Next time." In Eugene, Louise hadn't joined the proud flailing at sunlit folk shows. But she danced at parties, liked being unmoored in the dark.

"These guys are from Düsseldorf." Dieter handed her the sleeve, which had a traffic cone on the cover, a simple orange shape. The band's name, Kraftwerk, splayed across the middle. "We'll go see them play. You can teach the locals how to dance."

She patted the cushion next to her. He joined her on the couch. The next song spread out, and with that languid sound, expectation crackled between them. The faint purple under his eyes, the stubble on his cheeks. Again that quick sliver of his apprehension, a small break in the confident facade.

"Do you always pick up women in the sauna?" she asked.

"You're the first one I've met there who was under the age of seventy." He slid closer. "But I would have noticed you in the city. Or in the Ritterhof. You're always looking so intently. As though you're figuring out how everything is put together."

"Always?" she said. "You barely know me."

He reached for her, a slow investigation. They were alone in the giant warehouse, a secret hidden from the dark city outside. Dieter got up to change the record, set the narrow mattress beside the drums. He retrieved a pillow and a blanket from the shelf, and she followed him to that soft place between the equipment, riding a line of welcome danger —they were in a space meant for working, their bodies exposed in the open room. His breath, his weight unfamiliar, and yet to be with him felt easy, as though she'd known him for a long time. Afterward she didn't sleep, closing her eyes against the thin beam from the streetlamp on the other side of the glass.

In the morning Dieter made coffee in a tin percolator. "It's almost like a normal house," he said. Louise stood by the window with a mug while he straightened the sheets. That neatly made bed belied what had just happened: still hazy with sleep, she'd touched him, felt his body against her own. Now he folded the blanket, then pushed the mattress to its place against the wall, a series of motions she'd soon know as routine.

ELKE

2008

AT PASSPORT CONTROL in the Düsseldorf Airport, the agent smiled at Elke and said something in German that she was too bleary to comprehend. He winked at her, then held his watery-blue gaze. The way he was straining to flirt embarrassed her. These were her people.

"Danke," she said.

"With a name like Elke Hinterkopf," he said in English, "I don't know if I should speak to you German or English."

"English, clearly." She was ashamed she hadn't understood.

"No problems," he said, showing his gums. "Enjoy your stay in Germany, Frau Hinterkopf."

Louise was behind her, next in line, and Elke lingered to hear what her mother would say.

"Ja, ich bin auch Amerikanerin." Louise returned his goofy smile. *"Das ist meine Tochter."* How odd that this was one of the only times Elke had heard her mother speak German.

She waited for Louise to finish, her nerves and anticipation spurred by the terminal's morning buzz. Airports had been a key setting of Elke's childhood, the landscape of her family's sad glamour. Other kids had divorced parents; most lived with their mothers, as Elke did. But the rest of them could shuttle to their fathers' homes in town for weekends or holidays. No one else had a German dad living in New York City. No one also called their father by his first name.

The first time Elke had gone to see Dieter in New York, when she was in first grade, she'd cried in the Eugene Airport; she wanted her mother to go with her. Louise told Elke that she was brave, that she could do it on her own. Always, each trip after that, Elke felt the same uneasiness as she left her mother to board the plane. She clung to Louise's reassurance: *I know that you can be brave.*

But this time Louise was coming with Elke. Elke was thirty-five years old now, and even so, her mother's familiar brightness was a relief, her beacon in a blue sweater and green corduroys.

"I feel like the pope every time the plane lands," Louise said as they moved toward the baggage claim. "I just want to kiss the ground."

Only a week ago, Dieter had called Elke with the news of her grandmother's passing. He'd asked her to tell Louise. Elke knew so little about the time Louise had spent living in Germany that she'd never really thought about her mother's connection to Hannelore before that. That they'd known each other once.

They moved along the corridor now, in a crush of murmuring Germans. Her father would be picking them up in his brother Norbert's car and driving them out to Bad Waldheim. The plan was for Dieter to meet them past the baggage claim: then this strange reunion Elke had set in motion would begin.

"Entschuldigung," a man said, snaking his body through the crowd. *"Danke,"* as Elke let him through.

"Bitte," Elke said. Maybe Elke had wanted her mother to come in part for recognition—she needed Louise to see what she'd done by herself. How she'd teetered along in Germany on her biennial trips here with her father, the language like high heels casting her body into an odd posture, making a show of every uneven step.

But really, she just thought Louise should be there. At first, the idea was strident—Louise owed it to Hannelore, who had always asked after her, who had sent her cards for Christmas and her birthday. Inviting Louise was a surprising impulse, but it had nagged at Elke until finally she'd asked. She'd thought carefully about how to do it, sensing that her mother would say yes if approached the right way. Her mother usually said yes. Elke told her that she could use her support, that she thought the trip would be good for her. These things were true.

Elke believed in gut instincts. She liked to be direct. It's why she'd ended her last relationship—Cedric was sweet but distant and actually a bit bland, and almost two years had gone by like that. Better to end it than keep going through the motions.

But for nearly a year now she'd been single, and though she'd thought that leaving San Francisco had given her a clear direction, that path had also dissolved. Soon after she'd arrived in New York for the new job, the rumors of financial collapse had started; at work, sober analysts projected layoffs and a hiring deep freeze. An apt forecast, it turned out. Elke was fired. And the fact that hundreds of thousands of other people had also lost their jobs that summer and fall was not a comfort.

Elke's gut instincts had not been leading her to great places lately, and yet here she was with her mother in the baggage claim of the Düsseldorf Airport. Louise was alert to the bustle around her, studying a bleached blonde rasping at her children, an old man wiping his mustache with a scarf.

Suitcases dropped from a metal chute. Elke looked at the circling belt, all those neat packages of other people's things. Riding momentum and a wash of feelings—grief and anticipation and unease—Elke had launched her mother's return. But since then Elke's misgivings had nibbled at her resolve. It was crazy to bring her mother with her to Germany.

Things could easily go wrong: her father might be moody, her mother awkward. The German relatives might be uncomfortable, too.

Talking to Richard hadn't helped. She'd spoken to him on the phone a few days ago, and his irritation was palpable. Of course she knew this trip wouldn't be easy for him—no one wanted to think about a spouse's previous life. But she also didn't feel she had to apologize for it. Her grandmother had died, and she wanted her mother's support. She'd thought the fact that they'd be going to Margot's show would please him, but instead that detail only seemed to make things worse.

"It's just such great timing," Elke said.

"Right," said Richard. "Time for psychedelic drone."

"I feel old," Elke said. "I don't know what that means."

"I don't either. And I'm from the psychedelic generation. So the show's in Belgium?"

"It's only an hour away from my grandmother's town," Elke said. "Dieter's going to borrow my uncle's car and drive us there."

"I didn't realize Dieter was going to the concert, too." Richard's tone was careful, tamping something down.

"I invited him," Elke said. "I thought he'd be interested in the music. And it's better this way—he's used to driving over there. The Autobahn is crazy."

A beat, and then Richard responded. "Berlin's supposed to have some fascinating memorials. Monuments all over the city."

"Sometime you and Mom should go to Berlin," Elke said. "On your own trip."

"Maybe."

"I would have invited you this time," Elke said, trying for a joke. "But that would be a little weird."

Richard laughed, a bitter snort. "Louise and her caravan of husbands."

"She's been divorced from Dieter since I was a baby."

Elke could hear Richard's breath. "The timeline wasn't actually all that simple," he said. "I'm sure you remember how wild those early days were, when Dieter came around."

She wasn't sure she knew what he was talking about. She did remember that her father had come to Oregon when she was a kid, but was Richard there, too? She was having a hard time filtering out what she actually remembered from what she thought she remembered because she'd been told about it. And now, more crucially, what had she not been told at all? None of her parents, her three parents, had ever spoken to her directly about that time.

"I was pretty young then." She must have been four or five. Richard had been around for all of grade school—he was the one who'd come to her school plays and her cross-country meets, the one who'd lived with her mother. He'd been a loving, steady presence in her life. He'd acted as her father, even though she already had one.

Her conversation with Richard had left Elke feeling guilty. And now, as her mother leaned in to yank her suitcase's ribboned handle, Elke still wondered if her invitation was a mistake.

"It won't take us long to get out to Bad Waldheim," Louise said as they rolled toward the exit. She was forgetting that Elke had been here much more recently than she had. Which one of them would be leading here?

Elke could see her father through the baggage claim's glass walls, pacing by Norbert's navy Mercedes. He was coatless, wearing two flannel shirts, the collars stacked; he pushed on his silver hair with one hand. Of her three parents, Dieter had been the easiest to convince of this trip—when Elke suggested that Louise come, too, she'd sensed his surprise. But he didn't argue.

"It would mean a lot for me to go to Germany with her," Elke had told him. "And I think it would be good for her to pay her respects." Her father was a Leo on the cusp of Virgo, a complicated astrological border. Elke knew her pitch would have to be direct, appealing to both ego and an embattled sense of self-worth. The zodiac was a quiet interest of hers, a slightly embarrassing tool—Elke had used it extensively in her work as a recruiter. She wasn't completely sure she believed it, but when the combination of her intuition and the zodiac's clear guidance led to a successful placement, she was willing to recognize its logic. She wanted to rely on something larger than herself. An explanation, a reason for things.

Elke and Louise went through the automatic door. "The women of America are here," Dieter said as they emerged. A smiling agitation— he hugged Elke, holding on, clapping her back a few times. There was her father's slightly musty smell, and on top of that now, the trace of a rare cigarette masked by herbal candy, the lozenges that Elke's *Tante* Gisela had always pushed into her hands.

Elke watched him greet Louise; he braced her shoulder, kissed her cheek. Louise's smile, cautious and close-lipped, made Elke feel like a kid in some terrible movie, plotting to get her parents back together. Except it wasn't *back*. She'd never known them any way except apart.

"Fresh off the red-eye," Louise said.

"Your flight was fine?" Dieter asked, more of a direction than a question.

Elke nodded. "I brought you something," she said, pulling from her pocket a bag of pretzels from the plane. Their running joke. When she was a girl and they'd flown to Germany together, Dieter would request extra peanuts and then squirrel them away, surprising her with snacks days later. He'd take everything—the socks and the toothbrush, the little envelopes of salt.

"I'll save it for the right moment," Dieter said. He was pleased, exposing his gold molar.

"Let me take your suitcase," he said to Louise. "It's rather big." He swung the luggage into the trunk.

"I brought a few pairs of shoes and my raincoat," Louise said quietly to Elke. "I like to be prepared for weather."

The last time Elke's parents had been in the same place was her high school graduation in 1991. How much had she registered then, as a self-absorbed teenager? She felt a fascinated apprehension now —studying them as the unit that had produced her, but bracing for their discomfort. She read unease in both of them: the set of Dieter's jaw, the way Louise muttered little *hmm*s, as though muzzling her own thoughts.

"So we go to Bad Waldheim," Dieter said. Louise motioned for Elke to take the front seat. Norbert's car was immaculate—the lines in the just-vacuumed carpet, the little bag for trash.

"I'm sorry about your mother's passing, Dieter," Louise said. "How old was she?"

Dieter had one hand on the gear shift, the other tight on the wheel. "She was ninety-six," he said. "The decline started getting much faster in the last year. So we knew it would be soon. I saw her this summer. She didn't know me, of course."

"Sometimes there were little flickers of recognition," Elke said. "But those faded, too."

"Elke said she wasn't in her house anymore," Louise said.

Dieter shook his head. "An old-age home, since the dementia set in. But Norbert hasn't sold her house yet—his daughter, Julia, was living there with her family until a few months ago. I'm going to stay for a few weeks, to help him take care of things."

He turned on the car's stereo and accelerated onto the highway. "Elke told me that you retired." His CD was starting—free jazz, the drums rolling in.

Louise was leaning her head to the middle of the back seat, her voice in Elke's ear. "It's a big change for me. I'm a bit nervous about it. But it's exciting—I'm going to have more time for my own work now. I'm looking forward to that."

"I read the review of your show on the internet," Dieter said. "The article in the *New York Times* with this sculpture on the highway over-pass." Elke had read it, too—it had been an important invitation for her mother, to be part of a series of public art installations along transportation corridors in Seattle. But the review was hard for Louise to swallow. *Mining traditions of earthworks and outsider art, "Light Above" places reflective materials over swiftly moving traffic, catching and refracting light both natural and man-made. While the piece's central gestures are tired—the broken glass is derivative of more well-known land artists —Willis's work manages a whimsical flair.*

"The review got a few things wrong, in my opinion," Louise said, "but I was grateful for the coverage." Elke knew her mother was upset by the description. Louise wanted the piece to create an emotional, meditative stillness over the chaos of the highway, but the review hadn't mentioned that. *It's embarrassing,* Louise had told Elke.

"Are you still making the sculpture on your lawn?" Dieter asked.

Louise said yes. "It's been important to me to keep it going." Elke sensed that for her mother, the *18th* project was like one of her children, a thing she'd observed and doted on and tracked for years. Louise loved calendars and charts. She'd noted Elke's and Margot's heights on the frame of the linen closet, logged their milestones in a notebook.

"I have other projects I'm still maintaining, too," Louise said. "I have an ongoing piece by a nuclear reactor, a collaboration with my students."

"Sure," said Dieter. "I've read about this one on your website."

"It's been a surprising project," Louise said. "I started it in the late seventies, but unexpected things happened. Those changes have structured the piece."

"What was unexpected?" Dieter asked. His frank mode of interrogation hadn't ever softened to the American style of small talk.

"The piece began when the plant opened. There were protests, and I thought the work would simply serve as a response. Just a way to get my students to engage. But the plant itself was so compelling. There were cracks. Leaks. All kinds of distressing problems. And that captured my imagination, too. The plant's processes, its relationship to its environment, was completely fascinating." Louise was breathless. Elke could hear her mother's nerves twining with the two cups of coffee she'd guzzled on the plane. "That project was always a collaboration with my students. So I'm going to miss that part of my job, too, though the plant is closed now. The decommission is finally over."

"She went to the implosion," Elke said.

"That process was disturbing, too," Louise said. "They buried radioactive waste in the ground. The site is called a park now."

The music was getting louder—the saxophone like indignant geese. Dieter was charging along the left lane. The Autobahn's blue signs blurred past. Elke hadn't been to Germany in four years, and she feared that without her grandmother there would be no reason to go back.

"Enough about me," Louise said. "What's going on with your music, Dieter?"

"The usual things," he said. A little defensive, puffed up. "I'm playing with a few other guys. Maybe you know that I was booking shows at a venue in Manhattan, but that place closed."

"You play at home," Elke said. "He has gear all over the house."

"Sure," said Dieter. "My house is my studio."

"It's nice you have studio space at home," Louise said. "I'm lucky to have that, too."

"Actually, I've been meaning to tell you that I found one of your paintings at my mother's house. From when this one was small." He lifted his elbow toward Elke.

"I can't say I remember it," Elke said. She slipped against the leather seat as they left the highway.

"What did you find?" Louise asked.

"I think it must be from your series," Dieter said. "That summer when Elke was an infant. It's still there if you want it."

He was gruff in this offer, and returning to her father's cadences made her remember how crazed he could be, his reserve occasionally cracking to reveal a frantic energy just under the surface.

Though Elke was used to her father, it was hard to explain him to other people. Dieter in his double sweaters, friends with all the nuts on his gritty block in downtown Brooklyn. To be there with Dieter had always meant traipsing through apartments on his super's rounds as he fixed locks and drains. It meant going to his shows with the ever-shifting group at the club on the Lower East Side, where she'd watch him range over the drums, tacking along with a guitar, a saxophone, an upright bass, as the men at the tables around her called out a determined *yeah* or *mmm*. And she listened to records with Dieter in his living room, to his endless tales of their genesis. Dieter's own music was an essential part of his house, too. He often retreated to the basement, sending keyboard melodies or the faint pulse of the drums through the floors of the brownstone. This was his private music, the sound of her father thinking, and she liked the way, while he was playing, that the notes and patterns wove into her own thoughts.

Dieter had offered her early tastes of adulthood—he gave Elke well-sugared coffee when she was in middle school, and a beer with dinner the winter after she turned sixteen. She'd come during her February break that year, not her usual July. She already had a job lined up for the summer as a camp counselor in Eugene. She had her eye on college and a car; she was saving money for that escape.

She greeted his suggestion of a beer with cool approval, which she thought the situation merited. They sat in his living room, the only room in the house that was actually warm. Was this a reason to call her mother—the heat didn't work properly and Dieter didn't seem to mind? It was February and Elke slept in her coat, the hood cinched under her chin.

"I'm sorry if you find it cold," Dieter said. Genuine apology mixed with a smug observation: "Americans tend to overheat their houses. It's healthier to sleep in a cool room."

She slept on the couch after that first night, waking up to the smell of coffee, which she accepted with a practiced loftiness, too. Over breakfast, Elke and Dieter talked about the wall coming down in East Berlin a few months earlier.

"I find it quite moving, to see people pull the wall apart with their hands, to see them climb up on the rubble," Dieter said. "I wish I could be there."

"Do you ever wish you still lived in Germany?"

He shook his head. "It's not the right place for me." The same answer he always gave her, but this time he said a little more. "It's gratifying, though, to see the way things change."

Elke had watched the coverage on TV with her mother and Richard. Louise sat close to the screen, watched the pieces get hauled away. Elke didn't tell Dieter about that.

"Did you ever go to East Germany?" she asked him.

Dieter shook his head. "It's inaccessible to us. Even to get to West Berlin is difficult — the city is like an island in East Germany. To get there you must drive on a long road through the eastern part of the country. It's forbidden to get out of the car."

"Weren't you curious?"

"Of course," Dieter said. "But life is not providing us with everything we want."

This sense of limitation was Dieter's mantra: *we must save, we must make do with less.* As Elke got older, she realized his strict frugality wasn't necessary — Dieter had been steadily employed for decades, and without rent or a mortgage, his expenses were low. He'd inherited his house in the mid-'80s from his former boss, a landlord who'd owned buildings all over Boerum Hill. Dieter's property value had shot up enormously as Brooklyn gentrified, and still Dieter lived as though he had to squeeze every paycheck.

Elke wasn't a stranger to thrift. Her mother rinsed sandwich bags and patched foil. Richard kept the thermostat low during winters in Eugene — but he didn't turn the heat off entirely. Dieter's behavior indicated a deeper, spiritual poverty, an inability to imagine another mode of living. He had a trick for everything — the bread on sale the second day, or the Metropolitan Museum with its "pay what you wish" policy.

"This is my wish," he said, sliding a nickel to the cashier.

He didn't eat out, he repaired things he'd found in the garbage, he redeemed cans. That winter when Elke was sixteen, she and Dieter were walking home from the supermarket on Atlantic Avenue when his bag tore and a jar of borscht hit the sidewalk. Dieter grabbed the broken jar and drank from it, despite its sharp edges. Cars zoomed past and the air was bitterly cold, and when Elke tried to pull the jagged glass away from his mouth, he put up his arm to block her.

"Stop your hands," he'd yelped, wild-eyed. Elke wasn't sure whether to laugh or shrink away. Her father wasn't laughing. They walked the rest of the way without speaking, but when they got to the house, she helped him wrap the broken jar in newspaper, so it wouldn't cut the person who picked up the trash.

As they pulled into the driveway in Bad Waldheim, Norbert's wife, Gisela, came out to greet them, waving emphatically, flanked by two beagles. She wore a sweatshirt that spelled out: TO WEAR WITH A LOT OF JUNGLE. The dogs were barking next to her, it was raining slightly, and in Elke's sleepless haze, the shirt's mysterious message made a certain sense.

"*Haa—lloo,* Louise," Gisela said. Her cadence clinched the insanity of Elke's plan. That rhythm was so typically German, and yet she'd never be able to explain it to anyone. Something she didn't notice or think about until she was here listening to it, hurtled back to the distant familiar.

"*Ja, wie geht's?*" Louise said loudly.

Norbert had come outside, too. "Louise, it's good you are coming so much distance to see us," he said in bellowing English. He had thick white hair, a moderate slope to his stomach, and an otherwise trim vigor as he shuttled their things from the car.

"It's been a long time," Louise said with a fierce smile. *I know you can be brave.*

"*Das kleine Elkelein,*" Norbert said as he embraced her. She was almost as tall as he was.

Norbert clapped Dieter's shoulder, talked to him about the car. Listening to her father speak German had always been a comforting blur for Elke. She could lean back and intuit his meaning. He was literally speaking for her. This was her way of knowing the language—listening to her father. So much so that she believed her understanding was deeper—she could sense the meaning though she didn't really have the ability to speak. Her father had given her phrases and fragments so she could chat with the relatives: food, weather, school. He'd dictate letters and birthday greetings over the phone, for Elke to send to Hannelore.

To be in Bad Waldheim had always meant sitting with her *Oma* at the table in the green garden, laid with Kinder Eggs or the jar of Nutella beside the *Brötchen*. Hannelore smiling, squeezing Elke's hand. The lace-curtained room upstairs with a hot-water bottle left at the foot of the bed, even on what Hannelore called a cool night in the summer. Elke could make her grandmother happy simply by accepting what she offered. And she sensed that Hannelore was soothed by her presence, by their easy rapport. With Dieter it was more complicated —Hannelore's warmth toward him was marbled with sadness. He'd gone so far away. Now, as they went into the house, Elke stayed close to her father, tried to cushion his grief.

Gisela brought them to the living room, where Elke was freshly startled by the décor, the trophies of Norbert's hunting trips. Deer heads and sets of antlers were displayed prominently. As a child visiting here, she'd been terrified—stuffed birds and a fox with teeth bared. Dieter had told Elke that in the past, Norbert, stridently thrifty, used almost every part of the animals he killed, making sausage with ingredients he kept secret from his children, saving deer fat to grease his gun. Maybe there was a use for the heads and skins, too; Elke imagined he might have tried to make a coat or a hat. But in the end, Norbert's vanity won out, giving way to this tangible proof of his triumphs.

Dieter waved his arm toward the wall. "The museum has a new exhibition."

Gisela folded her arms over her chest. "No animals are permitted in the bathroom. I am telling that to Norbert."

"Real eyes they are not," Norbert said. "They don't seeing you with glass."

Gisela suggested they rest for a while, promising coffee when they awoke.

"Then you are feeling fresh," Gisela said. Elke and Louise were sharing the guest room and its double bed. With her mother beside her, Elke dropped off right away.

LOUISE

1971

LOUISE'S FIRST CRITIQUE was scheduled for October, a date she approached with eager dread. In the studio, she mixed paint while Ulf and Joachim made beefy marks on the other side of the room, their brushwork assertive and clean. She squeezed out blue and yellow, her body thrumming, and willed the colors to reveal a direction.

She'd brought her battered copy of Josef Albers's *Interaction of Color* with her to Düsseldorf, and his words became a mantra. *Color is fooling us all the time.* She found that subjectivity reassuring. To ground herself further, she invented an assignment—painting the view through the window. In Eugene the art studios had been surrounded by gardens, idyllic and pastoral. This new view, through a small window level with her eyes, offered just a flash of water between the buildings. Nature cutting through something static and established. A column of dynamic water flanked by wood and stone, lidded by various skies. The challenge would come from replicating the changing light's reflection. She looked out in rain or in fractured sunlight, pushing to see texture and variation. *Colors present themselves in continuous flux,* Albers had written.

She, too, was in a state of flux. Everything was uncertain—her work, her critique, her German life. And most especially Dieter. She thought about him all the time. The subtle lines of his ribs under her hands, the way his pulse made a slight tremor in his neck. Frau Kerbel's house had a cloistered phone on the first floor — for emergencies only, Frau Kerbel had said. So Dieter would usually just show up at the studio, stopping by several times a week to see her. Without the usual trappings of courtship — phone calls and dates — they were thrust into something that quickly felt both committed and undefined.

She wasn't quite sure what he thought about her, though he was usually the one to come to her. "Louise of America," he'd say as he bent down to kiss her. When she brought him in to see her work, he squinted at her canvas for a long time. She stood off to the side, bracing herself for his response. "It's a little blurry to me," he said. "I don't know if I understand it." This type of honesty was common here, and so different from the American mode of blank praise. But she listened because he was really looking, much more carefully than Ronny Dominick ever had.

Dieter moved closer. "When I look at these lines, I hear music," he said, pointing to the place where the river broke. "It makes me think about playing the drums."

She relished his response, found further connection as they walked through the city together, showing each other little things they noticed. A forlorn dog staring from a window, a kid's scarf stuck in a tree. In the Altstadt, Dieter pointed to subtle damage on the buildings: the lines traced into stone, the marks of bullets and bombs. "Barely perceptible," Dieter said.

Looking at the city's new buildings, Louise had found a quiet insistence on the present: the poured concrete, the glass and steel. Brutalist architecture, Dieter explained it, a deliberate break with the more ornamental past. The clean lines felt timeless, completely without history. They were blank.

Louise told him about the heavy concrete buildings on the U of O campus, also built in Brutalist style. But in Eugene, Louise had joined student protests against those massive fortresses, calling for structures that would incorporate both beauty and function into their lives.

"Concrete is cheap," Dieter said. Even so, Louise thought, Brutalism was about control. It surprised her that no one here was going to fight that.

The Kunstakademie was housed in a grand building from the last century. Damaged in the war and then restored—the building was still stately, in the way it had started out.

"Things aren't old like this in the States," Louise told Dieter as they walked through the narrow cobblestone streets. She was offering a compliment, but he shook his head.

"It's artificial," Dieter said with a tight smile. That bitterness a little wedge.

After the war, the Altstadt had been rebuilt in the same style it had been before, with small adjustments. The half-timbered houses strung with phone lines, the streets widened to accommodate cars. Aside from those little details, though, looking at it, you'd never know about the recent rubble.

On the surface, the Altstadt was pretty and quaint, like a fairy-tale village, and Louise was charmed in spite of what she knew. She didn't tell Dieter how she felt.

During those first weeks of the term, she began to lunch with Dieter's bandmates in the *Mensa*. Gerd, the catlike guitarist, lifted a finger in greeting. "This is Dieter's friend Louise," Gerd said to the group at the long table. His awkwardness—the long pauses, the blinking stare —was compounded by his use of the vague German *Freundin*, which was interchangeably platonic or romantic. Louise felt gawky and shy as she sat at the table. But Gerd's girlfriend—his *Freundin*, though his tenderness toward her made the romance clear—a sculptor named Ute, was warm and emphatic, and Louise liked her right away. Ute, short and busty, wore big sweaters over miniskirts and clogs, a tight bundle of inner fire, her hands always moving to punctuate her various convictions.

Ute told Louise about her professor Joseph Beuys. "A genius," she said, cutting her *Rouladen* with an elegant, two-fisted poise. His pedagogy was inspiring, with seminar discussions in a circle, and total freedom for students to work in whatever mediums they chose.

The last few years at the Kunstakademie had echoed what was happening all over West Germany, Ute said — protests over access to education, over students' say in their schooling. "We had the demonstrations like you had in USA in sixty-eight, too," Ute said. "We saw this everywhere in Europe, that the whole culture is changing. But here the protest has to go deeper. We can't trust authority. Look what that led to with the Nazis. So we're demanding to think for ourselves."

Even so, the Kunstakademie remained strict, and the administration wasn't happy with Beuys. That fall, he'd tried for open enrollment for his class, invited hundreds of students who had been denied admission by the academy. Louise was enchanted by Beuys's sense of possibility. "He says that art is for everyone," Ute explained. "But the school won't let it go on."

In the afternoons, Louise took long walks through the city by herself. Breaks from the fumes, she told herself, time for the paint to dry. Really, though, she wanted to get away from her sense that her new work was uninspired. She'd made several versions of the window painting: technically proficient but otherwise boring, and so she walked everywhere. Walked and looked. She didn't know what she expected to find. She'd never been to Europe before, had never even left the West Coast. In the U of O library, Louise had researched her unexpected new home. A huge amount of damage in the war, she'd learned. Lots of buildings were destroyed. But there was no mention of people. The books didn't tell her where the concentration camps had been, or what had happened to those fortunate enough to survive. And what about the perpetrators of those crimes? Absorbed in the slipstream, that willful blindness that Dieter had described.

She discerned a guardedness in the people around her, especially the older ones. They were so cautious, without American-style chitchat or smiles to strangers. She noticed, too, how Germans marked off what

was theirs—the mandatory lockers in the library at the Kunstakademie, the fences and hedges framing the yards. In stores, customers were
adamant about boundaries, using the little stick to separate their items
on the belt. They were intensely private, even with their groceries.

On the long avenues, she noted the flower boxes pitched high on
hard ledges, the sun umbrellas on repeating balconies overhead. Outside an *Imbiss,* a line of men in blue municipal overalls sat straight
along the bench in front of the store, gripping pint bottles of beer. Her
route took her across the canal that ran down the Königsallee, a row
of department stores with their names in neon, that flash tempered by
elegant cursive. She went into a supermarket and studied the packages. Yogurt, a sour, alien thing. Carbonated water in heavy glass, and
dark bread studded with seeds. She learned to make the right noises by
watching others navigate the shops. The assessing *so* as she arranged
coins for *Brötchen* in the bakery. An empathetic exhaled *ach* or *doch.*
Longer exchanges would give her away, but with these sounds, at least,
she could pass.

With Frau Kerbel, Louise had also settled into familiarity, which meant
that she was subject to the landlady's indirect criticism. Frau Kerbel,
with practiced weariness, would stop Louise in the stairwell: "I should
buy less for *Abendbrot.* If you're never going to be here. It's a crime to
waste."

Louise was used to aphorisms; her parents used scripture as a warning, and she continued to receive these premonitions in letters from
home. *Prayer protects. Foreign soil is Satan's turf.* They were so fearful of
the unknown. But her life here was entirely new. Gradually, with less
to say, or less she could explain, Louise wrote to them in larger cursive
to fill the page faster.

Although the newness could be dizzying, Louise had fallen into a
routine, which helped steady her. Many nights she'd bring discreet
sandwiches from the *Mensa* to Dieter's studio after she was finished
working, after he was done with Astral Gruppe rehearsal. The two of

them could be alone together there, listening to music in the chilly room. In that setting, she was sure of his devotion — Dieter had a particular genius for sensing her mood, shaping her feeling with the music he put on. Prolonging the celebration after a party, he played Can and Amon Düül, and he and Louise spoke loudly to each other about the evening, laughing about where they'd been. Then something gentler when they went to bed — Indian raga and Pharoah Sanders. With every record, he set the tone of the space they shared.

She brought the Albers book to his studio; she wanted to give him something, too. She read to him: *In musical compositions, so long as we hear merely single tones, we do not hear music. Hearing music depends on the recognition of the in-between of the tones, of their placing and of their spacing.*

Dieter, pushing her hair behind her ear, said that music was always about time. Impossible to separate the two. She wrapped her arms around his back, pulled him down beside her on the couch. He could be aloof, austere, but to be here with him, alone with him, was different. The elegant touch he had onstage belonged just to her.

She went with him to shows — Ash Ra Tempel and Neu! and Faust. The music was clean and cold and spare, with men standing over machines, the audience zeroed in with folded arms. Or else the bands were ecstatic, messy, free, with the crowd pulsing in time. In a gallery in Cologne, the singer of Mind Traum released a live lobster into the crowd, unbanding its claws and letting it scrape over the cement floor. The lobster cut a path through the recoiling audience as three drummers kept a steady, ominous beat.

At a club by the water, the music seemed to echo the landscape — guitars and violins were droning, circular, continuously returning to the same note for several hours. Everyone sat on the floor and listened in the dark. It was immense and enveloping, without beginning or end. *We want to make a different sound,* Dieter had told her. And sitting there, drifting beside him, she understood what he was after — the music offered a way into a fleeting, ideal space.

She went to Astral Gruppe shows and watched Dieter and Gerd glance at each other onstage, the two men waiting for their mutual break into an unhinged strut. Gerd taught classes in architectural drafting, tucked his napkin into his collar in the *Mensa,* and that quiet precision belied the manic energy that emerged when he played. Dieter and Gerd's symbiosis was the band's nucleus; Louise envied their charged collaboration. Her work was so solitary.

But when she watched Dieter, she felt connected to him, too. She recognized his focus as he listened, that squinting grimace that marked pleasure rather than pain. The public version of something private: in the packed room, everyone was with him, but he belonged most of all to her.

On the morning of her first critique, Louise brought the best version of her window paintings to the classroom on the third floor, at the end of the long hallway lined with leaning frames. Ulf and Joachim were clustered around the easel with the rest of the class, flanking Herr Knecht, a sweet-looking man who could be quite nasty, portly and topped with a fluff of white hair.

She'd divided the canvas into three planes, the static wood bounding the water, which she'd layered with meticulous detail to replicate the subtle motion and glinting light.

"With this piece, I'm using color to mark change," Louise said. "The canvas becomes a dynamic space. Here I want to capture the way light shifts over time." A phrasing she'd rehearsed, a direct translation of something she'd once said in Eugene. She wasn't sure this new painting met that old goal. An uncomfortable feeling—the tight armpits of a shirt she'd outgrown.

Knecht surveyed the work with a heavy, blinking gaze. "Let's see, *Fraulein* Villis," he said. No one here could pronounce the *W* of her last name. "You must get closer." Knecht was working with purple that term, and now, as he moved his thick hand, she saw the color lodged in the creases of his palm like extra capillaries. "You must look harder if you want to convey the kind of live energy you describe."

"These marks do have an agitated quality," said Heiko Binder, a sardonic towhead who painted photorealistic boats and cars. "But I don't see change."

"I see shifting tones," said Jens Mayer, "but these colors together don't invoke the passing of time for me. The palette feels a bit flat." She'd admired his work—Jens painted with a sure, visceral touch—and his criticism came with an extra blow, because she realized he was probably right.

"Maybe you need to work yourself into a state of this energy you're talking about," Herr Knecht said. "For the canvas to come alive, you must come alive, too."

Deflated, Louise left the critique to have lunch with Ute. Even the potatoes and sliced cucumbers made a jumbled composition on her plate.

"They didn't get it," she told her friend. "Especially Knecht. He barely said anything." She was frustrated that they hadn't understood her painting, but even worse was her sense that their criticism was warranted. Maybe it was an accident that she'd wound up at this rigorous institution. She'd been a strong student in Eugene, but the art department was conservative, and she realized now that her success had come from her ability to follow and replicate rather than think on her own.

"So maybe they don't understand it," Ute said. "The important thing is that you understand it." But that was exactly the problem—Louise felt stagnant, uninspired. She hadn't found a new direction for her work.

Ute told her about the installation she was preparing for the student show at the end of the term, and after lunch Louise visited her studio. *Indigestion,* Ute was calling the piece. She'd arranged photographs of Nazi silverware in place settings on the floor; she'd found the knives and forks at a flea market. "I wanted to buy them so I could destroy them," Ute said. "But I didn't want that awful *Saukerl* selling them to earn something."

Germany's recent history had sat on the edge of Louise's consciousness before she came here. Her outrage was directed at civil rights and Vietnam. And in Eugene, Louise could ignore those injustices if she wanted, retreat into her studio to sketch a still-life. Ute was saying that here it wasn't possible to tune out.

Ute lit a cigarette. She asked Louise about Dieter. "Gerd says he talks about you all the time," Ute said.

"I'm glad to hear that," Louise said. "Sometimes it's hard to know what he's thinking."

"*Ja.*" Ute nodded, passing Louise the cigarette. "Dieter is always brooding. He's deep. But I think he finds something deep in you as well."

"I guess I just want him to tell me that." Louise took a long drag.

"Maybe he finds you a bit mysterious, too. Though I think Dieter likes a sense of mystery," Ute said.

Louise hadn't thought about it that way — that she'd been closed off, too. She'd thought it was obvious to him; everything he showed her was something she wanted to see. And she craved his attention: Dieter meeting her at the door of his studio, his hands on her shoulders, on her hips, the warehouse empty around them.

"It's clear to me what you're thinking about him," Ute said, her broad cheeks stretched further by her grin. "So maybe you should just talk to him about it."

"How is it with you and Gerd?" Louise asked. "He's kind of a quiet guy."

Ute gazed down as she stubbed out the cigarette. "Yeah, maybe so."

Interesting, Louise thought — even though Ute was pressing Louise to be open, she herself was reserved when pushed.

A few nights later, Louise and Dieter were sitting beside the Rhein, and she told him about Ute's project with the silverware.

"All that stuff is still here," Dieter said. "Even though we pretend the Nazis never existed. It makes me feel crazy, like I can't trust my own eyes."

"It's an impossible contradiction," Louise said. In Eugene, her politics had been separate from her work. Painting was a balm for her anger, her confusion, but it wasn't a response.

But now Louise remembered her friend Larry Bryson, whose number had come up in the lottery, who, at his going-away party, was attacked by his friends at the basement keg. They got him drunk and then broke his arm and his collarbone, that violence an act of love. Of protection — with his injuries he was sent to Korea, rather than to combat in Vietnam.

Louise told Dieter about Larry, the simultaneous shock and relief he must have felt during the attack by the keg. "How strange that must have been," she said. "To feel grateful that they had hurt him."

"Completely strange," Dieter said. "Confusing. But that kind of impossible combination is all I've ever known. We don't talk about the war, though we have an East Germany and a West. We don't mention the Holocaust, as though that will make it disappear. But some of the Nazis are still working in the government. We can buy those Nazi forks."

He pointed to the river. "That's why I need a sense of infinity," he said. "That's why I make music. Everything is so close here. The water tricks you. It looks expansive, but you can easily see the other side."

They talked about it — he saw music as a kind of landscape, something big and vast that he could inhabit, an open space to explore. Louise could see that for Dieter, for Ute, a political consciousness and an artistic one had to be intertwined. That was what she'd been missing in her own art. She'd been painting in the same way she had in Eugene, but it was incongruous with what was happening here.

She told Dieter about the ocean. She'd driven to the coast with her parents from the time she could first remember, to camp in the cool, foggy summers, and she missed that place, missed sharing it with them.

Her father pitched a tent behind the dunes, where open sites were dotted with Douglas firs. The ocean often only a sound, an idea in the dense clouds. The view obscured and imagined.

Dieter listened as she described it. "This sounds like your natural habitat," he said. "The painter looking out at the infinite sea."

"And here I am staring at the Rhein," Louise said. "The river is painterly, at least."

"A limited infinity," Dieter said. He was still watching her. "My cousin told me he can go to the ocean in New York City." His expectation was hopeful, shy.

"It's hard to picture," Louise said. "The ocean in the city." She'd never been to New York.

"I think you'd like it there, too," Dieter said. She seized his recognition. That glimmer of a shared future. She remembered what Ute had said—*maybe you're a bit mysterious to him, too.* She told him that she wanted to go with him, and he pulled her close, moved her legs over his.

In her studio, Louise thought about what she'd seen in the Altstadt, that hidden layer in the city's buildings. She thought about the Oregon coast. The sound of the tide, roaring behind the fog. A muted flash of lightning behind a screen of clouds—she wanted to paint toward that. She began a new painting, an abstract landscape, with blocks of red in the foreground, and a faint pink line emerged, barely more than an idea, pinning the composition together. A hidden ocean, its sound visible on the surface of the painting—a pulsing, constant force.

Ulf and Joachim shared an occasional cigarette or tube of gouache, and she joined them to talk through her ideas.

"Landscape is tired," Ulf said, cupping his hand over a match. "That's for my *Oma* at her *Ferienhaus.*"

Joachim shook his hair from his eyes. "But the way you describe the landscape is something more interesting, Louise. It's not for *Oma.*"

Joachim's words bolstered her. She spent entire afternoons adding to the painting and then scraping her marks away, searching for that elusive click, when her mark made everything come together, made it whole. The fall slipped by in those fluid hours. She had no plans to return to the States, and not only because of the cost of the trip. Her mother was right; Louise was held in the grip of something, though it wasn't evil. To go back to Oregon would break the spell, stall Louise's transformation. She wasn't becoming German—she was in-between, not of it but not completely outside either. She spoke English only with Dieter, and even that was mixed with German. Both of them wanted to practice the unfamiliar.

"I like the way you put words together," Dieter said. "Your sentences in German make a window of the way you think." And actually, her thoughts were shifting over, too, a weird sensation. Those repeated phrases were a private incantation, the words of agreement setting a rhythm for her steps. *Ja, natürlich, ja, genau.* And her favorite expression, *alles klar,* which could be both a question and an answer. Everything was clear, as it should be, all right.

Then came the onset of Christmas, with its red ribbons and fir wreaths, and a market by the river selling warm *Glühwein* from cramped stands. The cold white lights made Louise miss her mother's cranberries and colored bulbs.

Dieter took Louise to see his family for Christmas Eve. They rode the S-Bahn out of the city, to the house in Bad Waldheim where he'd grown up. Dieter's mother, Hannelore, was a stout woman in a wool dress who had a swift and surprising lightness on her feet. *"Es freut mich, Sie kennenzulernen,"* Hannelore said. She used the formal *you* in her greeting; her lilting accent truncated her words. Louise leaned in to listen as Hannelore led her to the kitchen, with its embroidered curtains and potted plants. The textbook definition of *gemütlich,* the room sweet and warm and close.

"This is what we do for Christmas Eve," Hannelore said. She lifted the lid from a tin of cookies. "If you're an American, maybe you don't know such things." Hannelore said this bluntly, but with a shy reserve. She pointed to the platter she'd arranged—the round *Nussbällchen* dusted with sugar, the *Kipferls* set in curved rows.

"We have cookies for Christmas," Louise said, "but not as beautiful as these."

Hannelore nodded, pleased. Louise could hear Dieter in the living room, talking with his brother, Norbert, who lived nearby, who'd come over with his wife and little kids. Hannelore had moved the family to Bad Waldheim from southern Germany when Dieter and Norbert were young so she could work in her cousin's grocery store. Norbert had taken over now as manager of the store. Charged with that role, he was assured, cocky, with groomed sideburns and a toddler on his lap.

Louise stayed with the women in the kitchen. Norbert's wife, Gisela, was loud and sunny, her hair cut into a shag. Gisela fell a step behind Hannelore, broke down her dense instructions for Louise.

"We do it like this," Gisela said of the bread, the meat, the wine.

At the table, Norbert studied Louise. He had Dieter's same rangy height, but he was thicker, with soft padding around the bones of his face. "We're glad you're here," Norbert said. "Dieter doesn't usually bring a girlfriend home. Especially not an American one."

Dieter squeezed her knee under the table. "Norbert is a hunter," Dieter said. "He didn't catch these creatures"—he pointed to the *Würstchen* and cold cuts—"but one of these days you'll get to sample his talents."

"Someone has to be," Norbert said. "Dieter just bombards us with his music."

"When I was a teenager," Dieter explained to Louise, "I loved the music I was hearing on the radio so much that I made the light switch in the kitchen turn on the radio, too."

"At quite a volume," Hannelore said. Her laughter was infectious, and Louise was carried along.

Norbert leaned back in his chair, still smiling at the joke. "So, Louise, you're a student?" he asked. She could see he already had his answer, was veering toward some antagonism.

"I'm studying painting," she said.

"No matter what they study, the students are always protesting," Norbert said. "Always making a fuss. But I don't think things are so bad."

"Maybe if you actually listened to the protesters, you'd understand why they're doing it," Dieter said. "Come into the city sometime."

"What am I going to see in the city?" Norbert asked. "The guest workers hanging around the train station? Those Italians are so annoying. They get right up in your face and talk too close."

Dieter exhaled sharply, but Hannelore interrupted the argument with the platter of sausages and *Wurst*. "Take more," she said. "Don't let it go to waste."

Louise looked at her plate without much appetite: the *Wurst* and its geometric composition, with meat squares of unknown origin set in eraser-pink circles. She was offered these same mysterious slices at Frau Kerbel's, and the repetition was beginning to wear on her.

"Always cold cuts, even on Christmas," Louise said quietly to Dieter in English.

"We didn't always have this." He chewed with earnest conviction. "I didn't have a sausage until I was eight years old. It was very difficult after the war."

Louise was chastened and a little surprised; Dieter had never sought pity before, but now she could see his defensiveness. His feelings were more complex than he'd let on.

Later, in the living room, Louise watched Hannelore light the candles in the tree's branches. Dieter set a pail of water in the corner of the dim room. The beauty of the custom—the glinting light against the deep green needles—came in part from its risk. Louise felt lonely and cozy at once. The astringent fir, the holiday mood, made her miss her parents in a way she couldn't deny. She remembered threading cranberries with her mother. With stained fingers, together they'd wound the red strand around the tree. She thought of her father, who'd carved apples for ornaments, whittling faces into the fruit. He dried the apples over the radiator, to preserve their precise expressions; they'd hold just into the New Year.

Though her parents' words were often warnings—*false idols lead to false faith*—their enthusiasms had taught her something else. Her mother admiring the light cracking through a mottled gray sky. Her father leading her over the narrow path through the forest behind their house. Her mother had told her once that she'd wanted to have more children, but the Lord's plan was different, and Louise sometimes imagined it, if she'd had playmates, if she'd not been alone in a quiet adult world. Unknowingly, her parents had shaped her into the artist she'd become.

That night, she and Dieter slept in separate rooms upstairs; Hannelore gave Louise a hot-water bottle for her feet. Louise waited for Dieter to come to her, but she was disappointed—he didn't disobey his mother's wishes.

In the spring, the Grateful Dead played a concert at the Rheinhalle in Düsseldorf, and Louise went with Dieter and Gerd. They shared a joint on the way, and as they tracked along the river in the soft April evening, she told them about the last time she'd seen the Dead play, a sunny show at a farm outside Eugene, with kids and dogs romping in the grass. "It felt like a family picnic," she said. "If everyone in the family got loaded."

"Now you'll have your family reunion with Jerry and the boys," Dieter said. Louise laughed, and felt unexpected pride, to show him something of hers.

She'd never claimed the Dead as her own, but now, as she peered through the huge crowd in the theater and found the familiar bearded figures onstage, she felt a warm exasperated fondness, "Truckin'" a primal echo of home.

It was uncanny to hear those songs here, as part of an anonymous mass. At first, the Germans only nodded their heads cleanly, but the band was tight and confident, and as the music strutted on, the people around her became less stiff. They swayed and hugged and dipped their knees, dancing in the aisles before the ushers herded them back. Louise danced, too.

During the long, meandering "Dark Star," Dieter held her hand and listened with his eyes closed. The music was enormously loud. Gerd moved his head, let his body follow the sound. Louise could hear something of the open, searching way that he played the guitar in this song. She'd always thought of the Dead as hippie stuff, but she was hearing it differently now. As the band wound into their trance-like third hour, she thought that really their music was visionary, intuitive. And Gerd had channeled that influence into his own sound. In the thick press of people, Louise felt it urgently—she had to do that, too.

When the band finished, Louise's ears were blown out, her body thrumming and spent. Dieter sang as they walked home through the Altstadt. *We can share the women, we can share the wine.*

That pleasing sense of dislocation reverberated through the spring. Louise went with Ute to gallery shows in Düsseldorf and Cologne. On Neubrückstrasse, she saw work by a British artist who photographed the path he'd worn into the grass by walking back and forth. She loved the way the artist's process was palpable in the finished work. The Kunsthalle had a show of American land artists. Photographs and films, documentation of work set outside, and the landscape prompted her visceral longing.

Louise told Ute about her parents' house in Oregon. She'd spent so much of her childhood wandering in the pine forest. Time was elastic back then—she had entire afternoons by herself. Her father marked a trail and trusted her to find her way. As an adult she realized the distance wasn't all that great, but as a solitary child her territory felt monolithic, infinitely possible, and hers alone.

"Maybe you need to paint on a different surface," Ute said. "Or in a different kind of space."

Ute's words charged her. She thought about the possibilities—an installation, with her paintings set outside. Or maybe she could get away from the canvas entirely, think about sculpture, work three-dimensionally. She could make a different kind of mark.

Louise had been reading the newspaper at Frau Kerbel's to practice her German, and that spring she'd tracked the new round of American bombing in North Vietnam, the brash moves led by a now distant Nixon. There had been mass protests on the streets of San Francisco, Chicago, New York in response. To be so far away, deciphering the German reports, left a single note shattering in her ears. She wasn't there.

A lonesome feeling—she had no other Americans to commiserate with—that came with some nagging guilt. She had to speak out. So she found some consolation when Dieter suggested they go to a demonstration in Cologne, protesting West Germany's involvement in Vietnam. They drove there with Ute and Gerd; in the square, hundreds of people pressed around the fountain, hoisting hand-lettered signs. *USA Out of Vietnam. No War for Deutschland.* The crowd cheered in response to a man yelling through a bullhorn: Germany must stop participating in American violence. The war in Vietnam must end. His rhetoric pitched the U.S. as the aggressor, the leader of the terrible charge, and though Louise had participated in identical protests in Eugene, she felt caught in an odd limbo now. Not defending the U.S., and yet she was of that place, a lone American carrying the weight of her government's actions. Maybe that was something like what Dieter felt about Germany. She was holding him, was gripped by his arm, with him and still separate. Her body so vulnerable amidst that shifting mass of people, and yet still part of the crowd's excited pulse.

Next to them, Gerd was chanting—*peace now*—his face contorted with fierce conviction, breaking his usual reserve. Ute clapped her hands in an off-kilter pattern. Louise sensed their urgency—this was a chance to show another way of being German. The noise of so many voices fused into a current of sound.

Louise thought about her window painting, the way the static wood buildings made the moving water especially vivid, framed again by the small window. *Change is a result of influence,* Albers said. She was always looking from some remove. Her name had a different pronunciation here, her sandwiches were composed of odd meats. Her perspective was different in this place. But the real change had to go deeper. She was starting to look outward, and her work had to do that, too.

In May the Baader-Meinhof Group organized a string of bombings in West German cities. They were leftist militants; their manifestos claimed their outrage over Germany's denial of its Nazi past, their objection to the involvement in Vietnam. But though the group was condemning government aggression, that message was perverted by their own violence: they bombed office buildings and American army bases in Frankfurt, Augsburg, Karlsruhe. People were killed.

"Those *Arschlöcher* make me sick," Ute said in the *Mensa.* "They're total hypocrites."

Gerd made a sign for his van's back window: *This vehicle is not inhabited by the Baader-Meinhof.*

The public outcry was intensifying—in response to the Baader-Meinhof terrorism, Willy Brandt, the West German chancellor, passed a decree that banned radicals, left wing or right, from working in state jobs. Baader-Meinhof and Nazis were at two ends of the political spectrum, but the new law counted as radical a much wider swath in-between. Going to an antiwar rally was grounds for dismissal, as was mere suspicion of a particular bent.

"It's dangerous," Dieter said. "I thought better of Brandt." Brandt had been part of the Resistance during the war, Dieter told her; a couple of years earlier, during an official visit to a Holocaust memorial in Poland, he'd dropped to his knees in front of the monument, in a spontaneous gesture of apology.

"No public figure ever did anything like that before," said Dieter.

"He said it was unplanned, that he felt the weight of what Germans had done. To me this was so powerful. And now his actions are so extreme. Just when I think Germans are taking a step forward, then we take a step back." Louise thought so, too, though she only nodded carefully—she didn't feel entitled to criticize in the same way.

Even Frau Kerbel was talking about Baader-Meinhof—Frau Kerbel who watched vapid *Schlager* pop shows on TV and was resolutely zip-lipped about politics. One evening Louise found her in the kitchen, hunched with a cigarette and the *Rheinische Post*. Frau Kerbel pointed to the newspaper's headline: ARE THE BAADER-MEINHOF INFECTING OUR YOUTH?

"Monsters," Frau Kerbel said, shaking her head. "With their long hair." She put the paper down. "You should be careful with the friends you're making here. I don't allow these kinds of people in my house."

Frau Kerbel had met Dieter a couple of times, had made it clear to Louise that he wasn't to eat the *Abendbrot,* which left Louise both annoyed and amused.

Now she felt attacked. "My friends aren't terrorists." She was losing her patience with Frau Kerbel. And she'd grown tired of the long concentric circles between Frau Kerbel's and Dieter's studio and the Kunstakademie. Her Saturday trips to the sauna by the Hofgarten had lost their novelty—she bathed at Ute's house now. And she suspected there really was a bathtub in Frau Kerbel's house. Water rushed and gurgled in hidden pipes, for stretches longer than a toilet flush.

She had never worked up the courage to confront her about it, though. She'd just addressed it obliquely, asking if the lack of bathtub was common. She'd never seen Frau Kerbel at the sauna.

"We've always had extra people living here," Frau Kerbel said. "We had to take people in since my husband and I were first married."

The first mention of Herr Kerbel. This missing fleet of men.

"After everything happened," Frau Kerbel said, "we had a housing shortage here."

Frau Kerbel wouldn't even say the word *war*. And she wouldn't answer Louise's question about the bathtub.

Louise didn't dare search for the tub, but she did complain to Dieter. "I'm surprised she lets me use her toilet."

"I'm sure she thought about how to avoid it," Dieter said.

They were sitting on the couch in his studio, the windows cranked open to a warm breeze. Voices carried in from the street, the happy rumbling of a Saturday afternoon.

"We could find a place with a toilet and a bathtub," Dieter said. "You could say goodbye to Frau Kerbel."

"But I would miss her," Louise said, climbing onto Dieter's lap, laughing.

"You're lying," said Dieter, pushing her hair from her face. "Tell me what you really want."

She wanted all of it, she told him—to live with him, to live without Frau Kerbel. His confidence buoyed her. This shared life would mark a notch on the belt of her assimilation, and she wouldn't have to cling to the scanty evidence of their domesticity anymore—the smuggled sandwiches, the mattress pulled down beside the drums. She would get to see him all the time. But still, doubt nudged in. She didn't know what it would be like to live with him, to surrender herself entirely to a shared life. This was a big step, one she couldn't easily retreat from.

They crunched the numbers, figured that Dieter could still save money as long as they were frugal. Louise had two more years of the fellowship, and when she finished, they could go to New York.

"My cousin can help me with a job," he said, "and it will be good for your art there, too."

New York was where Louise, as a painter, was supposed to go. Part of her longed for Oregon's landscape, the visual stimulation she found there—the packed trees, the ocean lost in fog. But she wanted to be with Dieter. They would go to New York together, a future *we*.

RICHARD

2008

RICHARD WAS CROUCHED in the prescribed spot on the flat part of the roof, looking down at Louise's project. Replicating what Louise did once a month: climbing out the window of her attic studio, using the camera to catch the tiles leading to the woods at the edge of the yard. The winding hills beyond Hendricks Park reminded him of his childhood in Southern California. The steep canyons, the sense of dark mystery.

Louise had sketched what he should see in the viewfinder so there would be no question about what she wanted. He'd already set down the piece she'd left behind. The new edge flush with the pink side of last month's piece. Louise had been drawn to squares lately, their neat fitting together.

He held up the camera, looked but didn't press. Louise had left him with this task while she went to Germany. She hadn't asked him to go with her. While Richard had attended conferences in Europe—in Rotterdam, in Copenhagen—he'd deliberately avoided Germany. That wasn't his place.

He climbed back into the house and paced around the room, past Louise's pinned plans for a new project with canopies of dyed cloth. Usually he liked being up here, amidst the traces of his wife's thinking. She kept her pencils and pens in a pile—she liked the spontaneous chaos of her materials, she'd explained.

Louise was unemployed and gallivanting around Europe. It wasn't her fault that she'd been let go, but still, her reduced income was going to be a challenge. She was planning to teach classes on the side, but not full-time—she'd like to devote herself to her art, apply for grants, try to show her work. Richard wanted her to be able to do these things. But they'd have to be strategic in order to hold on to the house.

They'd been here for nearly twenty years. They'd bought the house with a huge mortgage in the flush '80s, when Margot was a baby. Elke had been ten when Louise and Dieter's divorce finally went through, the process prolonged by Dieter's protracted green card quest. But Dieter had started sending Louise child support long before the actual divorce, and Richard and Louise put that money toward the down payment on the house.

Now Richard went to his office on the second floor, to dip into his email. He was glad to see a new message from Margot. *After the show we stayed in this nearby town, a planned community from the 1960s. Big square buildings, a college, but with a preserved farmhouse in the center. Four hundred years old or something. Low ceilings and a stone bar with beer made by monks. Local monks, apparently, though I didn't see any.*

PhD material, Margot's advisor had told Richard after the graduation ceremony at Reed. She'd written her senior thesis in political geography, on the detrimental effects of multilateral trade agreements on subsistence agriculture in Chiapas, and she'd let Richard read it. She was brilliant. She said she wanted to take some time off after graduating to research programs, to get her materials in shape. But now an entire year had gone by and she still wasn't talking about applying anywhere that fall. *Give her time,* Louise kept telling Richard. But too much time was how people got stuck.

Elke and Mom will be at our show in Hasselt tomorrow night—Elke said that Dieter is going to borrow his brother's car and drive them there. It'll be so weird and cool to see them in Belgium.

Richard left the computer. He paced the upstairs hallway, past the girls' bedrooms. Margot's was still decorated with her teenage convictions—the PETA poster, the flyer for a Bratmobile concert. Elke had converted her space to a blank guest room as soon as she left for college. She was more secretive with her things.

But then, Elke had always been somewhat mysterious to him. He'd locked eyes with Margot the moment she was born. She was his completely. And though he'd been a father to Elke, undeniably that relationship couldn't be the same.

The girls were different. Though Elke had grown up in the same household as Margot, Richard still witnessed an ancestral welling up. Maybe he was tapping stereotypes about Germans, but he saw it so clearly. Elke's self-propelled sense of order, her acute awareness of time, something she certainly didn't share with the rest of them. Richard and Louise always willing to linger over coffee, Margot needing to be coaxed out of bed. And there was Elke, her coat and shoes on ten minutes early, goading the rest of them to the car. Elke used to organize her Halloween candy into tiers, still pulling out Snickers in December. Margot ate it all in a weeklong binge.

Richard had been drifting along the hall; he'd wound up in front of his own bedroom. He looked in on their empty bed. He didn't go back up to the studio. He hadn't taken the photo, but he didn't feel like doing anything for Louise just then.

In the car, Richard picked the music he wanted to hear. He was not often behind the wheel—he rode his bike to work, used panniers to transport groceries—and he liked listening to music in the car. *Morrison Hotel*, up loud. Louise's minivan had a surprisingly good sound system.

He was driving without destination. He stopped at a drive-through coffee shack—Jitters, not to be confused with Jiggles, the strip club advertised on billboards on I-5 up near Salem. Margot had made that mistake once when Richard had expounded on that small pleasure of driving—a stop at Jitters, not the same on a bike, he'd said—and looked at him with horror. Her misunderstanding had become a family joke. Espresso, he'd clarified since with buoyant enthusiasm. He had it now, two shots in a paper cup like you'd get at the dentist.

He'd go to Market of Choice, he thought, and buy something heavy to carry home in the car—beer, canned goods, squash. Never mind the rumors he'd heard, that the store was actually run by a closet conservative who peddled health food in a regional empire. The CEO a hypocrite who'd just made a sizable donation to the McCain campaign. McCain-Palin, for God's sake. But right now Richard didn't actually care about that. He wanted to drift through the aisles and look at bright things.

Dieter had always been just outside the perimeter of Richard's life, never completely in focus. The first time Richard had met Louise, in 1978, Elke had been there, too, an almost five-year-old who'd had to have been spawned by someone. Richard had been in the park doing research for his dissertation, photographing a dirt path that cut between the playground and the parking lot—the result of people walking, not the official route paved by the parks department. That one framed the grass. It took much longer.

A woman was there, pushing a girl on the swings. "What are you doing?" she asked.

He thought she was talking to the child. He was crouched down, getting a low shot of the trail's expanse. When he looked up again, he realized she was watching him. She wore a magenta T-shirt, red shorts; her hair was wild; she was bright and immediately present.

"I'm photographing this path," he said.

"Are you an artist?"

"Maybe," he said. "But these pictures are for my dissertation." Richard launched into an explanation. Desire lines, these paths were called: the way people tromp over the grass, skipping the sidewalk and wearing down a path better suited to their needs. Footsteps caused erosion; Richard liked how direct it was. Unconsciously, people were more assertive than they ever could be in the rest of their lives.

Louise was listening as her hand met the little girl's back. "Higher," the child said.

"Think of footprints stomped out in the snow," Richard said. "When the official path gets covered, people figure out their own routes."

"It's a poetic concept," Louise said.

"I think so, too," Richard said. "But desire lines are also useful. Sometimes these casual trails are better. More efficient, more scenic. Easier. And they provide a record of how we collectively use space. Together we all influence each other."

"I'll keep using them, then," Louise said. She introduced him to Elke. He noticed she didn't wear a wedding ring. Not that a ring was the sole indication of her availability. But he wanted to see her again —he liked her hair and her ready laughter and how thoughtfully she responded to him, the gentle, funny way she talked to her daughter. The child was extremely quick. He couldn't imagine a husband in the picture. The two of them were a tight unit. And Louise seemed at once competent and vulnerable, like she might need some care, too. Richard felt he could give that to her. He wanted to be close to her, a feeling he found both unnerving and thrilling.

He kept going back to the park, always at the same time, in the hopes of seeing her. He'd been trained to track routine. When he did run into Louise, he'd tell her about his research, not mentioning that his repeated trips to the park weren't necessary—he'd already gathered enough data. He loved photography, he said; that much, at least, was true. He had an ongoing project with abandoned structures, decaying buildings. He liked how they made visible the passage of time. Taking pictures helped him think through his ideas—he wanted to study how people used space, how they left marks—and he loved how she seemed to get that, nodding as he spoke.

He tried his best with Elke, who was wary of him at first. Kindergarten in the fall, she told him shyly, and he sat on a swing and talked to her; she liked dogs and things that were purple. He got to know them both, but his bigger questions remained—the location and identity of

Elke's father chief among them. Louise still hadn't mentioned him, and Richard didn't want to push.

"You could come have dinner with us," Louise said after their third run-in. "If you're walking our way."

He was biking, actually, across town to his place near Hendricks Park. But he wheeled his bike and walked with them through White-aker. While Louise cooked dinner, Richard played Candy Land with Elke and let her win. After Elke had been tucked in, they drank the last of the gritty jug wine that Louise had transferred to a carafe and sat on the deck, looking out at the yard. Most of the space was taken up by vegetable beds.

"This is where my creative energy is going these days," Louise said of the garden.

"Alexander Pope said that all gardening is landscape painting." Rich-ard had been reading all day.

"Painting in the dirt. Elke would like that."

"Elke is a nice name," Richard said. "Unusual." To him, Elke sounded like a hippie name, not that different from what his friends at the no-nukes meetings called their kids: Rain, Lotus, Dawn.

"Her father is German," Louise said.

The start of an answer. Richard nodded and poured them both more wine, bracing for this information.

"I went to Düsseldorf to study art after I graduated from U of O." Louise drank slowly, her eyes tightening. He could see her considering what to say.

"And I was married for a short time." She laughed and then stopped, which Richard attributed to nervousness. Later, when remembering that evening, he would wonder if she laughed because she was, at that point, still married, something that only became an issue for Richard when her husband appeared in Oregon a few weeks later.

"Is Elke's father still in Germany?" An invasive question, but Rich-ard had to say something, and, besides, he wanted to know.

Louise nodded. She was flushed, a bit apologetic perhaps, and though Richard had more questions, he didn't ask them just then. He was thinking of his own experience. He hadn't been part of anything so dramatic: no marriages, no life in another country. No children, and Louise must have been older than him, he was realizing, if Elke was going to be in kindergarten and Louise had gone to Germany after getting her undergraduate degree. He scrounged for a detail to prove his worth. Richard was twenty-six then, not ready to be a father.

Louise looked similarly stricken. He wished they had more wine. "It's not ideal," she finally said. "But the entire situation is not ideal."

Richard didn't press that—he barely knew her—but he held on to her careful delivery, her wistful expression. His questions were right there, already formed, ones he would carry with him for a long time. Who was this man? Why had she left Germany? Even then, when he wasn't entitled to jealousy, he felt the thick mass of it forming in his stomach.

"Your desire lines remind me of what I used to do as a kid," Louise said. "My parents let me wander in the woods all the time."

"By yourself?"

"I was an only child," she said. "Somehow I always found my way back."

"I wish I'd had something like that," Richard said. "I grew up in a subdivision in Orange County. A model bedroom suburb."

"That has its own opportunities for exploration," Louise said. "Your concept is like making art, really."

"In what way?" Richard relaxed into the conversation. This was easier.

"There's no set direction," she said. "It's working with the unconscious, I guess."

"It's human nature to want surprise."

Louise nodded. "If I cut Elke's sandwich into different shapes, she's thrilled."

"Right," said Richard. "That pleasure in the unexpected."

They kept talking about desire lines, but he was wrestling with what she'd said about Elke's father. *Not ideal.* Would ideal mean that her ex-husband lived in Eugene? Would that mean they'd still be married? Maybe it had just been Germany that Louise needed to leave, or perhaps she'd wanted an American life for her daughter's sake. Richard's questions kept spooling out, though he didn't ask them that evening.

Dieter had been there for as long as Richard had known Louise. And over the years, as a way of dealing with that fact, Richard had taken subtle things from Dieter, which gave him soft pleasure he wouldn't divulge to Louise. Ideas for research. When Dieter dragged his feet with the divorce and embroiled them in long negotiations with an immigration lawyer, Richard thought about the political implications of walking. He'd investigated desire lines in a migratory context. Migrants, he might add, who had a much tougher time than Dieter, with the cushion of his Western European passport, his white skin, and his sham marriage to Louise.

Borders as arbitrary lines, footpaths as direct ones. Richard had channeled his anger into his work; after the divorce was finalized, he'd celebrated by writing and publishing a paper about the U.S. border with Mexico that became a chapter in his book, which had helped him secure tenure. But things hadn't gone so well since then. Richard's fieldwork fell out of favor with the architects who dominated his department—outdated, they said—and though he was tenured, he was repeatedly turned down for promotion. He plateaued at assistant professor. But with tenure he was safe, and he continued to research what he wanted.

Richard drove home with his groceries, still feeling agitated. He'd arranged to Skype with Louise at noon his time. He left the bags in the kitchen and went straight up to the computer, and when he logged in, Louise was already waiting—her face was huge and pixilated on the screen. Elke was just over her shoulder, in front of some Germanic furniture. Richard wondered where Dieter was, and the relatives.

"How's the jet lag?" he asked.

"I'm propped up on caffeine," Louise said.

"We'll feel better tomorrow," Elke said, leaning in toward the camera. "Margot's show is part of an all-day festival, so their set is early. And anyway, Dieter's going to drive."

Richard saw his own displeasure boxed on the screen and tried to arrange a neutral expression.

"Was the next piece OK?" Louise asked. Her expectation was clear despite the graininess. "How'd the photo come out?"

He knew if he tried to lie, his face would give it away. He told her that he hadn't taken the picture.

"Is there a problem with the camera?" Louise asked. "Use my old one. It's on the shelf in my studio."

"That's not it," he said. "I just haven't done it." He was ashamed to say this out loud. He hated feeling her disappointment.

Louise squinted. "What are you talking about?" She probably thought he was joking.

"I haven't taken the picture," he said quietly.

She laughed nervously, her concern barely restrained. Tension crackled. Elke had leaned back, a wary sentry at Louise's shoulder.

Now Louise understood he wasn't kidding. "I need you to do it," she said. Her gaze pierced through the screen, that narrowing he knew well. The deepening brow crease. "I'll call Nina and ask her to do it if you can't."

He'd taken them right up to the brink, but he could still pull it back to safety. Extend the olive branch. Louise was waiting for his response. She was blinking. She pushed her hair back. He could almost smell her. Conditioner tended to catch in the creases of her ears. She always smelled good. He missed her, missed the easy version of Louise, the easy version of them. Now they were stuck in this limbo, at the precipice of further acrimony.

"I've got some things to take care of before my class tonight," Richard said. "Let's talk again after you see Margot."

Louise nodded, still pissed. He was avoiding her eyes — how odd, but also how easy, to avoid contact with a disembodied screen. She was thousands of miles away. He logged off.

He was alone again. He'd been alone all along, even with Louise's image on the screen. But now the room echoed with its actual emptiness. He felt unsettled. He was annoyed, but also guilty, exposed. He didn't like the feeling of Louise being mad at him.

He composed an email to her, tried to type out his thoughts. *The reason I didn't take the picture.* No. He backspaced over those words. *I'm sorry I didn't take your picture.* But he couldn't complete the apology. *Why did you have to go? Try to see things from my perspective. It's actually pretty selfish of you to think I'd be happy to work on your project while you reconnect with your ex-husband.* He left the email in his drafts folder.

Louise had left him with the address and phone number of where she'd be staying. Bad Waldheim. He typed that into Google and pulled up the map. A curved grid, with a river bending around the town center, those pale blocks of green and brown. He zoomed in so he could read the names of streets and roads. He slid himself along some *Strasse,* imagined moving through the square until he felt dizzy.

He got up and went outside. A foggy day, the weather matching his mood, and he walked through the garden, from the eggplant to the hydrangeas and finally the tomatoes, Louise's end-of-summer prize.

He'd always been attracted to Louise's sense of freedom, the way she followed her instincts. She'd inspired him to maintain that sensibility as a scholar — sticking to what interested him even after the architects in his department called him timid. Planners were supposed to shape the way people used space, not the other way around. To study desire lines was to deny the purpose of the profession. He had a responsibility to influence, they said. Richard did see influence, though — but as conversation, symbiosis, collaboration, and Louise had agreed with him, found beauty in the potential balance.

He knew he was supposed to let Louise follow her instincts. And he understood why Elke wanted her mother to go on this trip. But right now, across the planet, Louise was going to see Margot's show, and Richard wasn't there.

He hadn't taken the picture. He could do it now. He could do it later that day, and apologize the next time they talked. But he knew, with a guilty certainty that nevertheless bolstered him, that he was not going to do it. He left the garden and went back to the project, and riding that certainty, picked up the dark blue square he'd set that morning. He returned the piece to the garage. She could do it herself when she came home.

LOUISE

1972

AT THE END of the summer, they moved into their new place in Ober-bilk, a few blocks from the central station and Dieter's studio. Their street was lined with blank apartment houses, and the neighborhood was seedy, a bit run-down — there was a strip club around the corner, a menacing hum in the air. But rents were cheaper here, and the new apartment was sunny and clean.

Now they had three rooms and a shallow balcony, a kitchen with a refrigerator, a bedroom with a door that closed. The bathroom with its hard-earned tub. Louise and Dieter took baths that first morning in the apartment, and the triumph of the new plumbing was muted only slightly by Dieter's pointed thrift. Before reaching for the towel, he stood in the tub and brushed the water from his body with his hands, as though the towel might be taken from him before he was dry.

While Louise made coffee, Dieter put on a record in the other room; he turned up the volume so they could hear it in the kitchen, where, at the small table by the window, they spread *Brötchen* with butter and thick plum jam. They were listening to the Amon Düül album with its wandering flute, its reliable drums. The easy beat steadied Louise against the coffee; she wanted to linger there, watching the sun move over the planes of Dieter's face.

Before he went to work, Dieter brought the featherbed to the balcony. The German bedding style was frustrating: the thick featherbed but no top sheet. The previous night had been too warm for a blanket. Too much or nothing at all; Louise craved some kind of in-between.

"Lüften," Dieter said, as his long arms stretched over the balcony's drying rack. There was a certain energy to his movement — nearly frantic but always controlled. "It needs air."

They should do the same thing with their clothes, Dieter said, to put off trips to the laundromat, to avoid the trek home with a wet bag.

"Doesn't the laundromat have a dryer?" Louise asked, frustrated with his scolding tone.

Dieter shook his head. Stubborn, unyielding. "It wears out the clothes."

In the studio, at Frau Kerbel's, she and Dieter hadn't needed to squabble over chores. Now there was no getting around it — this apartment, with all its fresh possibilities for disagreement, was theirs together.

The start of the term was swept up in news of the Olympics in Munich. Everyone was talking about it — the last time the Olympics had been held in Germany was in 1936, in Berlin, the events then a platform for the Nazis. These new games were a chance for Germans to show the world they'd changed.

Though Munich was in a distant corner of West Germany, six hours away by train, Louise could still feel that sense of hope in Düsseldorf. The chatter on the streets and the signs in the shops proclaimed it — the "Happy Games" the chosen moniker. In the newspaper, she read about the careful attention to the message these Olympics would send. The official colors were a range of soft pastels, not an aggressive red, yellow, and black. The font on the tickets was modern and clean. The organizers even wanted to limit beer consumption, so that no one got too sloppy.

Most interesting to Louise was that the planners wanted art to be part of the new German culture, too. They invited artists to design the posters, made a *Spielstrasse* in the Olympic Village, an entire block of galleries and performance spaces, of poetry and theater and film. Even Embryo and Agitation Free would be playing in the *Spielstrasse,* Dieter said.

Louise and Dieter went to Gerd's apartment to watch the opening ceremonies on TV. A group from the Kunstakademie had gathered, eager to see what they could of the art. Gerd crouched beside the TV, his beer squeezed between his knees, and gave a little lecture about the Olympic architecture. The design for the village was peaceful and open, with sloping lines and wide paths. The stadium had a transparent roof made of Plexiglas — no shadows, Gerd said.

The stadium was built into a hillside planted with flowers and trees. "The structure is rising from the earth in a gentle way," Gerd said. "Not looming over us, not telling us what to think."

The TV camera zoomed in on signs urging visitors to pick flowers and walk on the grass. Louise found it poignant, the rule-bound Germans trying so earnestly to lighten up.

The group in Gerd's living room was loud and festive, offering punchy critiques. It was simplistic, they proclaimed loudly in front of the TV, to think that this spectacle could erase Germany's crimes. And yet they watched.

Louise and Dieter went to Gerd's each evening, for swimming and gymnastics, for beer and conversation. Louise liked the neat arc of suspense and resolution. The reassuring guidance of the commentators, the definite beginning, middle, and end. Someone had to win.

She liked, too, the way the city was united by this temporary collective pride. It wasn't patriotic — in the TV coverage, the German flag was never displayed. Not on the buildings, not in the stands. But she noticed a new levity in the streets of Düsseldorf. Live radio broadcasts played in the stores, and customers swapped gleeful stats. Louise saw proud children carrying *Schultüte* on their first day of elementary school; the huge paper cones of pencils and candy celebrated the rite of passage. Germans were obsessed with birthdays, she'd learned, with rituals that marked stages of life. She found it fitting that the *Schultüte* kids coincided with the Olympics, both events a measure of change.

The week carried on like this until the day the news broke. Louise was in her studio when Ute came to tell her: during the night, Palestinian terrorists had stormed the Israeli team's apartment. They'd taken hostages, and now there was a standoff—but the news wasn't clear at all.

They went downstairs, where people were gathered around the radio at the Kunstakademie's front desk. The standoff was ongoing. All events were canceled that day. Ute's face was stricken. They should go to Gerd's, she said to Louise; there must be news coverage on TV. They left, cut through the streets bustling with the usual morning business. Most passersby seemed unaware of the news, but Louise caught the eye of a stunned stranger, the woman offering a bitter reflection of the week's camaraderie.

On the TV at Gerd's apartment, a man in a mask stood alone against the hard lines of the hotel's concrete balcony. The Olympic security forces were stationed outside, outfitted in pale blue. That color, chosen to be soothing and hopeful, now felt brutally inadequate. The reporters kept circling through the same updates. The lack of change was maddening.

"Why aren't they doing anything?" Gerd snapped at the TV.

Through the afternoon, the rest of the group trickled in and sat with them on the floor. The police were still trying to negotiate. The terrorists made demands: to free prisoners in Israel. To free Andreas Baader and Ulrike Meinhof from German prison.

Ute groaned. "Those stupid Baader-Meinhof are part of this, too."

Louise felt Ute's visceral, trembling shock. Everyone in the room kept saying it—with all the careful planning that had gone into these Olympics, how could this have happened?

Dieter came in the late afternoon, straight from work with his bag of tools. When Louise went to the door to greet him, he was wooden, unyielding in her arms. He sat apart from everyone else in the living room, cross-legged and hunched in front of the TV.

The news came that one of the Israeli athletes had been killed. The police tried and failed to get in. Louise felt ill—she'd been clinging, with jaw clenched, to the possibility that things could still be all right. Now the room was thick with cigarettes, jangling with her friends' stale nerves.

Gerd offered beers—a way of numbing, of sharing, as they grimly watched. From the sofa, Louise watched Dieter blink in the blue light from the screen. That morning, he'd put on the Beach Boys' *Pet Sounds;* he'd come back to bed and reached for Louise in the bright room. She'd listened to that album hundreds of times in high school but had never heard it this way: devotional, an utter guarantee. A sincerity she'd scoffed at as a teenager, but listening that morning, she'd claimed it, believed that it was hers.

Now that belief felt impossible, more foolish as the hours went by. Dieter remained entirely separate from her, up near the front of the room, alone and folded, one hand combing through his hair. And though she sensed his devastation, he would not, perhaps could not, share it with her.

It was night when the terrorists took the hostages to the airport; they wanted to fly to Cairo. Louise couldn't understand the chain of events. Her body was stiff, vigilant, her head dizzy. Now the German police were surrounding the airport. This was their last chance to save the hostages. The reporter was still on the tarmac, the camera fixed on the darkness beyond.

The TV cut to the anchor at his yellow desk: the terrorists had been killed by German snipers. The remaining hostages were alive. "Thank God," Ute said. In the crowded room, Louise could feel her friends' bitter relief. They were echoing Ute, murmuring to each other, and Louise let out her held breath, leaned back against the couch.

Gerd was pacing the room. "Finally they did something," he said. "It took too long but they figured it out."

Dieter stood and stiffly straightened his legs. "It's a miracle they're alive," he said, "but that doesn't change the fact that this occurred."

He was responding to Gerd but looking at Louise, his face hard. "We shouldn't be happy."

He'd returned to her, but not in the way she'd wanted. His remark confused her, upset her. She wasn't happy. She went to the bathroom and then to the kitchen, away from the television, and away from Dieter. But the TV's urgent trumpets called her back. She watched the news anchor's face—somber, sober. The initial news was wrong, he said. He was sorry to report that the hostages hadn't made it. "They've all been killed."

A swift punch, a rip through the room. His words were a mean, impossible trick. How could he have made that mistake? Louise felt what she'd dammed up in her body come loose—she'd been waiting all day, desperate for change, but she hadn't allowed herself to anticipate this. Her friends were muttering, swearing, crying quietly, their grief broken all the way out. Now there was nothing to wait for, nothing to watch. No possibility but this.

The dark sky was edged with purple as Louise and Dieter walked home. The space between them was curdled and thick. She hadn't been happy, she needed to tell him, but the anchor's mistaken announcement was far away from them now.

"They should have done more to save them," Dieter said.

"But how?" asked Louise.

"That's a stupid question." He was staring at the middle distance, refusing to meet her gaze.

"Do you know the answer?"

A shadow passed over his set face. A crumbling that frightened her.

"It's a paralysis," Dieter said. "Germans will never escape it."

"This was a terrible tragedy." Louise said this in English—she couldn't think of the German word. "But it could have happened anywhere."

His cheekbones were like wood under canvas. He stayed in her English. "You're wrong," he said, getting louder. "You'll never understand it." His voice was pointed, cruel.

She stopped while he kept walking. He didn't come after her. She circled the blocks for a while, but she was exhausted; she had nowhere to go. When she got to their building, after she pressed the light switch in the hallway, she didn't start her usual race against the timer as she climbed the stairs. She took the last flight in the dark. Her hand found the lock by habit, and when she got into bed next to him, she turned to face the wall.

In the morning, at the table in the kitchen, Louise turned on the radio and spread *Quark* on dense brown bread. She ate the sour slice: the breakfast she'd wanted, the tangy *Quark* she'd picked out at the store. But she remembered how it was in the supermarket, the way the customers grabbed for the little stick to separate their items on the belt, keeping Louise at a studious remove.

Dieter stood at the sink with his coffee; he faced her but didn't talk. The radio news report was throaty, agitated noise: *"Als man heute versucht, die Motivation für diese furchtbare Tat zu begreifen, sind mehr Fragen als Antworten vorhanden."* Louise didn't concentrate on the words, drifting instead on the grim current of near-understanding.

When Dieter left for work, she found his clothes from the night before. She picked up her blouse and jeans, and the smell of cigarettes reminded her of the anxious room at Gerd's. She took it all to the balcony, spread their things over the rack.

As she walked to the Kunstakademie, the city was muted and weary. The Olympic posters hung in shop windows, their bright colors a stinging rebuke. People moved slowly; Louise was clouded, adrift. She thought through her fight with Dieter—he was shutting her out, telling her she had no place here. In the studio, she studied her marks on the canvas, thought of Hartmut Knecht in his stained smock. *You must get closer,* he'd told her. But how? She couldn't get through to Dieter if he wouldn't let her in.

At lunch, she and Ute talked about the night before. "The Germans weren't prepared," Ute said in a tone reserved but forthright. That was

what made it especially tragic. The authorities hadn't made an effective
plan for security; they hadn't armed their guards. To display Germany's
reformation, Ute said, they'd made a show of their open approach. But
they'd taken it too far. They'd botched their attempts at rescuing the
hostages, had failed in their ambush at the airport. The Israelis had
been killed, and the Germans hadn't saved them. Ute's flush crept into
her ribbed turtleneck, those parallel lines pointing down.

Louise recognized Ute's shame and was surprised by a shot of grati-
tude: she was American, she didn't belong here. She shared Ute's grief,
but not her remorse. When Dieter had told Louise that she'd never
understand, she'd been offended, shut out. Now her feelings were more
complicated. She remembered Dieter's face the night before, its quick
collapse at the news. He was ashamed, too; his discomfort had made
him lash out. She could see it now in a way she hadn't been willing to
the night before—his devastation was different than her own.

That night, a usual one for Astral Gruppe rehearsal, Dieter stayed out
late, and Louise went to bed before he came home. She woke and left
early, still grappling with her conversation with Ute. And she couldn't
face him if he wouldn't apologize, didn't want to be the one to give in.

The games had resumed, but the group was no longer gathering at
Gerd's to watch them. But Louise was with them again the next night,
at the Ritterhof in the Altstadt, a Thursday ritual after critiques. Louise
went to the bar with Ute; on a cart in the corner, a color TV broadcast
the evening's events. Silently the group agreed on a table on the other
side of the room. They settled into a discussion of Joseph Beuys, who
was trying for open admission to his class again that fall. If the school
denied him this time, the students would protest—they planned to
occupy the Kunstakademie's administrative office.

When Dieter arrived, he sat a few seats away from Louise. He leaned
on his forearms with a cigarette, spoke emphatically to Gerd. "That
song should begin with synthesizer only," he said. "That'll make the
progression more intense."

Louise was talking to Ute but listening to him. "I'm not sure what I'll put in the show," Louise said. "I haven't locked into anything I like."

"Drums, sure," Dieter was saying. "But it has to be subtle at first."

Louise went to the bathroom, and on her way back, she passed the TV. A race in a stadium, with runners lined up on the track. And there was Steve Prefontaine with his mustache, the hero of Oregon. He'd been a student at U of O at the same time as Louise, but she'd ignored sports then, particularly Prefontaine's arrogant rise to glory. The best runner in the world, he'd claimed, and the worst part was that he was right. He always won.

"The American with the enormous ego," the commentator was saying now. The runners stretched, shaking their loose, thin thighs. Prefontaine wore a white jersey with deep cuts under the arms, so that much of his torso was visible, his fragile ribs exposed.

Louise's parents were sure to be watching. Everyone in Eugene must have been tuned in, and she felt ownership at that, an unexpected pride.

"Perhaps today Prefontaine will prove he deserves this great ego," the second announcer said.

"His results up until now have been remarkable. Such incredible dedication to his training."

"His mother is German, so maybe that's why he knows the sense of discipline."

Of course, Louise thought—he couldn't escape that influence. But there was something distinctly American about Prefontaine. He tossed his hair as he waited, and his confidence gave her a fierce longing for home.

The runners started with the shot; quickly they abandoned their lanes. Prefontaine was at the center of the clump, his flap of hair swinging, his white singlet bright against the stands. The race was 5,000 meters—a distance Louise couldn't figure. But as the numbers rolled up at the corner of the screen, she felt the urgency of time. An entire fleeting universe: men in green blazers with whistles and watches, and others in white jackets, their boxy cameras trailing cords. The huge stadium, the small group moving in tandem, Prefontaine running alone.

How she might capture that movement with paint. The way the colors blurred together as the light radiated from the screen. A bright square, floating over the amorphous dark. The liquid motion contained and still spilling out.

Louise saw Dieter crossing the room toward her. He couldn't have known her reasons for watching. Prefontaine and his crowds at Hayward Field in Eugene, the cars backed up on Eighteenth Avenue. Pre's traffic, Louise and her college friends had said with derision. The connection she felt toward him now unnerved her, this ache for something she hadn't needed before.

Pre lit out ahead, held the lead through the long laps. Dieter was leaning on the wall by the jukebox, but she didn't look away from the race. The minutes ticked by. A bell signaled the last lap. Pre was in front —he would win it, he always won—but then he drifted back to a tight clump. The group, pressing and receding, swallowed him. A stern Finn took the lead. Prefontaine would medal, at least, the commentators were saying, the silver, or maybe he'd take the bronze. But in the last meters before the finish, another runner, who hadn't even been in the frame, burst through and replaced him at the line.

Pre finished fourth and Louise heard only the waving rush of the crowd. The last runners were still roaring in, with tragic dignity: the race was already won. Pre took off his shoes and slowly left the track. The potential that had gripped Louise moments earlier was gone now. She stayed even as the coverage changed.

She saw Dieter waiting. He put coins in the jukebox, and a song started, something angular and fast. She went to him, let him reach for her. At the table, they were careful with each other. He touched her hair, her shoulder, her leg. The TV was a flashing abstraction, a square of light across the room. Louise stayed at the table, worn and aching, as though the race had been hers to run.

———

The Olympics ended just as the term was getting underway. Ute encouraged Louise to try to switch into Joseph Beuys's class—Louise could be part of the ring discussions, get some new ideas. But Louise never got to ask for permission to change; as expected, the administration wouldn't allow Beuys his open enrollment. Students protested, camped out in front of the Kunstakademie with stenciled signs and fabric canopies. Louise joined the demonstration on the first day. Beuys was milling around in a hat and a vest with stuffed pockets. His face burned with conviction; he had huge teeth, a mouth that split wide open when he laughed. He addressed the crowd in a booming voice. Life itself was a work of art, Beuys said. So how could the administration say that art was only for a select few?

In the gathered students, Louise felt again that hope that had been shattered by the Olympics. This was something they could actually change.

Louise was thinking about what she'd seen during Prefontaine's race. She'd felt a tender sense of connection to the way Pre had tried and come up short. She remembered how his motion had engulfed her, saw again his humble retreat from the track. She wanted to embody that, paint toward that feeling. Now she recognized what Beuys was saying—everything she was experiencing had to be part of her work.

The protests went on for more than a week, and then Beuys was fired.

But Louise was still charged. She started riding her bike from Oberbilk to the Kunstakademie each morning; she wanted to get to school faster. From the bike, all the things she'd noted on her walks were amplified, sped up—the geometric buildings, the boxes on balconies. She thought often about the vantage point that Pre's race had allowed her—those fleeting moments in the Ritterhof let her watch from a distance and from within. She was an outsider in this complicated place. But maybe that position was more interesting for her as an artist. She had the space to actually see.

She worked on a new set of paintings for most of the fall. She wanted to evoke the energy of the race, the way the colors had shifted and blurred together, how they radiated off the screen in the dark room. She applied paint in thick layers—a wide green stripe at the center of the canvas, and at the edges, deep blue, almost black, to dial up the contrast. She tracked small white squares over the expanse, in a flickering, uneven line.

She found a lightness on her feet, that perfect rhythm—to think and make a mark, to look and adjust. A limber quality, absorbed in moving and waiting. A slow chain, a meditative call-and-response. The feeling she'd missed from her undergraduate days: she would sleep in the studio if she could. A spell, an incantation—day to day, she didn't want to wash the paint from her clothes or her hands.

Dieter was busy with the band. They were recording an album; a label, a really good one, he said, wanted to put it out. "Maybe we can use one of these for the album cover," Dieter said when she showed him her new work. His favorite was the canvas with a gradually shifting yellow line, overlaid with dense strokes of blue and gray. "I want to keep looking at it," he said. "Each time it gives me something new." Dieter's praise was sporadic but carefully considered, and his words now marked her triumph.

During her critique, Knecht assessed her new painting with a slight smile. "You've been busy," he said, pulling on the tie he wore under his stained smock. Another victory. He was right. After class, she went back to work; she wanted to look again.

On a windy day in October, Louise realized that she had not had a real period for nearly two months, an irregularity in an irregular cycle that only jarred her when she stopped on her bike to count the days on her fingers.

Most startling was that she hadn't noticed. Her pulsing devotion to her work had swept over her usual sense of caution. She felt a bolt of panic. Time. She wouldn't have any time to paint. She wheeled her bike in a daze. She knew she would have to take care of it right away. But she didn't know how that sort of thing worked here.

When the rain started, she went to the Kunstakademie, where she'd planned to have lunch with Ute. They took their trays to the building's top floor. The school stored sculpture replicas there, copies of famous works for art history lectures. An outdated technology, from the days before slides. The hall was lined with columns and arches and headless women draped in stone cloth.

Louise told Ute right away. "I'm not sure," Louise said. "I haven't seen a doctor yet."

"But you're pretty sure," Ute said, her face creased with concern. "You'll have to decide what you want to do. It's not legal here. But there are ways, if that's what you want."

Louise didn't respond. She didn't know what she wanted.

Later in the afternoon, Ute found Louise in her studio, gave her a piece of paper with an address in Amsterdam. "I can find out more for you," Ute said. "It's legal there."

Amsterdam wasn't so far away, considering the distance Louise had already covered. But the risk felt much bigger. Expensive, maybe dangerous. Another country. Both choices overwhelmed her.

At home that evening, Dieter's certainty surprised her—she'd expected his hesitation to match her own. A child was far beyond any shared future they'd discussed.

"This is the way things are meant to be," he said. She told him about Ute's address in Amsterdam.

He shook his head. "I don't want you to do that."

She bristled at his resolute response. It was her body, not his. "We don't have enough money," she said.

"We'll get *Kindergeld*." And she could have the care of a midwife before and after the baby was born, he said. It wouldn't cost anything, and, besides that, he had a job.

"We don't have room."

"I can build shelves," he said. "I'll make a crib." But he knew what kind of space she was talking about. She didn't want to give up her work. He wouldn't want to give up his music, either. He told her they could still leave Düsseldorf when she was done with her fellowship. They could go to New York as they'd planned. The thought of so many unknowns made her apprehensive, but Dieter was telling her that he believed in their creative ambition. That sense of shared possibility jumbled in with her nerves.

For the next few days, she carried both options in her mind. Motherhood would undoubtedly limit her; how could she paint? And it would tie her here; the baby would grow into a child who'd speak and understand much more German than Louise did. The child would belong here in a way its mother never would.

At home in the evening, Louise stretched out on the sofa while Dieter showed her where he planned to build shelves. "I measured it," he said. "I think we can manage in the apartment while the baby is small."

Already this thing was forming, microscopic but taking shape.

"I was thinking," Dieter said, "about what it would mean to be a father." His face expectant, a nervous pride. "I didn't have that. My whole childhood was without him."

He sat down and pulled her feet onto his lap. She hadn't thought about what this would mean for him.

"What happened to your father?" Louise asked. "In the war."

"I never knew exactly," Dieter said. "He was fighting on the front in Russia, and he was wounded, and whether that killed him or the elements did — starvation maybe — I haven't found out."

"Your mother never told you about it?"

"We Germans don't talk about things — haven't you learned that yet?" His smile was a false one, lips closed and tight. She sat up with him on the couch.

"I guess it's possible to try to do it better," she said. "As parents. To do things right."

She thought of her parents' inevitable dismay at the news of her pregnancy. Their letters had become telegraphic, pithy and loaded.

"After the murders at Kent State, I was devastated," she said. "But my father said that the police did the right thing. That they'd responded appropriately."

"What did you say to that?"

"I'd been going to similar protests at my college. I told him that one of those protesters could have been me." She remembered the grim set to her father's jaw. He'd walked out of the room, and, livid, shaking, Louise drove back to Eugene.

"Will your parents be happy about the baby?" Dieter asked.

"I'm not sure," Louise said. "You and I are living in sin."

Dieter looked around the room. "This is certainly a sinful environment," he said. "But we'll get married."

His assurance anchored her. A husband would please her parents, she thought—in a letter, she could backdate the wedding day.

"It is possible to do it better," Dieter said. He told her he'd design the crib so it would fit in the corner of the bedroom. She pictured the things the baby would need—a changing table, a rocking chair. That fall she'd realized that her life had to fold into her work. She thought about her studio, the cool, quiet space. How would a baby fit there?

Dieter was still describing what he could build—really, the apartment had plenty of room, he was saying. They would be parents together, she thought. It was a way of starting over. Of doing things right.

That week, Louise went to see a doctor; she met a midwife who would visit the apartment during her pregnancy. She leaned into this care, thought about how the change in her body might affect her work. Give her new perspective. Germany was a place rife with contradiction—why couldn't she be an artist and a mother at the same time?

MARGOT

2008

IT WAS MORNING IN Antwerp, and Margot stood with Joel on the sidewalk, feeling the entire trip curdle around her. As Keith and Spencer packed the gear into the car—their fraught daily Jenga—Margot calculated the distance they'd need to cover that day. Three hours to Lille, a town she knew nothing about. Margot had never been to Europe before this trip; she'd lived her entire life in damp Oregon, first in Eugene and then Portland for college, and each city on their European route was a mysterious prize.

She climbed into the back seat. The car was a stark metal box when they'd picked it up, the cheapest model, strictly functional; now it was sullied by four people, strewn with their forgotten snacks. Every available inch was in use: their tote bags of electronic equipment, their toothbrushes and paperbacks. The duffels of dirty clothes, strewn with loose LPs and CD-Rs, the merch they'd tried to hide with underwear, in case their lack of work permits was questioned at British customs.

The tour was almost over. They'd begun in the UK two weeks ago, hauling everything around on buses and trains, then picked up the car in Brussels and started a diagonal lurch into the continent. Traced out on the map, the route looked like a dog lying on its back, a crooked smile. The routing, which centered around the festival in Gent, the show that was funding the transatlantic tickets, was not logical. Too much backtracking, a convoluted pinning-together of gigs.

Tomorrow they'd arrive at a destination still murkier: Hasselt, snaking back into Belgium. Margot's mother would be there. A week ago, Louise had told Margot she'd be in Germany for a funeral, that she and Elke wanted to come to one of Margot's shows. Which seemed extremely odd for several reasons. One, that her mother wanted to attend the funeral of someone in her ex-husband's family. Two, that her mother was traveling all the way to Germany to do that. And now this: Margot's sister, Elke, had written with the plans. *I'll be at your concert in Hasselt with Mom and Dieter. It's just an hour from where we'll be staying, in my grandmother's town.*

Her sister's grandmother was unknown to Margot, as was her mother's ex-husband. Her mother rarely spoke of Dieter, and even Elke hadn't ever told Margot all that much. He was just an accented voice on the phone at Christmas, asking for Elke or Louise, the source of pinched irritation on Margot's father's face when she announced who it was.

Now Keith was asking her a question from up front.

"What?" she yelled.

He turned down the music. "Should I play the show from last night?"

Keith recorded all their sets, though the four of them didn't always listen back. Hearing it again required a certain blend of emotion and circumstance—a mix of confidence and doubt, of the need to be reassured and to take each other down a few notches.

Joel said he wanted to hear it. "The end was killer." He drove with one hand on the wheel, one forearm stretched along the window. Margot was directly behind him.

In this configuration—Margot in back with Spencer, who was eating a banana beside her—she could study Joel. The surprise of his good posture, his shoulders pinned against the seat, and the uneven wisps of his hair, which she'd watched him self-barber. The tour had started with the band as a platonic quartet, but during the past two weeks, things had progressed with Joel: she'd first kissed him in Leeds, and ever since Sheffield, the two of them had angled for the spare room or the basement whenever such accommodations were offered. Mostly they weren't, though—the four band members usually had to crash in the same room—and so Margot and Joel went to the car or wandered through unfamiliar towns so they could surreptitiously make out. They wanted to keep their burgeoning relationship discreet, to preserve the band's fragile balance.

"I thought last night's set was lackluster." Keith was eating prawn-flavored potato chips, part of his ongoing survey of regional junk food. "It took forever to peter out."

There was a constant argument of how to end things. Whether to let the set trickle away or to cap off with something definitive. To lock eyes and plot a final blow, or else to keep pushing, teasing out the sound.

Keith opened his laptop, the site of his archive. The recording began with the hum of the amps. Margot took sick pleasure in their shared scrutiny, the four of them grandstanding over minutiae, criticizing slight moves and sonic gestures. They essentially played the same thing every night. Each of them had similar gear: simple inputs, just micro-phones and mixers hooked up to pedals to process the sounds. They used their voices, somewhere between speaking and singing, or else small objects that produced tones. Literal bells and whistles. The result was a huge drone, something textured and layered and full of complex-ity. That was the goal, at least.

"That was Spencer, right?" Joel asked, as the recording began with the first pulsing tones.

"The PA sucked," Spencer said. He'd finished his banana and left the peel on the middle seat. "I couldn't hear anything."

"The PA was fine," Keith said. "You just need to listen more care-fully."

"I'm always listening," said Spencer.

Joel was shaking his head. "You're both wrong. It was the audience yelling through the entire set. It was impossible to hear."

The night before, they'd played in a bar where Flemish frat-boy types sloshed high-octane pilsners and traded jovial insults until they got too consumed by the question of whether what they were hearing was indeed music.

"Bart seemed to like it," said Margot. "He wanted to talk about it all night."

Bart was the club's promoter, and the band had camped on his living-room floor the previous night, beneath a ten-foot terrarium, held captive as he sat on the couch for hours, chatting and cracking beers.

"I slept horribly," said Joel. "The light from that fish tank was like an interrogation lamp."

"You mean the lizard tank," said Margot.

"Bart's an odd dude," said Keith. Indeed—Bart had shaved the black hair off his arms down to his wrists, where a thicket formed, his arms inexplicably Clydesdale-style.

"I wish you would have asked us where we wanted to stay," Margot said to Keith. He'd agreed to it without checking with any of them first. He was usually their spokesperson—the band's de facto leader, their strident, visionary glue.

"Would you have preferred to sleep in the car?" Keith asked.

"Of course not," she said. "But you always decide everything without us."

They didn't talk for a few minutes, just listened to their sounds blasting through the speakers.

"What's that noise?" Keith asked, tipping his head. "That feedback is ruining a totally restrained comedown."

"I was using the oscillator," Margot said. She liked the way it sounded. That fluty, haunting wash was her own modulated voice. Though Keith was right—the tone was frayed by the amp's feedback. She was still getting a handle on the gear.

"The oscillator has had too much airtime," Spencer said. "Try to branch out."

"But you were using an oscillator pedal, too," Joel said to Spencer.

"That's different," Spencer said.

Spencer recorded things with a handheld tape player—church bells, AM radio, a thrumming air conditioner vent. He ran the cassettes through his mix, and the original sounds broke down, melted into rich tones or stuttered through a delay. His contributions were a secret language, a journal of the trip transformed through effects, and he was constantly taping, his thumb over the record button in gas stations and strangers' homes.

"It's getting cluttered now." Keith pulled at the corners of the chip bag, positioned it over his mouth.

"It's not cluttered," said Joel. "It's complex." He was defending Margot, but she hoped that he really believed she was playing well.

"I like it better when it's spare," Keith said into the bag. Before the trip, she'd known him at a comfortable distance, but the tour had thrust them all into a familial intimacy, with recognition of one another's smells and noises, and frank discussion of bathroom habits and needs.

Margot slouched in her seat; her bare toes reached a sock that she was pretty sure wasn't hers. "It's big and lush and ominous. To me that sounds good."

She did think their performances were getting better: more dynamic, deeper, somehow. At times the music was completely serene—but interesting. The quality of their aesthetic interaction had to function inverse to their human interaction. The worse they got along, the better it sounded. Traffic jams, rainstorms, indigestion—all of it improved the music. Strange things to wish for.

With four people, every configuration became important. The alliances shifted frequently. She and Joel, the discreet couple, or else the unit of Joel and Keith, who were obsessed record collectors, whose musical knowledge buttressed their strident opinions. Margot and Spencer, the taper, were on the other side of this gulf, coming at their musicianship from somewhere more primitive and, Margot thought, more pure.

Sometimes it was the three of them against Keith, whose dark moods hinged on his terrible eating habits. It was Keith's band—he'd come up with the idea and the sound and brought the four of them together, and he acted as though that justified the way he micromanaged everything, from the structure of the set to where they ate lunch. And yet really it was Joel, who built and repaired their equipment, who had the ultimate upper hand.

With these power shifts came a complex calculus of responsibility and blame — an invisible chore wheel spun daily. It was exhausting. Even so, Margot loved being on the road. She liked the compressed acquaintance with each place: this town was the birthplace of the pyramid scheme; this venue offered dinner but was stingy with the beer.

"I feel sick," Keith said. "Gurgly."

"Probably the shrimp chips," Spencer said.

"We need gas," Joel said.

"Maybe it was the chocolate soda," said Margot.

"The band fund is down to nine euros," Joel said.

"Don't spend it all in one place," Spencer said.

"We have to spend it," Joel said. "We need gas."

"It's not that far to Lille," Keith said. "We might be able to stretch the tank."

Next to Margot, the red light on Spencer's tape recorder was flashing.

"I just hope we start making better money," Joel said. They had only a few shows left: the tour would end in Den Haag, at a squat in an old school. A legendary venue, a popular stop on the noise circuit, and they could stay there for a few days, cool out and do some recording before flying home and returning to their various horrible jobs. Margot and Joel worked at a jewelry warehouse, where they had to pass through a metal detector before leaving for lunch. Spencer did data entry; Keith, delivery for Fire on the Mountain, a chicken wing place. Margot was looking forward to Den Haag — the big school with lots of rooms, where she'd have space to consider the trip.

"We have to play better," said Keith. "It's as simple as that." Keith had a long ponytail but no hair on top, and before this tour, Margot had never seen him without a baseball hat. But she'd woken up before him one of the first mornings and discovered his bare scalp. At moments like this, with Keith a grouchy scold, she was still able to access the vulnerability of his bald head, find some feeling of tenderness toward him, which she sensed she'd need to keep on deck.

"We'll get paid in Hasselt," Spencer said. "I think a lot of people will be there. We'll probably be able to get rid of those LPs, too."

"My family will be there," Margot said. "That's three more people for the audience." Though they wouldn't be paying spectators; Margot was going to put them on the list.

"Your mom's coming, right?" Joel asked.

"With my sister," Margot said. "And my sister's dad."

"Your stepfather?" Spencer asked as he labeled a cassette.

"No," Margot said. "My parents are still married. This is my mother's first husband. I'm not sure what he is to me."

"What do you call him?"

"I don't know," Margot said. "I've only met him once."

The only time Margot had seen Dieter was at Elke's high school graduation. Margot, who'd been six at the time, could remember only flashes of his visit. The strongest one was something she knew she wasn't supposed to have seen: Dieter and her mother in close conversation up in the studio on the third floor of the house. Their bodies pitched toward each other. Her mother in her striped blue dress, and Dieter bending in. Margot interrupted them, still wet from the bath, and Louise and Dieter, startled, stepped back. Her mother had seemed guilty, flustered, and Margot was unnerved by their intimacy.

"If you had done things differently," Dieter had said to her mother before they realized that Margot was in the room. "Maybe then Margot is my child." She remembered that he'd mispronounced her name — *Mar-gott*. The shock she'd felt when she realized that *Mar-gott* referred to her.

"He's German," Joel said. "Right?"

"He's German," Margot said. Her sister's name — Elke Hinterkopf

—was the giveaway. Margot Warren was solidly of Richard the American.

"I hope they like the show," Keith said. "Slag Heap is one of the other bands. They can get pretty harsh."

"I think they'll like it," Margot said. "My sister's dad used to be a musician."

"In Germany?" Keith asked.

"Right," Margot said. "My mom went to art school in Düsseldorf in the seventies."

"I didn't know that," Joel said. "I wonder what bands they saw."

"I wonder what band he was in," Keith said. "He might have been doing something really interesting."

"I have no idea."

"I can't believe you never told me your mom lived in Düsseldorf in the seventies." Keith was looking back at her, ravenous. "Why did she leave?"

"She was a student," Margot said. "She finished, I guess." Needling questions—she didn't know the answers.

"And this guy—"

"Dieter," Margot said.

"He left Germany with her?"

"He came later," Margot said. "But he moved to New York. They'd split up by then. I don't really know the details."

All she had for details was one envelope of photographs she'd come across in a box in the basement. Pictures of her mother and her father, and Dieter was there too. A kitchen, the three of them frozen in conversation. The snapshots looked as though they had been filtered through cream soda. Her mother in an embroidered blouse. Margot's bearded father, shaggy and impossibly young, and another guy with chin-length hair. Louise was in the middle of the two men, laughing at something outside the frame.

Margot took the pictures to her mother. "Who is that?"

"That's Dieter," Louise said. "His hair was long then."

Of course—Margot could see Elke's face now.

"Dad had a crazy beard," Margot said. "Where was this?"

Louise was frowning, running a hand through her hair. "Where did you find those?"

Most of the pictures were of Elke weaving through a row of flowers. Then a series of shots in the kitchen, a quick succession of the same themes.

"Dieter was visiting," Louise said. "Elke was little."

A visit was normal—it was Louise's reaction, not the information, that had made Margot uneasy. She sensed that her mother was hiding something. She'd put the envelope back in the basement, and looked for it again a few days later—further examination might provide more clues—but the envelope was gone.

"Maybe he's Dieter Moebius," Keith said. "From Cluster."

"That's not his name," Margot said. Dieter Hinterkopf. Her sister's last name. "And he's not famous."

"Dieter Moebius lives in Germany," Joel said.

"Fine," said Keith. "But if this guy was in Düsseldorf, he might have been hanging out with Kraftwerk. Or Can. I'm sure he saw them play."

"Did your mom see any cool bands?" Spencer asked.

"Probably," Margot said. Margot had never asked because her mother never talked about her years in Düsseldorf, but now it seemed shameful or odd that she hadn't, that this rich and pertinent piece of her mother's history—Louise might have seen Kraftwerk!—had gone unexamined until now.

Joel was watching Margot in the rearview. "What kind of music is your mom into these days?"

Her mother listened to what her father put on, Neil Young and the Byrds, the albums he played on car trips, hitting the steering wheel in time. But Joel and Keith wanted something juicier, and Margot rooted around in her memory.

"She used to have a Terry Riley LP in her studio." When Margot was

little, she'd loved to sit with Louise in the studio and listen to the record, *A Rainbow in Curved Air*. A title that made no sense, a wide-eyed
lunatic on the cover. Margot and Louise quiet as they sketched. Margot
was just doodling, but her mother's encouragement and the sweep of
the music had made her feel it was something more.

"Nice," Keith said. "My mom listens to right-wing talk radio exclu-
sively."

"My mom listens to Billy Joel," Spencer said. "I'm not sure which
is worse."

"My mom's not really into music," said Margot. "She's not a head."

"She sounds like a head," said Keith. "I'm looking forward to meeting her. And the German guy."

"What does your dad listen to?" Joel asked.

"Bob Dylan," Margot said. "The Rolling Stones. Basic stuff."

"Classic articulations of that era," said Keith.

This was how Joel and Keith looked at everything, music their constant frame for understanding.

"Sure," Margot said. "Fleetwood Mac. The Beach Boys. The Everly
Brothers."

"I'm getting a picture," Joel said. "'Bye Bye Love.' Those candy
songs."

"No, it was different," Margot said. "He had this one Everlys album
that was really gloomy."

"Like depressed cowboy music?" Keith asked.

"Right," Margot said. "Good old boys who hit trouble and went out
to the ranch."

"I think I know what you're talking about," Joel said. "*Roots*. That's a
sought-after album. They got kind of dark. Everything soured. There's
some sick guitar playing on that one."

Margot liked Joel's and Keith's encyclopedic knowledge. She enjoyed
their keen focus on a single album, how they'd worship it for an hour, a
week, an afternoon, each set of songs a complex lineage to break down.

The stories behind them were often incredibly sad. Right after this one was recorded, they'd say, the singer fell down the stairs and died; you can hear the premonition of tragedy in her voice. Or this one, Keith might say, written by a genius who spent two frenzied weeks recording every instrument before vanishing. Or the follow-up to a big studio album, made after a band's members fell in love with each other and then switched partners. The harmonies were recorded at home in a canyon somewhere, cocaine propping up the letdown.

Joel and Keith were excavators, unearthing albums that were forgotten or out of print. Time worked in both directions: they found fresh material that was actually decades old.

Margot had hosted a radio show in college and noodled on bass with her friends while they smoked pot in a basement jam room on Reed's campus. She was nothing like Joel and Keith, who displayed a seemingly physical longing every time they passed a record store. They ran a tiny label together, releasing limited runs of vinyl and cassettes with complicated packaging, selling their goods to like-minded freaks around the world.

She'd met Joel first, at work at the jewelry warehouse. They talked about music and sound, their hands busy with valuable goods, and she went with him to Keith's house in North Portland, to his spacious basement where all the Joel-built equipment was laid out.

That first time the group played together, no one talked about what was going to happen, and Margot felt she shouldn't ask. Joel explained the equipment to her only briefly. This would make the sound waver; this would thicken it with reverb. This one to delay, this to repeat, this to extend the length of that echo. The four of them set up in a ring on the floor. They used their voices, a flute, bells through microphones. A small keyboard sometimes, and Spencer had his cassettes. They hunched over the pedals, letting their sustained tones change and pile up.

Afterward they went upstairs and drank beer and talked. Keith knew what kind of sound he wanted to cultivate—he spoke about it reverently as he moved between the record player and the couch.

"It shouldn't be premeditated," he said, pulling on the brim of his hat. "It's got to be loose. But not sloppy—we just have to get ourselves to a particular state."

"It has to always be in front of you," Spencer said.

Joel nodded. "As soon as you know what it is, it's ruined."

This type of discussion became a crucial part of their music-making —they usually talked for longer than they played. At first Margot had no idea what she was doing. She sat with the equipment, and everything was loud and huge and hard to distinguish. She couldn't tell what she was contributing, and so she stayed behind when everyone went upstairs. Alone in the basement, she held a microphone to her mouth and tested each knob and setting until the sounds started to mean something. Her voice became something different than when she spoke. A true instrument, something she could use.

One of those nights, Joel came downstairs and listened to what she was doing. "It's all just routing signals," he told her, using his finger to trace the bird's nest of pedals and wires. "Inputs plus effects." The moment her crush crystallized: she found then a beautiful simplicity in the gear, and it was Joel who'd made it all, who understood the pedals' tiny parts.

After that things happened fast: they released a cassette and a CD-R, played some shows in town. And then farther away—they drove in Joel's car to Seattle and San Francisco, squished in with all the gear. They made an album that Joel and Keith released on their label—a run of a thousand LPs with hand-painted covers that sold out quickly over the internet. Always a sense of momentum, a relay from hand to hand. The invitation to tour in Europe had felt like validation.

Margot wanted all of it, including Joel. In Sheffield, when he asked her to take a walk with him after their show at the community center, where a crew of tweakers yelled and vibrated on the street outside, she could see what was going to happen. She went with him through the town, now shut down for the night, still with a sense of caution. She wanted to preserve the independent place she'd carved out with the band. She was there on her own merits, not as someone's girlfriend, though all these cities later, watching Joel drive toward the French border, it seemed that was what she was becoming.

LOUISE

1973

THE NURSES GAVE LOUISE fennel tea. She could see flowers on the trees outside the hospital window—the pink and white of early June —and she felt both a sense of calm and an overwhelming fear. Her labor had gone quickly, and while she knew that was fortunate, still the pain had been profound; her body was torn open, wrecked. She was stunned by the rapid transition. And now she was going to name this child, set her direction in the world.

Dieter wanted to give the baby an American name. But their child was already going to stand out, Louise said, burdened by a mother who wasn't a native speaker.

"But when we live in New York," Dieter said, "the German name will make her stand out."

"Maybe," Louise said. "But you claim that Americans are more open-minded. Isn't that why you want to go there?"

Louise liked the name Elke. They compromised; Dieter picked her middle name—Grace, after Grace Slick. And Hinterkopf at the end. The supposed reverence of Grace would please Louise's parents, though she still hadn't told them about the baby. She and Dieter had married in the winter: a brisk ceremony with a judge, Louise in a loose dress, with Ute and Gerd as witnesses. But even with the marriage, she convinced herself that the abrupt news would land better with the joyful announcement of the baby.

During the first days home from the hospital, exhausted, pitching between wonder and fear, she composed the letter, first in her head and then on scrap paper, and finally the real thing. She was married now, she wrote; she had a baby girl. She'd send pictures soon. The act of writing and sending exhausted her, confirming the magnitude of Louise's choice. Time had become both prolonged and rushed, her sensations muted by her quick gasps of sleep, her body's slow recovery. The baby was a strange delicate thing, Louise's attachment to her at this point an idea more than a solid feeling.

Louise's midwife came to the apartment almost every day, the same woman who'd visited throughout Louise's pregnancy, who'd listened to the globe of Louise's stomach with a wooden horn. Now Frau Müller, stout and kind, measured the baby and checked on Louise, who relished the reassurance. Yes, Frau Müller said, she's healthy, she's fine.

When a letter finally came back from her parents, it was full of the harsh incantations Louise had expected. No congratulations or well wishes. *An unbaptized baby invites damnation. The Rapture is coming soon.*

Louise cried when she showed Dieter the letter. And he suggested, gently, that maybe she didn't have to write back to them for a while. "She's our daughter," he said. "They shouldn't say those things about her. We're a family now." He was protective, defensive; they were doing this enormous thing together. She was steadied by the sight of Elke nestled in his arms.

She didn't go to her studio. Work more, work less, no one was monitoring her. She slept in snatches; she was bleary, teetering on a speedy high. But when she held Elke, felt the baby's regular rhythms of heart and breath, Louise was calm.

When the term ended in early July, Louise and Dieter calculated their expenses in the apartment in Oberbilk. Even with Dieter's income, even with the *Kindergeld,* money would be tight until Louise's fellowship renewed in September. They wouldn't be able to save for the move to New York.

"Klaus-Peter needs a place until the fall," Dieter told her. "He'll pay our rent and stay here, and we could go to my mother's house."

Louise hesitated. It was six weeks until the fall term started. She barely knew Hannelore.

"We could save money for our move to New York," Dieter said. "I could come to the city to work during the week."

She didn't want to leave the city, her friends, to be stuck alone with an infant.

"Let me think about it," she said.

"You could be painting," Dieter said. "My mother would help with Elke."

As she weighed his suggestion, it was that offer of help that swayed her. She was so tired. But there, she would be able to work.

Dieter borrowed Gerd's van and they drove to Bad Waldheim with Louise's canvases. Dieter's brother brought over a crib. The room that Louise had slept in that first Christmas was now her studio.

The room was small but the light was strong. Dieter moved the furniture and covered the floor with a sheet. He arranged everything with careful attention, helping her stretch canvas and pin it to the wall. She felt profound relief. She could close the door and work. And Elke would be safe. *"Wo ist mein Schatz?"* Hannelore babbled to the baby, delighted to hold Elke in her arms.

Dieter would take the train out to Bad Waldheim on Friday nights. In Düsseldorf he'd sleep in the music studio, go to work, rehearse with the band. Astral Gruppe would be recording their album in the fall, and having this time to develop the music was essential, he told her. Still, she felt her stomach lurch as he kissed her goodbye. She was nervous about being alone with Hannelore, and she didn't want to be apart from him, didn't want him to miss this time with Elke, though she did want him to be able to work on his music.

And he was helping Louise work, too. Dieter had told his mother that it was important for Louise to be painting, and this was something

Hannelore understood, a generosity she was willing to extend. Every day at breakfast, Louise gave the baby to Hannelore at the bench in the kitchen, a magical lifting of responsibility. Later, Hannelore would come into the room quietly when Elke was hungry, and Louise would bring the baby to the other bedroom to nurse, away from the paint fumes, before handing her off again.

Louise limited her palette, working from her memory of the colors of Prefontaine's race on the TV in the Ritterhof—the blues and greens of the stands, the brown-red of the track. She was excited to paint again, and buoyed by Hannelore's constant energy. Hannelore, stocky in polyester, had quick fingers, tiny ankles. She seemed always to be in motion, and she was sometimes very funny—part of her continual movement was a repertoire of comedic gestures. The rolled eyes, the offhand wave, the exhaled, dramatic *was?*

Hannelore's kitchen philosophy was one of maximum function: the rigid mealtimes that aided digestion, the ancient sauerkraut in its earthenware jar. There was a pleasing logic to it all. A soup from a soft head of cauliflower. Yesterday's meat turned to stew. Endless string beans from the garden, snapped at the table, and the sour milk's cool tang. Hannelore always watched Louise while she drank, made sure she finished the glass. It reminded Louise of her own mother, the frugality that had stifled her as a teenager but offered a surprising comfort now.

Hannelore showed Louise how to make *rote Grütze,* shaking sugar over raspberries and currants. They ate the thick compote in the garden that afternoon. Louise liked the pale stain it left on the bowl, the bleed into loose white cream.

"Dieter said there was no coffee after the war," Louise said. "That must have been hard." Louise's head was clouded, her eyes gritty. She longed for an unbroken stretch of sleep.

The crease in Hannelore's forehead deepened; she looked at Louise with Dieter's cool blue gaze. "It wasn't so bad."

Her tone was guarded, tough, and Louise became flustered. Hannelore had lost her husband—what would she have cared about coffee?

"I just mean with little kids," Louise said. "You must have been tired. I can't wait until Elke can sleep through the night."

"She's growing quickly," Hannelore said. "She needs to eat often."

"Right," said Louise. She'd have to be more careful about what she said.

The first weekend, Hannelore wanted Louise to cook for Dieter. She unwrapped a white paper package of kidneys and stood beside Louise at the stove. The orbs jiggled on the counter. The meat was a deep red, rich with blue and brown, a color she could smell.

Hannelore's shoulder pressed against Louise's arm. "Be sure it's cooked all the way through," she said, squinting at the pan. "Otherwise it's bad for the stomach."

Dieter ate the kidneys quickly that evening, wiped his plate with bread. He didn't get up when Elke cried in the night, barely stirred when Louise brought the baby into bed to nurse. The next day they walked along the river, sat with Elke and studied her features—Dieter's blue eyes and dark hair, and something of Louise around the mouth and chin.

Louise showed Dieter what she'd been working on. She remembered the lines of buildings she passed on her bike, the flowers along the balconies, the boxes of color flashing by. Last fall, with the time to stretch out in her studio, she'd tried to achieve that sensation through the slow accumulation of detail. Now she had to find a different approach. She'd sketched a series of small paintings; there would be twenty of them, and that sense of motion would depend on their ultimate arrangement, stretching around the walls of a room.

"That makes sense to me," Dieter said. "It will rely on all of it together."

"Right," Louise said. "The order will be important, too. The progression." She could see how the series would come together.

"*Zeitgleich,*" Dieter said. "Even as you move from one end to the other."

Louise couldn't remember what that word meant.

"Simultaneous," Dieter said in English. "All at one time."

He stood in front of the canvas she'd nearly finished, a two-foot square with flashes of white embedded in a field of blue fading to green.

"It's like a musical composition," Dieter said. "A complete atmosphere. I thought the one you showed me last fall would be the right album cover, but I like this one even more."

She was charged by his recognition. *Each time it gives me something new,* he'd said of her painting in the fall. "How are the rehearsals going?" she asked.

"The synthesizer is fussy," he said. "It takes so long for the temperature to be right. So we waste time waiting."

"At least you have a few more weeks before you start recording," Louise said.

He nodded. "We'll start in the fall."

"I'm looking forward to hearing it."

"Me, too," Dieter said.

It was so quenching to talk to him about her work—she'd missed this kind of stimulation. In Bad Waldheim, Louise was cut off from the news, from Baader-Meinhof, from Nixon and Vietnam. From the gossip of the Kunstakademie, too. This was both frustrating and liberating, to work without input or constraint. She struggled to contain the mess of her work—the stink of the oils, the thick paint down the bathroom drain. The close room and the small canvases unlocked her urgency. She had no idea how she would manage in the fall, what she would do with Elke.

She started going to bed early, since she'd be waking frequently for Elke, so that she could save all her energy for her work. She was already thinking ahead to the student show in the winter: the order, the proximity of her pieces. The color moving out of the frames along the wall. Naming the series prompted the same question as naming the baby: Would this thing be known by German or English?

———

It was an afternoon in early August when Louise asked Hannelore if she had photos of Dieter as a baby. She wanted to look for Elke in that early version of his face. They were under the umbrella in the garden, eating leftover *Pflaumenkuchen,* and because of the plums, Hannelore said, wasps hovered over the plates. Careful, she warned, they'll go right in with the cake.

"Photos?" Hannelore said. "Not really. We couldn't bring much when we moved here."

"What was Dieter like as a baby?" Louise asked. Elke was placid on her lap.

"He liked to scream," Hannelore said, amused. "But he grew out of it."

"You must have been busy," Louise said. "With two little kids. Was Norbert old enough to behave himself?"

"Norbert was five when Dieter was born," Hannelore said, flopping more cream on her cake. "He took himself quite seriously."

"I can imagine that," Louise said.

"He liked to be helpful," Hannelore said. "And my husband was still around when they were kids. He could help me, too."

Louise was confused. "I thought your husband was killed in the war," she said carefully. "That's what Dieter told me."

Hannelore chewed and swallowed. "He did serve in the war," she said. "But that's not how it happened."

"He died after he came back?" Elke's cheek was pressed against Louise's neck.

Hannelore nodded. "It was some time later," she said. "He was damaged by it. He was holding all of it inside." She picked up her fork and put it down again. "It was wartime—we had to go along with the politics or we would lose everything. We didn't have any power." She was growing more animated, and Louise saw Dieter in her face, that charge in the widening of the eyes, fixing her, compelling her to agree. "That's what killed him. Or that's why he did what he did."

Louise's body lurched toward this thing she didn't want to know.

Was she understanding correctly? Was Hannelore saying that her husband had committed suicide? "How old were the boys?"

"Norbert was ten and Dieter was five."

"So they understood what happened?" Louise looked down at the table, trying to find some space.

"Unfortunately they did," Hannelore said. "They were the ones to find him."

Louise was dizzy. *"Es tut mir leid,"* she said. The apology that never felt right—to say it in German felt incomplete. She struggled to find a verb that fit what she wanted to express, but that wouldn't step too far. Dieter was five when it happened; he'd had that tragedy as part of him for as long as he could remember. A piece of him he'd kept private, that he didn't want her to know.

Later, as she washed her brushes in the bathroom sink, anger crept in. How easily Dieter had lied to her. In the apartment in Oberbilk, when she was newly pregnant, when she was still deciding what to do, he had spelled out that entire story about his father. *It's possible to do things better,* he'd said. She'd gone along with him. But the story he'd told her wasn't true. She scrubbed the sink, ran the faucet to clear the drain. It wasn't right for her to be mad. Even so, the thought of seeing him was tainted now. She wasn't sure how she would keep it from him. But to bring it up would dig deeper into his pain, expose what he'd chosen to hide. Both choices felt impossibly hard.

The next morning, Hannelore was detached, bustling with her sauerkraut preparation. Louise wondered what more she'd be able to ask. Dieter would be coming in two days, and this might be her last chance to get Hannelore to confide. When they were in the garden together that afternoon, with the last wedge of *Pflaumenkuchen,* Louise decided to gently push. "It's a tragic thing that you told me yesterday," Louise said. "Dieter always said that his father died in the war."

Hannelore nodded, anticipation cracking over her face. "That's what we say about it." She set her coffee on the table. "My husband couldn't sit with what he'd done," she said. "And I didn't want to tell the boys about it."

Hannelore was gazing down. Louise asked her, softly, what she meant.

"Dieter and Norbert don't know about what their father did in the war," Hannelore said. "For Dieter especially, it would crush him."

Louise was repulsed and magnetized — she didn't want to know, but she felt that she had to. Elke was dozing on her lap, out of sync with Louise's drumming pulse.

"Dieter is so preoccupied with history," Hannelore said. "Since he was a teenager, he's said he wants to leave Germany. So that's why I think he's happy he found you. You can give him a way to escape."

What was Hannelore saying? That Dieter only loved Louise because she was American?

Louise was insulted, and the feeling emboldened her; if Hannelore could be blunt, then she could, too. And Hannelore had led her this far already.

Louise said the words slowly — what had Dieter's father done?

"He was at one of the camps," Hannelore said. "Children were there."

She was so matter-of-fact. There didn't seem to be room for the things Louise wanted, needed, to ask: Had Dieter's father believed in what he was doing? How had he and Hannelore talked about it? How did Hannelore stand it? Had she believed, too?

"My husband wasn't the same afterward," Hannelore said.

Louise looked down at the table. He had a choice, though, she thought. He didn't deserve pity, as shattered as Hannelore looked right now.

"Dieter doesn't know about this?" Louise asked.

Hannelore shook her head. "He and Norbert think their father fought on the front in Russia, which is what I've told them. They don't know he was at the camp."

Louise didn't know what to say. She was holding Elke, who was

Dieter's daughter, the grandchild of this man whose choices would be too much for Dieter to bear. Elke was part of that heritage, and Louise couldn't do anything about it now.

"Verstehst du?" Hannelore was asking Louise if she understood, more of a command than a question. But why was she confiding in Louise? How could Louise possibly understand this?

Louise nodded, asked her who else knew.

"No one," Hannelore said. "We moved here to Bad Waldheim after my husband died. My cousin had the store. I could work. And people didn't know."

"Where were you before?"

"In the south," Hannelore said. "That's where my husband and I grew up. Lots of people had situations like ours. It was just the fact of things after the war ended. But people still talk, and talk badly. It wouldn't have been comfortable for us there."

Elke was fussing on Louise's lap, and her interruption was a relief. *"Bist du müde?"* Louise asked the baby. Alone, she spoke to Elke in English, but she used German—stunted, a weird strain—around Hannelore.

"She has to nap at the same time every day," Hannelore said. "In her crib. Or she won't learn to sleep through the night." She stacked the plates, waving away Louise's offer of help. Louise stayed in the garden and circled the beds with Elke, trying to calm her own spinning mind.

That night, as Louise was leaving the bathroom, Hannelore stopped her in the hall. Standing there in her nightgown, Hannelore held out a photograph. Louise saw the two little boys, and the much taller man, who had Dieter's close eyes, his set mouth. Louise didn't even know his name. Hannelore pulled the picture back, retreated into her bedroom. As if Louise could memorize it, hold on to something that wasn't hers.

She needed a break from painting, Louise told Hannelore the next day. Really, she didn't want to leave Elke alone with her; she needed to keep the baby close, in sight. She walked down to the river, spread a blanket, and watched Elke gaze up at the sky.

Louise thought about the night the previous fall, during the Olympics — the way Dieter had lashed out at her. She remembered the complicated fact of his shame. To be with him, Louise would have to make space for that. There by the water, as Elke blinked at the blue expanse, Louise was afraid of both things — of losing him and having him, too.

In the evening, Hannelore offered Louise *Blutwurst,* with a spoonful of applesauce on the side. She'd just been to the *Schlachtfest* at a neighbor's farm, Hannelore told Louise, helping to slaughter a pig.

Louise let the words wash over her, not wanting to make sense of them.

"Der Bruder vom Nachbarn hat einen Hof, ich kenne die Frau," Hannelore said. She sliced into the purple sausage. *"Der Metzger war zum Schlachten gekommen, und wir haben den ganzen Tag mitgeholfen."* She was talking with her mouth full. *"Dafür habe ich jetzt gute Wurst mitgebracht, Blutwurst, Leberwurst, ganz lecker."*

On and on about the neighbor and the sausages. Louise's stomach was tight.

After supper Hannelore showed Louise how to make the Hinterkopf *Geburtstagskuchen* for Dieter.

"I've taught Gisela to make this cake, and now you can make it for Dieter," Hannelore said. "It's a tradition in our family." Louise wondered if Hannelore had told Gisela the family history. What else did she expect of her daughters-in-law?

Louise asked when the party would happen. Dieter's birthday wasn't for another ten days.

"The cake is best when it can sit for a while," Hannelore said. "We'll leave it in the cellar where it's cool." She instructed Louise on how to make thin layers of buttery cake, stacked and spread with currant jam.

"No one made this cake for you on your birthday," Louise said. Hannelore's birthday had been in July, and though they'd celebrated around the table in the yard, Gisela brought a poppy seed cake heaped with cream.

"No, that's not the way it goes." Hannelore turned to the sink to wash the pan, and Louise watched her hunched shoulders. Who had the upper hand now? Was Hannelore unburdened or more deeply ashamed? Hannelore had given Louise their family history almost as she would a recipe—just another way that a woman should care for a man. But what was Louise supposed to do with any of this?

The next morning stretched out in nervous anticipation—Dieter would be arriving that afternoon, and Louise thought about what he might notice in her face or sense in her mood. When he got to the house, though, he was immediately distracted by Elke. Louise suggested a walk, so they could be together without Hannelore watching. She needed to feel connected to him again, so she could try to figure out what to do.

They set out toward the river, taking their usual route through the neighborhood. As they tracked along the sidewalk, Louise pointed to a house with a chain stretched across the driveway, asked him what it was for.

"They don't want you to turn your car around in their driveway." He was pushing the stroller, and his expression was both defensive and bemused.

"What are they afraid of?" Louise asked. "What's the threat?" She'd noticed the German fixation on fences and hedges and gates—every house on the block had clearly demarcated its property lines.

"There's no threat, of course," Dieter said. "People here are private. They're insular. They don't like outsiders intruding on their space." She studied his face—Hannelore's story had upended what she thought she knew of him.

"It's hardly an intrusion," Louise said. "It's not as though someone's going to move in."

Dieter shook his head. "I think it's ridiculous, too."

The field at the end of the block was backed by a forest next to the river, where Louise brought Elke on their daily walk. It lacked Oregon's fundamental wildness; it was pretty, with evergreens and silver water, but entirely contained.

"I used to come here when I was a kid," Dieter said. "When we first moved to Bad Waldheim."

"How old were you then?"

"Five or six," he said. "I thought this was the most magical place."

He spread a blanket over the grass, and they sat with Elke between them, stretched out on her back.

"How did you feel about moving?" Louise wanted to test the ground, pull him closer. How awful for him to have discovered his father's death —she wanted to comfort him, but how could she bring it up? Dieter had lied to her about it from the very beginning.

"I was young," Dieter said. "And my mother's cousin was kind to us. Norbert and I both latched on to him."

She couldn't predict how he might respond if she told him what she knew. She remembered the way he'd snapped at her on that night after the massacre in Munich, when she'd stepped too close to his shame. And clearly he didn't want to talk about his father's death.

She felt uneasy now, stunted by what she knew. If she told him, he would be devastated. She didn't want to cause him pain. But to keep the truth from him would be a betrayal. That would be even worse. She touched his shoulder, touched his arm. He wrapped his arm around her, rubbed his thumb along the knobs of her neck. She had so little time with him this summer. She wanted to keep him close.

Dieter looked down at Elke, smiled into her face. *Children were there,* Hannelore had said in the garden. The other half of Hannelore's secret was more awful, and more confusing. Dieter's father had worked in a camp; he hadn't been the conscripted soldier Dieter had believed him to be. But was it even Louise's place to tell him that? And what about Elke? Did she deserve to know? Dieter had lied, but so had Hannelore, and now Hannelore was asking Louise to lie, too.

They went back to the house, and Louise showed Dieter the latest piece she'd completed in the series. She'd made four paintings, and she'd have the entire fall to complete the rest before the open studios in February.

"I like the sense of movement," Dieter said.

What was he hearing when he looked? Maybe she imagined that shadow of distraction, as though he was listening to something far away. His stern face, loaded with what the family had maintained for so many years. That complicated everything she'd already accepted. And it was too late to change that now — Elke was curled against his chest.

"Do you still want to use the first one for the album cover?" Louise asked.

"I'm not sure," Dieter said. His tone, offhand and still a bit edgy, struck her as embarrassed, defensive. He walked to the window with Elke. "I'll have to check with the group."

"Let me know," she said, disappointed. His slow nod didn't convince her that he would.

Norbert and Gisela came over for Dieter's birthday party, bringing a bag of hand-me-downs for Elke. Clothes she would grow into, the fabric printed with mushrooms and berries.

Dieter held the baby up to Norbert. "She's bilingual," Dieter said. "She cries in both German and English."

At the table in the garden, Gisela sat beside Louise. She held Elke and spoke to the baby in a stream of nonsense, shaking her bangs from her eyes. Louise wondered what Gisela knew of this family, how she accommodated its effect on Norbert.

When Hannelore went inside, Gisela leaned in to Louise. "You learned to make the cake, I'm sure," she said quietly. "It's for men only. No one will tell you that, but it's true. I've suggested to Hannelore that I make it for her birthday, but she refuses. I'm only supposed to make it for Norbert."

Louise liked this punchy side of Gisela. "At least we're allowed to have a slice."

"It's a little too jammy for my taste," Gisela said. Her son, Tilman, was picking crumbs from his plate, already an oblivious heir. And Dieter was across the table, asking for a second piece.

That evening, Louise and Dieter watched TV with Hannelore. The same *Schlager* variety show Frau Kerbel liked, with a man in square-heeled boots striding across the stage to restrained applause. A woman in a crocheted dress sang through a smile. The round stage was ringed with pots of flowers, and a tuxedoed band honked behind her on shiny horns.

"Manchmal," the woman sang. *"Manchmal liebe ich dich."* Her performance was sanitized, flavorless. Louise sensed Dieter's agitation; he was slouched with folded arms on the couch. He'd told her about the *Schlager* songs, their scrubbed and willfully naive version of German history, German culture. An air of complacent ease — everything was smooth, easy, fine.

"She looks drugged," Dieter said. "She looks psychotic."

Louise felt Hannelore watching her. "It's just a TV show," Louise said. Hannelore caught her eye — wary, complicit — and Louise looked away.

"Everyone watches it, though," Dieter said. Everyone was willing to buy into the show's empty jollity, he meant. And even so, he kept watching it, too. He didn't suggest that they go to bed.

DIETER

2008

THE BLOW-UP MATTRESS on the second floor of his mother's house was a better accommodation for Dieter than Norbert's crowded house. Crowded especially by Louise—an older, remote Louise, who'd been traveling separately on this planet for quite some time, whose laughter lit up ancient sensations in his mind. She was the mother of his only child and a stranger nevertheless.

When Elke had told Dieter that she wanted Louise to come to the funeral, Dieter had been surprised, to say the least. He'd agreed to it— he could hardly say no to his daughter, who'd put up with his extended absence in her youth. Perhaps Elke needed her mother there for some kind of psychic bolstering. And in a strange way, he found Elke's idea of a reunion flattering, even appropriate. His mother had loved Louise.

Dieter had been sleeping in his mother's house since he'd arrived last week. Most of the furniture was gone now from Hannelore's, which was why he was bedding down on the blow-up. But he wanted one last stay in the house, even in the empty rooms.

Each night since he'd arrived, Gisela had made him a tea with herbs before he left to go to bed, to cure his lingering jet lag. She was brewing it now for Elke and Louise, too, who both looked like they were already dreaming, slumped at the kitchen's bench.

Gisela gave each of them a mug. "If you want the body to under-stand what time it is, you must be firm."

Dieter drank the tea quickly; it was so hot it burned his mouth.

"*Langsam,* Dieter," Gisela said. But Dieter wanted to guzzle it down so he could retreat. To see Louise in Gisela's kitchen was unnerving. Louise, once his wife, now a good guest, was keeping her vital force in respectful check—her still-electric hair, her discerning eye. Louise and Gisela, both a bit more solid, their faces lined. The past had curdled into this weird version of the present.

"I'll see you in the morning," he said. He walked the few blocks to his mother's house, the evening brisk and melancholy. The short trip compressed the thousands of times he'd traced this path. The cross-hatched fence, the dim gardens. All of it was still there.

Time was working strangely, but that's what his life had been marked by—a series of timings that were not quite right. Sometimes bad timing, and sometimes just a bit off the beat. He had learned not to fight it; what other choice did he have?

Strange timing: Dieter had been born just as the war was ending. He'd arrived amidst that lingering, unspoken horror. A big baby with strong lungs, his mother had told him. That's all he knew of his early years. His memories of his father were cloudy—even the most terrible one was vague to him now, as though he was remembering being told the story, rather than living through it. He'd been only five years old.

But of course his mother never did tell Dieter anything about what happened. Whatever he knew of it had to have come from his own eyes. He and Norbert had gone into the house first, running ahead of their mother. Bad timing. But if Dieter hadn't seen his father, would he know now what happened? His father's suicide was never mentioned, and as Dieter got older, his mother began to tell people her husband had been killed in the war. They all had.

But since Dieter was born in 1945, that meant that he also had to say that he'd never known his father. So Dieter's fragmented memories of the man became private, impossible under the version of the truth that his mother had imposed.

The timing was off—the timing contradicted itself—if he could remember his father's tall frame bending to lift him. His father carry-

ing wood into the house, bringing the cold inside in his wake, pushing Dieter back from the stove. Dieter wasn't supposed to have those
memories—a smile, a shard of laughter—and so he allowed them to
become blurry. That's what his life in Germany had been. Pretending
that none of this was there.

This strange timing had chased him, patterned his life, and this was
why he'd played the drums. To fight it. To control it. Literally keeping
time. He'd found the same rhythm with the tones and pulses of the
synths. If he was improvising, if his time was off, he could make that
misstep seem deliberate. Seizing that sense of *off.* The reason he liked
free jazz, the reason he liked living in New York. The city offered the
sense that you could be missing things at every moment. The random-
ness a comfort: you could choose to turn left instead of right, to walk
instead of ride the train. And you would miss some instance of ecstatic
chaos, but there would always be another. Time was everything and
nothing at once; it controlled the city and yet the city seemed to go on
despite it. There was no time there—New York was open, ongoing.
And that was how he heard music.

Now, on the other side of the hedge, he could see his mother's house.
He unlatched the gate, unlocked the door. When Hannelore had gone
into the nursing home five years ago, Norbert's daughter, Julia, had
moved into the house with her family. Julia left the house last spring,
and Dieter and Norbert had undertaken a slow sifting since then; Hannelore hadn't been a saver. So each object that had remained was meaningful, if only for that fact—a tablecloth, an earthenware jar. Norbert
and Gisela had absorbed some of the furniture into their own house.
And Dieter, too, had taken things home. His great-grandfather's chess
set and the photos of his mother as a girl, with her braids pinned into
a crown. He had barely any pictures of his father's family—he and
Norbert had to share the few that remained, so that his image of his
father was always the same washed-out, calm expression, the sweet and
seeking eyes. His father in the class photo from his *Berufsschule,* one
young face in an anonymous line.

Tomorrow morning Dieter would continue painting the first floor while Norbert worked in the basement, filling cracked cement. It would be better to put the house on the market in the spring, the real estate agent had told them, but they'd get everything ready now, while they were together.

In the empty rooms, Dieter could fill in flashes of long-finished time. Here in the kitchen, he could imagine his mother cutting *Spätzle,* her face flushed over the steaming pot. Her love had been serious, something else to work hard at, and though she hadn't been demonstrative, he'd never questioned that love.

And despite his mother's weariness — she was always working, and she'd always seemed old, even when Dieter was young — she'd enjoyed herself. He remembered her happy in this house. A card game in the evening, a glass of red wine. Her loud laugh. Her delight with Elke. And though her displeasure at Elke's and Dieter's distance was a thick mass between them, his mother had always been thrilled when they visited.

That was the gift of their German nature, he thought — in this case, the stoic acceptance of Dieter's less-than-perfect family circumstances. He saw flashes of her upset. He caught her squinting when he described his plans, an expectation textured with her grief. An occasional touch of passive-aggression in her tone. And even so, he felt her resolute warmth — *it is what it is,* he sensed her telling him. She was steady and devoted, always there.

With the rooms empty, sounds were different — it was his own footsteps that bounced through the space as he climbed the stairs now, rather than his mother's, rapid then gradually slower over time.

In the back bedroom, he found the cardboard package in the closet. "Her painting is there," Hannelore had sometimes said to Dieter when he returned to Bad Waldheim. In exactly those words — specifying any further would take them to the brink of something more direct and uncomfortable. A discussion they didn't want to have.

Hannelore would mention the painting when he visited, both an offhand reminder and a direct lament: Louise had been here, and now she was gone.

Hannelore did ask Elke how Louise was doing, and right in front of Dieter, too: *"Wie geht es deiner Mutter?"* Elke answered in careful German, her response always the same vague assessment.

It was complicated for Dieter to talk to Hannelore about why he didn't want to come back to Germany. He couldn't bring himself to mention his father—that would only make things harder for them. He was afraid of what else his mother might reveal, what she might tell him about herself. It was easier to be together—really, it was the only way he could manage it—if they didn't get into all that.

In America, in New York, he'd found a place where the big problems, the problems of history, didn't belong to him, weren't his fault. And in a way, his staying in New York made him understand why Louise hadn't returned to Düsseldorf. Days piled up into a choice.

Now, upstairs in the room that had served as Louise's makeshift studio, he wondered if his mother had ever looked at the painting he'd found tucked in the closet here. The wrapping was so perfect and tight. Plastic and cardboard—he himself had packed the canvas, so long ago. He pulled it out now, the surprise of color still vivid and assured. The blue faded into green, in layers Louise had applied. It had been tacked to the wall the first time he'd seen it. Dieter cradling Elke's wobbly neck. Louise explaining her series, excited and charged. That moment near perfect in his memory, caught in amber. But the Louise who'd made this painting was not the same as the woman a few blocks from here, sleeping in Norbert's spare room. The intervening years had left their mark, the press of time something he couldn't actually control.

LOUISE

1973

ON ONE OF THEIR first nights back in the apartment in Oberbilk that September, Louise and Dieter went to an opening on Mittelstrasse, a group show of female artists that Ute had helped organize.

"I love this space," Louise said as she hugged Ute. It was hot in the gallery; Elke's hands were sticky on Louise's neck.

"An alternative space," Ute said. "For us women, the alternative artists."

Dieter was looking over their shoulders as they talked, then left the conversation to wander the room. He picked up a beer, and now was joking with a woman with flat yellow hair.

Ute had asked Louise to contribute something to the show. Louise might have offered a piece from her series, but she didn't want to break it up. She regretted that choice as she circled the room, which was crowded with work: drawings hung salon-style, a weaving that spanned its own wall. Ute had made a new sculpture, with torn dresses arranged in color-coded piles. People were laughing, loud, buzzing with their opinions about the art. They were part of something serious and shared, and Louise wandered the room's perimeter with Elke, feeling envious, left out.

The blond woman did a performance. She was tall and solid, confident in a short red dress. A handsome woman, Louise's mother would have said. A nice healthy girl.

She stared out at the audience, eyes wide as though possessed. She fell to the floor and rolled across the room. The spectators stepped out of her way. She moaned, stood up, moaned, and fell again. Elke woke up and cried, too, which prompted intoxicated laughter, and Louise left her place beside Dieter, moved to the back of the room, sat on the floor and nursed while the woman barreled on.

Afterward, Dieter was talking to the blonde again, leaning against the wall. The woman laughed constantly, preemptively, the sound rattling in the room.

Louise stood with Ute in the corner, with the wine bottles and the stained tablecloth, and Elke asleep in her basket at their feet.

"Who is that?" Louise had finished a few cups of wine, and though earlier she told herself she wasn't going to ask, she'd lost that need for dignity.

"Sabine." Ute was placid, composed, but her cheeks were blotched red. Klaus-Peter had joined Dieter and the woman against the wall. "She sings," Ute said.

Louise kept looking at her. Ute's teeth had a purple cast — indigo, with the gray of bone beneath the sheen of wine.

"She's singing with Astral Gruppe now," Ute said.

Dieter hadn't told Louise that. "I haven't heard it yet," Ute said. "Gerd says they're going to try her vocals on the album recordings."

Louise thought she could push Ute to say more, but she was afraid of what her friend might tell her. She left Ute at the table and walked across the room. "Klaus-Peter," she said. "I haven't said hello yet."

He leaned in to kiss her on the cheek. They spoke for a while, and the whole time Louise was aware of Sabine, of watching and being watched.

The night was winding down when Dieter finally introduced Louise to Sabine. "Nice you could be here," Sabine said. Dieter had skipped right over her name. The kind of person who expected recognition.

"I'm sorry that our daughter interrupted your performance," Louise said.

"Macht nichts," Sabine said smoothly. "Don't worry about it. Good art is spontaneous."

Louise touched Dieter's back. "It's late."

She watched him say goodbye to Sabine, and then Louise kissed her quickly on the cheek. She took advantage of the formality. She wanted to know what this woman smelled like, whether her skin was soft.

Earlier, Dieter had gathered the spent wine bottles and laid them on their sides. Now he went back to the table and finished off the last collected drops before they left. She felt tenderness despite her aggravation. His move was funny and sweet and pathetic all at once.

Dieter carried Elke on the walk home; Louise held the empty basket.

"You didn't tell me that Sabine was singing in Astral Gruppe now," Louise said.

"Am I supposed to tell you every single detail? Would you like to know that Gerd broke a string?"

"Of course not." Louise was delirious—from wine and lack of sleep, from her creeping suspicion. But even so, she registered his defensive tone.

"It's not certain yet," Dieter said, hugging her shoulders. "We're trying it, but her vocals might be too distracting."

They'd reached the apartment by then, and though Louise wanted him to tell her more, in this softer voice, Elke was awake and reaching for Louise.

Louise was enrolled in Knecht's class again that fall, and she planned to keep working on her series. She switched studios so she'd be with Ute and another woman, Birgit Becker, a sculptor who didn't mind if Louise brought Elke along.

Immediately, though, problems. Louise wound up with paint on her hands while Elke was red-faced, livid. Neither choice was ideal: walk to the sink at the end of the hall to the sound of Elke's screams, or stain the baby, who'd need to be washed then, too. From then on Louise dressed Elke in the same paint-smeared onesie each time she brought her to the studio. She knew it was risky to have Elke there at all—certainly breaking at least one rule—though she hadn't asked.

In the studio, Louise reached for the original thread of her thinking—that sense of contradiction she'd felt watching Prefontaine. Her own feelings of looking through an open door. The quiet sequence of the city's buildings that she'd noticed the previous fall. Her movement against the static field. And her discussions with Dieter on the second floor of Hannelore's house—that simultaneity, barely in reach. She tacked up her sketches, considered order and placement while Elke nursed.

But it was difficult to drift into sustained thought. She couldn't paint, couldn't tap in. She burnished the surface of one of the canvases from last fall, rubbed it with a wire brush. She tried watercolors, markers. She sketched. All in the gasps between diapers and nursing, in the quick mornings when she brought Elke to nap in the corner of the studio. She didn't touch the four paintings from Hannelore's; she would return to the series when she had more time. And she saved the one that Dieter had wanted for the album cover, the dotted green field, so it would be ready when the band completed the album.

Louise went to school less and less. Dieter was working in the studio with Astral Gruppe several nights a week, so she saw him only in harried windows. All their interactions centered around the baby. Elke's crib was in their bedroom; her diapers were strung over the drying racks. Dieter assumed that Louise would do everything for Elke, that his work was more important than her own.

"I have work I'd like to be doing, too, you know," Louise said when he returned late one night. She was nursing Elke, sitting up in bed.

"The recording is slow," he said. "We're tracking each instrument separately." Usually when he came back from the studio, his voice would be loud, his ears cottoned by the prolonged volume. This time he was soft, removed.

"And vocals?"

"We're trying them," Dieter said. "They might not fit."

"You just like to have Sabine around," Louise said. "She gives the band some sex appeal." She was punchy, desperate, unsure if she was being rational.

"It's not like that," Dieter said.

"You're interested in her."

He shook his head. "There's nothing going on." His tone was matter-of-fact, dismissive. Case closed.

She could have pushed more. But it was easier to let him come quietly into bed. He held her tenderly, but that was all; her body served the baby and nothing more.

Tangled into her quiet acceptance was Hannelore's story. Louise knew a deeper and more complicated side of Dieter's psychology, and that awareness raised both her pity and her ire.

Hannelore had unloaded her secret on Louise; she expected Louise to accommodate Dieter's damage but not actually tell him the truth. It was awful of Hannelore to do that, completely unfair.

Or maybe Hannelore did want Louise to tell him, because she couldn't do it herself. That wasn't fair either. And Louise couldn't imagine, with things between them so fraught, how to broach the subject with him. Maybe it would bring him closer. Maybe it would drive him further away. Louise relied on Dieter; they had Elke now, and on her own, Louise couldn't afford more than a single room. Her fellowship would be ending soon; she had one term of funding left.

Each day with Elke stretched so long, and yet the weeks blurred, time marked by the baby's development. Louise watched Elke study her own hand with profound focus. Elke shifted her eyes to Louise, the two of them bound in their devoted gaze. Their connection was essential and gratifying, completely immersing to Louise as her relationship with Dieter grew more strained.

For the *Rundgang*, the open studios that would happen in February, Louise cut up one of the paintings she'd made in Bad Waldheim — the repeating rectangles of the stands, the white lines of the track. Ute talked to Louise in the studio as she pinned the cut pieces to the wall. Elke was napping in her stroller, bundled up next to the open window.

Ute seemed antsy. She was pacing in distracted steps. "Gerd doesn't want Sabine to be in the band," Ute said. The sound of her name was startling.

"The singing isn't working?" Louise looked over her shoulder at Ute, but Ute wasn't meeting her gaze.

"It's not that," Ute said. Louise pushed the tack into the wall, her fingers thrumming. *Just say it,* she thought.

"Gerd's angry at Dieter," Ute said. "For being involved with her."

A visceral shock, for Louise to hear out loud what she'd suspected, the surprise of what she already knew.

"Gerd said it's been going on for a month," Ute said. That was a surprise, too. Louise had assumed Dieter had started up with her in the summer. But still, she couldn't believe she'd let it continue for that long without confronting him.

"It's not fair to you," Ute said. "I'm angry at him too. And for what it's worth, I don't like Sabine's singing. She sounds ridiculous."

"She sounds awful," Louise said.

"Dieter is being awful, too."

"I can't leave, though," Louise said. She felt trapped. Her fellowship's meager income would end soon. Married to Dieter, Louise could apply to become a citizen. After the fellowship, she could stay in Germany. Maybe she could teach, or try to show her work.

What was her other option—to go back to the U.S.? What would she be going back to? To Eugene? To her parents, who'd told her that her unbaptized baby was destined for hell? She could stay with friends in San Francisco. But that was what she'd do if she were untethered, when she could survive on saltines and sleep on a couch. Elke required much more.

"I would miss you if you left," Ute said. "Tell him he has to end it."

Louise looked at her bright pieces on the wall. Cut up, the series lacked the energy she'd felt at Hannelore's house. It remained untitled: she couldn't find a name for it in either language.

The pieces were where she'd left them, pinned to the studio wall, during the *Rundgang* the following week. Students elbowed for the best spots in the stairwell or the entrance hall, but Louise didn't think her work deserved that exposure.

She brought Dieter to see it, ashamed at the erosion of her original idea. "I left the painting you liked intact," she said. "If you still want to use it for the cover."

She dipped her knees to jiggle Elke, who was in her sling, pinned to Louise's chest. Dieter glanced around the room, ran his fingers through his hair.

"The covers are already being printed," he said. "The others chose the image. I didn't have much say in the matter."

How fluidly he could lie. Louise stepped out into the crowded hallway, and her disappointment over the album blurred with the broader loss of her life here. Dieter was in step beside her and, even without looking, she could feel the set of his jaw.

"This spring is my last term," Louise said. "The fellowship ends after that."

"My mother would be happy to have you again this summer," said Dieter.

"You can't leave me alone with Elke."

"Astral Gruppe is going on tour," Dieter said. "It would be much easier for you to be with her in Bad Waldheim."

"What about New York?" Louise asked. They'd paused in front of a giant slab of foam. Dieter was staring at it, his face creased.

"I can't leave now," Dieter said. "The band is at a critical moment. The album is coming out. We have to tour."

"Elke and I could go with you." Louise felt rushed, out of breath.

"It's no place for a baby," Dieter said.

She was dizzy now, riding the heat that had rushed to her face. "Why, so you and Sabine can be together? So we don't get in your way?"

Dieter took her arm, led her toward the stairs. "It's over now," he said quietly. "With Sabine. I've ended it."

She let loose with a burst of invective, lobbed English at him with acid force. Elke was crying in the sling between them. Dieter unsnapped the baby, lifted her out. It was finished, he kept saying to Louise. He was sorry that he'd hurt her. He held Elke, shushed her, kissed her head.

"What am I supposed to say to that?" Louise asked.

"There's nothing you can say," Dieter said. "It's for me to say. *Es tut mir leid.*" His apology felt simplistic, too polite—these words didn't give her explanation or actual remorse. Still, she needed to believe him. But what a precarious foothold. They left together, walked through the cold night to the other side of town.

Spring came early that year; during a blast of unseasonable warmth, Louise took Elke to the placid, gritty park in Oberbilk. She sat with other mothers along the playground and let Elke touch the sand. On the paths winding through the woods, she nodded to old people, glacial in formal clothing. She glanced at haggard men waiting, saw quiet exchanges, an occasional flash of bare skin. There was a snack bar in a clearing that sold sausage and beer. The low A-frame reminded her of the camp canteen where she'd worked as a teenager. Men sat in redfaced groups, bellowed friendly insults. She bought a bottle of Kölsch and sat with Elke at a stone table soft with moss.

She drew in her sketchbook; she wanted to capture the damp menace, the rip of danger. The people here were jolly despite their history, despite their guilt and pain. The men at the neighboring table reminded her of the *Schlager* pop songs' adamant good cheer. Louise was the mother of a German daughter. This place belonged to her now, too.

She'd realized, with quiet shock, that she'd been infected with Germany's denial: when she'd thought about what Hannelore had told her about Dieter's father's suicide, she'd pitied him, cut him slack. She'd let his affair with Sabine go on. In that way, she'd made his life more important than her own.

Last year, Louise had chosen to keep the baby in part because she thought it would help Dieter resolve his losses. Those losses were so much more complicated than she'd known.

Now that burden was going to be passed on to Elke. And maybe it was the thought of Elke that had kept Louise quiet; she couldn't bring that pain into their life as a family. But in her silence, Louise was acting out the collective failure to acknowledge the truth. She didn't want that for Elke, either. There was no way around it—for Elke's sake, for her own sanity, Louise would have to try to talk to him.

Astral Gruppe had a party the next week to celebrate the release of their album, and Louise brought Elke with her to the show, in a gallery off the Königsallee. The new records were fanned out on a table in the back. *All at One Time,* the album was called; the title was in English. But when she looked closely, she was dismayed. The cover was not anything close to their conversation about *zeitgleich* and Louise's paintings. The artwork consisted only of photos of the band. There were some on the back and stretched across the gatefold and, most prominently of all, a shot of the group on the front. The five of them. Laughing in the studio, serious along a brick wall. One with Dieter beside Sabine, looking over at her with definite mirth. Louise had inspired him, while her own work had failed. He'd stolen *zeitgleich* from her and not given her any credit. She put the record down.

Everyone was drinking beer. Louise had one, too, a cold bottle in the warm room, with Elke's head against her neck. She stayed in back and arranged her coat to muffle Elke's ears. Up front, Dieter reached to hold the top of the door frame as he surveyed the room. He was close to two meters, as Louise had learned to think of it, and he took up even more space. When posing for photos, he spread his arms out—all mine, he seemed to be saying.

The band started playing. Sabine, beatific and bursting from a shiny

dress, sang in a low, blurred voice: the words might have been in English, but Louise couldn't tell. Dieter was hitting hard, possessed. But
Louise was not with him, and she was separate from everyone else, too
—all of them watching, admiring him. The band a unit, oblivious to
everything outside, locked into their shared pursuit. Her anger drove
with his beat. She'd been part of this mass of admiration for him. She'd
allowed him too much.

But as much as she wanted them to sound bad, the band still had
the power to transport her—the music was so much bigger now, even
with Sabine's wailing. Whatever else Dieter had been doing with his
time, practicing had been part of it. Tight changes linked the drifting
passages. They had become really good, incredible, and it had nothing
to do with her.

When the set was over, Louise took Elke to the kitchen, which was
empty and dim, just off the main room. She unbuttoned her blouse;
as Elke nursed, Louise watched the party through the door frame. The
music was up loud, and people were dancing now, a couple dozen of
them jiggling in front of the turntable. Men lined the wall, their wide
belts and open collars confident and expansive. There were girls in
boots and short skirts, in leather and suede, the colors of their fabrics
blurred together. Shades of orange and purple and brown, and a happy,
messy quality to their yelled conversations, their exaggerated gestures,
all teeth and gums and waving hands.

Dieter was next to Sabine on the dance floor. They moved to the
blaring music. They didn't touch. They were merely in proximity to
each other, and yet their connection was palpable, particularly from
the way Dieter's long arms cut through the open space around her. All
mine.

While Dieter was dancing, Elke spit up on Louise's skirt. Alone in
the unlit kitchen, Louise took off her skirt and cleaned it at the sink.
She stood there in her wool tights, with Elke in her sling, and listened
to the roar from the other room. She was back here, a spectator to
Dieter's pleasure, with Elke already sleeping again.

Louise had only had one beer. But maybe the collective inebriation of the place had an osmotic effect. Everyone else was much further gone. She didn't put her skirt back on. Not a clear decision in her mind. A visceral response. She had to get out there. She took off her tights, the rough wool rolling down her legs. Her hands pushed against her dry skin, pulled at her underwear. She left her things in a pile and moved back into the party on the rhythm of her own pulse.

The music was loud, the Can album they listened to constantly then. The song that spanned nearly the entire second side: the toggling bassline, the drums crashing over the same melody and words. *Mother sky*, the singer was chanting. The words steadied her. She floated on them. It felt like he was talking to her. *Mother sky.* She pulled her scarf over Elke, who was sleeping warm on her chest. She danced in the crush of people; the room was crowded and hot.

Louise was on display, close to Dieter, and she kept her eyes down. She knew everyone was watching. Not because she was half-undressed; nudity was not that unusual. But the top half of her body was so matronly—Louise's blouse buttoned all the way up, her breasts heavy, Elke's sling on top. Elke's weight pulled on her shoulders, but even so Louise was light, boundless as her feet touched off the cement floor. She could smell the stranger beside her, his sweat and damp wool. He surveyed her through thick wire glasses, gave her a suggestive, approving nod.

Across the room, Ute had her hand cupped over Gerd's ear. Gerd was bending down to hear Ute, and looking over the crowd at Louise. Sabine was still dancing on her own. A mix of power and shame: Louise was in the middle of everyone. The music was pounding, repeating —they were looking at her now.

Dieter was coming toward her; he held her arms, tender and forceful, and led her back to the kitchen. Through the crush of people, the music still blaring. Her act was a quick anomaly in a long, loose night. Her embarrassment mixed with her anger—all of them had continued dancing, taking long swigs of their drinks. She'd wanted everyone to

stop, to see her humiliation and rage. She needed to feel them acknowledge her. But the party was still going on.

Dieter took Elke from Louise while she put on her tights and skirt.
"We'll go home now," he said. His voice was subdued, almost soothing.
They left quietly, without goodbyes.

She listened to the album a few days later, during the afternoon while
Dieter was at work. She turned it up loud and sat on the floor while
Elke crawled around the room. The first side was all long songs, with
the same brisk movement she'd heard at the show, and Sabine's keening
vocals. Louise stayed on the floor for the entire side, tracking the baby's
curly head. Elke kept looking back at Louise and laughing. *Ha ha ha.*
Her wet, enchanting grin against the roaring music.

How was it possible to feel all of this at once? That deep tug of love
as she met Elke's eyes, even as the music unspooled her sense of loss.
She flipped the record and sat on the floor again, pulling Elke onto her
lap. Long swaths of drone, textured, with layers of sound that melted
into one massive thrust. *Zeitgleich.* He'd stolen it from her. And though
she'd never figured out how to make her own paintings achieve that
sense of simultaneity, he'd found it in his music. Jealousy and disappointment curled in her stomach.

Dieter hadn't been honest with her, but she hadn't been honest with
him either. She'd been trying to protect him; she'd excused him because
of what she knew. But she couldn't keep it up any longer.

When he came home that evening, he sat weary on the couch, dis-
tractedly scanning the newspaper. Looking at his familiar posture,
slouched with his long legs crossed, she felt both tenderness and re-
vulsion. She tried to engage him, described Elke's crawling, asked him
about his day.

"It was a usual day," he said. He didn't even glance up. Anger lit her
body, rushed heat to her face. If he wouldn't look at her, then there was
no gentle way in. Nausea climbed up her throat. She'd waited too long
already.

"There's something I have to talk to you about," she said. Her shift in tone got his attention. He looked at her—curious, concerned. The words were forming in front of her, propelling her forward. "Your mother told me about your father. When I was with her last summer. She told me."

Dieter was frowning at her. "What do you mean?"

Her pulse drummed in her temples, in her chest. "She said that he wasn't killed in the war. That he died a few years later."

She could see him absorbing what she'd said, the shock withering him. "Why did she tell you that?" he snapped at her, his voice raw and desperate.

Louise told him she didn't know. He leaned forward in the chair, his elbows braced on his knees. "Why do you tell me this now? Why wait so long to do it?" He was lighting into her with questions she couldn't answer.

"You never told me either," Louise said.

He looked at her, distraught. "My father killed himself," he said. A blunter assessment than the phrasing she'd practiced. "I'm surprised that she told you. Our family never spoke about it."

"She didn't spell it out in exact terms," Louise said. "But she let me know what she meant."

"That became our collective story—that he was killed when he was on the front. We never discussed it, never agreed to it. It just happened that way. My mother started saying it, and then we did, too." He was on his feet now, pacing, agitated.

His distress made her dizzy, ill, but she was riding the momentum of her decision to tell him. She couldn't give him one piece and not the other.

"He wasn't on the front," she said.

He looked back at her, wounded, confused.

"She told me that, too," Louise said. "And I think you deserve to know. She told me he worked in a camp."

Time slowed to agonizing seconds as he processed what she'd said.

"Why would you make up that kind of story?" Dieter asked. "You're angry at me, but why would you lie?"

"I'm not lying," Louise said. "I'm telling you what she told me." Her voice was loud, shaking. "He worked in a camp. He wasn't a soldier on the front. Why don't you ask her why she kept it from you? Why not ask her why she told me instead?"

Dieter was breathing in quick gasps, his anger radiating out. "Why did you wait to tell me this?"

"I didn't know what to do," Louise said quietly.

Dieter knocked the lamp from the end table with an urgent swipe of his hand. The lamp hit the floor, and the sound of it crashed in the room. His force frightened her, sent panic through her body. But his charge was driving him away from her—he grabbed his coat from the hooks in the hall and rushed out of the apartment, pulling the door hard behind him.

The quiet that followed was punctured by Elke awake, Elke crying. Louise went to the bedroom and picked her up. Minutes ticked on that way—Elke, red-faced with gargling cries, then quieting, then calm. Louise brought her into bed, fell into unsettled sleep as she listened for Dieter's return.

In the morning, she found him in the living room, sitting on the couch.

"I'm sorry," she told him. "I wanted to do the right thing." He didn't respond. He took the baby from her arms and stood by the window.

"This is for me to try to understand," Dieter said without turning. "It's not for you."

He and Elke were both looking out at the balconies of the buildings across the street. He'd set the lamp back on the table, Louise noticed, and turned it to hide the ripped shade.

Louise made coffee, cut bread. They ate quietly, their weariness shared. Before he left for work, he reached to embrace her, and for a few minutes she stayed with him by the door.

———

Their routines kept them apart in the days that followed. Dieter was calm when he came home, but cordial and remote. They stepped carefully around each other, spoke in cautious, simple exchanges about what Elke needed—a diaper, a bath. The distance between them, and Dieter's cool glaze, was as painful as the way he'd yelled when she told him. But she couldn't take it back.

The strain stretched on for several weeks, a fog whose scope wasn't clear. And so when the letter from her father arrived, the imperative tone was almost soothing, despite the gravity of his news. *Your mother is very sick,* he'd written. *Come as soon as possible. I can send you the money for the ticket.*

Louise read the letter at the kitchen table, absorbed what her father was telling her. She knew she would go right away. It would have taken a week for his letter to reach her; it would take another week for her response to get back. She calculated what it would cost. The price of the ticket would be a hard sum for her father to come up with.

That evening, when Dieter got home, she showed him the letter, told him she wanted to go to Oregon for a month.

"Of course," he said. How awful, he was saying, her mother's illness was frightening news. He wasn't offering to go with her. And she didn't ask. She knew it would be easier without him, as much as she would have liked his support. With so much festering between them, she wasn't sure he'd be able to give her that. It was relieving, actually, to think about a break from their tension. Her husband had to work, she'd write in the letter. He couldn't make the trip with her.

"I'll pay for the ticket," Dieter said. "We have money in the savings account." That was what they'd put aside for their eventual move to New York.

"Ich werde euch vermissen," Dieter said. *I'll miss you.* And though he was looking at the baby in his arms, he'd used the plural form of you.

Ten days later, Louise left. The journey would be complicated: to London and then to New York; to San Francisco and Eugene and finally Cottage Grove. She saw Ute and Gerd before she departed, tidied her corner of the studio, but she didn't go out to Bad Waldheim. There wasn't much time. Elke's first birthday would pass while they were in Oregon, and Hannelore had been talking since Christmas about the party she wanted to have. But the party would have to be postponed. They could do it later in the summer, Louise thought, with a bowl of *rote Grütze* in the garden. She saw it in front of her, an image comforting and clear — the purple-red on the white bowl, the dark colors contained in that wide spread of green.

MARGOT

2008

OUTSIDE THE GAS STATION, Keith was counting coins. "Might as well use this now," he said. He handed Spencer the money and went into the store with the laptop. Margot went in, too, and looked at the magazines and cartons of pudding. Joel was circling the aisles, examining the vague jerkies.

"We really should go," Margot said to him. "We're already going to be late."

"Tell that to Keith."

He was posted up by the bathroom, his hands busy on the laptop, which was pedestaled on cases of soda. "There's Wi-Fi," Keith said without looking up from the screen.

"We still have two hundred kilometers," Margot said.

When the group reassembled, it was Joel's turn to drive, and Margot took the passenger seat.

"I have good news and bad news." Keith handed up a CD. "I downloaded some Krautrock to prepare us for meeting the German guy."

"That's not bad news," Joel said.

"The dude in Den Haag wrote to me," he said. "They got shut down."

"I thought squats in Europe were really established," Margot said. "They had government funding."

"Apparently not," Keith said.

"We could knock up for Bart back in Antwerp," Joel said. "He told us we were always welcome."

Margot thought of Bart's manicured arms. She wanted to keep moving.

Joel turned up the volume. "Can," he said. "Düsseldorf band. Well, Cologne. Close enough."

Margot had listened to Can before, but she hadn't really thought about her mother as the band's audience. The music picked up as green landscape rushed by. The rhythm was mysterious, propulsive; a voice tacked off-kilter over the drums.

"This song is amazing," Margot said. "It just keeps on going."

" 'Mother Sky' is maybe the greatest song of all time," Joel said.

When the album ended, Keith told them not to eject the CD. "I downloaded the Everly Brothers album, too," he said. "Family portrait."

Margot recognized the song. *I wonder if I care as much,* one of the Everlys sang, and Margot thought of her father, sitting by the stereo in the corner of the living room.

"Listen to what's going on in the background," Keith said. He turned up the volume, and thus instructed, Margot heard two voices harmonizing under a track of acoustic guitar. Then an electric broke in.

"That lead is incredible," Joel said. One note held without letting go.

"It's a drone," said Spencer.

"The apple doesn't fall far from the tree, Margot," Keith said.

This comment pleased her. But the song ended, and the next one had sad lyrics in tidy rhymes. Margot felt uncomfortable—she wished she hadn't said so much about her family. They were getting close to Hasselt, where her mother was waiting, and Margot felt she'd betrayed something private, or said something that wasn't quite true.

When they left the highway and drove into the town, Margot thought about what her father had told her any time they visited a new place. *Look at the way people choose to move,* Richard said. In big cities, he'd point to people cutting across the street diagonally, through cars stopped at traffic, ignoring the comfort of the crosswalk, stepping off the curb to bypass slow-moving foot traffic. The brain was the original GPS, her father had said a few too many times. Hasselt lacked that urban bustle, but even so, Margot could see it, the pedestrians' sense of direction clear.

She read the directions to Joel, and when they found the venue, Joel double-parked and they shuttled everything in. The show was a festival, and it had been going on all day, and in the crush of people, the big room hot and musty, she noted the smells of old cigarettes and beer, a nostalgic sort of stench. As she wound through the crowd, she sensed she should pay close attention, because she knew she'd miss this, the expectation and then the proud relief when the show was over. Soon enough she'd be home again and back at work, urging time to hurry as she stood still.

Margot saw her sister first. Elke, her hair in an elaborate knot, was beside their mother. And then Dieter—silver and skinny, with an eagle's knowing frown.

"I'm sorry we're late," Margot said as she hugged her mother. "The kilometers thing is tricky."

"The show couldn't go on without you," Louise said. Her face radiated enthusiasm. "I can't wait to see you perform."

"The earlier band made a super set," Dieter said. *Da errliah bahnd. Tsupah.*

"How's your trip going?" Margot asked her mother. Elke was distracted by something Keith was saying to Dieter.

"It's interesting to be back," Louise said. A role reversal—Margot had been the one to reassure her parents of her plans, telling them that the band and this traveling would work out, that she wasn't being irresponsible. But now Louise was sheepish. Her mother looked apologetic, a little forlorn.

"It was important to Elke that I come," Louise said quietly.

The next band was starting: a man and a woman sat facing each other onstage, each holding an electric guitar. The woman cried out, slow and lugubrious, the fine timbre of her voice stretched as she picked stark notes. The man played distorted riffs, and Margot cringed as her mother nodded her head beside her, then felt guilty about her embarrassment.

Elke was on the other side of Margot, her face lit by the screen of her phone.

"It sounds like Jefferson Airplane playing at half-speed," Dieter said behind her, his voice dim under the music.

He was exactly right, and Margot knew Joel would enjoy this comparison. She turned her head to Dieter. He was leaning toward her mother, telling her something, and the intimacy of this gesture, that and her mother's response—a softness in her face, a willingness as she tipped her head—unsettled Margot. She turned quickly, away from something she sensed she wasn't supposed to see.

Elke's face was still illuminated; she was oblivious to the whole thing.

"Want to get a drink?" Margot asked her. She'd been given two poker chips to redeem at the bar. Elke followed her through the crowd to the back of the room. Margot got a beer while her sister negotiated the ingredients of a cocktail mixed in a plastic cup. Elke was communicating completely in gestures. A finger held up, then pointing, then a flat palm. Elke's smile to the bartender was sardonic, just slightly flirtatious —she spoke no Dutch and yet had total control.

As a kid, Margot had worshipped her sister. Their age difference was wide enough that Elke was an enormous influence. Elke's clothes, her cassettes, those markers of her teenage self were left for Margot to inherit.

Elke had doted on Margot. When she left for college, she'd always asked to speak to Margot when she called home. *Margs!* Elke would exclaim, breathless over the line, and Margot, in grade school, was thrilled by Elke's reports of papers and parties. The dorm a world away. As the years and phone calls continued, Margot began to report on her own adventures, and Elke offered advice. Elke sent for Margot, and Margot visited on her own, trying on Elke's brand of independence. In Seattle and San Francisco, the sisters shared a shorthand—for their mother's eccentricities, for the lackluster details of their hometown.

Elke lived in cities. She was German. She'd traveled internationally on a regular basis; she was glamorous and free, and as a child, Margot had wanted those things badly. But now, with Margot reaching adulthood herself, Elke's choices had lost some of their sheen. Elke's work seemed pretty boring, and her last boyfriend was a jockish hedge-fund guy who'd rattled on about rates, though what he was measuring, Margot was never sure. It was possible Elke was square. Maybe now they were trading places, Elke handing Margot the baton.

"I'm so out of it," Elke said. She sipped her drink. "I feel like I'm sleepwalking."

And yet Elke had her usual assertive chic. Here she was, at a weird show far from home, jet-lagged, she claimed, and yet she was totally put-together. Business casual in boots and tight jeans and gold jewelry, her brown hair glossy and flat. Margot was the actual slob here—she'd been wearing the same cardigan for fourteen days straight.

Joel waved to Margot from the other end of the bar. She could hear his voice—*any beer, as long as it's Belgian*—and then he glanced back at her again.

"Is that your guy?" Elke asked Margot.

"Not really," Margot said. "I mean, maybe."

"You like him," Elke said.

"That sounds so high school."

"He's cute."

"We're keeping it under wraps," Margot said. "The group dynamic makes it complicated. It's hard to date on tour."

Elke nodded. "*Would you like to go out with me tonight?* Oh yeah, we're already spending every minute together."

"Exactly," Margot said.

Now Joel was coming over to them, and Margot saw him through Elke's eyes: his yellowed T-shirt, his uneven hair. But Joel was charismatic, and women noticed him—girls after shows and waitresses across Europe. But he belonged to Margot, maybe, and this stream of attention only intensified her desire.

Joel squeezed in next to Margot, stood beside her with his bare arm pressed against hers.

"When's your birthday, Joel?" Elke asked.

"I'm twenty-four," he said.

Margot looked at Elke. "He's an Aquarius."

"Got it," said Elke. She nodded at Margot. Aquarius and Sagittarius could work. A little weird, but Aquarius was not a difficult sign.

Louise and Dieter joined them; they were all crammed together in the vibrating crowd.

"Margot was telling me about your sculpture in your yard," Joel said. "That sounds really cool." Margot watched her mother's face light up. Louise also had a magnetism, a talent for listening—she could make teenage delinquents, pets, her own children, come closer and confide. "So you put the pieces down according to a schedule?"

"That's how it's supposed to work," Louise said. "A piece on the eighteenth of every month. Which was a few days ago. My husband is supposed to be maintaining it while I'm gone. But he just informed me that he didn't do it." She said this last bit as an aside to Margot, dumping that on her. There was something a tiny bit precious about her mother's project. And yet that obsession with her work was part of what made her mother interesting—a quality that Margot admired.

Louise's face was twisted with irritation. "We talked to him on Skype before we came here."

"Why didn't he do it?" Margot asked. This was extremely odd.

"I'm not sure," Louise said, gazing tightly past Margot. "He wasn't exactly forthcoming. It's a small thing I asked him to do."

"It won't have the right time stamp," Margot said. Her mother had a system for the project—though maybe not for any reason beyond its own perpetuation. Louise just put the photographs into a drawer.

"I'll have to pencil in the date," Louise said, her tone dangerous, sarcastic. "Maybe you can suggest that to your father."

Margot's parents had always seemed more or less stable, griping in predictable patterns—the way Louise left cabinet doors open for Richard to hit his head on, the way, after a shower, Richard dripped water all over the bathroom floor. Margot thought of that Everlys song they'd listened to in the car—*I wonder if I care as much.*

By then Keith had joined the circle, triumphant with a bottle of beer. "*Dubbel,* man," Keith said.

Joel lifted his glass. "This one's *tripel.*"

"We were listening to Can on the drive today," Keith said to Dieter. "Margot told us you're from Düsseldorf."

"I'm a child of the Rhein-Ruhr," Dieter said. "Then I lived in Düsseldorf when I was a young guy. Cologne, too. But I've been in New York since thirty years."

Keith was leaning in. "And you're a musician?" Margot could see Keith's barely restrained barrage of questions forming.

"I like to think so," Dieter said. "I've lost my audience."

"I'm sure you saw amazing stuff back then," Joel said. "Did you ever see Kraftwerk perform?"

"Sure," Dieter said. "They were the big thing."

"Did you, Mom?" Margot asked.

Louise nodded. "A few times." Why hadn't she ever told Margot about that? But of course, Margot hadn't known to ask.

"Louise showed up in Düsseldorf a follower of the Grateful Dead," Dieter said. "But I quickly reformed her." This was news to Margot, this supposed fandom.

"Did you see the Dead in the seventies?" Keith asked.

"I did," Louise said, "but not necessarily because I wanted to." Ah —that was the mother Margot recognized.

"What about Tangerine Dream?" Margot asked.

"They stood with their backs to the audience," Dieter said. "Just in love with the huge machines and the sound they were producing."

"It sounds awesome," Keith said.

"I enjoyed it." Louise's tone was serious. "I was painting all the time.

There was a fantastic energy. All the artists I knew were so dedicated to their work."

Louise always framed her time in Germany around art school. Not the music, not her former husband the musician, not watching Kraftwerk play.

"Typical German industry," Dieter said. "But it was fun."

"What was your band called?" Joel asked.

"Astral Gruppe," Dieter said.

"No shit!" Keith said. "They did that album on Brain," he said to Joel. "With all the pictures of the band on the gatefold."

Joel was ecstatic. "*All at One Time.* The sidelong jam is nuts."

"The vocals are incredible, too," Keith said. "That operatic witchy thing."

"I didn't know you'd heard it," Margot said.

"I didn't know you were connected to it," Joel said.

"I'm astounded," Dieter said. "This album is out of print. It's nearly as old as Elke—she was a baby when it came out."

"Ancient," said Elke.

"It's hard to find," Keith said. "I downloaded it, actually. I'm sorry."

"It's pricy," Joel said. "I think I saw it for two hundred dollars on eBay."

Margot could see Dieter was pleased.

"That was Astral Gruppe's only record?" Keith asked.

"The band was over soon after that," Dieter said. "Otherwise I made a solo project."

"Did you release anything?"

"I recorded," Dieter said. "Mostly with synthesizers as my instrumentation. But I never had any releases."

"Joel and I have a record label," Keith said. "Just something small. We reissue stuff that's out of print. Astral Gruppe is the kind of thing we'd love to put out. And I'd really like to hear your solo project sometime."

"I'll have to dig the recordings out of my time capsule," Dieter said.

"Where are you going next?" Louise asked Margot abruptly.

"Brussels tomorrow," Margot said. "But it's a little murky after that."

"Our show in Den Haag got canned," Keith said. "The squat was shut down. So that means we can't stay there, either. We were supposed to hang out there until the end of the tour."

"Oh, wow," Dieter said. *Vow.* "I should put you in touch with my nephew. He's making shows in Berlin. Experimental stuff. Who knows, maybe he's interested in what you're doing."

"Tilman used to be this big techno guy," Elke said. "He brought me to these insane clubs in the nineties."

Margot's mother was doing that weird thing with her mouth where she moved her lips as Elke spoke, anticipating the words. Louise did it to Margot sometimes, too, her encouragement both smothering and sweet.

"Whoa," Joel said. "I'm jealous."

"He was a DJ for a while," Elke said. "He put his turntables on a float in the harvest parade when he was in high school. They had a fog machine."

"Maybe we should check out Berlin," Joel said.

"We're going to be there," Elke said. "Mom and I are going to Berlin in a few days."

"You guys could be our groupies," Joel said. "Come to all our shows."

"Our paths just keep on converging," Elke said. "Listen to me, I sound like Richard."

Margot laughed with Elke, but Louise didn't join them.

"Berlin is a great city," Dieter said. "Almost as good as New York." He wrote on a scrap of paper, handed it to Joel. "Here's his email. I'll be seeing him in Bad Waldheim in the next days. I can mention it to him if you'd like."

Spencer was signaling to them from across the room — it was time. Margot followed Joel and Keith to the stage; she hunched over her gear and connected the cords, waiting for the red wink of the pedals' lights. The set began with a slow build into a massive drone. Joel had his microphone against his mouth and she could hear the shape, but not the exact sound, of what he was doing. Spencer switched cassettes and that noise, too, was changed by his chain of effects, the adjustments he made with the knobs.

She'd followed their lead since joining the band, imitating the physical way the rest of them got into it. Feeling the pulse, up on their hands and knees. Now she hovered over her pedals, hunched before the amp. A trembling genuflection. A primal ritual. She played a note on the keyboard that rang out over the low texture. The bare tone shot through her delay pedal, repeating her mistake. She played the note again, then again, imbuing this accident with purpose. She could tell Joel was listening—he always listened closest. He responded to her, building a thick drone and leaving her sour note behind.

But the sound was thinner than usual, and when Margot looked up, she saw that Keith wasn't playing. His arms were crossed over his chest; his face was angry, scrunched. This hadn't ever happened before. Usually Keith liked to be heard. But if he didn't approve of the way the set was going, too bad. She turned up the volume on the echo pedal. The wave of her sounds folded back, and she could hear Joel and Spencer getting louder, too. Keith stood and stepped over the equipment, his feet heavy, awkward, fast. He was leaving the stage, cutting a fraught path through the crowd, interrupting the audience's forward gaze— people were recoiling, confused. But the music didn't stop. Margot and the others kept going, letting the sound sit up high until Margot started pulling back and the whole thing came down, slowly. They rode out the ending to an almost excruciating level, which Keith hated. Too drawn out; the set should have a clean finish, a definitive break, Keith always said. But the three of them were capitalizing on each tiny sound.

Suddenly Keith was there despite his physical absence—his voice, over and over.

"Stretch the tank," Keith said, disembodied Keith, that big sound of him coming through the PA, saturated with reverb, disintegrating, so that his voice slowed and washed out. Spencer must have put this fragment of Keith's voice through; he was hunched over his pile of cassettes, hands frantic on the mixer. This was breaking the rules too.

Margot didn't want the set to end. But the digital recorder was still going despite Keith's departure, and Margot knew she would enjoy listening back.

Then there was applause. Margot stood up. Her right leg had fallen asleep. She limped over to where her mother and Elke and Dieter were waiting at the edge of the stage. She felt herself grinning—from the needles in her leg, which made her laugh, from the triumph of what the three of them had pulled off without Keith.

Dieter smiled back at her. "Your music is as intense as I hoped it would be."

"Dynamic," Elke said.

"Hard to control those dynamics sometimes," Margot said. "Usually we all stay onstage."

Joel was beside her, shaking Dieter's hand.

"With bands," said Dieter, "the music gets better when you all hate each other."

"It was really interesting to see what you're doing," Louise said. "I couldn't picture what you meant by the microphones, but I get it now."

"It was great to meet you," Joel said to Dieter. "If you ever feel like sharing those recordings, let us know. We'd love to hear them."

Dieter nodded. "I'll keep it in my mind," he said. "And tell me if you'll ever be playing in New York."

Louise reached to hug Margot. "We're going to drive back now," she said. "We're all pretty pooped."

"Thanks for coming," Margot said. "I'm really glad I could see you." She hugged Elke, shook Dieter's hand, walked them outside for a final wave goodbye.

Two guys came up to her. "This was exceptional," one of them said. "I'm watching you while you play. Such cute little patterns."

The other guy nodded. "I love the female sense of rhythm."

"Does rhythm have a gender?" Margot felt combative, and she left them to join Joel and Spencer, who were guzzling that powerful Belgian beer by the door.

"Your sister is a babe," Spencer said.

"Thanks," Margot said.

"I'm more interested in Dieter's recordings," Joel said.

"That's a relief," Margot said.

"I'm serious," Joel said. "The loner synth stuff is probably amazing. And if he let us reissue the Astral Gruppe album, I would lose my shit."

"The nephew could be interesting too," Spencer said. "In Berlin. We should follow up with that."

The beer had left her removed but not quite intoxicated. She didn't want to go back into the hot show, where they would have to wait out the other bands before they could retreat to their accommodations, a room in the basement with bunk beds. Margot would have rather slept here on the sidewalk, where it was quiet and cool. A strange thing to wish for.

Then she saw Keith, crossing the street and pulling on the brim of his hat.

"I thought the set sounded good," Spencer said to Keith. "You shouldn't have left. Walking off stage is tantamount to betrayal."

"You were too loud," Keith said.

Spencer had been schooled by Montessori and a college in the desert with no grades. It seemed to Margot that in Spencer's twenty-five years his opinion had never not been valued, his creativity never discouraged. *You were too loud,* Keith had told him — these words set off his red button of alarm. From here there was no turning back. Spencer threw his bag onto the sidewalk, toothbrush head dangling dangerously from its open zipper, and emitted a wordless bark.

"The end was amazing," Joel said.

"The music's not interesting if it's always the same," Margot said.

"Of course you agree with him," Keith said, scoffing. Margot glanced at Joel — Keith was being such a jerk. Joel flashed her the briefest smile.

Keith saw it, too. "You two can stop sneaking around, you know."

"It's obvious you guys are together." Spencer, still bruised, swigged his beer. "We're not idiots."

"We're not all pulling our weight," said Keith. "We've got to try harder. All of us."

Though there were a thousand things this could mean, Keith's criticism was likely directed at her. Margot wasn't a very good musician. She wasn't really a musician at all. She'd have to try harder as she moaned and rang bells. Fine. She would try harder.

"That's really what I think," Margot said. "About the way the set ended. It's my own opinion."

They weren't listening to her.

"We need to be on the road by ten tomorrow morning," Keith said. "I want time for that record store."

"I'm not driving first," said Joel. Margot followed them inside.

LOUISE

1974

LOUISE CHANGED HER DEUTSCHE MARKS to dollars at Kennedy Airport in New York. She separated the money into two thin stacks, parceling out what Dieter had given her for the return ticket, promising herself she wouldn't touch it. How strange it was to return to a place where she could understand everything without straining. Waiting to board, in New York and then San Francisco, she listened to passive-aggressions she knew were directed at her, at Elke screaming, her back arched in the stroller. She kept at it until Louise unsnapped her and let her crawl over the carpeted floor.

When they finally arrived in Eugene, Louise found her father waiting at the luggage carousel—she could pick out Trent's tucked flannel from the escalator. At this distance, she searched his face for what she'd been expecting: his anger, his fear and grief. She could see only his usual squint.

Her father reached for her and Elke in the same embrace. Trent, wiry and compact, had always appeared larger than he actually was. It was his deep quiet that gave him size. Despite the massive trench between them, despite the nervous expectation she could now distinguish in his expression, he was unchanged. He wasn't going to scold her, not here, not now.

They spoke in snatches in the car—the flight, the recent rain. She didn't mind when their talking lapsed. She needed this liminal quiet.

As they left the city, the car filled with pine and cedar, the mineral drift of moss and wet stone. The old smells tangling with what had become familiar—Elke's soapy, slightly sour head. A potent mix of now and then that drummed with Louise's pulse. Her father had come alone. During the last days in Düsseldorf, for the entire convoluted trip back to the States, Louise had pictured her mother in a nightgown, clutching a mug of tea. A foolish image, but it was too late to prepare anything else.

She watched the tendons on her father's forearms as he drove across Cottage Grove's quick downtown. Elke took in the drugstore, the bank with its slow clock. With the succession of smaller roads leading out of town—the gas station, the rye fields—Louise's pulse raced. She felt Elke's small body against her own, tried to match the baby's regular rhythms of heart and breath.

The house was the same, with its raised basement and wooden stairs to the front door. The vegetable garden, the shed, the open mouth of the woods.

In the kitchen, her mother was dressed and bustling. She felt half the size of Louise, as though she might crumble in her arms. Mary held Elke and broke into a nonsensical song. She didn't scold Louise for her prolonged absence. But when Louise looked closely, the punishment was clear: her shrunken mother, her eyes huge, her once-thick gray bob in a desperate stretch over her scalp.

They sat for lunch. Colors bold and simple: a white plate, the green linoleum. The mustard jar, and ham in plastic, a visceral, luminous pink. Louise couldn't stomach the meat's garish hue. Before they started to eat, her mother began to pray.

"Let the doctor have steady hands," Mary said. "Let him remove the thick and terrible poison from my body with your divine power as his guide."

Mary was a reticent woman except for this free expression she'd learned in church. The minister encouraged participation: as acts of devotion, the congregation could call out or shake or even cry. It had scared Louise when she was in high school, and it frightened her still.

But now, so much of Mary was diminished; she hadn't even lifted her sandwich. "What does your husband do?" she asked. "Is he an artist?" Louise could see her mother struggling with that last word.

"He's a musician," Louise said. "And a carpenter."

"Does he have religion?" Mary was looking at Elke, who clutched soggy bread. Louise knew what her mother was really asking—had the baby been baptized?

"Not at the moment," Louise said.

Lunch was cut short by Elke's shrieking, and Louise took the baby to her own childhood bedroom, where her old crib was waiting. Mary said that she would lie down, too, and after Elke finally fell asleep, Louise, bleary but too agitated to rest, went downstairs, crossing the living room's hooked rug. Her father's books about the apocalypse lined the shelf—*Perhaps Today* and *The Late Great Planet Earth*—their titles still forecasting the same doom.

She drank coffee with him. "I've closed the garage," Trent said. He was a mechanic; he worked by himself. "For the past few weeks now." Of course—it was the middle of the afternoon and he was at home. "Your mother has treatments every day."

"I could take her," Louise said.

Her father shook his head. "You can come with us." He didn't trust her. But there was no way to change what was done. He told her then, in unsparing language, about what had already happened: the tumor, the radiation, the tests.

Louise calculated—if her mother got better during this next round of treatment, it would be all right to leave again. She wouldn't stay away for so long this time. She would visit and bring Dieter, too.

Trent watched her, tapped his fingers on his mug. "I cleared the trail for you. Lots of branches down this winter." In the woods behind the house, Trent had marked a course of several miles, dotting the trees with spray paint. He'd taken Louise there as a young child and then let her explore on her own. She could wander, he'd told her, but she'd always have the blue blazes to lead her home.

"I've missed it," she said. "I'd like to take Elke on a hike."

And so they settled into a routine. In the haze of uneven sleep and constant caretaking, Louise worked in tandem with her father, tending to Mary, shrunken and forthright, and Elke, soft and needy and sweet. Together they took care of laundry and meals, and that shared purpose offered a kind of relief. They washed the windows with vinegar and newspaper, with Louise in the house and Trent outside on the ladder, tapping on the spots she'd missed.

They took Mary to her treatments at the hospital in Eugene, and the trips into town deepened Louise's visceral return: the resolute friendliness at the donut counter, the benign stink of patchouli wafting from the head shop next door. She knew again the gentle eccentrics, the blank-eyed girl selling crafts in the park. But in the little errands came the surprises of reverse assimilation: the unsolicited baby advice from strangers, the jars of peanut butter in the A&P. Louise had forgotten Oreos and Ritz Crackers; she tried not to think about *Quark* and *Lebkuchen* and thick sunflower bread. She used her stash of dollars for Elke's diaper cream and cottage cheese, stopping her father at the register as he tried to pay.

Louise consulted her mother about Elke's sliced banana and scrambled eggs, and in these conversations they found safe territory. Louise needed the advice, and she could see her mother's pleasure when she asked. They discussed the garden, too—Louise weeded and watered while Mary played with Elke on a blanket in the grass. "I want to get more annuals in," Mary said. "I was thinking a nice shock of red. Impatiens, maybe."

"Pink ones, too," said Louise. "Maybe here by the hydrangea. So they'll fade in a spectrum." She liked talking to her mother about color. She'd forgotten about the elaborate designs Mary sketched each year— the vegetables in their fenced plot, the flowers that flanked the house.

Louise sat with Mary and looked through her worn folder of plans. Mary had used colored pencil to blur her green squares into the blocks of surrounding grass, and there Louise found echoes of her own thinking, felt the urge to paint, to draw.

One afternoon Trent took them to the coast, to the state park where they'd camped when Louise was a child. Now, at the start of summer, fog swallowed the shoreline. On the beach at Devils Elbow, Louise skated Elke's feet over the chilly Pacific, listened to her laugh at the receding waves. The Germans would approve, Louise thought — that brisk dip a way to make Elke strong.

On Sundays, Louise's parents asked her to go to church with them. She told them she'd stay home so Elke could nap, but she hiked instead, her own act of devotion. With Elke in her backpack, Louise pointed out the texture of bark and mushrooms, the shadows that shifted over the forest floor. She remembered what her father had taught her, to look back occasionally, to see what the going would look like as opposed to the coming.

When she knew Elke had fallen asleep, Louise let herself break down. Here at a remove from the pain of the house, she knew her mother wasn't going to get better. She could see the terrifying scope of a future without her. And with their little time together, Louise needed to apologize for cutting herself off. Her mother was sad and frightened, and she wanted to comfort her, but Louise was frightened, too.

She thought about Dieter — she knew that telling him about Hannelore had driven a wedge between them. She wasn't sure they'd ever return to normal. But maybe he was with Sabine now anyway, perhaps even in their apartment in Oberbilk since Louise was cleared out of the way. She thought of the missed time at the Kunstakademie and, worse, that maybe her absence didn't even matter. She'd been producing mediocre work. She cried and walked through the trees, with Elke asleep against her neck.

How much Louise had missed without realizing. The damp, mulchy earth, the gentle stench of the stagnant creek. The lift of astringent fir. When she heard Elke murmuring, felt her fingers in her hair, Louise stopped and took off the backpack, let Elke stumble around on the ground. Elke held Louise's fingers and took heavy steps; she crawled over rotting logs, examined ferns with frank wonder. Louise felt better then, grounded here. She and Elke were together, touching the moss and stones.

That night, reading the paper in the living room, Louise found an article about Steve Prefontaine; he was back at U of O and training again. He'd built himself a sauna, inspired by the Finn who'd beaten him in Munich.

"If that's his secret," Pre said in the caption beneath his photo, "then I'm going to make my own little Finland right here in Oregon."

She remembered the bathhouse by the Hofgarten, the bracing shifts between hot and cold. And she thought, too, of watching Prefontaine's barefoot retreat from the track.

"Pre was in the Olympics in Germany," her father told her after she'd passed him the sports section.

"I saw it," Louise said. "I saw the race on TV."

"We thought of you," her mother said. "We wondered if you were there." Louise, touched, chagrined, didn't tell them how far Munich was from where she'd been.

She watched TV with them. Her mother sat with her embroidery hoop, her father with one of his books—*A Thief in the Night*. Louise pulled out a sketchpad. But mostly she watched and didn't draw. She'd missed a lot while she was in Düsseldorf: Watergate, the end of Vietnam. Now she listened to Walter Cronkite describe Nixon's impeachment hearings. The TV cut to Dan Rather in front of the White House. "Upstairs at dinner in the executive residence," he said, brisk and even, "some family members were in tears." His delivery had an incantatory rhythm, and Louise sat transfixed. "The president was not."

Of course not: Nixon's sardonic calm needled Louise. She looked at

Walter Cronkite—did she detect his subtle glee? The next item was about West Germany hosting the World Cup that summer. "Perhaps this revitalized nation will overcome its crushing defeat in Mexico City at the last World Cup in 1970," Cronkite said. "This time soccer might help heal the German scars of war."

A tall claim. She thought about how Frau Kerbel wouldn't say the word *war,* how even Dieter skirted around his feelings of guilt. She remembered, with terrible clarity, how hurt he'd been to learn the truth about his father, how she'd complicated and deepened his shame. Maybe this time apart would give Dieter the chance to absorb what she'd told him, allow them both to cool off. She hoped that he was all right—looking back now, that conversation with Dieter felt nearly as remote as the World Cup, the report of a faraway loss.

Two weeks in, Dieter's first letter arrived. He'd written in English— concern for her mother, questions about Elke, a touch of local news. He was thinking of her, he wrote, but he didn't say that he missed her. Was that a gap in translation, simply a forgotten verb? Did he think he'd implied it? She left the blue envelope in her top drawer with what remained of her stash of dollars.

Elke began to walk in earnest in Cottage Grove. She turned one in June, and Louise made a cake and lit a candle. Dieter addressed his greetings then to Elke, sent his mother's good wishes. Germans had such a fixation on birthdays, but here, where the celebration had never been much, what mirth there once had been was dampened now by Mary's decline.

Though Mary was spending much of the day in bed, she continued to gather the family to pray. Even brief bouts of proselytizing exhausted her; she was lit up and then spent. *Let Louise and her little one ground themselves here at home and live under the light of your salvation so that she might come into your good graces again.* A ribbon of anger snaked through Louise's fear. She wanted them to talk about her real life, or the baby. *Don't let the wicked forces of foreign evil pull Louise away from us. Don't let Satan tempt her again.*

Alone with Elke, Louise tried to speak German. She read from the book she'd brought with them — *Wir mit dem Hund spielen.* But it had never felt right to speak German to Elke, and even less so in the fluorescent aisles of the A&P. *Mamamamama,* Elke said as she palmed Louise's face.

Car, Louise said, pointing. *Window, house, dog.*

At the end of June, the month was up — Louise and Elke had been in Cottage Grove for four weeks — but Louise hadn't bought a return ticket. Her mother's treatments had paused, Louise wrote to Dieter, but the prognosis wasn't good. She'd have to stay a little longer. A horrible letter to write. She didn't know how to express to Dieter that she missed him acutely, that even so, she was having a hard time believing that her life in Germany had been real. Her anger at him was muted now by an aching sense of loss, blurred with her anticipation of further grief.

Time sped up just as it slowed. Each morning she looked at her mother and wondered about holding on. How stupid Louise had been, how cruel, to cut off from her parents so completely. And yet she still didn't understand them. Awake with Elke in the middle of the night, Louise went downstairs and flipped through her father's books. *The Rapture could happen today! Be ready so you aren't left behind.* Until now, she'd avoided the specifics of her parents' religion, a refusal that had come in part from snaking apprehension: what had seized them could get her, too. Now, flipping through the pages, she sensed the comfort these bold promises must have offered. Still half-asleep, lonely but not alone, the books almost made sense — a recognition that unsettled her.

Somehow she'd emerged from this strange place. Impossible, she'd told herself in college, as she made her plans to leave. Louise was an artist, a radical, she was so different from them. But now she studied her parents. She'd taken for granted their constant projects. Her father carved apples and wood. His work as a mechanic gave him a tactile understanding of the world. And even his connection to the land was a way of seeking. Her mother sketched those elaborate plans for the garden; she canned and pickled and sewed. Perhaps her prayers, too, were a creative act.

As the days went on, Mary softened her rhetoric. *Let me walk in the kingdom of heaven with you, Lord, where the flowers are in perpetual blossom and the very sight of them in their colorful splendor will be like a drink of water for a parched traveler. Keep Trent and Louise and Elke safe until you come back to earth again. Let them reside in that splendor in your name and image.*

Louise didn't know how she would find this splendor. Elke's curls were getting darker; she was curious, delighted to be up on her feet, but despite this progression, Louise couldn't see beyond the most immediate future—the next hours, at most what needed to happen the next day. She was using the dollars from her ticket fund now. Her father was careful in the supermarket, discussing with Louise how to stretch the meat. No more meandering drives to the coast.

Louise got a letter from Ute—she was shooting video now. Joseph Beuys had finished a show in New York. He'd locked himself in a gallery with a coyote. *I Like America and America Likes Me,* he titled the piece, and he'd had an ambulance transport him from the airport to the gallery. He wanted the coyote to be the only part of America that he actually saw.

Louise wrote back to Ute, and she wrote to Dieter, too—when she returned to Düsseldorf, maybe they should think about going to New York, maybe it was time to make that move. But he was vague in his response—*we'll discuss the plans when you're back here.* He was touring with Astral Gruppe that summer, playing lots of shows. The band was getting a good response; the album had sold out its first pressing. His sentences were matter-of-fact, self-deprecating and still charged by ego. She missed him. She could hear the cadence of his speech when she read it, that rhythm a window to a place she'd known.

Summer unfolded into clear, hot days. Neighbors stopped by with muffins and casseroles. The news came that Nixon had resigned, and Louise felt only a distant, bitter triumph. Time kept moving forward, and as she noted Elke's incremental changes, she tracked the landscape, too. The wheat fields inches taller, the brush along the road burnished to a deeper shade. Setting off for a hike with Elke, Louise saw an old shutter left to lean against the shed. The chipped green paint revealed an earlier coating of white. The shutter made an obvious frame against the tall grass, but it was the fading color that caught her eye. She relished that flare of inspiration; later, in the kitchen, as she scrubbed her hands with her father's rough black soap, she longed for the physical end to a session of work.

She wrote to Dieter at the little desk in her bedroom. *I miss painting, I miss the studio. But what I'm seeing here is giving me new ideas.* She began thinking about installations, her own marks set against the trees. She remembered how when she was a child, the "Hidden Driveway" signs on the road had made her believe that if she looked hard enough, she'd find a nearly invisible route out of the woods. That idea enchanted her once more; she imagined the rich tint of oil paint, loud against the limited palette of brown and green. She thought about it then — what if she didn't go back? In the quiet woods, it was harder to hear Dieter's voice.

She wondered what Elke would someday know of her parents' relationship. Louise had realized since returning home how little she knew of her own parents' lives before she was born: they'd married young, left their families in Bend's high desert, a terrain striking but so different from the wet green woods they'd found. She recognized the bravery in that, what it must have been like to leave what they'd known. They visited those relatives just once a year. "This is all we need," Louise's father used to tell her as he led her through the trees. Now she could understand what he meant.

Trent hiked with her one afternoon, offering to carry Elke in her pack. Louise followed him over the path he'd cleared. He spoke to her without turning around. "Your mother would be happy if you baptized Elke," Trent said. "It wouldn't take all that long."

Louise watched Elke, alert beneath the firs, as they passed the occasional trunk dotted with Trent's flash of blue. "I'll think about it," she said.

They crossed the dry creek bed; Trent talked to Elke about the deer tracks along the edge.

"The deer must have wanted a drink," Louise said. "How frustrating."

Trent tipped his head back, smiled from beneath his hat's brim. "Wrong time of year for that," he said, and together they continued on.

Back at the house, Louise sketched the hydrangea's bleached petals, the pink shot with gold and green and brown. She brought the drawings to Mary in her room.

"I always liked the hydrangea," Mary said. She asked Louise if she had any more.

Louise had brought only one sketchbook with her from Düsseldorf; the first pages were filled with her plans for the series.

"I wanted a sense of motion," Louise said, showing the sketches to her mother. "So if they were lined up on the wall, you'd see their progression all at once." Mary traced a finger along the page. She and Trent hadn't gone to Louise's student shows in Eugene. And though Mary had railed against Louise's decision to study art, Mary herself was an artist, a contradiction whose full relief Louise could only now discern.

"I didn't finish it, though," Louise said. "I only made a few pieces in the series."

"You'll get back to it," Mary said.

Louise remembered a time when their places had been reversed. A day when Louise, twelve or thirteen, was home sick from school. Her mother returned from work at lunchtime—she did the phone and the books at Trent's garage—and after she turned on the Crock-Pot and made toast for Louise, Mary tied her hair back, pulled a T-shirt over her dress. Louise had never seen her mother smoke before, but Mary lit a single cigarette at the kitchen table with such clear ease that Louise knew it was not an anomaly. Then her mother washed her hands and removed the T-shirt. She ate a striped mint and left for work again. Her pious mother had a vice, and an elaborate system for covering it. But she hadn't hidden it from Louise. That memory comforted her now —maybe her mother could forgive her imperfect choices.

Mary was looking at Louise, her face soft. "Your husband must be missing you and Elke."

Louise nodded. "But you can't be in two places at once." She told her mother about Düsseldorf—the city's long avenues, the windows and ledges lined with flowers. The sun umbrellas on balconies high over-head. You could look up and see the bright triangles of the umbrellas' undersides. Even the language felt geometric. Those logical clauses, the neat grammar, the slow stringing together of unfamiliar sounds.

"Must be strange," Mary said, "to have your child speaking another language."

Louise nodded. "It will be. When she actually starts talking."

"That's right. It's all babble now anyway."

That's all it was for any of them, Louise thought her mother was saying. How hard it was to understand and get through. She left the hydrangea drawings where her mother wanted them, pinned to the wall beside her bed.

That evening, after Elke went down, Louise walked on the road and thought about what her father had suggested. As the sun set, she traced the shoulder's line. At that time of day, the light was nearly psychedelic —she was caught in the strong beam, a blinding white intensity. She wondered what Dieter would say about how ready she was to give in to her father's request. But she knew she would do it. She could treat the baptism as a pantomime, a ritual, a chore. Alone on the road, she walked quickly, so the thrum of her pulse was the thing that marked time.

That Sunday, the service opened with a song by the reverend and his wife, both of them with guitars. They were skilled players — the wife especially, finger-picking with a fluid, elegant touch. A third parishioner sat at the drums, made emphatic hits. Oh, Dieter, Louise thought, how could she explain where she'd wound up?

The church's pews were built from dark wood; some of the rows were missing, their space filled with folding chairs. The stained glass reflected pale blocks over the carpet, and the walls were strung with banners, with verses of scripture cut from felt.

They were singing now, the minister and his wife and the drummer, in a striking three-part harmony. Such talent — they might have used it in so many other ways. *You'll get back to it,* Mary had said. Louise wanted to believe her.

The congregants shook their bodies to the music, dancing in the pews. Their hands cut through the space above them. Their arms moved like sacks at their sides. A man in a thin beard jogged in the aisle; an old woman laughed out loud.

"I want to talk to you about the ultimate trip," Revered Fulton said from the pulpit. "I want to tell you about the return." The pews creaked as the congregants shifted, the old wood adjusting as it held.

He called Louise to the altar, scanned her with quick lizard eyes. His hair was graying, longish, curling behind his ears. He wore a ring set with turquoise, a cross on a heavy chain. "Elke Grace Hinterkopf" — how mangled her name sounded in the minister's flat tongue — "today we will baptize you in the name of the Father, the Son, and the Holy Spirit." He sprinkled water over Elke's head. "What's to come is better than what's been."

Elke screamed and Louise cried, too — she did not believe his prediction. Everything that had once been open to her had closed. She let the tears run down her face as she jiggled Elke and shushed her. Since her teenage years, Louise had refused her parents' suggestion that she be baptized. Now Louise had made Elke do what she herself was unwilling to go through.

"The spirit is in the room!" Reverend Fulton said. "We are witnessing the testament of mother and child. We've saved another sinner today. When those trumpets make their call, Elke Grace will not be left behind."

I'm sorry, Louise whispered to Elke that afternoon on their hike. She told Elke she'd try to let her make her own choices when she got older. The forest was hot and still, a witness to her apology. The sound of her voice lingered in the woods, echoed by subtle noises — a drifting pine branch, distant birdsong, a squirrel scratching over bark.

Mary went into the hospital at the end of August. Her room was shared with another patient, whose machines kept a steady, ominous drone, but the view through the window was verdant and calm, and Louise promised Mary she'd visit her every day.

On the drive home, Trent talked to Louise, his words unrolling as though rehearsed.

"You could take a class," he said. "Finish your teacher certification. You might as well make use of your time."

Time was an unknown factor — the doctors predicted days or weeks — but to calculate on her mother's life seemed crude, distressing. The shape too big to discern.

"I called the university," Trent said. "I don't know what you've already done. In terms of the courses. But they said they could help you."

She was touched by what he'd done. College was an arena unknown to him, one that she knew, in the past at least, he'd even feared.

"If that would be all right with your husband," Trent said. "For you to stay longer."

"I want to be here with Mom," she said. "But what about Elke?"

"I'll watch her. You can use your mother's car."

Louise took a loan from the bank for the tuition. At the ed school, it was easy to ask questions and get clear answers, to lean back against someone else's suggestion. Two more classes for the teaching requirement, another few credits so she could teach art.

The trips to campus compounded her homecoming. On the quad, it was all there again: the longhairs giggling after their Frisbee, the girl in a bathrobe bleating on an untuned flute. The anti-nukes people pushing their clipboards. The frat boys in Ducks gear, little kings in yellow and green. All of them were chewing on local gossip. The Dead were going to do another concert for the Springfield Creamery. Steve Prefontaine was bartending at the Old Pad.

Outside the library, Louise ran into Ginny Bowers, her freshman roommate. Ginny wore overalls, a bandanna knotted over her hair. "Wow, West Germany," said Ginny with a blurry smile. "I passed through Stuttgart while I was backpacking. That German hospitality is incredible. I'd screw these German boys, and their mothers would leave out an apple cake the next morning because I was a guest in the house."

Ginny, brassy and unkempt, was comforting, familiar. "It's good here, though," Ginny said. "Good old Eugene."

Louise nodded. "I've been out in the country with my parents," she said. "Looking for kinship with Walter Cronkite."

"He's more radical than you'd think," Ginny said. "When McGovern got the nomination, I swear I saw tears in his eyes."

Louise had missed all that, too. She felt like a stranger in her own life.

"Let's get together sometime," Ginny said, and Louise promised that they would.

Mary died in mid-September, a stark call in the middle of the night, and in her mother's dim room, Louise felt slamming fatigue and surprising relief. The sense of heavy limbs. Was she supposed to tell Elke what had happened, or was this another loss she would just intuit?

They called the relatives in Bend and arranged for a funeral at the church. Parishioners brought foil-wrapped food to the house. Reverend Fulton helped with the grueling bureaucracy: the burial, the paperwork. "When you hear the call, let us know," he said to Louise. "It won't be long now."

She hugged him; she did appreciate his help.

The fall set in with the burning of the rye fields outside Eugene, an end-of-harvest practice that Louise resented for its heavy-handed emphasis. The thick black smoke, the landscape in collusion with her mourning, was a physical mark too obvious, lacking the dignity she craved.

She decided she would spend a little more time in Oregon. She'd take care of her father and finish her credits, and then she'd try to go back. Trent reopened his garage, and Louise found a communal house in the Whiteaker neighborhood; one of the women who lived there could watch Elke while Louise went to class.

"We keep peace here," the woman told Louise. She wore a straight part and round glasses, a baby in a sling. She was Joanne Kelly, and the house had a name too: the Green House, painted a soft yellow and perimetered by vegetable beds. Louise took the misnomer as a good sign. An echo of Josef Albers—*color is fooling us all the time.*

ELKE

2008

ELKE'S EARS WERE STILL stuffed up by the time they got back to Bad Waldheim, still full of the volume from Margot's band. Gisela had supper waiting for them—cold cuts, perhaps fabricated from something Norbert had killed. There was cheese on the table, too, and plenty of bread. A salad with hard-boiled eggs. Elke helped herself to these other things, spreading the leaves to cover the plate.

"You are not eating the meat," Norbert said. "Both you Americans." He was across the table from Elke; his skin was pink and waxy, tight across his cheeks.

"I became a vegetarian when I moved back to Oregon," Louise said. "It's been a while now."

"Here, take some more cheese," Gisela said, passing the platter to Elke.

Norbert sipped from his beer glass. "We're watching your election in America. I don't think Americans can elect a black man." His eyes squeezed as he laughed.

"Obama's leading in the polls, actually," Louise said.

"But look at your history," Norbert said. "It's hardly possible for your country to do such a thing."

Elke's pulse was beating in her temples. "It's more than possible," she said. "There's enormous support for him. It's exciting."

"Elke's right, Norbert," Dieter said. "You shouldn't judge things you haven't actually seen."

"Obama's going to win," Elke said.

Norbert shrugged dismissively. His smug response annoyed her. In the heat of planning the trip, Elke had imagined lots to do and see in Düsseldorf and Bad Waldheim, sites and activities that would make her origins real. But she hadn't really thought about the fact that Norbert's close-mindedness was part of her origins, too. Now there was still an entire day to fill until her grandmother's funeral.

"When is Tilman coming?" Elke asked.

"He comes here tomorrow," Gisela said. "He's living in Berlin still. With the Turkish."

"The entire city is Turkish now," Norbert said. "They are sending their children to the schools, but they don't even wanting to speak German."

Elke sat between her parents. Dieter was chewing rapidly. That hurry to swallow, so that he could hit back at Norbert.

"It's hard to learn a new language," Louise said.

"They don't like to be German," Norbert said.

"This doesn't seem so strange to me," Dieter said. "I go to Chinatown in Manhattan and I don't hear people speaking English. It's as though I have gone to China."

"They don't wanting to be German," Norbert said.

"They're Turkish," Louise said. "Why should they be German?" She pulled the crust from her bread, her lips squeezed into a constructed calm.

"Why do they come here, then?" Norbert asked.

"I'm sure there are a lot of reasons they come here," said Elke.

Norbert shook his head. "They don't wanting to be German."

At that Dieter erupted into a barrage of German that Elke couldn't follow, and Norbert yelped back at him. A bad way of thinking, Elke thought her father was saying.

"Why can't they be both?" Louise asked.

"Look at Dieter," Norbert said. "He lives in America."

"He isn't American," Louise said.

"He speaks English," Norbert said.

"He's still German," Louise said.

"German-American," Dieter said. "I've become hyphenated." His tone was facetious, though Elke knew he proudly considered himself a New Yorker.

Elke looked at her father. "I'd say you're German."

"You'll see it when you go to Berlin," Norbert said. "They believe they are still in Turkey."

Elke couldn't look at him, didn't want to see his pink face.

"Perhaps the world isn't as tightly defined as it once was," Louise said.

Dieter was nodding, hunching forward. Elke had been worried about how her parents would get along on the trip, but here they were, teaming up to battle Norbert.

"It's hard when things are different," Gisela said with gregarious urgency. "It's only that it's changing."

They ate in silence for a few minutes. The next day loomed—an enormous gulf, one likely filled with still more meat and intolerance.

Elke could feel her mother struggling to fill the space—Louise shifted in her seat, made her little *hmm*s. "So Julia is arriving tomorrow, too," Louise said.

Norbert leaned back in his chair. "With the kids."

"Tomorrow I must prepare," Gisela said. "Some cooking and baking for so much people."

"I love to cook," Louise said. Her tone was polite, removed. "I'd be happy to help you."

"*Ja*, OK," Gisela said, with gleeful emphasis on the second letter. "If you like, we are having some cake now." She stood up and strode toward the kitchen. "It's left over from Norbert's birthday, *aber schmeckt noch gut*," she called over her shoulder.

"If Norbert is willing to share it," said Dieter.

"Of course," Norbert said.

Elke asked him for his birthday.

"It was Tuesday," he said. "The fourteenth."

It surprised Elke that he was a Libra, given his stubborn force. But anyway, she'd need to see the chart, trace what else was there. And Libras could be surprising.

Gisela reappeared with a wedge on a platter. "The Hinterkopf *Geburtstagskuchen*," she said. "Hannelore would be happy that we eat this."

"I remember this cake," said Louise.

Elke remembered it, too — the dense cake with its thin layers of jam.

"You must have learned how to make this, too, Louise," Gisela said.

"I did learn, once," Louise said. "But I never made it on my own."

"Not for your girls?"

It would have been odd for Louise to make this most German of cakes in Oregon; Louise didn't do German things. And though Elke knew, logically, that her mother once had that fluency, she'd been unable to picture it. By asking her to come with her to Bad Waldheim, Elke was asking Louise to prove that her life here, Elke's heritage, had been real.

"I thought the cake was only for men," Louise said.

"We stopped that," Gisela said. "I couldn't make it for Tilman and not Julia. She would have screamed."

"Why was it only for men?" Elke asked.

"Hannelore was old-fashioned," Gisela said. "It wasn't really true, that it's for the men."

"It was a different time," Louise said.

"We're all eating it now," Dieter said. "Men and women together." His tone a familiar one to Elke — the joking edged by his anxious desire to please.

After dinner they watched a soccer game on television, sinking into plush couches shaped around a table where the men rested their beers. Gisela poured amber schnapps for Elke and Louise. Elke slumped into the deep cushions and tracked the ball while her father and Norbert yammered about statistics.

Someone was shaking her arm. "I'm turning in now," Louise said. Elke had fallen asleep.

But once she was in bed beside her mother, Elke was awake, left staring up into the darkness.

"Norbert is something, with all the animal heads," Louise said. "Vegetarian paradise."

Elke was pinned under the duvet's dense cloud. Her mother's joke made Elke feel a little bit defensive, even though Elke agreed with her. But still: Elke was German, her mother was not.

"Why did you come here in the first place?" Elke asked.

"For art school."

"I know," Elke said. "But why Germany?"

"I had a fellowship. It was a great opportunity."

"It just seems so random."

"What's random about it?"

"That I was born here," Elke said. "That I'm half German."

Louise was silent next to her. Maybe it was wrong to push, but the dark room unlocked a sense that Elke could.

"Did you think about getting an abortion?" Elke could hear her mother breathing just inches away.

"That's a difficult question," Louise said. "I didn't know you then. I didn't know how my life would turn out."

"So you did think about it."

"I was twenty-three," Louise said. "I didn't have money. I was estranged from my family and far away from home. So yes, I did think about it. But it wasn't an easy thing to do back then. It was illegal. And dangerous."

"So if it was easier to get an abortion, you might have done it," Elke said.

"That's not what I'm saying. I loved Dieter. I thought it would work between us."

Both of them were on their backs, lying still. Elke had not asked these questions of her mother before, and maybe it was bratty, but she felt she deserved to know.

"Can't you just believe that you were meant to be?" Louise asked. "I'm telling you that. I can't imagine my life without you." She sounded worried, her voice small, as though she were the one who needed reassurance. And Elke felt both cruel for digging in and upset by the answers Louise was providing.

"I don't understand Norbert and Gisela," Elke said.

"You're not necessarily supposed to understand your family. My parents were extremely conservative—some of the things they said would have horrified you."

"Grandpa was kind of nuts," Elke said. "That apocalyptic stuff. At least he was discreet about it."

"He'd toned it down by the time you appeared," Louise said. "I left, don't forget. After my mother died, he wanted to keep me around."

Elke thought about how her mother had broken away from her parents. How bold Louise had been, how cavalier. How had she managed on her own?

"What did Dieter do for you?" Elke asked.

"What do you mean?"

"Financially," Elke said. "Was he paying child support?"

Louise said yes. "Even before the divorce."

"I thought you got divorced when I was a baby."

"We split up at that point," Louise said. "When I took you to Oregon in seventy-four. That was the end of it for us. But the divorce took a lot longer because of Dieter's citizenship."

"Weird," Elke said.

"I thought you knew all of this."

"I think you forget that I was a child."

"Our marriage was on paper," Louise said. "I was living with Richard. Dieter was in New York. The marriage was just for the government."

"How did Richard feel about that?"

"He hated it," Louise said. "But he was willing to do it for your sake."

This touched Elke, thinking of Richard. But how could her mother have expected that from him?

Louise was shifting beside her in the dark. "I don't know what to do about the project," Louise said. "I don't know why Richard didn't take the picture."

"I'm sure he'll do it," Elke said. Though she wasn't, actually—she, too, found it strange that Richard had resisted, that he'd been so salty over Skype.

"We'll talk to him again tomorrow," Louise said.

"I bet he'll have taken it by then," Elke said. She hoped she was right.

In the morning her mother was dressed and worrying when Elke opened her eyes.

"I'm going to email Nina," Louise said. "I'll ask her to go to the house and take the photo." She was in a chair by the window; Elke hadn't heard her get up.

Louise kept talking. "But maybe that would upset Richard, to think that I went behind his back."

"But Richard didn't take the picture. He's inviting that response."

"It's complicated" was all Louise would say.

Downstairs, there was breakfast in the kitchen. Coffee in a wicker thermos, yogurt, and cold cuts, and the dogs under the table, waiting for a treat. Elke sat at the table with her mother, on a bench trimmed with floral fabric.

Gisela was chatty, wound up. Norbert was slipping *Schinken* to the dogs. Dieter hadn't come over from Hannelore's yet.

"Today things are getting a little wild," Gisela said. "When Julia comes in with the kids—" She put her hands up, then waved them away from her face.

"Just put me to work," Louise said.

Gisela smiled — already well-caffeinated, clearly.

"It's the least I can do," Louise said. "You've hosted Elke all these years."

Gisela tipped the wicker pot over their cups. "Before we're baking the cakes, I must clear out the room where the kids sleep," Gisela said. "Norbert has left a big mess in there since he returned from the *Jagd.*"

"Sure," Louise said. "We can help." Elke wondered if her mother knew what she was agreeing to. The *Jagd* was the preserve in the country where Norbert went to hunt.

"I was going to go into Düsseldorf," Elke said. She felt like a child again, wanting something simply because it had been refused her. Louise moved her lips without sound.

"Go, go. Your mom is helping me," Gisela said.

Panic flashed over Louise's face — *don't leave me here alone,* she might be thinking. But Louise had just made such a fuss about helping Gisela.

"That's fine, Elke," Louise said. "Why don't you go in for a few hours and then help us in the afternoon?"

Elke knew she and her mother were still on tender footing after their talk the night before. It was selfish for Elke to leave her, when she was the one who had begged Louise to come in the first place. But now Elke wanted to be alone.

The train ride and its clear forward momentum consoled her: twenty-seven minutes to reach a place where she could slip in and explore. She got off at the Hauptbahnhof — all pretzels and shouting teenagers — and left the station, crossing a glass-domed courtyard. Green leaves swallowed bike racks. Sunlight cast prisms over a peeling fountain. At once elegant and gritty, and somehow hopeful, an antiquated vision of the future.

Out on the street, she followed an overpass, where, in the shaded daylight, shambled men sat solitary, nodding out, or else chattered in small groups. The morning so desolate and still.

She kept walking, along a wide avenue lined with zippy '60s-style buildings, all bright colors and geometric shapes. A bookstore sign spelled out in a classy minimalist font. She passed café tables under a striped awning, and lavish cakes in the window of a *Konditorei*.

Dieter had taken Elke to Düsseldorf before, but now she was think-ing about it as the site of her parents' courtship, their shared life. She could imagine them here—Louise and Dieter actually liking each other, intertwined. Her mother rushing to the art school, her father striding over cobblestones. She finally had a place for them as a pair. She had for so long wanted to understand how they had ever been a unit. And now, alone, in the absence of them both, she was beginning to see where they'd made sense.

She studied the people around her. A man in cut-off jean shorts, ex-posing a good stretch of thigh despite the only moderate temperature, who wore socks and plastic shower sandals, who was guiding his young son, dressed more seasonably, into a store. A woman wearing a hijab passed them on her way out, carrying roses wrapped in paper.

They don't wanting to be German, Norbert had kept saying the night before. But to be German came with plenty of baggage. And yet Norbert was so rigid about German identity, so anxious to protect it. Though even Elke, Norbert's own relative, was not German in the way Norbert would like to define it.

Elke didn't consider herself German, not exactly. But what might her life be like now if she'd grown up here, if she'd lived here all along? Given her current untethered state—she was single, childless, unem-ployed—it was appealing to imagine other routes.

She was thinking about her mother's life here; Louise had been so young, the same age as Margot, wide-eyed and brash, and yet she'd cared for an infant in a foreign country. How difficult that must have been. And here was Elke at thirty-five, her own life undeniably easier. She felt guilty for giving her mother a hard time the night before.

She stopped at a café on a side street. *"Ein cappuchino, bitte,"* she said.

"Here is your change," the woman said in English. She dropped the coins into a dish on the counter.

Elke took her coffee to a table. What if her mother hadn't left? What if she'd been raised here? If they'd stayed longer, perhaps she'd be able to fake the accent. Perhaps she wouldn't have an accent. She ate the foam with her spoon, not caring if she looked American.

The cafe had Wi-Fi, and Elke read her email on her phone. A new message from Margot: *It's so perfect that we met Dieter in Hasselt, because Joel got in touch with his nephew and he's going to help us out. Tilman has a couple of shows we can jump on, and he even said we could stay with him for a night. Where are you and Mom staying? And when do you arrive? We're trying to figure out what else to do in Berlin, and where to stay, since we have time to kill before our flights back to the US. FYI, we're having major band issues and it might just be me and Joel. Things have gotten much worse since Hasselt.*

Interesting. Elke could tell Margot all about Cousin Tilman, who was seven years older than her, stoic and sardonic and not necessarily all that friendly—Norbert through a bohemian filter. Once, when Elke was a teenager, Tilman had walked in on her in the bathroom at Norbert and Gisela's house. She was clothed and brushing her teeth, fortunately, but he was wearing nothing but a pair of striped briefs, and he wouldn't look her in the eye for the rest of her weeklong visit.

Margot's childhood had been simpler than Elke's. Margot hadn't had to stitch together the borders of her family. She'd grown up with two parents in the same house. And that resulted in a snug confidence that irked Elke just a bit. Maybe Margot's age was part of it—Elke could remember being similarly over-assured about her opinions in her early twenties. Elke did enjoy that recognition, seeing Margot the way she herself once was, but despite the similarities, she knew Margot was different. So thoroughly American. Like Richard. Like Louise, too.

The contrast between Elke and her family had always felt most pronounced whenever she'd returned from being away. Certainly the trips to Germany had underscored the fact of their difference, but her visits to New York had, too. She'd come back so aware of their elastic approach to time, their certainty that everyone wanted to hear what they had to say. Their stubborn belief that everything could be equal. *We'll split the check right down the middle.* Or: *Everyone gets a fair slice.* Richard used to tell that to Elke and her friends when they squabbled over treats. But Elke knew that sometimes the slices were just different. Her own father had taught her that.

Elke wrote Margot a simple reply. *Mom and I get to Berlin in two days —let me know your plans. Joel is a real go-getter. Typical Aquarius, right?*

Elke talked astrology only with Margot, the Sag, who didn't try to hide her interest in the zodiac. Margot, with her thrift-store dresses, her little boy's bowling jacket, gave irony a wide perch. Elke had liked Joel's even-keeled confidence when she met him in Hasselt—a quality she'd once slotted into many a finance position. But she was wary of his getting too close, of digging into something that Dieter had kept tucked away.

Dieter had never played Elke his band's album. *It's packed in storage,* he'd say when she asked. She'd googled the band a few times, though she couldn't find much information beyond the title. Even so, Dieter's record was out there in the world. Out of print but it could be found. Even by Margot's boyfriend. It bothered Elke. Her whole life, Dieter had been her private source of curiosity and frustration and admiration. Now Joel was claiming this connection without any struggle to earn it.

As she walked through the Altstadt's quaint village, Elke reviewed what Richard said to her on the phone, tracing the things her mother had said last night. What had happened with her mother and Dieter and Richard back in the '70s? It troubled Elke that she couldn't remember.

And now Richard hadn't taken her mother's photo, and her mother was upset. It was mean, vindictive, of Richard to refuse to do it. Richard was an Earth sign—his Capricorn grudge-holding had flared out. Elke didn't want to be stuck in the middle, expected to mediate.

She cut through a verdant park and walked down a wide avenue, then turned to a quieter block. A large sign proclaimed SAUNA. This seemed like a fine way to pass her time. And though she wasn't prepared

—no bathing suit—she imagined she could do without. Usually they gave you something in these places, a paper gown or a robe. At least a towel.

The quiet lobby was tiled in a soft green; through the glass behind the cashier, Elke could see a pool. She put her coins on the counter —maybe she would just try to *look* German—and accepted a key on a rubber bracelet. No towel. Maybe they were in the changing room. She followed signs, and beyond frosted glass, found banks of lockers shrouded by flowered curtains. No gender indicated, and both men and women milled about, casual in their undress.

She wasn't sure if she should take off her clothes. She'd been given no instructions, not even a scrap of fabric to hold against her body. She put her purse in the locker and went to investigate the pool. Children yelled, an echoing noise. The water beckoned—a brisk challenge, an escape.

She had no suit. Her bra was black, her underwear pale pink. Not convincing, but if she had a towel, she could cover her underwear until the last minute and then jump in.

She really needed a towel.

She looked at the families in bright bathing suits. Mothers who brought entire bags of folded towels for their squirming offspring, who would have to be coaxed into drying off anyway. And fathers in their tiny spandex briefs, exuding a bulging confidence that Elke wanted to assert, too.

She strolled past a bench, skimmed a towel off the top of a folded pile. Across the tiled floor, she was blasé all the way to a bench where she stationed and removed her clothes.

The water was refreshing, but Elke felt exposed, paranoid. The saunas would be easier since she could easily muster the required nudity. Her soaked underwear sagged as she climbed out of the pool. The families were looking at her. Maybe she would be hauled out, arrested for stealing a towel.

She found the sauna in a separate wing from the pool. In the changing room, she stripped and cultivated nonchalance. She opened the door to the sauna and found a spot on the wooden bench. A man waved his towel over his head. Elke closed her eyes. When she couldn't stand it anymore, she stepped outside, onto a deck beside a train overpass. She clutched her towel around her body, but others didn't seem to mind the proximity to public transportation. They were naked, lighting cigarettes as steam drifted from their limbs.

She stood alone, still loopy from the heat. She thought about Margot's email. She knew she should write her sister a longer and more generous reply. She'd invite Margot to stay with her and Louise in Berlin; Elke had swapped her apartment in New York with a supposedly spacious place in Kreuzberg. They could spend those days together. This was for Richard as much as it was for Margot. It would make Richard feel better, Elke thought, to think of his family together. Without Dieter. It would just be Louise and her daughters, doing touristic things. And then maybe Richard would take care of the project and Louise would calm down. Surrounded by naked steamers, buoyed by her new resolve, Elke tightened her stolen towel and braced for the hot return.

LOUISE

1978

SHE WAS RIDING BEHIND Richard through the hills south of town. The road was rural and empty, the stillness broken by the rattle of her cruiser's frame. Louise struggled on the incline, but Richard was waiting at the top of the hill, his hair glinting in the light. He wore cut-offs and black sunglasses, sneakers without socks. "We'll have to do some mild trespassing," he said.

"I don't have to pick up Elke until three," Louise said. "If we get arrested, I have all morning to spend in jail." Elke's nursery school had another week to go. Louise's year was already finished, and summer's promise gaped wide.

She'd met Richard six weeks earlier, at the end of April, but they'd quickly fallen into a routine. Twice a week, after teaching his survey, he'd drop by for dinner. When his semester ended, he'd kept the schedule. What she knew about him intrigued her. His research fascinated her; she loved the way he talked about his ideas. He'd told her that he'd grown up in Orange County; he'd surfed as a kid, and she could see it now, as he pushed his bike through the grass. That loose, limber faith in his body.

They'd met at Schubert Park in Whiteaker, the neighborhood where Louise and Elke had lived for the past three years. She'd never made it back to Germany. Slowly her resolve fell away. As a toddler, Elke had refused the German books. "No *Hund*," Elke had said, pushing her hands over her ears. Then Louise's letters slowed, and eventually she

stopped suggesting that she was trying to return to Düsseldorf. She
wrote to Dieter about Elke's progress, about her own projects with her
students. And he wrote about his music; without the band he was making recordings on his own. He was working as a carpenter but feeling
antsy in the job. He was trying to make it to New York, he wrote, but
she no longer believed he would.

She and Elke had first moved into a room at the Green House, the
two of them sharing the bed. The communal household had rotating
childcare and vegetarian rules — Spanish rice and cheese lasagna, vats
of lentil stew. But Louise had grown tired of the team parenting at
the Green House — *one carob cookie each.* The passive-aggressive notes
about leftovers or dishes despite the collectively lax housekeeping. Too
many meals starring raw garlic and brown rice. The neighborhood was
at once gritty and verdant, friendly and strange. The day drinkers who
gathered at Tiny's Tavern reminded her of the *Imbiss* scene in Düsseldorf, the men scowling with their beers on the bench outside the store.
That winter she and Elke had moved to their own squat bungalow a
few blocks away.

Now Richard looked back at her. "We can leave the bikes here," he
said. The broken fence curved around wide, overgrown fields. Set back
from the fence was a farmhouse, knee-deep in straggly vegetation. An
actual tree jutted up through the crumbled roof. In the distance was a
silo, folded in and faded red.

Louise pointed out the old delineations of property, the droopy
barbed wire and ancient spray paint.

Richard traced his foot along a dirt path, barely there, a long-ago
shortcut between the house and a wooden shed. "This desire line is
subtle, but it's still an informal route," he said.

"It reminds me of the work of an artist I saw once," Louise said. "He
walked back and forth so that he wore a line into the grass. Then he
photographed it."

Richard was listening, with that slight anticipatory smile. "A desire line in place," he said. "Was the art the photograph or his act of walking?"

"That's an interesting question," Louise said. "I'd say the walking." She told him about painting in Germany, her studio looking out on the Rhein.

Richard nodded. "I've always thought that city planning hits those same notes that painters think about. When we talk about visual cues in the built environment — color and light and shape."

Louise could tell he was a good teacher. But this was more than imparting knowledge. It was an invitation for her to get closer, to engage with him, and she liked the light way he wore his confidence.

Richard had his camera out now, and he stepped away from her to circle the house.

When he was an undergrad at Berkeley, he'd hung out with sculptors and painters, he'd told her. He began to take his photography more seriously, especially when he started doing his graduate research. The camera slowed him down, helped him find patterns, showed him lines and shapes. And that led him to more questions, new ideas to think through.

He'd brought over his prints a couple of weeks ago. He liked visiting abandoned spaces, he said. He was fascinated by decay. A gas station's forgotten pumps, or a highway overpass, the cement cracked by weeds. He had an eye — his pictures were well-composed. But most striking was that he found a latent emotional quality in these places, something lyrical and desolate.

Louise trailed behind him as he went into the house. They were walking and looking in tandem, not together but not apart. There was a little distance between them. An electric space. She sensed the lines of his body, of his arms. Her nerves sat with her own assurance, both of those feelings at once. Louise had been cautious with him because of Elke, and he'd respected that. In public, he touched her in innocuous ways that were nevertheless charged.

At the Green House, guys had come for the big group dinners and hugged for too long, that hippie embrace that could easily melt into more. These men were never quite what Louise wanted, with their onion smell and blank grins, but she sometimes let them linger before she broke away. One night she smoked a joint with one of the long-haired visitors and the rest of the household on the porch after the kids had gone to bed. After a few rounds from the jug of Cribari Brothers, it was just the two of them. *How about a little more of that, sister?* His van was parked in front of the house, in earshot, she hoped, of Elke's cries from the second floor. The air was musty, the encounter quick and unsatisfying, leaving her only more lonely. She missed Dieter.

Now she had Richard. Around Elke, Louise called Richard her friend, an ironic echo of the discreet German *freund.* He didn't spend the whole night in Louise's bed. What was happening between them occurred quietly after Elke was asleep. But being with Richard was entirely different from her furtive encounters at the Green House. Richard was responsive, attentive. He smelled of fresh air.

Louise went through the open door frame, stepped into the surprise of cool and dim and damp. The kitchen's curtains were still parted above the sink.

Richard was crouched by the door, focusing his lens. "Have you worked in other mediums?" he asked. "Besides painting?"

"Not since I was a student," she said. "Of course, now I try to do everything along with the kids. So I've had to relearn the kiln, which I hadn't used since I was an undergrad."

She'd discovered since she started teaching that, once her nerves settled down, she liked talking; that after her taciturn parents, after struggling to speak German, there was an ease to assuming authority, to speaking back to what she'd absorbed. And English allowed a complexity that she'd missed.

She watched Richard photograph a cluster of green bottles, left by another trespasser. She anticipated what he was capturing, saw it through his eyes. Looking at the door frame's softened wood, she felt the stamp of time. The house, with its crumbling walls and quotidian details, was a kind of clock. The windowpanes stood out in pale squares against the dim, and that made her think about painting. A canvas left outside could reflect the pressure of time. She wanted to experiment with that idea, set color against sun and steady rain.

"Hey," Richard said, catching her eye, lifting the camera strap over his head. He went to her and touched her face and hair. She led him back outside, to the dry grass behind the house. So much vivid texture: the dusty fields around them, the frayed collar of Richard's shirt. And the yellow crunch beneath their bodies. The afternoon was blazing, silent, still.

He leaned back for a second. "If we get arrested, I'll put up your bail."

"Thanks," Louise said, pulling him down again.

A few days later, at the end of a warm afternoon, Louise and Elke were in the front of the house, weeding the perennial bed. Louise had kept her mother's garden sketches, returned to them when her grief flared. She'd made her own as she planned the garden here. The new house was small, but it had a decent yard, a porch off the kitchen in the back. A half flight of stairs led from the living room to a little room over the garage, Elke's bedroom, whose sloped ceilings reminded Louise of the attic at Frau Kerbel's. Louise finally had her own room, and she'd set up a worktable by the window.

Elke was collecting dandelions in a vase for the table. Louise had taught her to trim the stems for the bouquet first, then dig out the root. That's what they were doing when the taxi pulled up — Louise with her gloved hands in the dirt, coaching Elke with the spade.

The local taxi service was a fleet of station wagons painted yellow and green. The driver lifted a suitcase from the trunk, and Louise saw his passenger's hands first, long fingers paging through a wallet. Then legs reaching from the back seat, and that's when Louise recognized him.

"It's Dieter," Louise said. Elke wouldn't know; Louise's contact with him had dwindled to sporadic letters. Louise grounded her hands on Elke's shoulders. Dieter counted bills and shook the driver's hand. An American confidence. The taxi drove away.

"It's time for me to see this place where you are living," Dieter said. And without any warning or time for her to prepare, he put his arms around her, a total embrace. She bent her wrists to keep dirt from his clothes.

Elke, who'd been watching Louise for a cue, hugged Dieter with quick arms. *Hug a neighbor, hug a friend* was a song Elke had learned in nursery school, complete with wan obligatory embraces—a life lesson in social insincerity. *Hug an estranged father* Louise thought, but Elke didn't look so troubled. She was already leading him inside.

His suitcase went in the living room—that would come later, the question of where he would fit. She filled a glass of water, invited him to sit down.

"I opened the window on the airplane," Dieter told Elke. "I wanted to bring you this cloud. So I put it in my pocket. Hang on."

He slapped the invisible substance into Elke's outstretched hand. "Hold it," he said. "Don't let it float away."

"It's fluffy." Elke was willing to go along.

Louise sent her to the herb garden to pick basil for dinner. "The big green leaves."

Dieter's gaze was quizzical, probing, as though he were the one trying to understand why she had suddenly appeared and not the other way around. "I realize this is unexpected," he said.

"How long are you planning to stay?" Louise was sideways in her seat, watching Elke in the yard.

"I bought a one-way ticket," Dieter said. "I need to spend some time with Elke." His accent was thicker than she remembered, each word heavy and deliberate. And the lovely sound of her daughter's name pronounced properly—*Ell-keh*. No one said it like that here, not even Louise.

"You should have told me you were coming." A one-way ticket? What did he think he was going to do?

"I thought it would be a surprise." Dieter's hair was shorter, trimmed flush with his chin, lending him an earnest quality, as though his spontaneity were actually an eagerly awaited gift.

Elke ran in and spread her bounty on the table.

"Good work," Louise said. "Now I need sage—the fuzzy one." Though she knew what she had to say to Dieter was going to take longer than this chore.

He went to the living room and retrieved wrapped presents from his suitcase. *"Ein froher Gast ist niemands Last,"* he said as he returned to the kitchen.

A once-familiar aphorism: a cheerful guest is always welcome. What could she say to him in German? Elke added sage to her pile and accepted Dieter's box.

"I think you'll like this." Dieter handed Louise something, too. The shape gave it away—an LP. And she knew she would, whatever it was. She had a portable turntable that she carried between the living room and her bedroom along with used copies of *Rumours* and *Tapestry* and *Harvest*—uninspired choices, perhaps, but reliable ones. She'd gone to the record store downtown, in an old Victorian house with a rotting porch, and, feeling nostalgic, asked for Can and Tangerine Dream. Imports, though, were expensive, and she convinced herself she didn't need them.

Dieter's gift was a Terry Riley album. A racing thrill: she didn't know it, was eager to listen. But it bothered her that she was still susceptible to what Dieter could offer.

Elke's gift was a sort of puzzle or maybe a game. A box of small wooden tiles in different colors and shapes. Triangles and diamonds, rectangles and squares. It came with a set of grids and patterns to replicate. *Puzzlespiel,* it said on the box.

"You can make these mosaics," Louise told Elke. "And you can make your own designs, too."

They set up the tiles on the living room floor and slid the shapes over the carpet, arranged boxes and patterns and lines.

"The two of you can share it," Dieter said. "Now let's hear Terry Riley. It sounds good when it's loud."

She listened while she made dinner—leftover lentil burgers, a Green House recipe. The music was free and immersive, covering Dieter and Elke's conversation in the other room. Louise toasted bread and sliced tomatoes, and despite her misgivings, she could feel herself riding along.

"Come add your herbs, Elke." Louise had made a spinach salad; she had sunflower seeds, cheddar cheese. The basil and sage wouldn't taste right, but she didn't want Elke to sense her apprehension. Everything had to be happening for a reason, even the task of gathering herbs.

"I almost know how to read," Elke said at the table, "which means I get to go to kindergarten."

"Oh, wow," Dieter said. *Vow.*

In the past, when Elke had asked about her father, Louise had described Germany and told Elke that she would have the chance to see him again. Increasingly, though, Elke wasn't appeased by Louise's vague promise. *Tell me when.* Louise felt her answer was dishonest—*when you're older*—but she wanted to believe that Elke would know Dieter.

Louise tasted the salad. The basil did indeed clash with the cheddar, but Dieter didn't seem to mind. "Delicious," he said. "From which animal do you make this burger?"

"We're vegetarians now," Louise said.

Dieter raised his brows. "An American diet."

"No more *Wurst.*"

After Elke was in bed, Louise took the record player to the porch, sat with Dieter at either end of the sagging old couch, left by the previous tenant.

She was playing the record quietly now. "What's the story of this one?" How strange, uncanny, to have him sitting here in her house in

Eugene, talking about records. Time had collapsed. When she'd imagined their reunion, it was in Germany. Dieter in the Altstadt or against a casement window. But he was there on the plaid couch, beneath the ancient Ducks pennant tacked up by the last renter.

"I went to the concert in Cologne," Dieter said. "Don Cherry and Terry Riley. This was unbelievable. So I found all the recordings."

"Do you like Cologne more than Düsseldorf?" Louise was circling around her real questions: she was already girding for his departure.

"In some ways," Dieter said.

"You'd had enough *Altbier.*"

His smile was direct and real; she felt it in her stomach. "I liked the *Kölsch,*" he said. "But not enough to stay."

"What do you mean?"

"Werner will sponsor me," Dieter said. "Eventually I'm making my way to New York."

"You're immigrating?" Dieter had been spinning this idea since she met him, but it had been a long time since she'd believed it.

"I'll be an American guy," Dieter said. "A New Yorker." He grinned at the prospect, but the smile went inward. She couldn't share it.

"Why didn't you tell me?"

"It's not an easy process," Dieter said. "I wasn't sure if it would go through."

"You've missed four years of her life." Elke's sandals were in the corner—she was a literal clock of all the time he'd missed. "You couldn't even tell me you were trying to come?"

"For a while I thought you were coming back," he said. "Then it was complicated to arrange my immigration. But I should have told you, you're right. I didn't want to disappoint Elke if it didn't work."

"So you'll be in New York." For a flash she'd seen him in Eugene.

"Eventually," Dieter said. "I'd like to spend some time here with Elke first, to make up for what I've missed."

A week, she thought, two? But she owed it to Elke. "She just turned five," Louise said. "She'll be in kindergarten in the fall."

"You left." Dieter's voice was even, careful. "You left and you told me you were going to come back. But I've accepted that Elke is an American now, so I'm going to be here, too."

The yard was dark. She couldn't tell him no.

"We have time to talk about that yet," Dieter said. "Right now, I have to tell you a little secret."

Louise felt momentary panic; his knees jutted out, a proprietary sprawl on her couch. "I haven't slept in a while," he said. He laughed to himself again. But she also sensed an opening: *I'm not in my right mind*, he was saying. *I'm giving you an excuse to let things happen. To make things happen.* One quick move on her part might set it off—to touch his shoulder, to stand intentionally close. How easy it would be to do that, the reason she'd put herself where she couldn't reach him, at the opposite end of the couch. She had Richard; their relationship was just beginning, but it felt serious and right, and she didn't want to screw it up.

She wasn't sure where to put Dieter. The sofa in the living room wouldn't accommodate his height. Elke could have slept in Louise's bed and Dieter in Elke's room, but that would disrupt the household so hard-earned.

There was the porch, though, and the very couch they were sitting on. Sheltered by a roof that extended from the house, and, besides, the Oregon summer was a respite from the wet months. She knew innately that pattern of warm and dry. And on the porch, Dieter would be out of the way.

The next morning, Louise took Dieter with her: they walked Elke to school and bought groceries at the Red Barn. She showed him the tubs of yogurt. "We don't have to import it from Germany," she said. When the cashier peppered Dieter with small talk—questions about the weather, about his cooking plans—Louise stood by and watched, amused.

"I don't know what she's planning to cook," Dieter said. Louise could see his confusion—why did the cashier want to know?

At home, she soaked beans and made cornbread, easy tasks except for the fact that Dieter was there, too. Examining the bulk bins, walking down Blair Boulevard in his striped T-shirt, looking better than she wanted to admit.

She called Richard and invited him to dinner, letting him know that Elke's father was in town. She wanted to make clear to Dieter that she was involved with someone else. And another thought snaked in—*let Dieter see how that feels.*

She made chili while Dieter read the newspaper on the porch, and after they picked up Elke, the three of them worked in the yard. Louise weeded the herbs; she was crouched there when Richard arrived, wheeling his bike over the grass. His long fingers curled over the handlebars, his backpack was slung with casual grace.

"Garden inspector," Richard said. "The tax is three strawberries." Louise watched him scan Dieter, his confidence eroding as he assessed. All she'd told Richard was that Dieter was out of their lives. Far away, she'd said, but now she could see Richard's face mirroring her own panic and curiosity, trapped between the impulses to remain in the yard or run.

Dieter, too, was prickly, puffed up. He thrust his hand forward. "I am pleased."

Lemonade, Louise suggested, and then she'd start cooking; they all needed something to do.

Inside, she washed lettuce while Elke spread her tiles on the table. "It's German," Elke said to Richard. "It's a German game." Elke had been wary with Richard since he became a regular visitor; he was the first threat to her tight bond with Louise. Richard responded to her with sweet enthusiasm, used compliments to soften her up.

"How do you win?" Richard asked.

"It's not that kind of game," Dieter said.

Louise lit the burner under the chili. She didn't know how to explain all this to Richard when she didn't understand it herself.

"I'm going to develop that roll of film from our research walk, Elke," Richard said. "You were an excellent assistant."

Elke nodded, pleased. "I'm good at research."

"We documented desire lines in Hendricks Park," Richard told Dieter.

Dieter sat back with folded arms. "I'm not familiar with this expression."

"They're a kind of casual trail," Richard said. "When people walk on routes that are outside the official path. Over the grass instead of along the sidewalk."

"Marching to your own drummer," Dieter said. "Is that what you say?"

Louise ladled the chili, delivered the bowls. "Something like that," she said. "Dieter's a drummer, that's why he asks." She was bantering with Dieter and smiling at Richard, a weird, concurrent exchange.

Richard got up from the table. "I'm in urban design," he said. "So I'm no drummer, but I'm studying what the different drummers prompt, if that makes any sense."

Dieter still wasn't giving in. "Perhaps I will need to see the pictures."

"You should come on one of our walks," Richard said, as though Dieter were another five-year-old who would respond to simple encouragement.

Over dinner they talked about Elke's upcoming nursery school graduation, the bulk bins, Dieter's game. Louise realized she had forgotten about the cornbread.

Richard usually stayed after dinner—he'd read in the living room while Louise gave Elke a bath. Tonight he had to get home, he said, and Louise went with him to retrieve his bike from the yard.

"How long is Dieter visiting?" Richard stood holding his handlebars, already poised for flight.

"I'm not sure." She squeezed his shoulder. "He's sleeping on the porch."

"I saw the sheets," Richard said, but he didn't look reassured. Louise kissed him, and then, because they were in front of the kitchen window, said good night.

For the next couple of days, Dieter cut Louise a wide berth. After Elke had gone to school, he asked about the library, came back with a bike and a stack of books. *I learned this term, thrift shop, as though the virtue was for sale.* Louise was static at her drawing table, aimless in the yard, circling over her feelings about Dieter's arrival.

Certainly there was an ease: at Elke's graduation, Louise sat with Dieter and introduced him as Elke's dad because it was true. Her own father sat with them, too. She'd told Trent over the phone the night before; she wanted to prepare him for the surprise.

"Elke's father is here," Louise said. "He'll be at the graduation to-morrow."

A pause, a tense silence.

"You didn't tell me he was coming here," Trent said.

"I didn't know he was coming," said Louise. "He's here to see Elke, not me," she added.

"All right," Trent said. "I'll look for you at the school." His voice was steady on the line. But she could see the raw feeling when he found her in the auditorium: the high set to his shoulders, the strained tendons along his forearms.

"Good to see you," Trent said, loud and slow as he shook Dieter's hand. Trent settled next to Louise and pulled out a book. His interests had widened — fluoride, political conspiracies — and he taped paper over the jackets now, to obscure their titles and images. Some modesty had kicked in after a prophecy of Armageddon in '77 hadn't panned out.

Dieter's presence might have closed the mystery in the eyes of other parents, or perhaps deepened it. People smiled and waved to Louise, and she knew her father was uncomfortable—he didn't know what was going on.

The ceremony was bumbling and sweet. *Today we're moving up,* the children sang. *Today we're crossing the bridge.* When it was over, Trent smiled broadly and congratulated Elke, posed with her for Louise's camera.

Elke grinned up at Trent. "Grandpa," she said, "I'm a graduate now."

"I'm mighty impressed," he said. And then he took off, leaving Dieter with another handshake and sturdy nod.

Trent's quick exit echoed Louise's own misgivings. On the surface, Dieter, with his jean jacket and long hair, was like any other guy coasting through Eugene. He wanted to fit in. "Sure" was his resounding answer, and only his more complicated responses betrayed his stilted English. But despite his best efforts, his German opinions kept coming out: he was critical of the neighbor's rusted car on cinder blocks in the front yard. *My God, what a mess.* He was surprised that Louise didn't peel carrots, that she left dishes in the sink overnight.

He kept closing the front door that Louise had left open when they were home during the day. She told him that everyone did it. Summertime, they needed air. She thought that maybe this could echo the German sensibility about *lüften,* but her West Coast interpretation apparently was all wrong. The open door would have been unthinkable in Germany, and even Dieter, so determined to leave that place, was bound to its rules.

"What if someone comes in?" he wanted to know.

"I'd ask him what he wanted." The real threat was to a sense of order —if the door was open, anyone could see into your house. It was her turf, though, and she didn't close it.

There was no reason for them to speak German here, except for the occasional private word launched over Elke's head. "What a *Scheisskerl,*" Dieter said when recounting some particularly irritating behavior of his brother's. Using only English gave Louise a sense of control —Dieter was a visitor to her world, and he slept on the porch all week.

Richard skipped their usual Thursday dinner, and when she called him to check in, their conversation was brief, strained. Come over next week, she suggested, and he told her that he would.

On Friday, after Elke was in bed, Louise sat with Dieter on the porch. It was raining, the noise steady on the roof.

"A real *Landregen,* my mother would call it," Dieter said. "It'll rain for weeks."

The mention of Hannelore was a bumped bruise. Louise sent photographs of Elke to Hannelore for her birthday and Christmas, matching Hannelore's greetings for Elke. But she felt guilty that Hannelore hadn't seen Elke since she was a baby. And now Louise was thinking about what Hannelore had told her about Dieter's father, how decisively Dieter had reacted. *This is for me to try to understand. It's not for you,* he'd told Louise. She wondered how he'd grappled with it since, whether he'd talked to his mother about it.

That was dangerous territory, though, and she wasn't sure how to broach it. Instead, she asked him about something else that had been bothering her — the question of how long he would stay.

"I don't want Elke to be upset when you leave," she said. "I want to be sure she's prepared."

He looked surprised. "I'd like to spend a few more weeks with her before I go to New York," he said. "If that's all right with you."

She couldn't deny him that time with Elke. He was making their daughter happy. But what about Richard? She didn't want to wait weeks to see him again.

"I was afraid that Elke would hate me when I got here," Dieter said. "How would she even know me?"

"That's not what happened, though." Louise knew it was partly her fault that Elke hadn't known her father for so long. She owed him a little more time.

Dieter flipped the record. He'd brought out Louise's copy of *Rumours,* and the Velvet Underground LP he'd brought home that day.

"A great price," he said. "Used. Why would someone get rid of it?"

"Good question," Louise said. "We've benefited from that bad choice."

She'd poured more wine and she liked the taste, a bit sweet against the garden's mulchy smell, the record's easy beat. "Have you been making music?" she asked.

"With synthesizers," he said. "Klaus-Peter got new equipment. I used them for some recordings."

"By yourself? No band?"

"Right," Dieter said. "I'm not sure it's my *Lebensaufgabe*." The word meant a calling in life, a term that captured that classic German reflectiveness—a philosophical coming to terms with what your life should be.

"What is your *Lebensaufgabe*?" she asked.

"I'll have to find out," Dieter said. "In New York."

"I'm sure you could get a band together there," Louise said. "Put an ad in the paper for local weirdos. You'll find them."

"Good idea," Dieter said. He stretched his arm along the back of the couch. "You'll never guess what happened with Beuys." His fingers were close to, but not touching, her hair. "I've been meaning to tell you."

She could see he'd been saving it, something to pull out for her at the right moment. Shining expectation, his pride in presentation.

"Beuys finally won the lawsuit," Dieter said. She didn't tell him that she'd already heard this in a letter from Ute. She wanted to hear it from him. "So now he has his studio back. The Kunstakademie granted him lifetime access."

"Better late than never."

Dieter was pulling lightly on her hair. "Why aren't you painting?"

"No space," Louise said. "No time." She'd set up a corner of the huge art room at the Cedar School for her own work, but she wasn't using it. She liked the job, though the move out of the Green House made it impossible for her to save any money. A regular school would offer a real salary, but Louise prized the Cedar School's radical mission, showing

these kids—fresh-faced thieves and druggies—a way out with char-
coal and clay. She thought sometimes about what Beuys himself had
claimed, that teaching was his greatest work of art.

"But you painted at my mother's house," Dieter said. "Surely you
could do it here."

"I've been drawing." She sketched at night when the house was
quiet, made notes and plans for projects, but she was ashamed at how
little she'd done. "It's what I can fit in right now."

"I'm not critical," he said. "I just want you to be happy."

The song had ended, and the porch was quiet except for the sound
of the record spinning, the needle caught in the lock groove.

"I'll get back to it," she said.

"Me, too." Would he make music in New York? Could he be a
carpenter and live with his cousin and claim his *Lebensaufgabe*? The
thought of it made her wistful.

"Remember when we heard thunder during the snowstorm?" Dieter
asked.

A night during Louise's first year in Düsseldorf. They were in his
studio, watching the unusual storm. The thunder and the snow felt
incongruous. They'd laughed about it.

The rain couldn't reach her now, but she moved to the center of the
porch, and Dieter got up, too. "I think it will rain yet," he said.

They hadn't touched at all beyond their initial greeting a week earlier. But now, he put his hand on her back. *Hug a neighbor, hug a friend.*
It was all so easy—once he touched her, the rest happened quickly.

She locked the door to her bedroom. The details were what she'd
forgotten, what brought him back: his thumb behind her ear, his ribs
under her hands. There he was, as he'd been. These details different
from Richard's—the surprise as she touched Dieter's head, interrupting her expectation of Richard's shorter hair. A cataloging that detached
her from the fact of what she was doing.

Dieter was taller than Richard, his arms and legs longer, and that
space he occupied in her bed, as she wrapped herself around him,

brought the past hurtling back. She'd walled off these feelings: watching Dieter's loose arms ranging over the drum set, watching his body from the crowd. That old intensity—she hadn't let herself think this way in a long time. Now she was with him again; she was here but also in Düsseldorf, in his studio, in their small room in Oberbilk.

When she was with Richard, she was aware of the kid sleeping in the other room. With Dieter, the kid was theirs. Being with him felt right. When it was over, though, she told him they'd made a mistake. Lying next to him, she couldn't see his face.

"Not yet," Dieter said. "Just wait a bit for that."

She stayed with him and listened, beneath the rain, for any sound of Elke moving in the house. Eventually she said it. "The living room should be dry."

She found Dieter drinking coffee in the kitchen the next morning. He'd left his sheets folded on the arm of the sofa, and Louise put them back on the porch. Elke wouldn't need to know even that.

"It stopped raining," he said.

She sat down with her mug. "It hardly ever rains here in the summer."

"I'll keep that in mind." He was sly and easy; he wasn't upset. The night before was an exception, not an opening. They could agree that it shouldn't happen again.

Elke came in and asked for cereal. The day was marked by Louise's caution: a gesture could be a signal, and she couldn't let Dieter interrupt her life here. That night, after Elke was asleep, Louise told Dieter that she was going to read in bed. Tired, she said. She was.

Richard showed up again on Monday evening, and Louise put a fourth plate on the kitchen table, setting his place beside her own.

Elke wouldn't eat the spaghetti. She was usually voracious; since her early days at the Green House, she'd relished avocado, black olives, Tabasco, the weird stuff the other kids refused.

Elke shook her head. "The noodles are too slippery."

"Ice cream is slippery, too," Richard said. She felt Dieter's gaze as she smiled at Richard.

"That's right," Louise said. "And if you want ice cream for dessert, you're going to have to eat more of your dinner."

Elke's long hair curtained her scowl. "It's a different kind of slippery."

Dieter was sitting across from Louise. "Not all children get to eat such food," he said. "They would beg for slippery noodles." He caught Louise's eye, a shared blip. But Elke wasn't swayed. She ate with exaggerated slowness.

After dinner, Louise walked Richard out to his bike. "I'll call you," she said. He was emphatic this time, not letting go, and Louise didn't pull back.

"Don't forget," he said. As he rolled away, she stayed in the space he'd taken up, as though that would keep him with her. She didn't want to go back inside and face Dieter just yet.

That night Louise worked at her desk after Elke was asleep. She was thinking about what she'd seen with Richard at the abandoned farmhouse. Green glass in sunlight, and the windows in smudged blue squares. The rotting structure left to measure time. She remembered the textures as she and Richard went through the soft wood frame and down to the hard yellow grass.

She kept Elke's tile game spread out on the table. *Puzzlespiel.* She drew patterns of repeating shapes, sketched ideas for a project, maybe with canvas cut in squares. She would leave the pieces outside, use color to track their change.

One night at the end of June, when Dieter had been there for nearly three weeks, she was sitting with him on the porch, slumped on the weak springs. To be with him again—his laugh, the stilted elegance of his speech—unlocked what she'd pushed away. She'd missed him. And she wanted explanation.

They were listening to the Terry Riley record: cool and engrossing, quietly triumphant. Louise flipped the record more than once—the electronic sounds transfixing, Don Cherry's horn resounding and clean. Easy to keep playing it, and Dieter didn't stop her.

She asked him about Hannelore. "Is she upset that you're moving away?"

"I'll visit," Dieter said. "I needed to leave. The culture is beyond hope. There are still terrorists blowing things up, but even that doesn't make change. It's always going to be silent." He paused, stared at the dark yard. "I haven't talked to her about what you told me. About my father. It's too difficult."

She was jolted by his direct mention of his father, surprised that he was bringing it up. She nodded, let him keep talking.

"It's hard for me to be close to her," Dieter said, his face clouded with his report. "It's been painful to try to understand what she did. What my father did."

"Maybe it'll be helpful to get some distance," Louise said.

"We'll see." Dieter shifted on the couch. "Düsseldorf feels different now. Gerd and Ute are talking about moving to Cologne, too."

He was changing the subject, but she didn't stop him. She didn't know what else to say.

"There was nothing there for me anymore," Dieter said.

"You haven't left anyone over there?" Louise was aware of her jealousy, irrational or not.

Dieter shook his head. "I haven't met any more American painters," he said. "So I had to come here."

His tone was lighter now; he seemed relieved to shift gears. But Louise was annoyed.

"What about Sabine?" she asked.

"You know that she's long gone." He looked down, bothered not by his guilt but by her bringing it up. "It was a confusing time," he said. "Mistakes were made."

"You sound like Nixon."

"That's not a comparison I appreciate." Dieter was smiling, but she shook her head. She wasn't going to let him dodge her questions.

"It wasn't important," Dieter said. "I'm sorry about it, you know. About Sabine. It was a mistake to get involved with her."

"You made a mistake," Louise said.

"That's right," Dieter said. "Just like your dear Nixon."

"Then why did it take you so long to come here? What have you been doing all this time?"

A fraught pause—he'd just told her that he'd been in pain. And though Hannelore's revelations weren't Louise's fault, she couldn't help but feel guilty. She hadn't handled that well.

Dieter, though, kept moving forward. "I was believing you were coming back," he said, and pulled her legs over his lap.

A moment of possible revision. Time caught in the lock groove. At that moment on the porch, she wanted him too. Her full spectrum of feeling—her anger and regret and grief—had a forceful outlet. His urgency swept her, matched her own. In her bedroom, behind the locked door, her hesitation fell away. They were connecting in a way that had otherwise been out of reach. Still, he returned to the porch before dawn. She asked him to. She didn't want Elke to think that she and Dieter were back together.

But she was imagining exactly that. What it would be like if Dieter stayed. They were still married; they could fall back into the neat shape of a family, cooking food and listening to records in the evening. Dieter biking around with Elke, Elke relishing his attention.

Elke liked telling stories—she'd made up an imaginary world she called Sillyland, and her winding and bizarre descriptions reminded Louise of her mother's prayers.

"In Sillyland," Elke said at the dinner table, "Dieter has a bike store. He gives everyone air in their tires. Even dogs."

Another moment of possible revision, with the three of them a unit. At Snowy's, the ice-cream stand downtown, the scooper was one of

Louise's students, Bobby Garner, a lapsed shoplifter with a mustache struggling to gain traction over his lip.

"Here you go, Mr. Willis," Bobby said to Dieter as he handed him the cone. Dieter laughed, but Louise was glad that Elke was distracted by her ice cream.

In May, Louise had taken her students to a protest against the Trojan nuclear plant near Portland. She had them conduct interviews and bring the responses back to the art room. Bobby had surprised her with the depth of his feeling, producing intricate drawings of the reactor's stark silhouette, with neat cursive forming grass from the phrases he'd heard at the site.

Louise had shown Bobby's drawings to Richard, who'd come to the protest, too. "Why is this kid shoplifting?" Richard asked. "He's got much better ways to deal with his shit."

Richard was a tight place in Louise's stomach, a knot she stepped around. When she sketched her new project, she remembered the afternoon at the farmhouse, everything bright and still. She'd felt complete.

She could no longer claim that certainty. It was wrong to be involved with both of them, she knew that, but her reunion with Dieter was necessary. She was having it out with him, facing the abrupt way things had ended in Düsseldorf. And though the timing was messy and awkward, she didn't want to give up what she'd started with Richard. She had to keep tracing the way with both of them. This situation was temporary, she told herself. Dieter would be leaving soon, and then she would resume, or resume beginning, her real relationship with Richard.

He showed up for dinner again the following Thursday. A mix of relief and dread: each person at the table needed something different from Louise. These men were tolerating the strange situation. They both wanted her, a flushed and shameful triumph. A lady of easy virtue, Louise's mother would have said.

"You have to eat at least five bites of broccoli," Louise told Elke.

Elke chewed a minuscule crown as she counted to five.

"How's the grass stepping?" Dieter asked Richard. Something a little dangerous in his tone.

"Business is booming," said Richard. Smooth and sure.

Elke put her broccoli on Dieter's plate.

In the yard after dinner, Richard scanned Louise's lower back with one hand under her T-shirt. "Can't you come over to my house some time?"

She wanted to do that, she told him.

"I have some photos to show you," he said. "Call me if you want to see them." It was up to her, he was saying.

Richard's place was near Hendricks Park. On the way there, Louise passed the roadside memorial for Steve Prefontaine, the spot where he'd crashed in '75. Driving home from a party, the paper had reported, celebrating after a win. People still left things for him here, flowers and candles, medals and shoes. Pre's Rock, people called it — the loss now part of the landscape.

Richard's apartment took up the second floor of a house, and Louise went in through the open door. She'd already told Dieter to put Elke to bed. Childcare was easier with two parents in the picture, allowing her to go on a date. An absurd thought. She knew she was making Dieter jealous, a feeling she'd batted away with guilty pleasure on the drive.

In the kitchen, Richard pulled cans of beer from the fridge. "How's Elke?"

"She's growing eggplant," Louise said.

"I love eggplant." His voice was even but not neutral — she'd have to work for this.

"I'm sure she'll give you some." The beer was perfect, cold and watery, the can sweating in the hot room. "She claims she likes the color, but not the taste."

"I wouldn't know what to do with it," Richard said. "But I'm guessing you do."

"Trial by fire," Louise said. "We have a ratio of three eggplants per person."

Richard leaned on the counter. "You've been busy."

"It's been good for Elke to spend time with Dieter," Louise said, flustered. "But I'm not working this summer. I have lots of free time."

Would he forgive her, would he let her back in? "Invite me over for eggplant," he said.

"I will. When the tomatoes start, then we'll really be in trouble."

Richard brought out an envelope of photos. Lines cutting through the grass, marks made by footsteps. Routes established first by deliberate action, and then unconscious retreading of that original path. There was a desolate quality to these pictures, and something voyeuristic, too. A path made by people long gone. An end times vision that Louise's father might appreciate — an empty world after the Fall.

Richard put more photos on the counter. "I had a set made for you."

The sleeve of his T-shirt was pushed up, and she touched the place on his arm where the fabric had blocked the sunlight, a clear line between summer and winter skin.

His bedroom was small, set in the corner of the house, facing a cluster of pines so that the branches nearly crawled into the open window. This space, with his blue sheets, his books stacked beside the bed, was separate from the rest of her life. Richard wasn't wary anymore. He was open, directive. His legs were like his arms, the tan fading higher up. His legs and arms were stronger than Dieter's, his skin softer. And something else — Richard was intuitive, responsive. They didn't have to worry about being quiet like they did at her house.

"Don't forget about me," Richard said later, when he walked her out to her car. "I've missed you."

"Come for eggplant." She knew she was welcoming trouble. But she wanted to see him.

She drove home with the windows down, careful on the turns. The place where Prefontaine, whose perfect speed had eluded him in Munich, had for once gone too fast.

July rolled on. Louise took Elke to lessons at the pool in Amazon Park. She gardened, made plans for how she'd deal with the eventual haul: tomato sauce for the freezer, green beans in jars. Dieter wore the same outfit for days in a row, airing his clothes on the porch. Louise showed him the dryer at the laundromat on Blair, but he refused to use it. Fine, but that meant he had to lug the clothes back to the house in a wet bag, string it all up in the yard. This time, Louise didn't do it for him.

She took Dieter to the regular Sunday dinner at the Green House. A nice compromise; she liked to be with the group around the table, but she also liked to leave before discussion of the tofu bucket began. And even worse—Blake had developed the distressing habit of greeting all the moms in the group with some mild attempts at French kissing, snaking in a little tongue.

"This is Dieter," Louise said in the backyard. "Elke's dad."

The group nodded, offered them sangria. The men were cleaning the fire pit; Joanne and Karen were shucking corn. Elke found the other kids—Sage and Orion, still in diapers, and Amber and Milo, the oldest at eight, the strident ringleader. The kids were fractious and fiercely close from their early years together in the house.

"Dieter, watch me!" Elke cried. She waved her arms as she hopped on one foot, and he crossed the yard to join her.

Louise left her drink on the table and followed Joanne to the kitchen, where a vat of water was boiling on the stove. They dropped the corn into the pot and leaned back to avoid the splash.

"So he's back, huh?" Joanne was tending to a pan of beans.

"I guess so. For a little while."

Joanne nodded. "He's crazy about you, I can tell."

This surprised Louise. For so long in Düsseldorf, she'd found Dieter enigmatic, wanted him to tell her what he was feeling. "You've barely met him," Louise said. She hadn't told Joanne much about her marriage, only that things had been difficult in Germany, only that she'd left.

"He's got that intensity," Joanne said. "Maybe it's a European thing. But the way he looks at you. The energy is palpable." With tongs, she extracted corn from the steaming pot. "They only need a minute."

"I'm not sure what's going on."

"What about Richard?"

"That's the thing," Louise said. "I didn't know Dieter was coming. I still want to see Richard. We have something really good together."

"So just go with it for a while," Joanne said, licking beans from her finger. "Elke seems happy. See what happens. What's Richard's sign?"

"His birthday is in January."

"Capricorn, probably," Joanne said. "That's a great match for you."

"Elke is happy," Louise said. "It's been good for her to have Dieter around. But I keep thinking about Richard. I don't want to give him up."

"Who says you have to?" Joanne asked. She handed Louise the pot of corn to bring to the table.

Outside, the men had drained the pitcher of sangria.

"Joanne found me," Blake was saying. "Not the other way around."

"I wanted a partner for the solstice," Joanne said. "Blake just happened to stay put for a while."

Louise wondered what the men had discussed. She watched Dieter absorbing the scene — the pack of sticky children, the flies buzzing over the compost, Blake and Peter shirtless, in cut-offs, dusty from the fire pit. She felt oddly defensive, even though she herself had chosen not to live here anymore.

"No, Wally!" cried Milo, running across the yard. Wally, the Green House's massive, shedding Maine coon, strutted toward the table, clutching a bird in his mouth. The kids gathered around the cat, fascinated and scared.

"Let him go!" Elke yelled. "The bird is alive!"

"You can't save the bird," Dieter said. "It's nature. Of course the cat wants to kill it."

"Let go, Wally!" Milo touched the cat gingerly, but in vain—Wally worked his jaws and then dropped the bird beside the table. The cat sat on his haunches and watched the carcass with glowering pride.

Elke, sobbing, found Louise, who pulled her onto her lap.

Dieter was matter-of-fact. "You can't control animal instincts. They want to hunt and kill."

"Easy, man," Blake said to Dieter.

"There's no use trying to change nature," Dieter said, getting louder. His eyes were bulging, charged.

"The bird is dead," said Elke. Her shoulders shook, and Louise wished Dieter hadn't been so graphic. The littlest kids were toddlers; some discretion was in order.

"It's OK, guys," Blake said. "Go inside and wash your hands for dinner. Joanne made enchiladas, and they're going to be really yummy."

The children filed through the screen door, and Louise lifted Elke off her lap. "I brought brownies for dessert," Louise said. "Go wash up and I'll save you a place."

"OK," Elke said, wiping her cheek. Dieter was at the other end of the table, and it bothered Louise that he didn't notice Elke's distress.

Blake shooed the cat, and with newspaper, scooped the bird and deposited it in the trash can in the driveway. "I'll wash my hands, too," he said, waggling his fingers in the air.

Louise returned to her abandoned glass of sangria. She'd found her footing here, sort of, but she wasn't sure that Dieter could. And yet she was still pretending that it was possible. That thought bothered her, too.

A few nights later, on the porch with Dieter: "You and Elke could come with me to New York," he said. "Nothing's happening with your art here."

"Something is happening," she said, annoyed. What did he know of her art? He knew a former version of her, but he didn't know anything of her life here. His timing was off. He'd ignored her when she'd suggested this four years ago, when she was ready to leave Oregon.

It was all a question of timing, really: what would have happened if Dieter had come before she met Richard in the park? And what if she hadn't met Richard in the park? What if Dieter had come back two years before that, or even last year? How much deeper they might have gone. But perhaps that would have been a mistake. And what if Dieter had come a year from now? She'd be fully devoted to Richard by then, maybe, and none of these questions would have surfaced at all.

She tried to tell Dieter about the sketches she was making with the tile game, the larger version she was imagining, with colored squares cutting a path through physical space. Dieter was flipping the record. "I don't understand the purpose," he said.

"It's not about purpose," she said. "You make art sound so clinical." They were constantly treading this fraught line, between flirtation and antagonism.

"Of course art has a purpose." He sat down next to her on the couch. And she had a choice—this was the question he was always posing—it was her bedroom, it was up to her to invite him there.

She slid her arm behind his back, rested her head against his shoulder. She'd run out of ways to argue. When he started kissing her, it was a relief, actually, to stop talking.

In her room she pulled him on top of her, a forbidden, frenetic energy in this return. But he was somewhere else, disconnected, grabbing at something rushing past. His skin was sticky against her own, sour with the smell of his sweat. He finished quickly and when he touched her, she couldn't sink into it—he seemed to be watching her, needy, expectant, her pleasure a reflection of him.

She rolled away, lonely beside him, unable to tap into their old recognition. Dieter got out of bed and put his clothes on, quietly opened the door.

She spent a couple of nights a week at Richard's house — leaving after Elke was in bed and returning very early with hair wet from the pool. Amazon Park was on the way home from Richard's; lap swimming hours started at 6 a.m. Deep summer was a haze — bright and dusty, the evenings still blazing, Louise never getting enough sleep. The early mornings were a mystery, clouded and cool, a gasp in the string of long days.

Each time she went in the water, she panicked. A struggle at first; she thrashed toward the other side. It always took a few laps to find her breath. There were no ropes dividing the lanes, just painted lines. In the water she found a clarity that eluded her in the rest of the hot, tired summer. Her strokes grew smoother, more refined. She watched the long black line and the scratched blue floor. The sun burned through the clouds, making trembling patterns beneath her.

She got home just before Elke woke up. Dieter had made coffee by then. He'd greet her with cool indifference, but he'd have a mug waiting. Louise cut fruit in the silent kitchen, buttered bread for Elke's cinnamon toast.

She felt a daze similar to when Elke was first born; with scratchy eyes, she tottered on caffeine's precarious edge. She made notes for potential installations — a painting she would set outside, perhaps in the woods in Cottage Grove, or maybe on the coast, where the fog swallowed the ocean. She thought about the sun's patterns against the pool's pale floor, shifting against the thick lines. She made sketches and plans, remembering Richard's beard against her face, the refuge of his cool green room.

One morning Elke told Louise that she'd had a nightmare.

"A horse was chasing me," Elke said as she bit into her toast. "And I kept yelling, but my voice didn't make any sound."

"Did you fall asleep again?"

"Dieter told me it wasn't real," Elke said. "Then I think I did fall asleep. Because I woke up." She laughed with her logic, but Louise was rattled. Elke had woken up, and Louise wasn't there.

Then the next day, Elke said, "He were at the library," repeating one of Dieter's frequent slips.

"He was," Louise said. "That's what you're supposed to say. He was at the library."

Elke looked back at her with a flash of adult awareness. "I know that." Louise could see in her expression both Elke and herself. She could see her own scrutiny, the thing she'd been allowing herself to ignore.

"You have to set an end date," Louise told Dieter that evening. "If you're going to live in Eugene, you have to find your own place."

"Elke's happy," Dieter said. "Let her have the rest of the summer with me and then I'll leave."

It was on a Friday in August, as the canning projects were shifting to tomato sauce and blueberry jam, when a box arrived at the house, wrapped in brown paper and addressed to Dieter Hinterkopf, care of Louise Hinterkopf. A package sent from Hannelore, the only person who would call Louise by that name.

She brought it to Dieter. Tight layers of wax paper, and then a dense and sticky cake, all those thin layers spread with jam. The Hinterkopf *Geburtstagskuchen*.

Louise crumpled the brown paper, pushed it into the trash. Elke had learned to spell her name—she would be able to read the address—but Hinterkopf wasn't Louise's last name.

"Yesterday went by and I completely forgot," Louise said. Dieter hadn't mentioned his birthday, either.

"We can celebrate tonight," he said. "This cake is probably nearly as old as I am at this point. It must be eaten."

Louise thought back to the last time she'd eaten the *Geburtstags-kuchen,* to Hannelore, and that August when Elke was an infant, when Hannelore had shared with her the story of their family. To her initial decision not to talk to Dieter about it. And she finally had told him, but to what end? It seemed to have only deepened his pain.

To distract herself from that thought, Louise made gazpacho—tomatoes and cucumbers, basil and parsley and garlic, into the blender with vinegar, Tabasco, salt—and left the bowl to chill. She asked Elke to draw Dieter a card.

Richard showed up that afternoon, too, sunbaked in a worn blue shirt, and suggested they go for a walk. She and Elke went with him to Schubert Park, leaving Dieter with his book on the porch.

As they walked, she told him about her idea for the new project. "Painted squares outside," she said. "I think I'll set them in a line." She stopped by the park's gate and pointed to a patch of trees. Maybe she'd bring the pieces here, as a test, to see how time and weather broke them down.

"It might be interesting to take photographs," Richard said. "You could do them on a regular schedule." He wanted to engage with her ideas in a way that Dieter wouldn't.

I don't understand the purpose, Dieter had said of her plans. He wasn't willing to try.

"I like that," Louise said. "The pictures could measure the decay."

Elke interrupted. She was bored, she said—could they go to the playground? Richard pushed her on the swings.

"That's not how you're supposed to do it," Elke said. "Dieter runs under the swing." She jumped off and went to the monkey bars, leaving Richard deflated behind the empty swing.

"Let's go away for the weekend," Richard said when Elke was out of earshot. "I'll take you to the hot springs in Breitenbush."

A funny suggestion, because Louise was the one with the car, but still she liked the way he'd phrased it.

"Dieter could stay with Elke, right?" He was asking her to make a public statement, and his confidence pleased her. "We can leave on Saturday, come back Sunday night."

"Let's do it," said Louise. "We could use a vacation."

Her father was in the driveway when they returned, looking into the open hood of Louise's car. "I came to check on the belt," Trent said. "I didn't like that rattling the last time you came out." He scanned Richard, scanned Louise.

"Dad, this is my friend Richard," Louise said.

"Help me out, son," Trent said. "Hold that right there." He transferred the pliers to Richard's waiting hand and pointed to Louise for her keys.

"It's working!" Elke cried after Trent tried the engine.

Where was Dieter? Louise found him reading on the porch.

She asked Trent to stay for dinner, though she was embarrassed. Exposed. She'd seen Trent's books and pamphlets—sinners of all stripes, which certainly included adulterers, not to mention bigamists, would be left behind after the Fall.

In the kitchen, she pulled the gazpacho from the refrigerator, opened a jug of Cribari white. A hot evening, and she added ice to four glasses —lately her father had been amenable to an occasional drink. She put an ice cube in each bowl of soup, too.

"What's your line of work?" Trent asked Richard at the picnic table in the yard.

"I'm a doctoral student in urban design," Richard said. "I'm hoping to submit my dissertation next year."

Trent squinted at Richard.

"Richard teaches," Louise said. "He's a professor." Water pooled in Louise's bowl of pink sludge, but the ice worked, each spoonful a blast on the throat.

Trent nodded with approval. "And what about you, Dieter?" Like a fairy tale or 1950s courtship, her father grilling these potential suitors.

Dieter took it in stride. "My training is in carpentry," he said. "In

Germany I was a cabinetmaker. There's a particular satisfaction to craft-
ing something with your hands."

"And are you doing that work here?" Trent asked.

"For the moment, no," Dieter said.

Trent registered that. Louise cleared the table, but Trent said he
wouldn't stay for dessert. She was relieved by her father's departure; she
wanted to end this dinner, end the display.

"Nice to see you fellows," Trent said before he left. "You should come
out to the house for a hike sometime. Louise can show you the trail."

In the kitchen, she found a taper candle. "We have a birthday," she
told Richard when she brought the cake outside.

"Yesterday," Dieter said. "It's already passed." His tone was offhand,
almost rude.

Elke wanted to sing, and she presented her card.

"A masterpiece," Dieter said.

"It's a drawing of Sillyland," Elke said. "That's you and me and
Mommy. That's us. We're all there."

"This cake is delicious," Richard told Louise. "As usual."

"I think so, too," she said. "But I didn't make it."

"She knows the recipe, though," Dieter said. "This cake has been in
my family for generations."

"I didn't realize you were a baker," Richard said to Dieter.

"I'm not," Dieter said. "Elke's grandmother made it."

"She mailed it here," Louise said. She put her fork down. The cake
was too dense, too sweet.

"Where in Germany do your parents live?" Richard asked Dieter.

"My mother is in a small town in the west," Dieter said. "Close to
Düsseldorf. My father isn't alive."

"I'm sorry," Richard said.

"He died in the war when I was still a baby," Dieter said. "So I didn't
know him." He was still fluent with that lie. Even though Louise didn't
expect him to give Richard the complete story, it was jarring to hear
him tell that version again.

"Where was your father?" Richard asked. "Where did they send him?"

"To the front," Dieter said. "To Russia. He had to go, I suppose."

"He could have said no," Richard said. "I mean, he could have defected, right? It's not like he was Jewish and going to be carted off."

"You're right," Dieter said. "I hope if I were in that situation, I would say no."

"I'm lucky I didn't get drafted," Richard said. "For Vietnam. I was at Berkeley then. I don't know what I would have done if I got called."

"No, it's impossible to know," Dieter said, getting louder. "And it's easy to make that kind of statement when you haven't been tested."

Richard's remark had seemed to Louise a kind of olive branch, but Dieter kept going, his voice brittle and charged. "Everything is easy for you," he said.

Dieter extracted his legs from under the table and moved swiftly through the yard, disappeared around the side of the house. His words settled on the table. Louise let out her breath — she'd been bracing herself for Dieter's continued outburst.

Elke was staring down at her plate, and Louise pulled her closer on the bench.

"No one could know that," Richard said. "How could anyone know?"

Louise tried to meet his eyes, but he was standing up, too. "No one could know that," she said. She smoothed Elke's hair. "We can read a few stories now, sweetie. And then it'll be time for bed."

She'd reached the breaking point; she couldn't push this unwieldy trio any further. Louise said good night to Richard, and then sat with Elke until she fell asleep.

Dieter returned an hour later, found Louise on the porch.

"I'm sorry that I left," he said quietly. "I wanted to say good night to Elke."

"She's sleeping now."

"I hope I didn't upset her."

His face was guarded, but Louise had to push forward. "You didn't tell the truth," she said. "You told Richard your father died when you were a baby." She could see she was hurting him, but she needed to get through.

Dieter was looking at her, angry. "Do you expect me to show off my family's problems to people I barely know?"

"No," she said. "I don't expect you to lay it all out."

"You don't know what this feels like," Dieter said. "There's no way to explain my family. What do you want me to do? Tell everyone?"

"I don't know," she said. And though this answer satisfied neither of them, she was too tired to keep hashing it out. She could see that it wouldn't be possible to find resolution with him. She left him on the porch and went alone to bed.

After her confrontation with Dieter, Louise was eager to get away. She and Richard left the next morning for the hot springs, two hours into the forest from Eugene. The grounds were clothing-optional, they were told upon check-in at the lodge.

"Clothes should be worn at meals," a man in a tunic said. There was a sauna in a cedar cabin, thermal pools, trails groomed of their brush.

Richard found a spot in the woods for the tent. They hiked and soaked that afternoon, and after dinner, tofu quiche served at the lodge, they returned to the springs. Louise stripped her clothes and tied up her hair. She climbed in, let her chin and earlobes dip. Richard sat across from her, and she stretched her leg out, rested her foot on his knee.

The pools were set in the trees, and clumps of people in various states of undress drifted back and forth from the bonfire behind the lodge. The smells of wood smoke, of sulfur. The sounds of murmured conversation and a slightly flat guitar.

Over Richard's shoulder, in an approaching group of people, she saw a gangly man toss his hair. Dieter was haunting her — ridiculous that she was thinking of him even now.

"The location is magnificent." But that was definitely Dieter's voice, and there he was, looming over the pool, flanked by Blake and Joanne.

"Where's everyone else?" Joanne asked.

"What are you talking about?" Louise was livid, dizzy. She heaved herself out of the water and reached for her towel.

Joanne's misgivings made a slow wash over her face. "Is it just the two of you? I thought there was more of a group going out."

Dieter was silent, arms folded. Was he insane?

"Just the two of us," Richard said. He'd gotten out and wrapped his towel around his waist.

"Where's Elke?" Louise pulled her dress over her head, yanked the towel down.

"Karen stayed with the kids," Dieter said.

"This isn't what we planned," Louise said. He was absolutely nuts.

"Everything is fine," Dieter said. "Elke is having a good time with the other children. I wanted to see the American interpretation of our wonderful German tradition of the sauna."

"We're going to camp tonight," Joanne said, scrambling. Her face caught Louise's panic. "We brought the one-man tent for Dieter."

Blake pulled his shirt off. "We're here now," he said. "We might as well enjoy it."

"I think so, too," Dieter said, unclasping his belt.

Richard stalked off in his towel, his back disappearing into the trees.

Blake and Dieter yelped as they eased into the water, and Louise was left standing with Joanne.

"Where's the bathroom?" Joanne asked.

"Everywhere," Blake said, laughing. He was already fully submerged.

Joanne apologized as she and Louise walked to the lodge. "Dieter told us that you were bringing a big group out here. He made it seem like it was a fun trip."

"It was supposed to be a fun trip," Louise said. Inside the lodge, the tunicked clerk was wooing a radiant and intoxicated woman, who was sitting on his desk. *You look really beautiful, man.*

"Just go to bed," Joanne said. "Blake and I will hang out with Dieter."

Louise found Richard by the bonfire, clothed again, slugging from a plastic cup. Pungent joints moved around the circle, trailed by a bottle of rum. A man was singing much louder than the guitar. *It's hard to get by just upon a smile.*

They took the long way around the lodge, so they wouldn't pass the pools, and Richard didn't speak to her, striding behind his flashlight's dim beam.

When they reached the tent, she crawled in and sat on the giant sleeping bag, two zipped together, and waited in the dark while Richard unlaced his boots. He sat with his legs sticking out of the tent, his back to her. He was incredibly slow — she could hear him pulling at the laces with methodical precision.

"Even the best-laid plans," she said. He still hadn't spoken. Every sound resonated from out in the darkness: the faint guitar, the beat of a drum, voices carrying through the trees. She sensed the straight line of his shoulders, his body decisive as he eased off his shoes.

"You're making a mistake," he said. "You're torturing me." His voice was resigned, a tone she'd not heard from him before. It frightened her. The tent was tiny; they were just inches apart. She was sorry, she told him.

"I want to take on your daughter," Richard said. "But not your ex-husband." He didn't move. "You can't be with both of us. I can't go on like this."

She reached her arms around his back, pressed her cheek against his neck. His hair smelled of burning wood. She could feel the wildness of his pulse, the tension in his back. Somewhere in the forest, Dieter was zipped into his one-man tent, stewing and unpredictable. And with the noise around them — branches settling, laughter carrying from the fire — she felt an irrational fear. It might be Dieter crashing through the trees.

"You," she said. Richard crawled in behind her, closed the flaps. She pulled off his shirt, his jeans. If he did leave, then this would be their last time together, and dread was twisting into her desire. She climbed on top of him, tasted rum in his mouth. She was aware of every sensation—the smell of dry pine, the cool air on her skin. The woods were alive with sound. It was the two of them now, together in the tent, and though she couldn't see beyond that contained space, to be with him there marked her triumph, gave her a quenching sense of relief.

RICHARD

2008

RICHARD WAS DRINKING A BEER at the counter in the kitchen, forking at leftovers. His unresolved fight with Louise was nagging at him. There was something so unsatisfying about a long-distance argument. He still hadn't sent the email he'd drafted, trying to explain to her why he hadn't taken the photo. He could go upstairs and send the message right now. But wasn't it obvious? Sometimes she could be incredibly, perhaps willfully, dense.

Long ago, he'd packed away his jealousy and resentment. Together he and Louise had edited out Dieter's time in Eugene. The story of their beginning boiled down to their cute run-ins in the park. That was the safe version they could tell other people, and with time he'd come to believe it. But there was also that unspoken triangle, the terrible vision that had tormented him then, of Louise entangled with Dieter. That was also part of their origin story.

The awful end of the camping trip. He didn't see it as a victory at first. True, he'd been the one to wake up in the tent, with Louise pressed against him in the sleeping bag. He unzipped the windows so the dry pine air drifted through the mesh and then lay down again, enjoying the previously unheard-of luxury of a lingering morning with her. Louise reached for him — would he forgive her, she was asking, and he let her ask.

But then they had to go eat breakfast, and inside the lodge Dieter was waiting, hunched at one of the round tables, chatting with Blake and Joanne. No choice but to join them with their eggs.

"Where's the coffee?" Louise asked at the table. Caffeine wasn't allowed on the grounds, Joanne explained, a long-standing and strictly enforced rule.

"Jesus," said Richard.

"Let's just go and get some." Louise said she'd seen a diner out on the road. "We can all fit in my car."

"You guys go ahead," Blake said. "Joanne and I are off coffee."

The diner wasn't far from the hot springs; its Sunday morning parking lot was full. The place was packed with people in church clothes, buzzing with pious energy.

Louise left for the bathroom as soon as they'd been seated. Richard was alone with Dieter. Had they ever been alone together? Dieter was sideways in his seat, with his long legs crossed and jutting out from under the table. He was unshaven, wild-looking, as though he'd stumbled in from the woods, and Richard thought there was something pathetic about the way he tucked his bobbed hair behind his ears, his constructed confidence.

"Coffee, guys?" the waitress asked, standing over them with the pot.

"Two, please," Richard said. "She'll be right back," he told the waitress, pointing toward Louise's chair.

"I'll take two as well," Dieter said.

Louise laughed when she returned to the table and found the two steaming mugs in front of her empty seat. "I'm not that desperate for caffeine." Her breezy tone didn't convince—her shame was clear on her face. *Why*, Richard wanted to ask her. She didn't have to put up with Dieter's irrational behavior—his overlong visit, his impulsive moods. It could all be so simple if she'd just let it be. He held her gaze, and in that beat, she seemed to be telling him, *I know, I know.*

The tables were pushed close together, and next to them, a woman packed into a shiny dress listened with disapproving interest.

Louise flagged the waitress. "Do you have muffins?"

"Marionberry and corn," the waitress said. "Are you ready to order or are you waiting for one more person?"

Richard looked at Louise. "I guess I am waiting for someone."

"I'll have marionberry, please," Louise said to the waitress.

Dieter took one of the coffees and swiftly dumped its contents into Richard's cup, which was still full, and now began to overflow. "There," said Dieter. "Now we have the right number."

The coffee streamed over the table and onto Richard's lap. He jumped up. "What the hell?" Dieter wouldn't even look at Richard and began instead mopping the table with a paper napkin, as though the mess were Richard's fault. Richard wiped his hands, his distress spilling into the next table: two sour women, older and younger, both with tight expressions, generations of dissatisfaction.

"Excuse me," the younger one said to the waitress. "These people are disturbing my mother."

"If you folks don't mind," the waitress said to Louise. "I can move you once another table clears up. You can just stand over there for now." Louise took her purse and slinked toward the front of the restaurant, her tangled hair floating behind her.

Richard threw his wet napkin on the table, but Dieter stayed, loud, emphatic. "The show has ended," he said. "Go back to your breakfast. I am leaving now with my wife and her boyfriend. It's a difficult thing, if you could imagine." With his syntax breaking down, his accent sounded heavier; he was lost, out of place.

The waitress was frowning. The customers listened with paused forks. Louise had one hand on the door, but she was trapped there watching Dieter, who was out of control. She looked miserable. Richard felt a pulsing connection to Louise—he had to protect her.

He counted out singles from his wallet. Each dollar slapped down on the table. "Dieter," Richard said. "It's time to go." Then he turned and followed Louise out of the restaurant. She stopped by the car, reached for Richard's arm. As though steadying herself, as though without him she might actually fall.

"I'm sorry," she said.

Richard leaned against the car's hot hood. She was next to him. He could smell her faint sweat, the smoke from the campfire, and he remembered the intensity with which she'd touched him the night before, the way she'd cried out for anyone and no one to hear.

"I don't want him to live in your house anymore," Richard said. "I understand that Elke needs to spend time with him, but he can't live with you, too."

"A week. I'll let him have one more week to figure out where he's going to go. Don't give up on me."

He could see Dieter leaving the diner, crossing the parking lot. "You have to make a choice." Richard pushed her hair from her face and kissed her. She kissed him back.

"I've chosen," she said. "Sometimes you have to do things wrong to realize how you would do them right."

That was it, Richard could see now. He opened the refrigerator and extracted another beer. Louise may have made some bad choices at the beginning, but together they'd set things right. And yet despite that fact, even though he knew just how much time had passed since they'd been in that diner by the hot springs, he couldn't help but wonder what Louise was doing in Germany now.

DIETER

2008

DIETER HAD WORKED ALL MORNING, painting the kitchen at his mother's house. He was grateful for the task, the chance to be alone. Now he was hungry, and he walked back to Norbert's house. When he got there, he found chaos in the kitchen. Julia had arrived with her husband and kids; the room was all softening butter and contested toys, with Gisela at the center, delegating tasks.

Louise was baking a *Kugelhopf* with Julia's son. *"Ja, gut,"* Dieter heard Louise saying as Felix greased the pan. Her voice so American. How much German had Louise retained? She'd been *bummeling* along so far, but mostly everyone had spoken English.

Gisela pressed against Louise. "It's better if you don't use so much butter for the pan. It makes the cakes soggy."

Gisela the inveterate advice-giver — from dog obedience to her homeopathic remedies, she always knew best. It drove all of them crazy.

Dieter found a *Brötchen* and ducked away to the computer, in Norbert's office, under the soulful gaze of a moose. There was a new message from Joel. *Show in Berlin?*, the subject in bold print.

Hey, man, just checking in. We're in Brussels right now. Your nephew has been a huge help—I don't know if you heard from Elke, but we're going to Berlin, and Tilman is hooking us up with not one but two shows! Tilman rules. You should come to Berlin too—we'd LOVE it if you'd play one of the Berlin shows. You could do a solo set, or whatever you want—it will be cool to hang either way. Tilman is psyched. Thanks again for putting us in touch with him. By the way, Keith and I are 100% ready to reissue the Astral Gruppe album. We'd do the same artwork, gatefold, heavy vinyl, really nice job. We'll do your solo recordings, too. Let us know what you think. Till soon, dude.

Not one but two shows—this was how the world worked now, instant questions and answers. And Joel wanted Dieter to play.

A show could be anything—a huge presentation or a glorified hangout. Dieter had played in bars, in basements, in old factories. On a stage, on a sidewalk, on a boat. Playing live had always thrilled him —he'd scratched the itch by going to hundreds of shows in New York, by sitting in whenever he was asked. And now he was being asked to do it again.

Tilman would be getting to Norbert's house that evening—Dieter could speak to him about the show directly. Tilman had long been after Dieter to play, but the thought of performing in Germany unnerved him. That would cut too close to a tender place. Those days were over, Dieter always told Tilman when he'd suggested a show in Berlin. Never mind the fact that Dieter had played in a weekly pickup gig at a bar on Houston Street pretty much the entire time he'd lived in New York.

More flummoxing, though, was Joel's second question. He wanted to reissue the Astral Gruppe album. Dieter hadn't heard it in quite some time. The last time was right after he'd split up with Franny, his foul-mouthed, wild-eyed girlfriend of seven years, the red-haired booker at a club on the Lower East Side where he'd been to countless shows. He'd put the record on when he'd had too much to drink, was feeling nostalgic, alone and untalented. But it had overwhelmed him to hear it then. It brought him back to Düsseldorf, to being a bad father and hurting Louise. He played through the whole thing, sloshed on the sofa with closed eyes. When the second side finished, he'd put it away. That was ten years ago. He wasn't sure he wanted to hear it again.

And what if he found the record wasn't really that good? What would that mean for how much he had destroyed because of it, for the way he'd shaped his life then? It seemed easier to keep it all filed away.

We'll do your solo recordings, too, Joel had written, and the boy's confidence both irritated and flattered Dieter. Joel hadn't even heard the solo stuff, which meant the content didn't actually matter. Joel wanted something he thought Dieter represented, and while it wasn't such a bad feeling to be wanted, Dieter was still hesitant to expose himself like this.

The solo recordings were different than the band's music. Dieter had made them after Louise left Düsseldorf. He'd always been a listener, but then, especially, he needed something to fill and cover the space around him. Louise sent a letter when her mother died, told Dieter that she was taking a class and helping her father, and it would be more time before she returned. Dieter read the letter in the stairwell of the building on Bilker Allee, and it was then that he knew he'd lost her. Elke and Louise were gone. Devastating—he had failed his daughter.

He'd thought of going after her. But he'd been so angry at her— she'd dumped this news about his father and then left him squirming under its weight. He was shamed by what Louise knew about him, about his family. To face her and confront what she'd told him felt impossible. He was stuck there, fixed in his confusion and pain.

So instead he went to the studio, because he didn't know what else to do. He used Klaus-Peter's synthesizers—at dawn, in the middle of the night. It began simply as a series of tones. The elaborate setup, the patient wait for the right sound. But then, as he learned the machines, he found rhythms, replicated what he'd been doing with the drums. The sound of moving forward. During that terrible year, as Louise did not return, he needed the music more. He wanted to record it, a document of this time, a part of the mistakes he had made.

Playing alone was different—a holy ritual. He'd spoken to Joel so blithely—sure, I was screwing around with some synths, he'd said— but the truth was these recordings were much more than that, and seeing Louise in Bad Waldheim had already unmoored so many of those feelings he'd packed away. He wasn't necessarily ready for all of it to be out in the open.

He drove to the train station to pick up Elke. He got there early and paced the platform, orbiting a man selling sausages from a grill he wore on a strap around his neck. Self-contained, self-reliant, making a little cash.

Dieter wondered if Louise would mind him tagging along on this trip to Berlin. He didn't necessarily want her to see him on a stage where she could so easily consider his past missteps. She'd hated him once, probably, and though she was friendly enough now, he wasn't sure he should be there, horning in on her time here.

What a strange proposition: Dieter had been genuine when he offered Louise and Richard's daughter the connection to his nephew, but he hadn't expected it to blossom so quickly.

He'd learned to embrace the central principle of improvising, though —to keep playing the wrong note until it sounded right. So if Margot wanted him to perform with them, Dieter wouldn't say no. If Louise was OK with it. If Elke didn't mind.

People had begun trickling off the train. Here was Elke. She lifted a finger in greeting, thanked him for picking her up.

"I'm spending the day painting," Dieter said. "I needed a break, too."

She was studying him, asking about Louise though she didn't say anything, both of them aware that this was an unprecedented thing —the three of them thrust together, mother, father, daughter.

They took the stairs from the platform. "I heard from your sister," Dieter said. "Or from Joel, actually."

"They're going to Berlin," Elke said.

"Do you know that Joel asked me to join them for a performance?" Dieter asked.

"In Berlin?" She looked at him over the roof of Norbert's car; neither of them had opened their doors. There was something fierce in her expression of surprise — her gaze more pronounced, her features popping out. He saw his mother, saw his brother in that gaze.

"For me it's a strange question, too," he said. "I haven't performed alone. I'm not a solo artist."

"You play by yourself all the time," Elke said.

"Not for an audience."

"I've been your audience," she said. Was she angry? Or was something else different?

"Is your hair wet?" he asked.

"A little bit." A smile from her then.

What had she done in Düsseldorf? Why had she wanted to go there on her own?

"You don't have to perform if you don't want to," Elke said. "You can say no."

"I'm not sure I should even go to Berlin," Dieter said. "Do you think your mother would mind my being there?"

"Why don't you ask her yourself?" Elke said this evenly — she wasn't exactly angry, but she wasn't pleased, either. She started walking again, toward the station's BAD WALDHEIM sign.

Elke had spent the first months of her life in this dusty town. If he'd done things differently, he might be speaking German to her now. He caught up to her, walked with her along the path.

"You came to Oregon when I was a little girl," Elke said.

Dieter nodded. "I waited much too long to see you."

"Was it just for me? Or were you going to see Mom, too?"

"Of course you were my priority," Dieter said.

Across the platform, the sausage guy had made a sale. *Ja, nur einmal, ha ha ha.* His life jolly, simple, contained.

"I can't really remember it," Elke said. "Only little snatches of the time you were there."

"You and I had a good time together in Oregon," he said. "That was the more important reunion. I realized how stupid I had been."

"Why did it take you so long to go there?"

"I thought Louise was going to come back to Düsseldorf." He regretted it as soon as he said it—the excuse was obvious, a limp thing he'd cast out.

"But she didn't come back. What was I, four or five years old by then?"

"I was afraid," he said. "I was selfish. I'm sorry about that. It's the big regret of my life, that I missed those years with you." There was nothing to say to her except for this, but still it wasn't enough.

Elke's face was stricken, vulnerable. "Was it your band? You wanted to stay to keep playing with them?"

"The band had already broken up," he said. "I suppose I thought more was going to happen with my music."

This answer didn't satisfy her either, and how could it? He was making it sound like his music had been more important than her. He'd never told Elke what had really kept him away for so long. He hadn't given her the full story, hadn't ever shared what Louise had told him about his father. He'd been devastated and angry and ashamed after Louise left Germany. Paralyzed by those feelings. Elke deserved to know about his father, Dieter believed that, but he couldn't stand to disappoint her further. And he didn't think it fair to burden her. What could she possibly do?

"I guess I remember Richard being around then, too," Elke said. "When you came to Oregon. That's why it's confusing."

"Your mother and I had some things to work out." He couldn't tell her the more complete answer: *Yes, your mother was sleeping with Richard even while she was sleeping with me.*

What was he supposed to say? *It was another time, everyone was loose then, we weren't the only ones to behave this way.* But it wasn't just a result of those promiscuous times. *Maybe Louise still loved me then,* he might have told Elke. *I thought I still loved her.* And even so, he could see now that he'd behaved like a fool.

They were back at the car. Elke was gazing over the train tracks. "Did you tell Joel you would come to Berlin?"

"I haven't responded to him yet. I wanted to ask you and Louise about it first."

"It's fine with me," she said. "I don't want to speak for Mom, though."

"I'll talk to her about it."

Elke looked at him over the car. "How are you doing?" she asked. "I realize this isn't an easy time."

And though there were loads of things she might have been referencing—the loss of his mother, the gain of his ex-wife—he was grateful for her compassion. It steadied him, to have Elke here. It wasn't easy to be back, especially in the face of his grief. But he thought he could tell her that it was easier now than it had once been.

"I'm OK," he said, a declaration he'd learned in America.

They were a bigger group that evening—with Julia and her family, with Tilman, who showed up just as Gisela was convening them for the meal.

"I'm glad we are here to honor our *Oma* Hannelore," Norbert said. "She would be pleased with the group we've gathered here."

The dinner conversation slipped between German and English. Norbert, as *Opa,* entertained the children in a lilting voice. It would be impossible to try to get a quiet word with Louise, who was seated on the other side of Elke, two seats away from him.

Tilman was across from Dieter, forking *Schinken* onto his plate. "You're staying at *Oma* Hannelore's?"

Tilman inspired in Dieter a proprietary fascination. A pride by proxy. Dieter had given Tilman a Captain Beefheart album when he was sixteen. Now he was past forty, scrambling and mildly unkempt, introducing Dieter to strange new sonic things.

"They've got a full house here," Dieter said. As if to demonstrate, Julia and her kids were making a small racket at the other end of the table.

"You could always move back to Bad Waldheim," Norbert said. "You could live in her house. We don't have to sell it."

A joke but not a joke, and as Dieter layered his bread with *Wurst,* he allowed himself to imagine it. He could sell his house and move back to Germany, ride out his old age in the cradle of his youth. But the familiar was cloaked in time's murky cloud. He didn't want this all the time, as much as it was right for the moment.

Gisela, beside Tilman, pressed more bread on Dieter. Like his brother, she had aged in subtle ways — seeing them only once every year or two made this progression incremental. A predictable disappointment: he knew he mirrored that slow and regular change.

Dieter had no idea if Norbert had ever told Gisela the truth about their father's death. Dieter guessed no. He'd never talked to Norbert about it, though it bonded them, the invisible thread that drew Dieter back. But Dieter had also never talked to Norbert about what Louise had divulged so many years earlier. He'd never talked to his mother about it either. And now he couldn't, which was both distressing and relieving. He'd never learn what else she might be able to tell him. He wouldn't hear the words she'd use to explain. But maybe he didn't want to.

Everyone at the table was busily eating, but Tilman caught Dieter's eye. "I'm glad they've convinced you to perform in Berlin," he said. "Just tell me what kind of equipment you need — I can borrow something, I'm sure."

Louise leaned over her plate, tipping her head. "Did you say something about performing in Berlin?" she asked in English. He saw her eyes, and past her the eyes of the once-nimble deer mounted on the wall behind her — a glassy expectation.

"With your daughter," Tilman said, continuing in English. "It's remarkable how the world shakes out, right?"

"The idea was just proposed to me," Dieter said. "I haven't decided yet what I'll do." Julia's boy was shouting in front of Hannelore's credenza, a massive piece of oak.

"You'll come to Berlin for a few days, stay with me, have some beers," Tilman said. "What's to decide?"

Tilman had inherited Norbert's pushiness, but tempered as it was by their shared interest in music, and a subtle mutual antagonism toward Norbert, Dieter had always felt a particular bond. Tilman's interest in Dieter as a musician had long flattered Dieter, validating him in a way the rest of the family didn't allow.

"Are you going to drone with Sky Mall?" Elke asked.

Dieter shook his head. "Solo percussion."

"Call up Gerd Schlagenhauf," Tilman said. "Get him to sit in on guitar."

This wasn't a bad idea.

"An Astral Gruppe reunion," Louise said. She was squinting now, and unlike the frozen deer, he saw her heating up, her eyes lit with primal agitation. "We're planning to see Ute, actually."

"An Astral Gruppe reunion would make Margot's boyfriend lose his mind," Elke said. This didn't exactly sound like encouragement. At the train station, Elke had told him that she didn't mind, but tolerance wasn't the same thing as a welcome.

"Too bad for Joel that a reunion won't be possible," Dieter said. "Astral Gruppe played its last show in 1974. It won't happen again."

"It's funny that Joel is so into your band," Elke said. "I didn't know that your album was available. You never played it for me."

"It's long finished," Dieter said. "A minor incident in a long span of time."

"Joel sounds like a real freak," Tilman said, with admiration in his voice. "I'm interested to hear what Sky Mall is doing. It's your daughter's band—what do you think of it?" he asked Louise.

"It's unusual," Louise said. "Striking. I appreciate your helping Margot out."

Tilman shrugged. "These concerts are already planned, so they are only joining the existing bill."

"Always the concerts," Gisela said. "He's never coming home for long."

"I'm here now," Tilman said.

"Work keeps us busy," Dieter said, giving Gisela a wink. She needed only a light nudge to loosen—a *Radlermass* at midday, some joking with her wayward brother-in-law.

"Louise, you're a teacher, I've heard," said Tilman. "That's even busier than a low-level concert promoter."

"Not so busy anymore," Louise said. "My school closed."

"*Schade,*" said Gisela, shaking her head. "But maybe there is another school for you?"

"That's actually not what I want," Louise said. "I'd rather focus on my own work now. Try to land another commission. Apply for things."

"But can't you do that while you are a teacher?" Gisela asked. "Teachers have such long vacation in the U.S."

"It got away from me," Louise said. "Teaching is incredibly time-consuming, if you're going to do it right."

"She makes a huge sculpture in her yard," Dieter said.

Louise mumbled a few *hmm*s, glancing over at Elke.

"I've seen this piece," Dieter said. "A long time ago now, at Elke's graduation. So the sculpture was much smaller then." Yes, he'd admired that work of Louise's then—she had a surprising, attentive mind, a way to represent her ideas that carried a kind of music, mysterious and known to him at once.

"But the pieces break down," Elke said. "That's the idea—that she keeps adding to it even as it disappears. So it more or less stays the same size."

"Something like that," Louise said. "It's cumulative. It's really about the process, about the unexpected things that can result from following a set of constraints."

Elke was so in tune with her mother. Nodding, chiming in. Her response needled him—Elke didn't understand his relationship to music. But he supposed he hadn't really given her enough opportunity to try.

"It's interesting, I think," Gisela said. "I'm having a hard time to imagine it."

"I can show you my website," Louise said. "That piece isn't the only

thing I do. My last commission was an installation on a highway overpass, and I've maintained a site-specific project at a nuclear plant since
the late seventies. I'd like to do more of that kind of thing."

The group began to drift. Julia was carting her kids from the table.
Gisela started clearing the plates. Dieter still hadn't asked Louise about
the show directly. But she hadn't said no, either. And if no one was going to give him a definitive answer, he would have to consult himself.
Did he want to do it? In a way, he absolutely did. He might be able to
prove to Elke that his time away from her hadn't entirely been in vain.
A chance for her to see his history, to understand the lineage of his
creative mind.

He left the table and in Norbert's office searched his email for the
message that Louise had sent him weeks ago. He still hadn't responded.
*I have a deep appreciation for what your mother did for me, and I was very
fond of her. But I want to be sure that my coming to the funeral is all right
with you. I hope that if you weren't comfortable with my being there, or
didn't think it was appropriate, that you would let me know.*

Now Louise was in the other room, playing games with Norbert's
grandchildren. But did Dieter want her to be there? There was something uncomfortable in this new visibility she'd prompted. And a
pleasing ache in examining the past. Louise had changed the course of
Dieter's life. She was Elke's mother. She was the reason he'd gone to the
States, and though that hadn't worked out as he'd expected, he'd made
a life he liked.

He returned to Joel's email. *Joel,* Dieter typed. *Agreed. See you in
Berlin.*

"We've got the match on," Norbert called from the other room.
"We're in the second half."

"Moment," Dieter yelled.

Dieter found the last message he'd exchanged with Gerd—almost a
year ago now. He pressed reply. *I'll be coming to Berlin soon,* he wrote.
*I'd like to see you, and even play with you if you're up for it. Nothing too
formal.*

Gerd had been his best collaborator, and maybe that symbiosis was a product of the time, lightning in a bottle that couldn't necessarily be re-created. But it might be fun. There in his brother's house, Dieter was nostalgic, a yearning that he'd long fought.

"You're missing it," Norbert bellowed. Dieter yelled back—he'd be right in.

LOUISE

2008

THE CHURCH WAS IN the old center of Bad Waldheim, the cobble-stones and half-timbered houses now punctuated by a cellphone store, a *Döner* stand. An appropriate setting for this ceremony—the right place to mark Hannelore's span of time. But Louise's memories of these narrow streets were clouded by nervous anticipation. The funeral was the reason they'd come to Bad Waldheim; during these first days leading up to it, though, Louise had felt like nothing more than an awkward houseguest.

She followed Elke into the church. How should she place herself in the pews? Though the gathering was small, Louise didn't belong in the front. But Elke did, and it would be weirder for Louise to sit by herself. Louise took the outermost edge, between Elke and the stained glass. Dieter was next to Elke on the other side, and then Norbert, Gisela, the kids—a return to a line Louise had once been part of.

Here on the fourth day of the trip, she was still unnerved by the ongoing cascade of once-familiar details. The digging up of buried terms. She was seeing twice, feeling the newness again. The seeded rolls in the bakery, the perfectly punctual train. The toilet with two buttons to flush, offering a choice of a small or large wash of water. And especially the toilet's platform, a forced reckoning with what you'd just done. That's what it was—the migrant's heightened sensation, the smallest things loaded and profound. Fresh surprise in the shape of a loaf of bread. People she'd once invested in understanding, that she later thought she'd never see again. Gisela and Norbert now their own kind of ghosts.

The minister began with a welcome. *"Wir kommen hier zusammen unserer Schwester Hannelore zu gedenken."* A relief to lean back into the ritual. Düsseldorf was a Catholic city—the nuns floating through the Altstadt, robes fluttering beside the Rhein. That Lenten restraint and release. But this church was Lutheran, Dieter had said. Hannelore had been a transplant here, and though Louise remembered her as vaguely righteous—the separate bedrooms when she and Dieter were unmarried seemed more the result of the times than any strict sense of virtue—Louise didn't know whether Hannelore would have believed the minister's prayers.

She remembered now, grateful to her younger self, the relief she'd offered her own mother when she'd agreed to baptize Elke. Louise had never told Elke about the baptism, though she'd tried to let Elke make her own choices since then.

Elke's choices weren't always so easy to predict. She was self-sustaining, a bit mysterious even as their early closeness remained. Louise was acutely aware of her daughter, was constantly trying to unravel and predict what she might do, how she was feeling. How different Elke was from Margot in that regard. Even as infants, their personalities had been clear. As a baby, Elke observed and babbled, happy to lean back and narrate to herself. Margot needed affirmation. *Yes, you made a tower,* Louise would say to Margot. *You're reading the book.* It was satisfying to give Margot what she clearly wanted, to recognize and deliver to her child.

What had this difference resulted from? The two fathers were an obvious cause. The time and place of the girls' upbringings—the list of differences was long. And Louise couldn't help but look at her own presence as a mother—her relative calmness when Margot was born, the relative stability. Maybe Louise had cultivated Elke's independence, Margot's need for confirmation—her girls sensed what she could provide. When Margot was born, Louise had ticked off everything she'd done wrong with Elke — the beer while pregnant, the nursing in clouds of cigarette smoke. Elke and her tiny lungs in the corner of the studio with its toxic paint. Louise had opened the windows, at least.

Dieter sat on the other side of Elke, his resting face stony, composed. He was still trim, but leathery now, and his forehead had grown larger, as his hairline had moved back. Before this trip, Louise hadn't seen him since 1991, when he'd come to Eugene for Elke's high school graduation. He'd brought that ridiculous CD for Elke, the recorded woman moaning through dinner, nearly orgasmic. *Baa-aaa,* she'd cried from the speakers in the living room. Like Sabine rolling on the floor in the gallery on Mittelstrasse, her ecstasy on display.

Dieter had asked to see Louise's studio then. She'd taken him up there after Elke's graduation party. Richard had gone to retrieve Elke from the state park, where she'd stranded herself with her bizarre boyfriend Kenny Salvage.

Dieter had gone right to the attic window. "You have a nice angle here," he said. And despite the details of her space — the pinned sketches of her *Hidden Driveways* project, the view of the yard strewn with party debris — she remembered being with Dieter in the evening, in the small house on the other side of town.

Margot, six years old then, was singing in the bathtub on the floor below, her voice traveling from the open door, but the sound was indistinct. It could have been Elke; the warm evening might have been one a dozen years before.

Dieter was frowning at the window. "I think what you're making is powerful," he said. "The concept is so intriguing. It's like an ancient calendar."

It was dark out there, just squares of light on the lawn. He'd dismissed her ideas for this project once, unwilling to imagine it, but now she believed he was really looking. "A calendar is a nice way to describe it."

"You have something good happening here," Dieter said. "You have a real family." He turned to look at Louise. "It's painful to see Margot," he continued. "She's almost the same age as Elke was when I came to Eugene the last time. I've missed so much of Elke's life." Dieter's face was seeking now. "I wish I'd done more." They'd been cordial so far, at arm's length, and it was gratifying to hear him talk this way. His acknowledgment made her wistful—just as they were reaching it, Elke was moving on to college. That would end Louise's reason for contact with him.

"Elke's growing up now," Dieter said. The line between his eyes deepened. "It's time for me to talk to her about my father, about what my mother told you."

Louise nodded. "I think she deserves to know."

"It's not an easy thing." Dieter's voice was defensive, a little testy. "I've been waiting until she's old enough. Perhaps I should have done it sooner, but I haven't." Louise knew it wasn't easy—she regretted how she'd waited to tell Dieter when Elke was a baby, regretted how she'd angrily sprung the news.

"You can't change it now," she said.

"No, we can't change what's already happened," Dieter said. "In that case then, maybe this would be my house in Oregon." His tone was lighter now, rueful. "If you had done things differently, maybe then Margot is my child."

He was close to her. She smelled what he'd been drinking; she could smell the fabric of his shirt damp with sweat.

"Mommy." Margot's voice cut through the warm night—she was standing at the top of the stairs, static. Her nightgown was on backwards, the tag flapped up below her chin. "Can you brush my hair?"

"You got yourself out of the bath by yourself." Louise took the brush, as gentle as possible.

"Too hard." Margot tipped her head away, exaggerating her distress. Louise wondered how much she'd overheard.

Dieter left Eugene the next morning, and Louise never got the chance to talk to him more about Hannelore, about what Elke deserved to know.

Now, watching his strained face in the pew, she wished she'd had that chance. She wondered if Dieter would tell Elke about his father now that his mother was gone.

"Wir hören jetzt das Wort Gottes," said the minister, lifting the Bible. The service went on, a murmuring that Louise could barely understand. Light streamed through the colored glass, and beside her, the others were grieving their own losses.

In another week Louise would be back in Eugene, without a job. It was a relief to step away from that uncertainty for a bit. But the complications of home weren't far away. She was still stewing over the fact that Richard hadn't taken the photo of her project. She knew he'd acted rashly out of pain, that in a sense he was punishing her for her trip to Germany. A distressing thought—it wasn't like him to be vindictive. Richard didn't know, of course, the complete story of her past with Hannelore and Dieter, the full range of events that she had to reckon with.

The thatch-haired minister was retreating from the pulpit. The service was over; the group was filtering out. Elke's face was stricken —Louise wanted to console her—but Elke was with Dieter, leaving Louise to follow behind.

The group walked through the cemetery beside the church, a loose clump along the path that led to the plot, through trees still bright with gold leaves. Louise watched the set to Dieter's shoulders, sensed Elke sharing his grief.

There was a plot for Hannelore; later there would be a stone. The names on the other graves were unfamiliar. Perhaps Hannelore's cousin with the grocery store was buried here. Of course, there was nothing for Dieter's father—she wondered what year his gravestone dated his death.

A stout woman distributed zinnias. Elke's eyes were cast down as the minister continued his impenetrable speech. Dieter put his flower on the casket, and the rest of the family followed: Norbert, Gisela, Elke, Tilman, Julia. Louise hung back with her long stem, alone at the edge.

She waited until the rest of the gathered group had paid their respects. Yellow and pink and green, and Louise's own white petals on the wobbling pile.

In the late afternoon, when Elke said she wanted to go out for a run, Louise suggested to Dieter that they get the painting from Hannelore's house. The three of them left Norbert's together, and then Elke took off, her bright sneakers flashing along the curb. Elke had a route, she'd said, down to the woods by the river, looping back the opposite way. Her familiarity with this place was sharper than Louise's, steeped in regular visits. Those woods where Louise had taken Elke as a baby—Elke was the one who knew them now.

Louise walked with Dieter beside a tall fence. Fences and hedges, that German claim to space, but even so these gardens could be in Oregon, with a similar dedication to a contained green world. There were birdbaths and tiny ponds, and statues of gnomes and trolls. Empty arbors in burlap. Marigolds hanging on. Louise had missed Germany. In her early years back in Oregon, she'd wanted a clean break. But as time went by, she sought small reminders—yogurt and dense rye. Quiet echoes, subtle enough that she wouldn't have to explain them to Richard.

Louise still knew the way to Hannelore's from Norbert's—a few turns and they'd be there. "Remember the chain that was across that driveway?" she asked. "Back when we were here with your mother."

"They can't get away with that anymore," Dieter said.

"Earnest xenophobia?"

"Exactly," Dieter said. "The xenophobia must be more subtle, like Norbert's." He smiled at that, but she wasn't sure she should join him. Norbert wasn't hers.

Dieter turned onto Hannelore's street. There was the house, with its square windows and stone sides. Time had shrunk it—her memory of it, at least. Thick trees shaded the sidewalk and the row of efficient cars.

"Things are more relaxed here now," Louise said. "I know it's a different time, that things everywhere are more casual than they used to be. But it feels lighter. People seem more open."

"It is a different time," Dieter said. "I was here during the World Cup two years ago, and for the first time people were holding up the German flag when Germany won. There was a huge outcry, of course. It hadn't happened here in my memory, that the flag could be waved like that."

"Not like in the U.S.," Louise said. "Americans are so nuts about the flag."

"Sure," Dieter said. "They'll put the American flag on their house and their car and maybe their underwear. But here, that behavior would feel dangerous. So when Germany won the World Cup, we had to think about whether we could be patriotic."

"Some felt that it was all right to do it, I'm guessing," Louise said. "I guess the flag raises the question of how much time is enough time?"

The little gate in front of the house was swung shut. The front beds bare, the green glimpse of the back.

"It's probably never enough time," Dieter said as he unlocked the door.

Inside, the empty rooms echoed. Louise drifted away from Dieter. She tracked over drop cloths, through the smell of fresh paint, filling the space with Hannelore's details — the embroidered curtains, the line of figurines.

Dieter found her in the kitchen. "Here we are," he said, holding what must have been her canvas, shrouded in cardboard. "It's strange that she didn't throw it away."

"She didn't keep things," Louise said.

"She wasn't sentimental in that way. Not a holder like me." Dieter cut the cardboard with gentle precision. "She was angry at you, too," he said. "That's another reason I thought she would have thrown it away."

Still that bracing honesty — Dieter hadn't adopted the American model of sugarcoating. And yet she knew he was right.

"I suppose the painting was a reminder of Elke," Louise said. "Of our time here when Elke was so young."

Dieter nodded. He took the cardboard off the canvas, and there it was—the field of blue fading to green. The first painting from her failed series. She could see it all again: the crowd on the TV in the bar in the Altstadt, how close Prefontaine had come. That light hovering off the screen. And she remembered how charged she'd felt as she watched in the corner of the bar—she'd found a direction for her work.

"A time capsule," Dieter said. "Saved from your scissors."

She propped it on the counter, took a step back. Louise could see how young she'd been. There was a cavalier confidence in her marks. And yet she remembered how desperate she'd been in this house, with infant Elke and her total need. How excited she'd been to paint, to lock into a rhythm. There was potential in her gestures; she could see it from a remove, with a teacher's assessing eye.

"I was grateful for the email you sent me," Dieter said. "Before the trip." He was stiff, cordial, as though thanking her for passing the milk. "I'm sorry that I didn't reply."

"I wasn't sure if you got it," she said. "It would have been nice to hear back from you."

"I appreciated it," Dieter said. "I was having a hard time ordering my words."

The late sun was streaking in—outside, fall's orange and blue and brown.

"Elke asked me to come," Louise said. "I felt I owed it to her, but I thought it should be your decision, too."

"It's OK with me," Dieter said.

"That's good," Louise said. "Since I'm here."

Dieter stood by the window, his face in profile.

"I feel bad that I never saw your mother again," Louise said. "She was so good to me when Elke was a baby."

"She liked having you around."

"She must have been upset that I took Elke so far away."

Dieter nodded. "She was angry when I left, too. I didn't come enough. Once I left, I was really gone."

"That's how I felt too," Louise said. "Though I felt that Elke could do it for me. The ex-wife isn't really supposed to come back."

Dieter smiled. "At least we got Elke over here."

It was the *we* that made Louise feel like she could push further. She wanted to give Dieter some padding and let him fall. "I can remember being here with your mother," she said. "Sitting out there in the garden with her when she told me about your father."

Dieter looked back at her, worn, blinking.

"I think you should talk to Elke about it," Louise said.

His face turned hard. "This isn't your story," he snapped. "It's not for you to tell me what to do." He walked out of the kitchen. His anger left her scolded, shamed. He'd lashed out at her like this long ago. But they weren't in that place anymore.

She could hear him moving in the next room, and then he was coming back in.

He spoke to her from the doorway. "I haven't been able to tell Elke," he said. "I haven't found the right time to do it. It's been hard to know what to say." Even now, even when they were speaking directly about what had happened, he was stoic, closed, frowning into the middle distance.

"I can understand that," Louise said. "It took me a while to talk to you about it after your mother told me. I was confused. In shock."

"Telling you was probably a relief for my mother," Dieter said. "Someone outside the family, outside the town." The veins on his hands were purpled and bumpy; his hands were pushing on his hair.

"I'm not sure it was a good thing for me to know," Louise said. "I didn't know what to do with that knowledge. I didn't know if I should tell you."

"Maybe that would have helped," Dieter said.

Helped what? Helped their marriage? Helped the fact that he was cheating on her?

She'd built up this moment of apology for so long. And there was something of a brutal letdown in actually doing it, because she wasn't sure it had accomplished anything, changed anything.

She crossed the kitchen. "What would it have helped with?"

"What do you mean?"

"You said my telling you might have helped."

"Who knows? It's a long time ago now." Whatever he'd meant moments earlier had evaporated—he wasn't going to revisit it. How frustrating he still was. That slack dismissal. She watched him rewrap the cardboard and seal it with tape. She accepted the parcel and followed him out of the house.

RICHARD

2008

IN HIS OFFICE on the second floor of the house, Richard lingered with his coffee. He had a stack of undergraduate essays on Le Corbusier waiting for him after lunch. He could see Louise's project from up here, the pieces wet from the rain. He hadn't brought the newest square back out. He hadn't taken the picture.

He checked his email. His message to Louise was still festering in the drafts folder. But he looked instead at a new email from Margot. *The band kind of combusted in the last few days. Now we're going on to Berlin, but it's just going to be me and Joel — we found plane tickets from Brussels for thirty euros, so we'll be performing as a duo now. Creative differences, etc. I won't bore you with the details.*

Richard wasn't bored. He was confounded. This saga of the band was ongoing, and Margot wasn't tiring of it. And always with the faceless Joel.

Since Keith and Spencer are staying in Antwerp, Joel and I will do the Berlin shows alone. Which might sound cool. Or might not. We're going to stay with Mom and Elke in their apartment swap, so at least it won't be a fruitless trip.

Richard pushed away from the computer and turned to the stack of essays. But he was still thinking about his unsent message to Louise. He knew he shouldn't send it. Logically, he knew that Dieter was not a threat. The last time Richard had seen Dieter was in 1991, when he'd shown up for Elke's graduation wearing a black leather pouch around his waist—a fanny pack, an accessory whose name was as horrible as its appearance.

Dieter had been a little weird, a little pathetic then. But his visit was comfortable—they'd all matured. Dieter stayed in a hotel and Elke chauffeured him around. He'd brought Elke a bizarre CD, which she had wanted to listen to right away, during dinner on the night Dieter arrived.

"Patty Waters," Elke read as she removed the plastic. *"College Tour."*

"It's a bit wild," Dieter said.

"So is college," said Richard. Elke went to the living room and started the stereo.

"This will be good preparation, then," said Dieter.

The first sounds were of a slow flute. Then a woman's trembling voice. A creeping bassline, and her voice picked up, guttural, charged, hinting at potential lunacy.

Elke was smiling as she sat down. "This is like that concert you took me to," she said to Dieter. "When those people started crying onstage."

"It was like going to church," Dieter said, and he and Elke laughed together.

"It's scary," said Margot, a six-year-old, delighted and confused. "Why is she screaming?"

"She's expressing herself," Dieter said. "It's music."

"It reminds me of that Bible lady downtown," Elke said. "The way her voice shakes when she yells about Jesus."

"I like to listen to this album in the bathtub," Dieter said.

"Relaxing," Richard said sarcastically. "A great way to unwind."

"It's not a tool for meditation," Dieter said. "For deep listening instead."

Dieter was Elke's biological father, but in practice the role had gone to Richard. He knew Elke's teachers at the graduation ceremony, her friends at the party in the backyard. He'd been the one to go pick up Elke when, the evening after the ceremony, she'd gotten stranded at a

friend's party at the state park in Veneta with the lugubrious Kenny
Salvage, Elke's sometime boyfriend who'd rambled with lethargic fervor
about acid rain for the entire ride home.

Richard was the one who'd been there for the long haul. And marriage was difficult; it could be a slog. He himself was not immune to
outside attraction. He was no saint. Good-looking grad students had
made suggestive comments to him in the indulgent '80s, when he himself was young and lithe, too. He'd had a semester-long ambiguous
friendship with a visiting professor in the mid-'90s, consisting of twice-
weekly lunches and heady conversation that turned to outright flirting
at a wine reception after a lecture, and Richard felt he was entitled to
this dalliance.

He hadn't pushed it further, though, and he was glad for that. The
place where he and Louise had finally arrived—commitment, a family,
a home—had required hard work, but it was secure, important. He
and Louise had taken long strides away from Dieter since his prodigal
return in 1978.

Dieter was no longer a threat, and yet Richard was sitting here
thinking about him. He still hadn't started on the papers. And now the
phone was ringing—more procrastination.

"I'm calling you with my computer," said Elke, her voice hollow, far
away. "Everything's fine, but I'm a bit bored."

"I'm glad I can alleviate your boredom." Richard hoped Louise was
bored too. He pressed the phone to his ear—he wanted the scrape of
a chair or crumbs of laughter, keys to what his wife was thinking so far
away.

"You should take Mom's photo," Elke said.

He wasn't sure what to say. Of course with the stupid Skype, Elke
had been privy to his entire conversation about the project with Louise.

"I realize this trip must be weird for you," Elke said. "But she's put
years into the project."

He was glad that Elke hadn't Skyped him; he didn't want her to see him reacting to her acknowledgment that he was upset. He felt like a child both scolded and consoled.

"Where's your mother?"

"She's downstairs," Elke said. "The whole family is here. I don't want her to know I called you and put you up to it. It just doesn't seem fair for you to mess it up on purpose. After all that time."

The project was a metaphor for their marriage, he thought Elke was saying—this long-assembled thing, its maintenance ongoing. But he felt stubborn, tough and dried out.

"It was childish of me not to take the picture." He was willing to admit that. "So you're going to Berlin tomorrow?"

"Right," said Elke. "I'm ready. It's been harder than I expected to be here. I don't know what I expected, actually."

He was pleased that she was confiding in him. Germany was a part of her life that he really didn't know.

"Dieter is coming to Berlin, too," Elke said. "Margot's boyfriend invited him to join their show."

Static on the line. He looked out the window at the juniper he'd put in when Margot was born. Margot's email had omitted that information. No mention of the German ex-husband tagging along.

"It wasn't my idea," Elke said. "There are a lot of cooks in the kitchen."

She was quick to fill in the details: Dieter would stay with her cousin Tilman, she was saying. The show would only be a brief part of their time in Berlin. She and Louise were excited to spend more time with Margot—they'd go to museums. Do tourist stuff. Elke was reassuring Richard about something that she didn't actually have to apologize for, and this made him feel pathetic.

"What's Düsseldorf like?" he asked.

"It's interesting, I guess," Elke said. "You'd like it—there are some great pedestrian avenues."

"The world-renowned Düsseldorf. A planner's dream." It felt good to laugh with her.

———

An hour later, after he'd made another pot of coffee, he passed his framed photos on the stairs. Louise had picked out her favorites: a disintegrating thatched roof, a stone wall in snow. A line of green bottles refracting shards of light. *Are you an artist?* Louise had asked Richard the first time they'd met. *Maybe,* he'd said. She'd recognized that in him; together their ideas had led to bigger things.

He worked on the computer that afternoon. He was thinking about Berlin. An interesting place, no doubt. The war damage, the rebuilding. The lingering infrastructure of the Nazi regime. The city stamped by that history, and the struggle now to memorialize it in appropriate ways. He'd read about these things. The postwar division of Berlin into East and West, the difficult movement between the two sides of the city. The former *Ossies* who still had allegiance to East Germany, a place that no longer existed.

Now he googled the Berlin Block, the city's iconic architectural style, all those apartment buildings with interior courtyards and thoroughfares closed to cars. He looked at blueprints, wondered about how desire lines might be affected by the rigid structure. And what about desire lines in the divided city? Had the Berlin Wall cut through existing paths? Were there East–West desire lines? Had it been possible to retrace them after the Wall came down in '89? Big questions, perhaps even fodder for a paper.

So he looked up psychogeography + Berlin—just to see what came up, where the search engine might take him. Urban design + Berlin + informal transportation.

He thought about his photographs on the stairs, his longtime interest in decay. He felt energized as he typed: posthumanism + Berlin. Sure. There was a scholar working on that at Humboldt University —an accomplished guy, a renowned institution. He let Google provide him with an awkward translation. He downloaded a PDF, read the bibliography of the paper. He recognized a few names. This was his field.

It might actually be quite useful for him to see this city with his own eyes. Research. Perhaps a new paper of his own. A chapter of his next book. Berlin — he hadn't thought of it as a case study. He'd always kept Germany off-limits. It was the site of Louise's first marriage; it wasn't for him, he'd thought. But now he wanted to talk to Louise about these questions. He wanted to see this place with her.

He went downstairs for more coffee, paced around the house. He had plenty of reasons for going to Europe. His entire family was there. He could see Margot's performance. Margot, whose band he'd never seen play. He could meet the faceless Joel. And Elke had called him, Elke who was half German — Richard hadn't ever had the chance to understand this side of her.

He went back to the computer. Priceline. Expedia. CheapTickets. His fingers fluttered over the keys. He was searching, getting results. He calculated — two missed days of classes, which could mean one canceled outright, one with an in-class writing assignment. A favor from a grad student, to sub for him. He kept clicking.

The ticket price was low — reasonable! — and the little timer was counting down. Fifteen more seconds and the page would refresh. One seat left at this price. Caffeine pulsed through his veins. He pressed the button with a trembling hand. And then he went to the couch, exhausted, to stretch out in the brutal comedown. He'd just bought a plane ticket to Berlin.

MARGOT

2008

MARGOT LEFT THE AIRPORT with Joel, headed to the Kaiser's supermarket by the Kottbusser Tor train station in Kreuzberg, where they'd planned to meet Tilman. Across the street, under the elevated train tracks, men in dark overalls and matted Mohawks paced beside a trash can fire. Good idea—it was freezing. In front of the supermarket, other men lingered; they clutched cans labeled STERNBURG EXPORT and snapped at each other with vicious laughter. Dogs with ratty fur and kind eyes stood beside them, vigilant and free.

"Germany is so punk," Margot said.

"It has to be," said Joel. "There's so much to push back on. You can't have fascism without punks."

"True," said Margot. "Those guys over there are doing important work."

Joel frowned at her.

"I mean it," she said. "I'm not being sarcastic." She wasn't, though Joel didn't seem to believe her.

A man approached, eyeing her. He was rangy beneath a huge down jacket. "Margot?" She nodded. They all said *Mar-gott*. "*Ja*, OK," he said. "You look like Elke. I'm just seeing her with your mother in Bad Waldheim. I've only left there this morning."

A shorter version of Elke, Margot thought, tipping back to examine his face. "I'm sorry about your grandmother," she said.

Tilman nodded. "Only two of you?" he asked. "I thought you were four."

"We lost some," Margot said. "In Belgium."

"Beer tourism," said Joel. "So we'll be performing as a duo now."

"The shrinking band," Tilman said.

"We may be one by the time we get back," said Margot. Snarkier than she'd intended, but she feared she might be right. This Berlin detour was entirely Joel's doing, and despite his insistence, she wasn't sure their music would sound all that great with just the two of them.

"OK," Tilman said. "I am taking you to the venue now." He picked up Margot's bag and began walking. Whether he didn't understand her completely—had he taken Joel's beer comment seriously?—or wasn't fazed, Margot wasn't sure. But she was glad that they didn't have to explain what had happened in Belgium. Some mild sniping about the hummus backstage had spiraled into a much deeper argument about taste. It didn't end well.

Now Spencer was staying with a woman he'd met at the show in Hasselt, a Dutch video artist who'd come on strong, and Keith had decided he would return to Antwerp and Bart the Clydesdale guy's offer of hospitality, to wait out his return ticket. Perhaps this would be the end of Sky Mall as a band, unless, Margot thought, whatever she and Joel managed to do worked out well, in which case they would repackage themselves as a duo, find another name. Or maybe Keith would cool off. (*Amateur hour*, he'd hissed in Belgium, as Margot defiantly dipped crudités.)

Any of these things could happen. More nagging, though, was the question of what she wanted. The band's precarious peace had broken, and now she was alone with Joel, to see if their sound together could be meaningful.

"Why are you limping?" Joel asked her. They were walking along the sidewalk, the evening's potential just setting in.

The sole of Margot's shoe had begun to detach in Belgium, and she had to scrunch her foot to keep her toes from flopping out. Six dollars at the Value Village back in Portland; she regretted bringing only the one pair with her on the trip. But this city could provide new ones, she was sure; she had her eyes open for something cheap and just fashionable enough.

She told Joel she was fine.

Tilman led them up a flight of stairs and into the venue, which was tiled and vaguely institutional, like a grade-school cafeteria or the locker room at a pool. Graffitied, a little grimy, sticky with mold and beer. A mysterious place to get to know, the expectation of strange people who were interested in what she was doing.

This was what she liked, night after night. The attention, the purpose, the mystery. She'd told everyone she wanted to go to grad school. And she did want it, but she also wanted freedom. The ongoing surprise. In college she'd been given a constant sense of possibility—her ideas mattered, and she was going to do something with them. And while she'd felt a different kind of excitement these last few months with the band, that had been sobered by the scramble to stay afloat. This life could give her freedom, but that would be punctuated with long spells of boring work, to keep on the treadmill of rent and student loans. When she was swept up in the music, she wanted nothing else. But so much of her time was in thrall to that, the hours and weeks of waiting to play.

A bald guy checked their levels. Margot and Joel would be on first —a twenty-minute set, since Tilman had shoehorned them onto the bill. Margot tried her signals; was it loud enough with Joel blasting through?

"Joel's sounds are powerful," Tilman said from the back of the room.

Margot cranked up her volume knob, tested a reverb-soaked moan.

"That's heavy, man," Tilman said.

Since they'd be playing first, they left their gear set up. They went to the balcony and had a beer, looked down at the punks and their dogs.

"Try to make it as full as possible," Joel said. "You can do something textural, and I'll do something more dynamic."

"I can be dynamic, too," Margot said.

"Just be sure you're listening to me."

Insulting that he said this. Worse was her sense that he was right. She hadn't always listened that well. She didn't really know what she was doing. Joel's scrutiny was uncomfortable; for all the time they'd spent scrambling to be alone, now it was actually just the two of them, and she wasn't sure how that would go.

Inside, the show was filling up. Tilman introduced Margot to his girlfriend, Arlette, who was French and constantly smoking, who seemed older than Tilman, starkly pretty and lined.

"I think you are playing now," Tilman said, and it took Margot a beat to unravel his garbled English.

Margot knelt over her gear, put the microphone to her mouth. How exposed she felt without Keith and Spencer there, too. She made a simple loop with her voice, layered another drone with the flute, the microphone gripped between her knees. Joel was slamming through an incessant, heavy beat, sending scraps from the oscillator through his delay. He was up on his hands and knees, feeling it in his body, and in the line of people pressed against the stage, Margot saw heads bobbing in response to what he'd laid down.

She could not feel it. Joel crouched in front of the amp, trembling with his own pulse, his lips moving in a distorted incantation. The crowd buffered the conversation from the bar, the Germans in rapt attention. The sound was huge, undeniable. The thing that she'd heard Joel do by himself in Keith's basement, the thing that had drawn her to him. He'd make the most exquisite loop and then call her downstairs, into an environment he'd made for the two of them to exist in, the tension of their at-that-point-unacknowledged feelings for each other sitting in that space. It was exciting. And the sound had been part of it —the sound had carried them.

But now that sound was Joel alone, and their feelings were acknowl-
edged, and Margot was only accessorizing. The red and green lights of
Margot's pedals winked at her. She blew into the flute again, twisted the
knob to stretch the echo. That's what she was—an echo. Texture. She
turned down each channel of her mixer, and he was still playing, his
body throbbing with the amp, seemingly unaware that she'd stopped.

"That was awesome," Joel said as they packed up. The lights were
on, and a disco song blasted through the PA. *You make me feel like
dancing.* People were talking, their attention punctured. The room a
party again.

A man in small glasses touched Margot's arm. "I find it interesting
to think about these sounds you are making," he said. "I'm not sure if
I like them."

"Thanks for letting me know." His breath was beery, clouded.

"Do you have vinyls for sale?"

She said no. Keith had kept the remaining merch.

The German guy wasn't deterred. "How does it make you feel, to
play such abstract music?"

Joel was shaking Tilman's hand. Smiling, basking in the afterglow.

She wasn't sure how to answer the German's question. It freaked her
out. If she wasn't enjoying it, why was she making this music?

The room had warmed up with the press of people, but Margot kept
her coat on as she watched the final performer, a man in a black vest
who'd taped contact mics to various parts of his body, which he'd wired
to a table of effects. His bare arms were ropy and pale. He stared out
at the audience, made prolonged, creepy eye contact as crackling noise
emanated from the PA. She fixed back on him, irritated by his cocky
assurance, still annoyed by how her own set had transpired. His hand
drifted down his torso, but she kept staring, forcing him to break his
gaze.

Afterward, she drank wine and chatted with Tilman and the woman
who ran the venue, Kate, who looked to be about Margot's age. She

was from Toronto, said she'd come to Berlin for a few days and just didn't leave.

Margot was next to the radiator. She gripped the bars and released them, burning and letting go. Kate asked her if she'd been to Berlin before.

Margot shook her head. "I'd never been to Germany before this trip. But my mother actually lived here in the seventies."

"Wow," Kate said. "Berlin in the seventies."

"She lived in Düsseldorf," Margot said. "She was an art student." *I was painting all the time,* Louise had said in Hasselt. Margot never knew her mother in her painting phase. Why had Louise given it up?

"The seventies were an interesting time," Tilman said. "As someone who was actually around back then."

Kate smiled. "I've never been to Düsseldorf, but the Kunstakademie is famous."

"I've never been there either," Margot said.

"It might have been your home, too," Tilman said.

"What are you talking about?"

"If your mother stayed."

"Well, then, I wouldn't be me," Margot said. "My father is American," she explained to Kate. But this didn't quite make sense, so she added, "My mother is American, too."

Tilman was still watching her. "It would have been interesting," he said. "If your mother stayed here with Dieter."

Margot looked back at him dumbly. What was she supposed to say? He was suggesting that if the events of her mother's life had gone differently, she would have never been born. "But my mom wound up in Oregon," Margot said. "That's where I grew up."

"It's funny, because we thought Dieter would stay in Oregon, too," Tilman said. *Orr-ree-gone.*

"Dieter lived in New York, though," Margot said.

"OK," Tilman said. "But first he went to Oregon, and everyone thought he would stay there with Louise and Elke. Maybe with your father, too. From what I understand, your mama had two boyfriends at the same time. Or a boyfriend and a husband, actually."

Was Tilman drunk? Margot didn't know what he was talking about, but she didn't want to give him the satisfaction of letting him know it.

"And yet here I am," Margot said, hoping he would take the hint and be quiet. "Definitely not German."

"That's because Dieter decided to leave Oregon," Tilman said. "I think your mother would have preferred that he stays, but Dieter always does what he likes."

"How old were you then?" she asked.

"Twelve or so," Tilman said. "Old enough to listen." He grinned wickedly.

And so maybe he was wrong, Margot thought. He'd just been a kid, was probably confused about what had happened. Besides, she couldn't tell if he actually believed this or was just being obnoxious.

"Dieter is too emotional," Tilman said. "He thought that leaving Germany would solve his personal problems. And he thought that leaving Oregon would solve them, too. But he just took his problems with him wherever he goes. He had much problems."

Margot squeezed the radiator. Kate had drifted away. Arlette was signaling to them from across the room—did they want to leave? Yes, Margot did. Louise and Elke would be arriving the next day, and Margot wouldn't have to stay with Tilman anymore.

Tilman's place was only a few blocks away. Margot imagined that the building—massive, blank, square—might be a remnant of communist architecture. But she didn't know if she was in the East or the West. They tromped up six flights of stairs to a tiny apartment, its small living room and kitchen combined, the bedroom just off that main space.

Tilman rolled out a thin mattress; the room was small enough that Margot and Joel would be half covered by the table. "Here you will sleep," Tilman said.

Margot eyed the bathroom longingly; she hadn't showered since Hasselt. Now she waited until the others had gone to bed. She crouched in

the shallow uncurtained bathtub, evoking a nude New Age prayer ritual. Small restricted movements with the hand-held shower head kept
the water from splashing the floor; she was borrowing a towel, and she
didn't want to waste it on a puddle. There were several types of brown
liquid soap, all smelling of cardboard and vague herbs, that reminded
her of health food stores from her Oregon childhood, before these sorts
of products had become trendy and sweet-smelling. Arlette had shiny
hair and a bright face, and it wasn't clear how these ineffective products
could possibly have contributed to her radiance. After Margot's own
shower, she had trouble raking a comb through her hair. In the mirror,
her skin was coated and dull.

She crawled under the table and lay beside Joel on the mattress. She
told him what Tilman said, spelled it out in a low voice in his ear. *From
what I understand, your mama had two boyfriends at the same time.* "I
might not have been born," Margot said.

"But anyone could say that," Joel whispered. "Any of us could have
not been born."

"Apparently Dieter lived in Oregon with my mom," Margot said.
"Which seems crazy."

"I think you're overreacting. You were born. And I'm glad."

"Everyone else must know about this, if Tilman is telling the truth,"
Margot said. "My sister can probably remember it."

"Was she supposed to tell you? You're saying that you're not even
sure it happened."

"But if it did, it's the kind of thing I would have liked to know."
Margot closed her eyes.

"How do you know that Tilman knows what he's talking about?
Wasn't he a little kid then?"

"He wasn't that young," Margot said. "He's in his forties now."

"Yeah, but he was in Germany when it happened," Joel said. "He's
not a primary source."

Margot was, though. She remembered Dieter's only visit to Eugene, when she was a child, six years old. Elke's graduation and the party in the yard. And after the party, when Margot got out of the bath. How proud she'd been to do it herself, rubbing her head with the towel. She'd heard her mother's voice in the studio and found the two of them talking, close and intent.

"I'm really looking forward to Dieter's performance," Joel said. "I wonder what it's going to sound like."

Why was everyone worshipping Dieter? He'd been in a band that did one album in the '70s. And he hadn't been a very good father—Elke had spent hardly any time with him as far as Margot could remember.

"I hope that he wants to do the release," Joel said. "His drumming style is incredible on that album. He sounds like Klaus—"

"I'm going to sleep now." Margot didn't want to hear Joel describe Dieter's talents. She didn't want to be here, on the floor of her mother's ex-husband's nephew's cramped apartment. But there she was.

In the morning, gray and dim, Tilman took them to a café with faded palm trees on the sign. He and Arlette ate soft-boiled eggs on toast. Margot ordered the cheapest thing on the menu, a bowl of yogurt sprinkled with bee pollen, the little chunks trailing gold. They drank coffee, and Tilman and Arlette smoked the entire time, exhaling over the plates.

Arlette was a photographer. She had work up in a local gallery. Every six months she did a lucrative stint on a cruise ship, documenting the passengers' recreation. The last one had been from Athens to Istanbul, and Tilman had gone with her, setting up her lights so he could get paid, too. It was a cruise for artistic types, and Arlette took pictures of them drinking cocktails and talking about their struggle to create.

"Our room had a curtain, not even a real door," Arlette said.

"The real artists got doors," Tilman said.

"We cannot have intimacy like this," Arlette said.

Tilman stubbed out his cigarette.

They walked around the silent city. Everything was what Margot wanted—unfamiliar candy bars, Turkish bakeries with spinach-stuffed rolls. She felt voracious even though she really wasn't hungry at all. It was the possibility, fleeting, of these unfamiliar things, and she felt a bittersweet longing for what was right in front of her. Joel had brought her here—this trip was mediated by his obsessions, and she was mediated by them, too. Tilman's story rattled in her head. Her mother had succumbed to Dieter. Perhaps Margot was no different, blithely following Joel.

They walked back through the park, Joel affecting a German accent while he asked Tilman about Krautrock bands. Maybe it would be better if Margot wasn't trying to play music with Joel, if each of them had their own thing. But music had been their connection, their coming together. If that ended, she wasn't sure what they'd have. In the contained universe of the tour, they'd become a couple, but what would it mean when they returned to their wider lives in Portland?

"It's different here in summer," Tilman said, leading them along a path that cut through the dry lawn.

"The parties make a carpet," Arlette said. "Everywhere is smoke from the food fires."

Margot suggested that she and Joel wander for a while; she wanted time by herself. She sensed that Tilman and Arlette were put out by their hosting and simultaneously insulted when Margot proposed doing things on their own.

"Really," Margot said. "We can find you again when it's time to meet up with my mom and Elke."

Eventually, she prevailed. When Tilman suggested a record store in Neukölln, Margot told Joel she'd walk around, meet him again in an hour. She didn't want to look at records, didn't want to hear the story of some long-lost edition-of-ten masterpiece.

"Fine," Joel said, miffed but looking past her nonetheless to the stacks in the store.

She walked alone along the middle of the wide sidewalk.

"Achtung," a man on a bike yelled. She was walking in the bike lane. He zoomed past her—with a cello strapped to his back, a beer in his hand.

What, actually, was she doing here? She was making this strange music, grasping at this scene that she was only tangentially part of—without Joel and Keith, she wouldn't be here, jumping out of the way of multitasking Germans.

And what about Joel? She'd wanted him acutely when she hadn't known if she could have him. And now that he was entangled, and reaching into her mother's history, she wanted to push him off, to extract herself from his reach. What had first attracted her—he knew everything, he could do everything—now annoyed her. He didn't have to know about Dieter, too.

She stopped in a store on the wide avenue. Shoe-finding would be a practical use of her time. Inside, the aisles were lined with boxes of juice, tracksuits, tall liters of mineral water. And bins of shoes. She found her European size, 38, in a pile of sneakers bound with elastic string. She picked a pair with blue stripes.

At the register, the counter was covered with newspapers and cups of coffee. The cashier, in a visor and thick eye makeup, snapped at another woman behind the counter, and Margot felt she was interrupting.

But the cashier smiled widely at her, swiped her hand through the mess on the counter. "Coffee, coffee, coffee," she said to Margot in English.

Margot was relieved by this—not by the English but by the direct address, the inclusion. She was slipping into the fabric of Berlin. She'd bought cool sneakers for the equivalent of seven dollars, and this was an achievement, too.

Outside, she removed her broken boots and took a photo of them on Germanic cobblestones, documenting what she'd be leaving behind. She walked back to the record store—*coffee, coffee, coffee,* she was thinking. *Zwei cappuchino, bitte,* she'd learned to say.

"Nice sneakers," Joel told her, cute and waiting on the sidewalk. He leaned in to kiss her—even an hour apart felt like a huge gulf given their constant proximity these past weeks.

"On sale," she said, glad to report her own triumph.

Walking into Görlitzer Park with Tilman and Joel later that day, Margot passed a giant crumbling structure, covered with graffiti and cordoned off by a chain-link fence.

"What's the story of this debris?" Joel asked Tilman. "Is it from the war?"

The stone pieces seemed to be on display, except there was no contextualizing plaque, no way to understand what the rubble had once been. History had happened here, perhaps.

"No, no," Tilman said. "Nothing like that. They were going to build a Turkish bathhouse, but the project stalled."

As they crossed the park's scrappy grass, Margot's new sneaker chafed her right toes.

She found her mother and sister sitting with Dieter at the outdoor café. Louise, with a blanket spread over her lap, held her coffee aloft, a sip paused in air. She saw them and waved ecstatically. Hugs and handshakes, and Margot fell into the chair beside her mother's. Each chair had a blanket; Margot unfolded hers over her legs.

"All roads lead to Berlin," Elke said.

"I'm glad to see you both again," said Louise. "But what happened to your band?" Her face wrinkled in expectation.

"Creative differences," Margot said. She didn't want to explain their convoluted dynamic. Keith was a control freak, Spencer was too sensitive. Joel was convinced he was always right. And if Margot looked at the situation closely, she might have to admit that she'd been stubborn, too.

"Things didn't look so good when we saw you last," Elke said.

"A dramatic exit," Dieter said. "That's one way to end a set."

Margot reached down to unlace her shoe, to give her toes some extra space. "Did you go to see your art school in Düsseldorf?"

Louise nodded. "And the museum. I took Elke to see where we lived when she was born."

"There's a little statue of me outside," Elke said.

"Do you like to have a coffee?" Tilman asked. The waitress was waiting over her chair.

Margot nodded, gesturing her please and thanks.

"I like your sneakers, Margot," Elke said.

"I just got them. But this one's hurting my foot." And there, upon further examination, clearly labeled on the inside of the tongues, one was a 38 and the other a 37. The sneakers had been banded together, presented as a pair.

"I'm so stupid," Margot said. She'd left the ankle boots on the sidewalk back in Neukölln. To try to retrieve them felt like failure. And they were probably gone by now anyway.

The cappuccino arrived, a bitter consolation.

"It's not your fault," Joel said. "Why should you expect them to be mismatched?"

"This shopkeeper thought she could cheat you," Tilman said. "Let's go back there tomorrow. I'll say you're my American girlfriend, give her a scolding in German."

This seemed distinctly not German to Margot—not orderly, not discreet. Too directly aggressive. But she knew Tilman wasn't really going to do that.

"So," Tilman said. "Have you seen the apartment where you are going to stay?"

"We haven't been there yet," Elke said. "But it's just around the corner."

"We have a bit of a space problem by me," Tilman said. "These guys can testify for that. We are cramped."

"I've stayed there before," Dieter said. "I don't need much. I'm certainly not a prince."

"With Arlette with me, now there is less room," Tilman said.

A prolonged stretch of quiet. The sounds of clanked china and murmured German. Tilman did not want to host Dieter. But no one else was jumping to offer the logical next step — that Dieter stay with them in the swapped apartment. Elke had told Margot the place was pretty big.

Dieter looked uncomfortable and old. Joel was leaning in, pressing his lips together, silently ecstatic with this continued proximity to Dieter.

"We can go take a look at the apartment," Elke finally said. "I think there's plenty of room. That might be more comfortable than Tilman's floor."

"That sounds better for you," Tilman said.

They all left the park, Margot with one sneaker left unlaced. They moved past a stand selling chicken and followed the overhead train tracks to a building set in the middle of the street. Upstairs, the apartment was spacious and bright — room after room linked by French doors, the trappings of some stranger's tidy, classy life. Potted plants and books on shelves.

"I can sleep on the couch," Elke said. "Then we should have enough bedrooms for everyone."

"I'm the one to do that," Dieter said. "You need your beauty sleep."

"I hope this is fine," Tilman said in a tone that implied that the arrangements were already settled. "Now I'm going to the venue to make sure the PA is ready for tomorrow. I'll see you all for the sound check."

Dieter said something to him in German, and Tilman laughed and left. They all stood in the living room, a collective unwillingness to touch or sit down — that sense of trespassing in a stranger's home.

"We should think about dinner," Elke said. "The apartment has a nice kitchen. I thought we could go shopping and then cook. There's a great market by the canal." So they traipsed out, a wobbly quintet.

RICHARD

2008

IN ZURICH, no planes were departing. "There is fog with thunder," the crisp clerk told him. "This storm is progressing slowly."

Richard asked about the train.

"It will not be any faster," the clerk said. She had earrings all the way up her earlobes, skin sensitive and prickled red, her hair a less natural shade of red. She was almost punk, like a teen runaway at the Eugene Greyhound station, and yet she still commanded authority. "The airline will not cover that cost. You must wait."

"When is the next flight?"

"It could be one hour, it could be more hours. Right now, who can say?"

"I was hoping that you could."

"When I can say, I will tell you."

Richard went back to his seat.

The night before, on the flight from DC to Zurich, he'd sat, slumped and buckled in, accepting refills of complimentary cognac from the ever-generous Lufthansa crew. He watched the tiny plane's path on the screen in front of him: he was somewhere over the Atlantic, rapidly traveling east. That image was comforting. The forward motion was out of his control.

He'd bought his ticket high on caffeine, and after a semi-lucid period of anxious reverie, he'd emailed the psychogeography guy at Humboldt University. Richard wrote that he'd be in town for another academic appointment—better not to invent a conference, a lie that would too easily trip him up. Perhaps they could meet to discuss his research. Richard was working on an article, a chapter of his book. He tried to make it appealing, tried to make his own research sound pertinent and contemporary and not flailing in the past as his most arrogant grad student had suggested. Richard's pitch must have worked, because the German agreed, and they set an appointment for the day after Margot's concert.

Richard stayed up late and read everything he could find. He absorbed the other guy's work, formed his own questions. This guy was looking at informal transportation, the patterns of cyclists in a city designed to accommodate bicycles much better than any American city. Really, there was a lot to consider here—the Germans didn't just accommodate bicycles, they championed them. Fodder for a cross-cultural study.

Richard knew that this trip was absolutely nuts. From Eugene, he'd flown to Denver, then DC, then London, then Zurich, and now he was waiting for the connection to Berlin.

He could get on a flight back to the States. No one would have to know what he'd done. This entire fiasco could remain a secret junket. Until Louise saw the credit card bill. He looked at the departures screen; delays aside, he could go anywhere. Stockholm, Ankara, Dublin. He could buy a ticket home. But to go back would mark his defeat.

He would buy himself some overpriced European snack. He'd find a corner where he could stretch out with his reading material: Alexanderplatz, the Berlin Block. He wasn't going to turn around now.

DIETER

2008

DIETER CROSSED THE BRIDGE with Louise and the girls and Joel. The market was on the other side of the canal. A dim afternoon, and the market's stands, canopied with tarps, made long, enclosed corridors. As a group, their pace picked up as they got closer — the potential of the market was palpable, rich. Socks, lentils, shiny peppers in a pile. Slippers and bolts of fabric. And a stand with records that Joel found immediately. He waved to Dieter to follow him.

"Cosmic Jokers," Joel said, holding up an LP. "This guy has killer stuff." The kid had really grown on him. What would it have been like to have a son? Joel sought Dieter's approval. He was more eager than Tilman. More American, basically.

Dieter flipped through the stacks, pulling out things that Joel might enjoy: Sonny and Linda Sharrock. Richard and Linda Thompson. He was showing off, enjoying Joel's interpretation of him.

"Double Linda," Joel said.

"Marriage as band structure."

Dieter kept digging. John and Beverley Martyn. Fleetwood Mac. All these couples, and yet Dieter knew how it always ended, what happened after the records were made. He knew he'd been a fool to get involved with Sabine. She wasn't his Linda, and he'd known it then, too. But Sabine was music, and music was an escape. Dieter hadn't known anything about being a father when Elke was born; he was terrified, overwhelmed.

Margot was motioning to Joel—she was going to walk around with Elke. Margot and Joel were another musical couple, though Dieter couldn't tell how long they would last. They were just kids. And yet their music was as powerful as it was strange.

Dieter studied Margot as she dug through socks at a neighboring stall. Where was Louise in this young woman? She had Louise's wild hair, though she was blond like her father. She was shorter than Elke, who was tall, like everyone in Dieter's family. Elke also had his mother's straight nose—the Weber *Nase,* though the Webers, his mother's people, were all gone now, or lost on distant branches of the family tree. Still, when he looked closely, he could see Louise in both Elke and Margot—the symmetry of her face and the expressions it formed. The squinting, slight exasperation, the reward of the radiant smile.

Dieter set off through the stalls. Here were Norbert's Turkish people, selling things Dieter wanted to eat—pastries with tahini and walnuts, pitas speckled with seeds. *Perhaps the world isn't as tightly defined as it once was,* Louise had said to Norbert in Bad Waldheim. And here in the market, with so many people who weren't German at all—not just Turkish, but people from Africa, from Syria, from Iraq—he wanted desperately to be part of this new world. This was a version of Germany to grab on to, one that could even make him proud.

The West African guy had Obama '08 T-shirts on his table, a gratifying sight. So many times on this trip, people had asked Dieter about Obama, their faces expectant with tender, cautious hope. The German papers were full of the American election: that morning Dieter had read that Germans were literally dreaming about Obama, the man appearing to advise them in their sleep. *Obama's going to win,* Elke had told Norbert. And people here wanted that too.

Dieter found Louise examining flat rectangles of bread—pillows, a soft landing. He trailed her from a distance, watching as she surveyed cucumbers and apples, bundles of dark spinach tied with twine. She assessed and selected, nodding, pointing, saying the German words. He got closer as she waited for olives and offered to carry her bags.

"Danke," she said, and went on with her order, negotiating for a brick of feta cheese. Dieter waited with the open sack.

The other day, in his mother's house, Louise had told him that Elke deserved to learn his father's full history. He knew she was right. He'd been afraid to tell Elke. He'd convinced himself he was protecting her, avoided her questions about his father, about his family. But he could see now that he didn't want Elke to have to go through the same thing he had, to be left wondering after he was gone.

"Zwei, bitte," Louise said, raising two fingers. She received the rings of seeded bread.

"Soon we'll need another bag," he said.

"I'm cutting myself off," Louise said. "We have enough food for a week."

On the way back to the apartment, they stopped at the Kaiser's supermarket for wine. Outside, guys waited to redeem their Sternburg bottles, drinking more beer as they killed time, with dogs and nothing to do. At least this wasn't what he'd become, Dieter thought, a Sterni outside the store.

They wove through the back streets to get to the apartment, a wide urban quiet that was impossible in New York. Paving stones and silver trees. Elke unlocked the door and hit the stairwell's light switch; clumped and laden, they climbed. From the window on the landing, he could see the garden in the back—a communal space with benches and trees, a green courtyard bordered by balconies. A typical German garden. All he'd wanted was to get away from here. And now this garden looked perfect to him.

Everyone set to work in the kitchen; Joel plugged in his iPod in the living room, turned up the volume so the music carried in. An early Amon Düül album—the flute and the thump of the drums.

Louise was at the center, explaining: the cucumbers, the peppers, the cheese. "Nothing fancy," she said. "A salad, the couscous. Olives and bread." He wanted to be part of her bustling energy, to be instructed.

He opened the wine. They brought out plates and platters, crowded the table in the living room with food. They sat and ate and talked about the details of the show the next day—Dieter had arranged some rehearsal time in the venue with Tilman. The rest of them would be going to Ute's gallery, and then to the art museum on Potsdammerstrasse.

"I'm happy that Ute and Gerd are in Berlin," Dieter said. "With Tilman here, too, it's been a real incentive to visit."

"Would you ever come back here?" Joel asked.

"To Berlin?"

"Or Germany. To live, I mean."

"A good question," Dieter said. "But my life is in New York now." He chewed an olive carefully, fished the pit from his mouth.

Margot put her own pit on her plate. "Why did you leave Germany?" she asked.

"It's easy to see that Germany is a complicated place," Dieter said. "I wanted something else. And Louise was an American. She changed the course of my life. I'm not sure I'd be in New York if not for her."

"Oh, come on," Louise said. Her tone was light, but her face was not. Watching, measuring. "You'd been talking about leaving Germany since before I met you."

"Talking and doing are two different things," Dieter said. "But perhaps you're right, I was destined to become a New Yorker."

"Why New York in particular?" Margot asked. Her expression was equally serious. Dieter looked at Louise, watching to see how she would react. He didn't know what narrative Louise had presented to Margot, or even to Elke for that matter. Louise was twisting her mouth, opening and closing slightly, preparing but not ready to speak.

"New York is music," Dieter said. "New York is constant time. I wanted a different rhythm. And I had family to help me there." It was hard to say this—Elke was the one he owed an explanation to, not Margot.

"Different than the German rhythm," Louise said. Together they were cutting out his time in Oregon. What more could they say? Would he have stayed in Oregon if Louise had allowed it? He thought that maybe that was true. But he also knew that Louise had been right to tell him that there was no place for him there. He'd wound up in New York. The backup plan had turned out to be the real thing.

Joel had left the table; he was kneeling in front of the stereo, fiddling with his iPod. "How about some Astral Gruppe?" he asked. "Let's listen to *All at One Time.*"

He had the album on his iPod—right, Joel had said he'd downloaded it from the internet.

"That's a bit egotistical, don't you think?" Dieter said. "To listen to your own band."

"I'm pretty curious," Elke said.

And Joel had already started the songs. For once Dieter was actually grateful for the cold digital format—there was no sleeve to embarrass him, to remind Louise of how terrible he had been.

But the music was the emotional part. He was afraid to hear it. Where could he go? He stood up and moved to the bathroom, a logical destination. But even alone he felt as if he were being watched, and in the small space he peed and washed his hands and looked at his face in the mirror, and he could still hear the opening strands. He sat on the closed toilet and listened to the sound of his bad choices preserved on tape.

"This reminds me of some of Klaus Schulze's solo stuff," Joel was saying. Dieter wished that for once Joel didn't have a comparison. It was too easy for them, that ready influence. Everything could be grabbed from the internet, the past a constant buffet.

Dieter knew he couldn't stay in the bathroom forever. They would think he was having a digestive emergency, some trouble with his bowels. He returned to his seat—now Gerd was launching into a full-on strut. No better collaborator for him—Dieter and Gerd had shared a language, it was brutal and savage when they really got going. A beautiful thing. And he sensed Louise nodding her head to the beat. He glanced over to see, but she was still, her face static behind the flicker of the candles.

"If this album is from 1973," Elke was saying, "then it's the same age as me." He wanted Elke to reassure him — this was what took you away from us, he imagined her saying. He wanted to know if she thought it was worthwhile.

The music was wild, rambling, charged. How young they'd been, how unhinged. He was far from that version of himself, but what a relief to hear it. The music held up. And maybe Joel's interest, his re-playing, was a chance for the album to take on new meaning. For other listeners, the songs wouldn't have to be about Louise and Elke leaving, about Dieter driving them away.

Now the dip down as the guitar pulled back — it was returning to him, all the modulations and tones. Sabine was singing. Chilling, transfixing.

"Are you supposed to understand the words?" Margot asked.

"I'm not sure I ever understood them," Dieter said.

Louise smiled a little — yes, he'd said that for her benefit. He still liked Sabine's vocals, thought they were essential, but he would never tell Louise that.

"I wonder if any Astral Gruppe fans will be coming to the show," Joel said.

"An intriguing thought," Dieter said.

The second side was starting. No need to flip. Klaus-Peter's gauzy layers — entire evenings devoted to getting the synth right. He could feel the drums rolling in, advancing from a corner.

"A lot of people love that album," Joel said. "That's why the reissue is going to be so awesome. We may have to do a second pressing."

The hard-panned drums had moved to the center now, that insistent thread pulling into the guitar.

"I'm still talking to the other guys," Dieter said. "They haven't agreed to it yet."

Joel turned to him. "I thought you already talked to them. In your email you said you agreed."

"I was referring to the show," Dieter said. "When I said agreed."

Margot was frowning at Joel. "You're being pushy," she told him quietly.

"I'm not strictly opposed to it," Dieter said. "But it's not only my decision to make."

Gerd and Klaus-Peter and Sabine—Dieter could almost see them again, as they once were, frozen in those pictures on the cover. That choice, to use the photos and not Louise's painting, had been a mistake. But then it hit him—now they could use Louise's painting for the cover, the original plan. This reissue could be a separate thing. A revision.

"See," Margot was saying to Joel. "You have to be patient." Her dissatisfaction with Joel spread sour over the table, and he followed her as they carried dishes from the room.

Elke was stacking the stained bowls. *Clank.* Somehow this evening had derailed—the kids were in the kitchen. The record had ended, and now there were only the sounds of water and dishes drifting in.

"I got dessert," Louise said. "Cookies with dates inside. And a marzipan Ritter."

The air was heavy, tense. Dieter was tired. The wine wasn't helping matters, but he finished what was left in his glass.

Elke came back. "We're thinking about going out," she said. "There's some huge dance club that we want to check out."

Joel and Margot appeared in the doorway, pulling on their coats. "There are multiple electronic music opportunities in a half-mile radius," Joel said. "We've narrowed it down to a grime party or a techno club."

"We're bringing both sets of keys," Elke said. "I may not last long. But we won't get lost." Elke held up her phone.

"And we have a map," said Margot.

"You'll be able to get by with only two words in German," Dieter said. "*Genau* and *genug.*"

"*Genau,*" Louise said. "Just nod your head and agree."

"Doesn't *genug* mean 'enough'?" Elke asked.

"That's right," Dieter said. "Incredibly useful. Just let Elke guide you. She knows what she's talking about."

He'd taught Elke to say *ich bin Ausländerin, ich spreche nicht gut Deutsch,* if she needed help when they were in Germany. To teach his daughter to say that she was a foreigner in his native land gave him a mix of pride and remorse. She was part of him, but she was not of this place. She was American, yet still she belonged to him.

"*Genau* and *genug,*" Joel said. Margot didn't smile.

They left. Dieter went to Joel's iPod, found the early Kraftwerk album that he remembered Louise had liked. Louise disappeared into the kitchen. He returned to his place at the table, alone with the music.

Then Louise came back in, with cookies on a plate.

"I have a question for you," Dieter said as she sat down. "Would you like to use your painting as the cover of the Astral Gruppe reissue?" He had promised it to her once. "The one we planned to use back then. The one from my mother's house."

She was thoughtful, squinting. "No," she said. "I don't think so."

"We could put it on the gatefold if you like that better." Her ready refusal surprised him.

"That record is a document of a particular time and place. It's where you were; it's where we were. The cover should be the same."

"We should have used it back then," he said. "It would have been a better cover."

"It's done now," Louise said. "There's no sense in changing it."

And that was what she had to say to him. It was impossible to trace out the other ways their lives might have gone. His choices had led him here, to a borrowed apartment in Berlin, next to but not with Louise. An imperfect circle.

"Who knows if this album reissue will even come about," Dieter said. "Margot told Joel he was being pushy."

Louise laughed. "I think she's annoyed with Joel. Too much psychedelic drone."

"Too much psychedelic drone could wear on anyone's nerves."

He ate a cookie, and then another. He felt the quiet settle between them.

"I was thinking about what you said at my mother's house," he said. "That you find it more relaxed in Germany now." He'd been relieved to hear her say that, heartened, grateful. As the keeper of his secret, she'd judged him, his family, his culture. And now she'd told him that things were different. That made him feel hopeful, calm.

"I'm going to talk to Elke about my father," he said. "It's time I did it."

Louise nodded. "Have you ever talked to Norbert about it?"

Dieter shook his head. "It's not a happy story."

"Did you ever try to talk to your mother?"

"I chose not to," Dieter said. "Maybe that was a mistake. Though I don't know what good it would have done. It would be difficult to smooth over all those years. But I made my peace with her."

"You did?" The way he'd said it sounded more like a question.

"I like to think I tried," Dieter said. "Maybe she found her own peace, at the end. Because for once, she truly couldn't remember. That burden was lifted."

Louise nodded, considered. "I've been thinking about what we were talking about the other day," she said. "Whether I should have told you sooner. Do you think that would have made things better between us?"

A difficult question. Louise knew his worst secret, the thing that had shaped his way through the world. He leaned on the table. The candle had burned to the bottom of the wick. It was pooling wax on someone else's tablecloth, the unseen inhabitant of this house, who had a life here, in Berlin, in Germany, who could look out at the green garden through the square window, secure in this place.

How could he answer her question? He studied her: what did she want to hear? "It's impossible to say. It happened the way it happened."

She didn't seem satisfied. She blew out the candle. "I better get this wax off." She stood and left the room; he heard her rattling a drawer. He followed her to the kitchen. He wanted to give her the answer that she wanted, to set her at ease. It wasn't fair for his mother to have done that to her.

"I don't know how it would have made things better," he said. What he wanted, too: someone to look back and tell him he didn't do everything wrong.

But she was crestfallen; this wasn't the right answer either. "Sometimes I felt like there was this impenetrable space between us," she said. "That there was this kind of sadness that I couldn't help you with. And I was angry at you. I knew that telling you would hurt you."

"You had a right to be upset." He followed her into the living room. She picked at the wax with the knife, collecting shards in her cupped hand. "Louise," he said. She looked at him. He wanted to console her. "You married again, you had a family. Our paths didn't go together anymore."

"Right," she said. "But the time we did have could have been better."

He put his hands on her shoulders. "It was good that you told me."

She cupped her hands, still holding the pieces of wax, his hands still gripping the top of her arms. He wasn't supposed to touch her, but this wasn't an overture. He was evening things out. Telling her that she hadn't done it wrong.

He followed her back to the kitchen. She put the wax in the garbage pail.

"It's brave of you to come back to Germany," he told her. "I know it must be difficult."

"It's your loss. Your mother. It's harder for you."

The kids hadn't done all the dishes. A few bowls left to soak in the sink.

"We could always say that things might have been better. But my life has not been unhappy," Dieter said. "Without you, I wouldn't have Elke. I probably wouldn't have New York."

She nodded. The window behind her reflected the movement of her head, caught a stark echo of the overhead bulb. It was a relief to say these things to her. He saw that she was lightened, too. They'd avoided this territory for this entire odd trip. Avoided the obvious: Dieter and Louise had something together, once; they might have continued it; they hadn't made that choice. And now they were together again only briefly, familiar strangers sharing this space. When she left the kitchen, he stayed there and finished the dishes, listening to the dim melody tracking in from the other room.

ELKE

2008

ELKE STOOD WITH MARGOT and Joel at the edge of the room, close to the bar, where it was a bit quieter. A physical kind of volume. The beat slammed and the crowd swayed slightly, stepping from one foot to the other, or bounced a bit, their faces impassive. An occasional ecstatic German flailed his limbs.

"The scene here is amazing," Joel said. "There are no hips moving in this entire club."

"Total inhibition," Elke said. Or yelled. "Even as they're totally un-inhibited." She felt embarrassed and somehow responsible. "I didn't know what the music would be like."

"I'm into it," Joel said. "Sounds like African Head Charge."

Margot squinted at him.

"UK," Joel said. "Experimental dub. Pre-techno."

"At least it's a typical German experience," Elke said. "We should be seeing more of Berlin than just the inside of an apartment."

Margot had transferred her squint—their mother's narrow, assessing gaze—to the dance floor now. A man in a shiny unitard gyrated around her. *"Genug,"* she said.

Joel nodded toward the bar. "I'll be right back with German refreshments." He pushed into the crowd.

"What happened in Düsseldorf?" Margot asked.

"What do you mean?" Elke asked.

"I mean in your grandmother's town," Margot said. "What was going on there?"

"A funeral," Elke said.

"I know," Margot said. "Sorry. I meant with Mom. Was she acting weird?"

"I don't know if weird is the word for it," Elke said. "I'm sure it wasn't easy to visit her ex-husband's family."

They stepped back as dancing bodies knocked into them—a shoulder, an arm.

"Was it hard for you?" Margot asked.

"It was sad to be there without my grandmother," Elke said. "It was strange to be there with Mom. I can't remember any of my life in Germany with her."

Joel was back, laden with beer. "Now this sounds like Palais Schaumburg," he said. "I wish we'd been here for Tilman's techno phase."

Margot took a bottle from him. "I understand that Mom came for the funeral. And I'm sorry about your grandmother."

"I asked Mom to come," Elke said.

Joel was nodding his head to the emphatic beat, smiling at a ponytailed guy waggling his hips. Elke felt like all of it was her fault: the ridiculous club, the atonal dance moves. She had to defend it even as it freaked her out.

"Tilman said something really crazy," Margot said. "He told me that Mom and Dieter almost got back together. That Mom was dating Dieter and my dad at the same time."

"When?"

"The other night," Margot said. "At our show."

"No, I mean when did he say that happened?"

"He said that Dieter came to Oregon. To win her back. He said I might have been German."

"That's ridiculous," Elke said. "I'm not even German." The beer was cold on her throat.

"You know what he meant," Margot said. "Do you remember what he was talking about?"

Elke could remember it, barely, in one or two distinct flashes. Dieter living in their house that summer, Richard being there too. Her grandfather coming for dinner, the table crowded with those men. But Elke's memory was patterned by what happened afterward, by the fact that Richard was always there with her mother, while Dieter was far away.

"I guess so," Elke said. "I was a little kid."

"I thought Mom started dating my dad when you were really young."

"She did," Elke said. "I think maybe they were both around for a bit, though I can't really remember." Behind the bar, a woman in a backwards baseball hat pushed bottles into waiting hands.

Margot was watching Elke. "Dieter was living with you and Mom."

"It wasn't for that long," Elke said. "I don't think. Why don't you ask Mom about it?"

"I'm going to." Margot's tone was fierce, determined.

"You're being a little dramatic," Elke said. *"Ja, ja, ja!"* the bartender yelled. "Why don't you focus on what Mom's dealing with right now? She just lost her job. And she's pretty upset that Richard didn't take the picture of her project." Margot's own father was the one to blame for that.

Margot was still agitated. "I'm going to find the bathroom," she said. "Hold this, please." She put her bottle in Joel's hand and stalked away.

Elke was alone with Joel. "Thanks for the beer." It was so loud there; she was practically yelling. "You're really getting an immersion into our family saga," Elke said. "Sorry to put you in the middle of it."

"It's OK," Joel said. He drained his bottle, started on Margot's. "Our band just fell apart, so this is filling that role. I need a certain amount of chaos in my life."

"The recommended daily allowance of tension."

"Right," Joel said. "It's like a vitamin." He had a great voice, a lulling bass. An Aquarian ability to soothe. Maybe Joel could calm Margot.

Elke didn't want to talk about her parents anymore, didn't want to apologize for something that wasn't her fault.

"Dieter's drumming style is so interesting," Joel said. "I can't wait to see him play tomorrow. He's got a great touch."

"I'm not a musician," Elke said. "I don't know how to analyze his style."

"Listening is just as important. Pay attention to the pulses."

It was awkward to confess this to Joel, who in some ways could understand her father better than she did. And now, with Margot returning—Elke could see her sister weaving through the crowd—Elke didn't want to dwell in that sensation.

She told Joel that she'd check out the dance floor. She pressed her way to the middle. Around these people, Elke felt intensely cool, as though the mere fact of her upbringing in the United States had bestowed upon her a sense of rhythm she was only aware of now. She could hide in the pounding music. She was tall in her boots and all alone.

The music was cycling through the same patterns, a repetition that held her aloft. She moved for a while, invisible, transfixed. Time passed that way, as she discharged the tension she'd stored.

A man was speaking to her. *"Sie tanzen sehr gern,"* he said. Lost in the blur of noise; she might have been able to get it if it weren't so loud. She nodded.

"Wie heissen Sie?" he asked right in her ear.

"Elke," she said. A word she could say like a German, the one word that wouldn't give it all away.

"Florian." He was as tall as she was, rangy and unshaven. Now he was saying something much more complicated. She had to tell him, shatter his belief that she was actually a German, not just the shell of one.

"Ich bin Ausländerin," she said. *"Ich spreche nicht gut Deutsch."*

"Elke the *Ausländerin,"* Florian said.

"I can try," she said. "In German. But we'll probably have to talk about food or the weather."

"I'd rather talk about other things," he said. "How does a foreigner have a name like Elke?"

"It's complicated," she said. The crowd was moving around them; she was standing still and yelling into his ear.

"What do you think of the music?" Florian asked in her ear. "Do you like the techno with many changes or with few changes?"

"I'm not sure."

Florian laughed. "Do you like to take a beer?" he shouted. She was still clutching her empty bottle.

They pushed through the throng of people toward the bar, where Margot and Joel were slouched on two stools, side by side in sullen conversation.

"You can't try to control what's happening onstage," Joel was saying.

Margot was poised to attack, with an elbow propped on the bar. "I wasn't suggesting that."

"This is my sister, Margot," Elke said to Florian.

Margot and Joel swiveled around to face them.

"Margot the *Ausländerin*," Florian said. There was definitely something transfixing in his smile.

"I'll take your word for it," Margot said, matching his brilliant grin.

"And what are you doing here in Berlin?" Florian asked Margot. Elke liked the way he leaned into conversation, liked the slope of his voice.

"I'm a musician," Margot said. She climbed off the stool, still holding his gaze. "I have a show."

"This is yours?" Florian asked, pointing his finger upward. Gesturing toward the music, but signaling something else, too—an open pathway, bantering right on the brink of flirtation.

Margot was laughing, shaking her head. "It's a noise band."

"OK, a noise band," Florian said. "This makes perfect sense to me." His body was pitched toward Margot, and she was responding to him.

Her shoulders pushed back, her face turned up to his. With Joel, Margot had projected platonic, kept a subtle distance. *Joel and I are keeping it under wraps,* Margot had told Elke. Now Margot was flirting in earnest, both coy and direct.

Was Elke competing with her little sister for this guy? What a ridiculous concept — Florian seemed to be older than Elke, way too old for Margot.

"Good," Margot said. "I'm glad it makes sense. Because Germans are so logical." Elke could see Margot feeling her power, testing it out. Just the way, as a kid, Margot had held court in a room of adults. But Margot was an adult now, a woman talking to a man.

Joel was clearly bothered by this. He stepped closer to Margot. "I'm Joel," he said to Florian, inserting that introduction awkwardly, way after the fact. "I'm in the band, too."

Elke felt bad for Joel — Margot was ignoring him. And why was Margot throwing herself at Florian? He was a complete stranger. A forty-year-old stranger. Elke's stranger.

"Our show is tomorrow night," Margot said. "You should come."

"OK, perhaps I will," Florian said. He turned to Elke, touched her arm. "What do you play in the band?" That charm was fixed on her again. Relief — Florian was just flirting with Margot the way you'd encourage a child. A doting uncle or big sister's boyfriend. Or big sister's techno club companion.

"I'm definitely not in the band," Elke said. "This is a family trip." Or something like that.

"She could join the band if she wanted to," Margot said to Florian. She'd drained her beer, a larger one than the first round Joel had purchased for them. Maybe Margot was drunk. She was embarrassing herself, and Elke felt both protective and annoyed.

"Should we take another beer?" Florian asked Elke.

She nodded, glad for the diversion. Florian signaled to the bartender, unrolled a string of smooth German.

"Margot, I'm really tired," Joel said. "I think we should get going."

A fraught suggestion. Margot's hair haloed around her face, the haphazard waves framing her discontent.

Elke certainly didn't want to go with them and fill the tense walk. They had their own problems to squabble over. And she wanted to stay there with Florian, who was standing expectant beside her, the entitled proximity they'd just barely established.

"I'm going to stay a bit longer," Elke said. "Do you know how to get back?"

Joel nodded. "I have the map and the keys."

"And I have the other set of keys," Elke said. She felt like their mother, sunny and spacious, trying to contradict her sister's odd behavior. Margot was turning away.

Florian put a beer in her hand. "I'm still curious about your name."

"My father is German." The classic explanation. "But I grew up in the United States."

"Your father didn't speak German to you?" Florian asked.

"He and my mom split up," Elke said. "So I didn't see much of him. And he's lived in the U.S. for most of my life. We speak English to each other."

"But you can understand something," Florian said. "You understood me before."

She followed him back to the dance floor. She let the music hold her up.

LOUISE

2008

MORNING LIGHT FILTERED through the curtains. Her dreams had been filled with murky urgency, but she'd slept — the walls were thick in that apartment, the windows double-paned. She hadn't heard the kids come in last night, or the sounds of the elevated train that cut through the street.

She left through the living room, past Dieter asleep on the couch. To the bathroom, to the kitchen, where they'd left the keys. Only one set was on the counter. One of the girls must have had the spares. Louise wrote a note: *Back by 8.* They'd probably still be asleep when she returned.

Outside, it was brisk and empty beneath the train tracks and the trees. She thought she'd have a coffee somewhere, but nothing was open. It was still early, and Berlin didn't seem to be awake.

She had the security of the map in her purse, but she wouldn't look at it unless she was absolutely confused; she'd take herself right to that brink. She'd heard so much English since she'd arrived in Berlin. That marked a change — in her student days, she hadn't had that crutch.

The night before, she'd talked to Dieter, and he'd seemed relieved, resolved. Louise had sensed him reassuring her, too. All that had passed was complete. She went by a gambling arcade; through the open door, she saw carpet and blinking machines. Men smoked at tables lit by low lamps. On a balcony just above street level, a woman brushed a husky, leaving lines in his soft fur.

They'd listened to the Astral Gruppe album, too. Louise hadn't heard it since Elke was a baby, in the apartment in Oberbilk, watching Elke's curls as she crawled over the floor. She wasn't sure she would have recognized the music if Joel hadn't announced it. Those waves of sound —and even Sabine's wailing—had become something else.

Dieter had asked to use Louise's painting for the Astral Gruppe reissue, the original plan from all those years back. But that would be an awkward revision. Everything that had happened since she'd left Düsseldorf—these were things she wanted. Richard, and Margot. They were her life. Her teaching, her ongoing work. There was something fated about that terrible time when Elke was a baby. Leaving Germany had set Louise's course.

Just ahead of her on the sidewalk, a man in running gear was sweating at the end of a jog. He took deep, lunging steps, serious in his strange stride. She followed him into a bakery below the train tracks, by the station with a flower market, where faded revelers were still traveling home. Louise picked out *Brötchen* to bring back to the apartment. The jogger bought a beer and drank with gulping resolve.

She walked back through the park, passing the shuttered café. Foot traffic had cut a dirt trail across the lawn. *The people have spoken,* Richard would say about those lines through the grass.

She imagined Richard steps ahead of her as they climbed Spencer Butte in Eugene. She remembered those very first times she'd spoken to him. The conviction, the unexpected beauty of his ideas. His laugh —she could almost hear his voice.

Deeper in the park, she traced the dirt paths: the trails crossed and came together, petered out or joined the official paved way. The park's road crested a hill, disappeared, and looped back. A deliberate move in planning, Richard would say—it was better for travelers not to see the entire path. *Pedestrians need mystery. They need turns.*

Louise thought about the painting she'd left at Hannelore's house, how she'd been chasing a sense of *zeitgleich* with that lost series. But maybe that simultaneity she'd tried to paint was not possible. With the *18th* project, she had allowed the line to unfold and then fade. It had not been, could not be, perpetual.

The project's constant measuring had given her a sense of control over time. The same way she'd used the entire house—tracking the kids' heights on the linen closet, taking the same picture of the girls in front of the juniper on the first day of school each year. She thought about the missing photo, Richard's skipped step in the sequence. Since the beginning of the *18th* project, she'd kept a dim vision tucked away, of bringing the piece to a graceful, natural close. She'd imagined this conclusion in the distant future, when she was old and decrepit and white-haired. It would fade out when she, too, had reached her end. Each piece of the project had always been an assertion. The end should be definitive, too.

Perhaps Richard had given her a gift by not taking that photo. Maybe that was the graceful, natural end. He'd been generous with her all along. He hadn't suggested that they sell the house, even though they both knew it was the logical decision. It was foolish to hang on to the big place, stupid to live beyond their means. They could find a smaller space, another garden. She could have a different studio—already she felt the pulse of excitement, thinking about the new work she might make. She wanted to write to him immediately, to call and suggest it, to see what he thought. *Stop,* she could tell him, *don't take another.* She'd keep going—she wasn't decrepit yet—but the project would not.

She would miss the physical aspect of working on it, noting the incremental changes. As the decaying pieces started to break down, they revealed brown grass underneath, in blotted squares or blurry triangles. And as the wood disappeared, it left little craters, which caught rain, which made mud. She would miss that continual revisiting. But there was something relieving, too, about letting go of the attention she'd devoted to the project, freeing up the space for something else.

A man was walking toward her. In that instant she saw Richard—
the wiry gait, the still-shaggy hair. A trick. The man pulled on his cap,
yelled to a dawdling dog.

She found an internet café, open only because it never closed. The
guy at the counter nodded and said, *"Fünf."* In the specified booth,
she found no new messages from Richard, but she wrote him another
quick hello. She'd thought he would have responded to her message
from yesterday morning, but maybe with the time change, winding
back nine hours—she couldn't figure it out, not without coffee.

She paid the guy, sliding out the proper change, while he spoke in
another language on a headset phone. She whispered her thanks in
German. *Bitte,* he murmured, both of them borrowing words.

In the apartment, she found Dieter ministering to a silver espresso pot
on the stove.

"Guten Morgen." She unpacked her wax bag of rolls.

"Elke's not with you?" Dieter poured the coffee into two cups.

"A solo ramble," Louise said. "I just slipped out on my own."

"I guess she's doing the same thing," Dieter said. "She's not here. The
door to her room is open."

Louise hadn't checked. She wondered if Elke had left before she did.
"And the others are asleep?"

"Sleeping off the disco," he said. The coffee was thick, bitter, perfect.
She heard someone go into the bathroom. Water rushed through pipes
in the walls. The routine sounds of morning, of the weird family life
they'd pieced together here.

Margot appeared, with her soft face and messy hair.

"How was the dance club?" Louise asked.

"It was interesting. Not really my thing, but it was funny."

"Germans can't dance," Dieter said.

"I noticed that," Margot said. "No offense."

"Quite all right," he said. "I don't bother to try anymore."

"Elke was up bright and early," Louise said. "She must have left even before I did."

"That's strange," Margot said. "We left the techno party before her."

"She was having a good time?" Dieter said. "She was so sure she'd want to leave."

Margot zipped her sweatshirt up to her chin. "She was deep in conversation with some guy."

Maybe Elke hadn't come home at all.

"We need more coffee," Dieter said. He set to work with the espresso pot.

"Elke has the other set of keys," Margot said. "I'm sure she's fine."

Joel was in the doorway, buttoning a wrinkled shirt. "She didn't come back?" He looked at Margot for an answer, but he was seeking something else, too. He was irritated with her.

Yesterday Louise had thought that Margot was the one peeved with Joel — her daughter's rare but emphatic harrumphing. But now Joel seemed to be annoyed, his own buoyant charm zapped by some unspoken tension.

"We don't know," Margot said, passing that flare of agitation back to him. "Maybe she went out for a walk."

"We're supposed to meet Ute at her gallery at ten," Louise said. "I'm worried about Elke. You left without her?"

"She wanted to stay," Margot said.

"What was the guy like?" Desperate scenarios were running through Louise's mind.

"He was German," Margot said.

"The situation seemed fine," Joel said. "Two consenting adults and all that."

"He wasn't threatening," Margot said.

Of course not. They never were.

"Not threatening to Elke, at least," Joel said. He accepted coffee from Dieter and slumped into a chair.

What was Joel saying? "You're not reassuring me," Louise said. "What's that supposed to mean?"

Margot darted her eyes from Louise to Joel. "Just ignore that," she said. "He's not talking about Elke. I'm sure she's fine."

"But she must know we'd worry," said Louise. A racing list of potential horrors—an accident, a mugging. Margot's breezy dismissal only made Louise more anxious. "This isn't like her. She had her phone with her, right?"

Margot nodded. "I'd call her, but my phone doesn't get service in Europe."

"I can't make calls either," said Louise.

Dieter pulled a phone from his pocket. "Technology is not helping us as it should," he said. "This is my German phone. But I can't call a U.S. number. Only German."

"What about a text?" Joel asked.

"Ah, a text message," Dieter said. He squinted at the phone, poked it with one finger. "Elke, *wo bist du?*"

They all were being a little too flip about this. "Did she have a map?" Louise asked.

"I think so," said Margot.

Dieter asked for Elke's number, poised to punch it in, and Louise recited the sequence, which she knew by heart.

"OK," Dieter said. "When she's texting me, I will call Ute so you know." His certainty was both soothing and a bit irritating.

Ute's gallery was in Mitte; over *Brötchen,* Louise and Margot traced a route on the map.

"We'll leave a note for her," Margot said. "With the address."

"Say hello to Ute," Dieter said. "I'll wait around to see if Elke comes back before I go meet Tilman. And I'll see you all for the sound check."

Dieter was remarkably unperturbed. Did adults get kidnapped? Elke might have fallen and hit her head. She was always on time. But they couldn't wait any longer, or they'd be late.

———

Ute was behind the desk at the gallery, her hair a luminous silver bob. She wore big glasses, big jewelry, a loose vest, clunky boots. Smiling Ute, jumping up to embrace Louise. How strange, they said, how wonderful to see each other again. How stupid that so much time had gone by. Ute went right into English, a language they hadn't spoken together in the past.

"To be in Düsseldorf again, and now to see you," Louise said.

Ute's jewelry clanked as she agreed. "When I've been back to Kunstakademie, I've felt time is collapsed and impossibly large at the same time."

"Exactly," said Louise.

"And you are also an artist like your mama," Ute said to Margot. "I'm looking forward to your music."

Margot smiled, clearly proud.

"Your husband was in Dieter's band?" Joel asked.

"Gerd played the guitar," said Ute. "He still does."

"Dieter said that Gerd's going to play with him during the concert tonight," Louise said.

Ute nodded. "He's looking forward to it."

"So you two were classmates?" Margot asked.

"And friends right away," Ute said. "This was an interesting time."

"Ute was a good role model for me," Louise said. "She worked very hard."

"*Nein, nein,*" Ute said. "But it was difficult then. For a woman artist to get attention at that time, she has to do something drastic. She has to be bleeding or peeing."

"Like for performance art?" Joel asked.

"Of course," Ute said. "She's not just peeing in the corner for no reason."

They were all laughing. Ute was warming up; the force that Louise remembered had fully emerged.

"Like Sabine rolling on the floor and moaning," Louise said.

Ute waved her hand. "She wasn't serious about her work. But if we are going to talk about serious, Louise, I still remember looking at your paintings in the studio with Elke in the stroller."

Ute's praise twined into Louise's agitation—where was Elke?

"So you knew my sister when she was little?" Margot asked Ute.

"Just as a baby," Ute said. "Our assistant in studio."

"Elke and I went back to Oregon before her first birthday," Louise said. "That's when your grandmother got sick."

"We missed Dieter, too, once he left," Ute said. "So many of our friends left Düsseldorf. So we came to Berlin, and that was a good move for us."

"Dieter went to Oregon, too, right?" Margot asked. She was both challenging and a little nervous, and Louise wasn't sure why she was bringing this up.

"He came to see Elke in Eugene before he moved to New York," Louise said. "Elke was still quite young." Louise looked at Ute—Dieter had visited Ute and Gerd many times over the years, he'd said. He'd kept up. What had he told them about his time in the States?

Ute was silvery, composed, as she herded them into the next room. "It tickles me to think of seeing Elke again," she said. "I thought she was coming today, too?"

"She's running late," Louise said. "You'll get to see her." It was nearly eleven.

"Is this its own piece?" Joel asked of the pebbles on the floor between the rooms.

"Space is defined by transitions," Ute said. "When joining these two rooms for exhibitions, it's important for us to think about what to put in the space in between."

"The same artist?" Joel asked.

"Right," Ute said. "This room always takes on a different role in our exhibitions. It's an important space. I'm quite enchanted with this idea of connection. I see much more of it now than there used to be. Connection between places, concepts, people."

"I heard 'Gangsta's Paradise' in the corner store last night," Joel said. "That was a surprising connection."

"It's not all about music," Margot said to Joel. "Ute's talking about something much bigger." She went into the adjoining room, and he drifted after her, leaving Louise with Ute.

"They ask good questions," Ute said.

"About the work, at least." Louise was still confused about Margot's sudden inquiry.

"Kids," Ute said. "They never want to think that the parents had a life before them."

"Margot's the same age we were then. It seems impossible."

"These days it's different," said Ute. "I see women putting pictures of the children on Facebook right beside the announcement of their exhibition. That never would have happened before. I always felt I had to keep my kids a secret."

"You use Facebook?" Louise felt creaky, behind.

"My son made it for me. I don't know what to do with it. I go on and then go off." The same Ute: the reassurance, politely forthright. "They are so young," Ute continued. "They are babies. Maybe things would have been easier for us if we were a little older at that time."

"You and Gerd stayed together," Louise said. "You were mature enough to make it work."

"I don't know if that's it. Dumb luck. A stubborn head."

"I was both dumb and stubborn," Louise said.

Ute laughed. "Not dumb," she said. "You had a baby to take care of right away. I'm sure that made it harder."

"It did," Louise said.

"We missed you when you left."

"I thought I would come back."

"But it's good for you in Oregon," Ute said.

Margot and Joel had returned. "I love the video piece about memory," Margot said. "It's so melancholy."

"I think so, too," Ute said. And here Louise remembered the more cautious and reserved Ute—here is my opinion, one I'm certainly convinced of, but I'm not going to insist you agree. There was something tough and impressive in that quiet conviction. That was Ute, that was German.

"It's an interesting time now," Ute continued. "We've reached a point in this country when we talk about the war, when we lament the tragedies, we can also recognize what ordinary Germans suffered."

"What do you mean by ordinary? Weren't Jews Germans, too?" Margot asked.

"I don't think that's what Ute meant," Louise said.

"Surely the Jews were German, too," Ute said, flushing. "I only meant that the other damages of the war weren't things we ever talked about. My parents had great difficulties during the war, but that was just life in wartime."

"I think it's hard to compare those experiences," Joel said. "I'm not religious, but my dad is Jewish, and I think he'd have a hard time comparing genocide to life in wartime."

"I think you're right," said Louise. "But Ute's not saying they're the same thing."

Ute was nodding rapidly. "I would say only that there was great pain."

They were walking to the front of the gallery, retracing their route in.

"Louise, I've been meaning to tell you that I've enjoyed your website," Ute said. They were going to talk about something else. "My favorite, I think, is the piece with the mirrors that catch the secret world in the forest."

Louise took her direction, glad for the compliment. "The *Hidden Driveways* piece. I started planning that one after Margot was born. My doctor had suggested a mirror during labor, since with the epidural I'd be numb."

"Ah," Ute said. "So that would tell you how you are progressing. How far you have to go."

"Exactly. We tried it, but Richard told me I probably didn't want to see it."

"So much blood," Ute said. "So much fluids."

Joel looked mildly disgusted, but in Margot's face, Louise could see her daughter's interest, that keen connection, and Louise wanted to keep going, for Margot to know.

"I loved that idea," Louise said. "The mirror could show something happening that I couldn't actually feel. It could expose something hidden. So I put the mirrors up on this winding little road. The idea was that they'd catch painted nylon strips in the trees that otherwise you couldn't see."

"I didn't realize that project was inspired by my birth," Margot said. "I'm flattered."

"This is fantastic," said Ute. "And it begins from the original place of power."

Over Ute's shoulder, at the front of the gallery, Louise could see Elke pushing on the glass door. A physical relief—there was Elke, stalking through the room. With a wildness in her hair and gait, a slightly off-kilter look as she approached.

Louise found Elke's eyes—*are you OK?* Elke gave her a slight nod, and Louise reached for her, grabbed her arm. That urge to hold on. "Where were you?"

"I'm sorry," said Elke, hugging Louise. "I lost track of time."

"We were worried," Margot said. Something a little edgy in her voice.

Elke stepped back, her eyes darting from Louise to Margot, simultaneously apologizing and nipping into something with Margot. The collar of Margot's jacket was folded up, a plaid scarf wound around her neck—she was bundled and oblique.

"I met someone," Elke said quietly.

"We met him, too," said Joel. He looked at Margot, annoyed, folding his long arms over his chest.

"Right," said Elke.

What was going on with them? "It would have been nice to let us know," Louise said. "Didn't you have your cellphone with you? You should have gotten in touch with Dieter."

A blast backwards to arguing with Elke when she was a teenager. That breathless, fruitless scolding—what was Elke thinking?

"My battery died," Elke said.

"This isn't like you at all." Louise let out her held breath, releasing the valve of her panic.

"I know," Elke said. "I overslept. It was an accident." With a sheepish smile, embarrassed and still savoring something private.

"When you're on your own, I know that you're living your life," Louise said. "But you can't do that to me again. You have to think about me when we're together."

"I do think about you," Elke said. "I've learned my lesson. I'm always going to pack my charger now. I won't go dancing on a low battery."

Elke knew how to disarm her. Louise laughed despite herself, though she still felt agitated. Creeping in was another question—who was this someone that Elke had met? Louise did want Elke to settle down, have a family. Perhaps he was an interesting guy. And why not meet someone in Germany? Elke was half German. And she'd be following in her mother's footsteps. Ha! A ridiculous thought.

Elke linked her arm through Louise's, apologized again. But something else was festering in the room. Louise wondered if her daughters' irritation was directed at her. Margot had questioned Dieter's time in Oregon, but Louise didn't understand why she was upset about it.

Ute patted Elke's shoulder, straining to smooth. "Little Elke," she said. "Of course. I can see your father's face."

Elke flashed Ute a bright smile—extra charming, making up for her misbehavior. "It's great to finally meet you."

"Actually, to meet again," Ute said, sprightly, bouncing back. "The last time I saw you, you were a baby."

"I don't quite remember it," Elke said, laughing.

"Your description of this driveway project, Louise, is making me remember a brilliant moment from our younger days," Ute said. "If we want to talk about something inspiring. We were making a big party after a concert—this was in the time when my husband and Dieter were in the band together, and the atmosphere was always unconstrained. So after the band played, we were continuing to listen to music. We were dancing. Your mom joined all of us and took off her pants on the dance floor, with baby Elke in the bundle on her chest. The music was heavy, everyone was drinking much beers. We were all fascinated by this powerful demonstration."

Her daughters were listening, with intrigue and squinting confusion. Get closer, pull back the layers of their dear mother's weird life. "The road to adulthood is paved with bad choices," Louise said. Just throw that on the pile of their dissatisfaction.

"Well, we all make bad choices," Elke said. She glanced at Margot. They both seemed so frustrated with Louise. It was impossible to placate them. All this had happened such a long time ago. She wouldn't do those things now.

"No, I think it was quite a feminist gesture," Ute said. "This proud woman, she is passionate and assertive. My God, with her baby and her exposed female's flesh, dancing to the music. As artists, the body is the best tool for our expression."

This was not an occasion Louise wanted to revisit, and yet Ute's critique bolstered her. It was a relief to recast that strange chapter. Louise had made choices, and certainly some bad ones, but she'd made marks.

Margot was watching her, bemused. "This sounds insane."

"It was insane," said Louise. Her daughters couldn't just let time be fuzzy—they wanted explanations for everything, an impossible crystal precision.

Ute herded them toward the door. "Now we'll have some bites to eat to give us strength to look in the museum," she said, flexing her arms. Louise followed them out to the street.

ALL AT
ONE TIME

2008

RICHARD STUDIED THE MAP as the plane descended. The most direct way, not exactly. But he was almost there. It was morning now, morning again; he'd slept on the airport carpet the night before, his coat a blanket, his suitcase scratching his cheek. The need for sleep blotted his concerns. And Louise had written to him—he'd checked his email in a little kiosk—as though she sensed his desperate dreams on the floor. *I miss you,* she'd written. *I tried to call. I wanted to hear your voice.*

On the U-Bahn, the stations flashed by in blocks of color. A dark hurtling and then the surprise of bright tiles pressed into the walls. Louise, he thought—those crisp and beautiful geometries. The train's doors opened only if you pressed the button, signaling your desire for release.

He had all day. He bought a pretzel from a stand in the station and went aboveground. There were no oncoming cars, but the Germans waited at the curb for the light to change. Richard crossed on his own. They watched him, nervous and disapproving. He laughed. Midblock crossing was essential to a city's health. It tempered congestion, eased the load on popular paths. That necessary dance of come and go. For all their talk, Germans were not necessarily efficient.

He found a shop to rent a bike. He left his suitcase there. The clerk suggested it. "It pleases me much to watch your things." She blinked, holding an unashed cigarette, and somehow Richard believed her words were true.

He brought his camera with him. He pedaled along a wide avenue, past outdoor tables where people lunched with beer. Then through the patchy woods of a huge urban park. Men muttered and gathered, or lifted their chins as he passed. The sound of a saxophone carried from a hidden grotto, scored these encounters with a mysterious unfolding dirge. He stopped when he wanted to take a picture—some uneven paving stones, the lines of a half-timbered house—and then he'd read the map and keep on riding. The TV tower his North Star. That was the job of a landmark, to offer that crucial sense of before and after. The body in relation to place. The dramatic arc unrolling in the trip. And it was the job of the planner to indicate the right direction. A city could be understood by its paths. So could a person, so could a life. The planner an artist of time.

He stopped in an outdoor café in another giant park. For coffee, for a marzipan croissant. The café had left blankets on the chairs, a thoughtful cozy touch, and he snuggled in and ate the pastry. Slick shards, flaking in his fingers, but the cappuccino didn't do its trick—now, sitting still after so much rushing forward, the warm drink had a narcotic effect.

He found a quiet patch of grass under a birch tree. He stretched out and dipped into strange dreams. Dim voices and traffic sounds drifted over him, like the gentle noise that might carry across the water if he were resting in the sun on the beach.

He woke up some time later, cold and disoriented. He could smell the stale stink of the plane on his clothes, the canned air he'd bathed in since Eugene. Then he remembered where he was.

I'm here, he was going to tell them. But really, how was he going to spin this impulsive trip? Louise would likely be angry at him—he'd abandoned her project and flown to Germany. He was crashing in on her return. But she'd left him no choice. Why couldn't he be spontaneous, too?

He heaved himself up from the ground. He'd been talking to himself, he realized, rehearsing his defense. On a bench only a few feet away, one he hadn't noticed when coming down for his nap, a man in a tracksuit had his arm around a woolly German shepherd, the dog up on the bench beside him, content. Maybe they just called them shepherds here.

He got back on the bike and looked for his family in groups of foreign women, scanning an open market, a street of galleries and unleafed trees. He even looked for Dieter—a man his wife had once loved, the father of Richard's daughter, a ghost who'd threaded through Richard's life. A pudgy guy, stooped and white-haired, was nibbling on a napkin-wrapped roll. After nearly twenty years, even that slob could be Dieter.

What a thrill to learn a new city with a bike, a camera, a map. For Richard, the beauty of urban design came in its challenges—structured properly, routine trips should flirt with the unknown. Even a simple commute or errand could become a meaningful journey, with the right balance of orientation and surprise. Of danger and confidence —the first time over a path was a choice, a hard and definite action. But as the path got trampled in, that sense of direction was lost.

Planners helped people orient themselves, though. They used signposts to indicate position and distance. Spatial nudges: a notch in the hedge, a line in the grass, a gradual thickening of trees. Richard and Louise had oriented each other. Years and years, a life together. They'd given each other that.

He looked at the map again and wound his way to Alexanderplatz; he wanted to see the communist facades. He'd read about this—a fight to tear down these old buildings, the argument instead to preserve. A relic of what once was, even if stark, even if brutal. A monument to another time even as the surrounding world shouted out, proclaimed it: *This is now.* Those buildings were ugly but they belonged there, and, looking at them, Richard had no question about where in the world he was. Better those ugly relics than some chain hotel.

He was exhausted. He'd been on the bike all day. But this was a pleasurable sensation, the weariness of body and mind—he hadn't slept, his legs ached, he'd earned his seat in Alexanderplatz, the straight lines shadowing his rest. He sat in the plaza; he put on his sunglasses and closed his eyes. He let himself float for a while.

He'd made the urban space his own, according to his particular whims and contexts, his jet-lagged state of mind. This was basic theory, too, but it resonated like he was a young student again. He opened his eyes and bought a falafel. He sipped from a cold bottle, let the *Hefeweizen* light his tired limbs. He was delirious, dreamy. *Sometimes you have to do things wrong to realize how you would do them right.* Louise had said that a long time ago. Now things were different; together they'd found the right way. He was going to tell her that, though he could see that she already knew.

It was the jacket she noticed first, all the way across the room by the untended bar. A windbreaker distinctly American, a bright announcement of weather and sport.

"I need more of myself in the monitor," Margot said. The slight dinge of the jacket's yellowy-green, the armpit tear sealed with clear tape.

"I'm sure it's loud out there," Joel said, pointing to the empty space in front of the stage.

"I need to hear it," Margot said. "If you're that loud, I won't be able to hear myself."

"Just think about the signal you're sending through," he said. "Keep it simple."

This made no sense—the man in the baseball hat squinting at her beside the stage was not a random German who looked like her father. It was her father. Proud, disheveled, embarrassed, zipped into his yellow coat. Maybe she was asleep. Maybe she was asleep and dreaming.

"I didn't miss it, right?" Now her father was in front of her. In an empty club in Berlin.

"What are you doing here?" She was seized with cold dread. "Is something wrong?"

"No, no, nothing's wrong. Berlin's a fascinating city." He noticed Joel listening at the edge of the stage and extended his hand for a shake. "This must be Joel. It's wonderful to meet you."

Joel shook his hand, bewildered. "You too. We've been having a great time."

Margot suggested to her father that he bring his suitcase to the room backstage. One of those very small ones that rolled, something her parents kept in the basement for their infrequent trips. But it was the middle of the semester.

"I'm meeting with someone at the university tomorrow," Richard said as they wheeled back there. "And I'm looking forward to your performance tonight."

"We're not playing until nine," Margot said. "It's only seven-thirty."

"I know I'm early. I just ran out of things to do," Richard said, punctuating himself with a barked laugh.

Margot was young and old, his child but taking care of him, too. "We have to pack our equipment," she said. "We'll be right back."

Richard went to the black vinyl couch. "I'll just close my eyes for a minute." He'd traveled halfway around the world.

Back on the stage, Margot unplugged her inputs. A strange web of incidents—since arriving in Berlin, she'd learned that her mother might not have married her father. She'd heard about her mother dancing half-naked with baby Elke. And now her breathless father had arrived.

A feminist gesture, Ute had said of Louise's pantless dancing—Ute was cool and funny and weird. Someone Margot would like to be friends with.

"Did you know your dad was coming?" Joel asked.

"You and I have been together for every moment for the past three weeks," Margot said. She wrapped her cable around her hand. "Do you think I knew he was coming?" Joel had been mad at her all day. Since last night, in fact. And Margot couldn't blame him—she'd acted like a fool. Of course it was stupid to flirt with Florian, some forty-year-old who was hitting on her sister. Margot wouldn't have done it if not for the copious amount of wine and beer she'd guzzled throughout the evening, trying to remove herself from the layers of awkward tension with her family members and her not-quite family members, trying to distance herself from Joel's overbearing enthusiasm.

But even if she'd been stone-cold sober, she still would have enjoyed feeling that power over Joel. If she was honest with herself, she'd liked it. She'd made Joel snap out of his musical mania and pay attention to her, not just her connections. Though she regretted her behavior, she knew why she'd done it.

"Your mom's here," Joel said.

Louise was back by the bar. "Elke's on her way, too," she said, cheerful as she crossed the floor. Margot climbed off the stage. She had to tell her mother that her father was here.

"Are you ready for your performance?" Louise asked as she reached Margot. "It'll be interesting to hear your music with just the two of you."

Margot nodded, but Louise was still talking, her face bright with expectation and concern. "You seemed a bit testy in the gallery today. I'm not sure why you made that comment about Dieter," she said in a low voice. "You know that I'm not here because of him. He and I got divorced a long time ago."

"I know that," Margot said. "But—"

"The thing is, it was complicated."

"I'm sorry I said that," Margot said.

"I made some choices that I regret now," Louise said. "But back then I had things to resolve with Dieter. I didn't handle it well."

"Mom," Margot said, trying to interrupt. But Louise was fired up, rolling on.

"You'll encounter things in your life," Louise said, "things that you want though they may not be right. Maybe you already have. So you have to find a balance. And it's certainly not easy. That time in Oregon was thirty years ago. It's probably hard for you to understand what a long stretch of time that is. I'm not that person anymore."

Margot interrupted her mother. "I was upset," she said. "I didn't really mean it."

"What was making you upset?"

"It doesn't matter. I have to tell you — Dad is here," Margot said.

"What do you mean?"

"I mean he's backstage right now."

"Your father is here?"

"I had no idea he was coming until he showed up ten minutes ago," Margot said.

"Why is he here?" Louise was frantically scanning the empty room.

"I'm not completely sure. He seems a little out of it."

Margot took her mother backstage. Her father looked battle-worn, rugged; he had his arms folded, asleep sitting up.

"Richie," Louise said. He opened his eyes. And though he'd just told Margot that everything was fine, nothing was wrong, her parents' moment of recognition was fraught with palpable tension. Time stretched out as they took each other in — her mother's surprised confusion, her father's stubborn pride.

"There's going to be dinner," Margot said. "Tilman should be here any minute." Her mother had just explained her past to Margot in a way that was honest and thoughtful, as though she trusted Margot to handle it. And Margot felt she could. Watching her parents move toward each other, Margot saw their years together — that vernacular of their gestures, their expressions, as they embraced beside the couch.

"I had a hard time getting here," said Richard. "I'm just catnapping."

"Why are you here?" Louise asked.

"For Margot's concert," Richard said. "For psychedelic drone."

"You didn't tell me you were coming."

Richard shook his head. "I didn't know I was coming."

You'll encounter things that you want though they may not be right, Louise had just told Margot. Like flirting with a middle-aged man to make your record-crazed semi-boyfriend jealous, Margot thought. It was uncanny, both uncomfortable and intriguing, the way her mother had echoed her own thoughts.

From the front came a steady thumping, the testing of the snare. Dieter must have arrived to check his own inputs.

"Where's Elke?" Margot asked Louise. Elke was probably mad at Margot too. Actually, Margot realized now that she'd been channeling Elke when she'd flirted with Florian, trying on Elke's brand of suave nonchalance. But it had backfired. Margot had been neither suave nor nonchalant.

"She's napping," Louise said. "She'll be here soon."

Tilman arrived, laden with bags. "OK, guys," he said. "Now we have some nice food."

"This is my husband, Richard," Louise told Tilman. "He just arrived."

"I wasn't expecting to meet the whole family," Tilman said. "Joel, maybe your mama is coming, too."

"That would be weird," Joel said.

This was already weird enough. Margot's father was sniffing around the food Tilman had brought — crackers and seeded bread and some sort of vegetable pate in a can. Cheese, a cucumber already sliced. A salad with homemade dressing in a jam jar. Quiche wrapped in foil. Margot was touched that Tilman had cooked for them — perhaps this was where he could actually play host. This club, this church of strange sounds, was his natural habitat. "Does anyone like a beer?" he called out.

The drumming stopped. Margot spread mushroom mush on crackers and doled them out, preparing for Dieter's awkward arrival. She had to buffer her dad. She felt responsible for him. Although Joel had set up the show with Dieter, without Margot, Joel wouldn't have found Dieter at all. None of them would be here in this moldy, beer-stained room if it weren't for her.

"Let's see where is Til," Dieter said as he came in.

Dieter and Richard. A long and surprised assessment. Handshakes and toothy, constructed grins.

"It's a nice surprise to see you here, Richard," Dieter said. He pushed a few crackers into his mouth.

"It's a nice surprise to be here. But I'm really enjoying myself so far. I've spent all day wandering the city."

Dieter nodded. "I'm sure it gave you a lot to think about."

"Definitely," Richard said. "Berlin's history of east–west division, and the way that planners have adapted to that is completely fascinating to me. And the city is compact and still feels spacious. You know, it's interesting that Germans don't jaywalk. It really contradicts the whole efficiency thing."

"I'm doing that now," Dieter said. "I learned to do that in New York."

"It's better that way. Everything functions better when people jaywalk."

"Surely," said Dieter. "But I think you can admit that we have a very fine logic in our city design here."

Richard was nodding, emphatic. Louise was loading her plate. "It's the little things," she said. "The warning to start shifting gears, just before the stoplight turns green. The bike lane on the sidewalk."

"Yes," Richard said, nearly ecstatic. "There's so much here we might emulate."

Margot recognized this mode of her father's—he was sliding in, gearing up for a confident strut through the corridors of urban design. He was comfortable. She wasn't sure why he was here, but here he was, telling them how to best organize public space.

"In planning we sometimes talk about design being melodic," Richard said. "All you musicians can relate. We talk about a harmony of elements. We talk about paths, how we can design paths to converge. We want that convergence to be melodic. And I really noticed that today, as I was biking around the city. A definite harmony."

"Perhaps atonal at times, but I think you're probably right," Dieter said.

"You were biking around Berlin today?" Margot asked.

Tilman took a long swallow of beer, spoke to Dieter. *"Der Dude sagt, wir müssen bis zwölf Uhr Schluss machen."*

"Schade, sehr früh," Dieter said, nodding. Margot had no idea what they were talking about, but that didn't matter. She wouldn't have to see too much of Dieter after this. She felt it then — she wanted to go home. Her clothes were dirty; she'd like to put on a different pair of shoes. Shoes that fit. She'd like to cook in her kitchen and read a book before bed. Her own bed, not someone else's floor.

It was almost time to go on. Margot was both nervous and bolstered. Her whole family was here. Even her father. She could not tell him at that moment what she was going to do with her life. Nor could she tell Joel, who was onstage already, absorbed in his chain of effects. She couldn't know how it would feel to be his girlfriend in a house in Portland, as opposed to this odd peripatetic romance they'd strung up. But she could join him onstage and attend to her pedals, wait as their sound traveled and built up.

After the house music went down, Margot got a few loops going, made texture with Joel. She cranked on the volume knob and stood up with the microphone. Her voice moved and transformed through the effects. She didn't sound like herself. That made her want to sing. She stepped back and forth, untangling the cord, tracing a path around her gear with the fragmented melody following behind.

———

Elke watched her sister onstage—Margot was on her feet, cutting a tight circle with her head craned over the gripped microphone. Her hair shrouded her face. Elke was proud of her sister's possession. An avant-garde diva, an alien chanteuse. The sound was enormous, and Elke had no idea what Margot was doing, and that made her even prouder. Joel was crouched, undulating—a slow humping of the amp.

Louise was next to Elke, practically miming the motions for Margot. Elke's father flanked her on the other side. And Richard was here now too, smiling, watching intently beside Louise. That, she knew, would only add to Dieter's anxiety about performing. But why was Richard here? *I wanted to hear the music,* Richard said to Elke when she'd arrived backstage. She'd hugged him, to check if he was three-dimensional, to cement the fact that he was actually there. He was musty and rumpled and a little unglued. But Elke wasn't hallucinating. Richard was in Berlin.

Elke had repeated this question to her mother— *Why such an insane trip?*—while they were waiting for Margot's set to begin. "Did you know Richard was coming?" Elke asked.

Louise snorted. "I'm as surprised as you are," she said, both agitated and amused.

Elke couldn't help but feel somewhat responsible and also a bit annoyed. It was as though she'd summoned Richard, by calling him from Bad Waldheim and talking to him about Louise. But Elke had wanted him to take care of her mother's project, not drop everything and rush to Berlin.

Elke kept scanning the room for Florian, to see if he was looking for her. She'd told him about the show. When she left his place that morning, he'd offered breakfast, said he wanted to see more of her. But no, she was late; she hadn't intended to fall asleep there, had thought she would take a taxi back to the apartment last night or very early in the morning, in fact. And she ran out before they could pin down a solid plan. But she'd told him about the show, and he'd made it sound like he was going to come.

Elke had liked being in Florian's apartment — the familiar German qualities, those memories of childhood lit up by revisiting. The traces of her family: the half-size refrigerator, the bottles of *Sprudel.* In Florian's bathroom, she was alone with the square window that folded open to a courtyard of birch trees. She noted the compact washing machine and drying rack, the nearly corrugated toilet paper, so sensible, pragmatic, never veering over to pleasure.

And yet that was what she'd experienced — Florian had surprised her with his assurance. But there was something so earnest that came with it, something so fundamentally German, that she couldn't get past. She was leaving in two more days, but he'd been interested in her. "Here is the number of my Handy," he'd said that morning. "If you want to send me SMS."

Maybe she shouldn't have left so quickly. But she'd had to — they'd be worrying about her, she'd told him that. He was a Taurus. Loyal to a fault. Dedicated to cultivating a comfortable home. She would have thought he'd understand her commitment to her family. She expected him to get in touch with her — he had her number, too. She wasn't going to SMS his Handy again. She'd already texted him a couple of hours ago. *Hallo.*

Now as she watched her sister's mysterious incantations, Elke — still a little bit hung-over, nursing that crispiness with a beer — let herself ride on the music. She wandered in her thoughts. Babies, bilingual ones. They could choose where to live, she and Florian. Maybe she'd finally learn to speak German. They could live in the States, or maybe here. German babies with American names. Or vice versa. Children who'd have a life like her own.

Margot's set was ending. The room got quiet, a stretched few seconds, and then applause broke the spell. People started talking, and German rap music blasted through the speakers. There was Ute with

Louise, shaking hands with Richard, introducing him to Gerd. Gerd was an architect, Louise was saying to Richard, launching the two men into ecstatic exchange.

Elke met Margot at the edge of the stage. "I really liked it," she said. "Even more than the show in Hasselt. This time I could see what you were doing."

"Now you can watch the Europeans ask me all their hard questions," Margot said. "*How does the music make you feel,* or *I liked this one little part but not the rest of it.* American audiences just push past you on their way to the bar."

Her sister was now an expert in this bizarre subculture. And it was cute but also striking—Margot had grown up. She was doing her thing.

"OK," Elke said. "Let me try. Why does this music speak to your soul?"

Margot shrugged, impish. "It just sounds good."

Elke's father was setting up onstage. Standing with more hunch than usual, curving his spine, shielding something. She'd heard Dieter make this private music but had never watched him perform it, and it was almost painful for her, to see the way his body and face anticipated it now.

"Is that guy from last night coming?" Margot asked. Her expression was nervous, seeking. *Just forget it,* Elke wanted to tell Margot. Really it was Joel who deserved Margot's apology. But that wasn't for Elke to say. Margot was smart enough to stumble around on her own. And maybe Margot was forcing a needed rupture with Joel, in a messy, human way.

"I don't know if he's coming," Elke said. It was after ten. What had she expected? That she'd fall in love with a German? She was going back to New York in two days. Germany was a place to visit, to make light conversation with complicated grammar, but it wasn't her home.

Now Richard and Louise were joining them. "That reminded me of some pretty far-out stuff I used to see in Berkeley," Richard said.

"I'll take that as a compliment," said Margot.

Richard laughed, tipped his head back. His hat, a plain one without logo or affiliation, gave him a certain authority. Like a coach, an official setting the score.

"Your father's highest compliment," Louise said, glancing at Richard with a wry smile. They stayed in their little cluster as the house music went down. Onstage, Elke's father sat at the drum set, his arms rippling and loose. She would never have interrupted him while he was playing in his basement in Brooklyn, but this was a public performance. *Pay attention to the pulses,* Joel had said. But here was something Elke claimed that Joel couldn't: she was merely seeing now what she'd always heard traveling through her father's house. The pride, the comfort, the ease that Dieter had in his little studio in the basement. He'd played so Elke could hear him.

Tilman was watching with his girlfriend, a haggard beauty in a leather coat. Cousin Tilman of the striped underwear, of the house in Bad Waldheim lined with animal heads. These were her people. Her heritage was not the same thing as her current life, and even so, even without her grandmother, she had reasons to keep coming back. She had her father, and she watched him smiling, grimacing, as the drumstick trembled. Now he pulled a violin bow against the cymbal, his freewheeling enjoyment in time with an unaired beat.

The sound system was huge—this was a place for kids to blast themselves into oblivion, not for expressions of the avant-garde. Every single gesture—a scrape on the cymbal, a brush of the snare—reverberated over the stone floor. Dieter's first takes had been tentative, too bright and aware. But he listened, settled in. Time passed, and he was the one who was measuring it.

He appreciated the applause when he stopped. He was sweating; his arms buzzed. He went to the microphone in its stand at the edge of the stage. He spoke in German and then in English. "It's special for me to perform in Berlin, which I haven't done since 1974. It was a much harder trip to make back then. So I'd like to dedicate this performance to my daughter, Elke, who I'm glad is here in the audience."

Now he let himself look at the crowd. At Elke with her proud expectation. Gerd waiting at the edge, ready for his cue. Margot and the inquisitive Joel. And then Richard, the long-traveling Richard, suddenly emerging from the deep tunnel of the past. Richard wore a cap and a bright jacket, like an eager child in the garden, chasing after his toy. Typical American, drawing attention to himself. But that was Richard, with Louise beside him. And if she found it a bit strange for a grown man to wear a cap to a concert, that was for her to decide. Louise was shoring up the row. They were all in a line, bracing for impact, waiting to see what Dieter would say.

"There are others here in the audience who I'd like to acknowledge. This music means something to me that is difficult to express." Dieter spoke in German first, then translated himself. He wanted to be sure that everyone understood. He found a rhythm in those pauses, a gentle back-and-forth. A conversation with himself.

He hadn't expected to say anything, but now he couldn't stop talking. "It's a funny thing, with music. We use it in all our ceremonies. So maybe this is a ceremony. A ritual for the international audience of Berlin. My mother was born in Schwabenland in 1912. Her life made nearly a century. My father's life was much shorter. But the most meaningful thing is to have children. They can step beyond your own life." His words unrolled like a carpet. "Children and music, they are things we tend like a garden. They measure the passage of time."

He wasn't making sense anymore; the light was blinding his eyes.

"Now it's time to invite my dear friend Gerd Schlagenhauf to the stage."

Gerd bounded up in high-top sneakers; he plugged in his guitar and struck a low note that cut into Dieter immediately. Gerd favored open tunings, and there was something mournful and haunting in the minor key. Dieter reached to underline him, to fill the space around him. That much hadn't changed: Gerd's articulation, all those records they'd listened to together, the hours of playing so that their conversation became intrinsic. It was lodged in Dieter's body, a resinous response he could still tap.

He glanced out at the floor. Richard was right in front of the stage, moving his body, turning his head. He stepped in front of Louise at the edge of the crowd, responding with his limbs. That was fine. Dieter continued to play.

Richard was dancing. Louise watched him, unsure where on the spectrum of irony and genuine expression he fell. No one else was dancing —the music had picked up, Gerd and Dieter were coming down hard, together, and yet the most anyone else in the audience offered was a subtle nod. Richard was moving freely, his arms and shoulders loose.

Louise stepped back, wanting to absorb herself into the crowd. There was something a little annoying about the exaggerated way he was taking up space. *Look at me.* But there was also something striking about his assurance.

A prismatic memory—Richard moving through Schubert Park in the late '70s, tracing a path. She was there and here, watching her husband—*look at the way people choose to move,* he'd said to her once. He was older now, his beard long gone. His hair was gray but still tousled; he had the same energy in his face. The progression had happened subtly, but added up to a huge range. Somehow this man flailing his body was the person she'd been with for thirty years. She felt the span of their marriage, its wide spectrum of humor and exasperation and love.

A prismatic memory, a simultaneous then and now: Richard was unhinged, like the stubbly man pacing the aisles during Elke's baptism in Cottage Grove. And there was Elke next to her, an adult, the one to lead Louise back. The audience pushed together, listening. A ceremony, Dieter had just said.

Ute tapped Louise on the shoulder, swung her head in emphatic time. Dieter was weird and witchy on the drums. He was like a bad cat, his sardonic gaze fixed on Gerd; he moved his arm as though performing a hex. He pulled it back, turning the drumstick over in his hand, behind him, bringing it forward again. Dieter's style had developed into this showy incantation, with more awareness, more spectacle. Still, though, there was some magic in watching him play.

"This next one will be our last number," Dieter said. "It's a nice time to be here, but it's also time to say goodbye." He'd become a performer, a charismatic, joking old man. "I want to thank you all for coming. It would have been strange without you.

"*Ohne euch wäre das seltsam gewesen,*" Dieter continued. Louise didn't catch the meaning—she was watching Elke and Ute, watching Margot whisper to Joel. Louise wished she could play it back, trace out Dieter's words and decipher their meaning. But he was already skimming the cymbals. He wasn't going to say anything else.

Later that night, in bed in the swapped apartment, Louise asked Richard about his dancing.

"I just felt something," Richard said. "That music is powerful."

"Look at how people choose to move," said Louise. She asked him, again, why he'd come.

"I wanted to be here," he said. "You needed a notch in the hedge."

"What are you talking about?"

"You needed a signpost," he said. "A marker in the landscape. Something to orient you."

He was exhausted, probably delirious. He wasn't quite making sense. And yet Louise thought she knew what he was saying—he didn't want her to get lost.

"You could have just come with me," she said. "If you felt that strongly about the notch in the hedge." She felt the rhythm of his breath, his body steady next to hers.

"I didn't realize I wanted to come with you at first. You gave me a signpost, too."

With the blinds pulled down, the room still wasn't completely dark. "You didn't take my picture," she said. "You let the project go."

He didn't say anything; he was silent, and passing between them was their full awareness of what he'd done, of where, together, they'd been.

"I was mad about it," she said. "I'm still mad about it. But it's time to end the project. Maybe you ended it already. I'm not sure. I have to think about it some more."

"You can still take the picture, you know."

She shook her head. "I've been thinking we should sell the house, find a new place. It would be good for both of us. It's exciting to imagine trying something else."

"You know I'll help you," Richard said. "If you want to do something with the remaining pieces."

"I would have liked to decide how to end it myself."

"I know," Richard said. "I made a mistake. I'm sorry. I'm telling you that."

"Sell the pieces off at auction," Louise said. "Mount an exhibition. I'm not just dumping them in the trash."

Or let them all disintegrate, let the grass grow back. She was already imagining how it might look. A decommissioning, an implosion—her mind was lighting up. New layers might be revealed under the still-intact pieces. New yellows and greens and browns. Richard had opened those possibilities.

It was early when she woke the next morning. Richard stirred but didn't open his eyes. She stayed in bed next to him for a while, in the unfamiliar space of a stranger's home.

In the kitchen, Elke and Dieter were drinking coffee. Still dim, with winter on its way, but the first light was coming in. Back in Oregon, it would be daylight saving time soon. She'd gain an hour—a nice feeling, to have time waiting at home.

The election was in a couple more weeks, too. Her anticipation was a held-breath mix of excitement and nerves. She needed to be home for that. Obama was going to win, Elke had told Norbert, and Louise wanted to believe her.

"Richard has his meeting with the urban studies guy this morning," Louise said. "And then he's got a whole list of things he wants to see."

"We might as well do some sightseeing," Elke said. "We're leaving tomorrow."

"You can always make another trip," Dieter said. "Tilman will welcome you."

Elke laughed. "Arlette will welcome me. She'll welcome you, too."

Margot and Joel and Richard trickled into the kitchen. The confusion of the night before had dissipated into this, all of them together in the room. It made sense to leave the crowded kitchen; for a little bit longer, they could move together as a group.

Richard went off to his appointment; they arranged to meet in a few hours, to look at monuments and memorials, to see how this city handled its history, how memory had been assigned a physical place.

In the afternoon they convened above the U-Bahn station in Mitte. Louise asked Richard about his meeting. Yes, he told her, they'd talked about a lot of things, and maybe there was something there for an article, a potential collaboration. "It was worth it," he said.

Together they all walked to the Holocaust Memorial — the Memorial to the Murdered Jews of Europe.

"The phrasing is interesting," Dieter said. "Who murdered them? It's not indicated."

"And yet I'd say the Germans have done more than other countries to examine their history," Richard said. "That's certainly something to consider. Look at the Turks and the Armenian genocide. Complete silence."

"And look at the way Germans feel about the Turks living in Berlin," Elke said. Her proximity to Dieter brought out her resemblance to him: the bones of her face, haunted and wise.

"Not all Germans feel that way," Dieter said.

The memorial was set in an open space between buildings, concrete plinths set in rows. The group spread apart. Louise was alone. The path between the slabs drifted up and down, so that she caught sight of other people and then lost them, her body like a boat on the tide. But her solitude, her contemplation was broken; she heard laughter, the sound of running, and not children's footsteps, either. At one juncture, the sun lit up the smell of piss.

As she emerged on the other side, she saw people smiling and posing for pictures, or laying across the slabs, eating sandwiches and looking at their phones. So many photos. So many people holding something up—a camera, a phone—to put those objects between themselves and the actual thing, the experience, the encounter.

She found her family again. "Isn't this supposed to be a somber place?" Beside them, a man had his hand in his companion's back pocket, his mouth ranging over her neck.

"It's a memorial," Richard said, "but it's part of the city, too."

"It's another way of not looking," Dieter said. "Averting the gaze."

Elke was squinting. "I think it's more complicated than that."

"I read a fascinating article about the architect," Richard said. "He intended for life to happen in and around the memorial. It's a part of this public space."

"You can't force people to observe things in a certain way," Margot said. Margot with Richard's root beer eyes, that calm intelligence.

"No," Louise said. "But you can hope they'd be respectful."

"Is there an element of respect in life continuing?" Richard asked. "That's what the architect would probably ask."

"But it's so easy for us to do everyday things here," Joel said. "We weren't there."

"A memorial always begs the question: Who is this for?" Richard said.

Elke looked at him, looked at Louise. "It's important that it's here."

"From a design perspective, it's pretty interesting," Richard said. "You can trace how people choose to move through this space. And in terms of paths, the way they rise and fall also clues us in to the psychol-

ogy of way-finding. When you can't see everything laid out in front of
you, there's some mystery, and that's very satisfying from a pedestrian
perspective—"

"OK, Dad," Margot said. "We get it."

They found the city bus and took it to the edge of a vast park. The
next stop was the Soviet War Memorial, constructed after the end of
World War II, Richard said.

In the park, Louise noted again the graffiti—here the marks were
set in fields of green, against leaves, against branches. A mark on every
single piece of the built environment—a trash can, a road sign, some
mysterious municipal hut. She could understand that impulse to document your presence. She wondered what she would have made of
this when she was a young student, what she might have painted after
walking through this park.

A man in leather was drinking peacefully on a bench. A quiet place
to let go, lush green absorbing his vice. They walked in a loose clump,
not talking, spread out. The path led through a brief forest, and coming
out of the trees was a surprise—a line of shaggy willows and a granite
statue in a tiled expanse. The trees demarcated a vast open space: Louise moved into a stone plaza framed by rows of marble slabs.

It seemed as though the whole city had collaborated to get her to this
unexpected place in the trees. To have all of them—her family, then
and now—with her there. Their visit was a monument but not a static
one. Rather a spreading out, a moving through. A ceremony: Louise
was touching this place in preparation for leaving it behind.

Her *18th* project had been its own kind of memorial, a forced reckoning with time. The project had served as a calendar, a clock, a measuring tool. There was a certain grief that went along with that kind of
assessment—marking the anniversary of a thing, marking its span, its
breadth—even as it was joyful or profound. This was how long it was,
how big, how wide.

Ahead of her, Richard was tracking along the walkway, which was
laid out in irregular shapes. Margot and Elke were murmuring plans for

the evening—a restaurant by the canal, a bar at the top of the mall in Neukölln that had panoramic views. Their voices carried and blurred in the wide, quiet space. They wanted that local beer, her children were saying. The one with a baby stuffed in a stein on the label. She listened to them laugh.

Clouds moved beyond the monument's stark angles, a slow white drift against blue. Louise stood still and watched her family—Margot was crossing the lawn now, heading to the stand of trees at the edge of the plaza. After a moment, Elke followed her there. Louise could see her daughters in the distance, past the granite and worn marble, under the lid of the sky. The girls wandered together, circled a broad willow. They looked back to see where she was. Louise followed the stone trail, one square and another set down. And then over the grass until she was with them again, her steps tracing a line through the expanse.

ACKNOWLEDGMENTS

My heartfelt thanks to:

My brilliant agent, Marya Spence, and my smart, perceptive editor, Naomi Gibbs; I'm so grateful for their dedication and their thoughtful work on this book. Thanks to Clare Mao at Janklow & Nesbit, and Lisa Glover, Erin DeWitt, and everyone at Houghton Mifflin Harcourt.

My wonderful professors in the MFA program at Brooklyn College: Josh Henkin, Julie Orringer, Amy Hempel, Meera Nair, and Ellen Tremper. And for the early encouragement and guidance, my undergraduate professors at Sarah Lawrence College: Paul Lisicky, Martha Sandlin, Myra Goldberg, and Brooke Stevens.

My MFA classmates, for the fellowship and inspiration. I'm thankful for the friendship of Michelle Radtke and Jonas Moody—fantastic writers, insightful readers—who helped me shape this story from the very beginning.

Judson Merrill, genius reader and excellent host of the Drafts on the Beach residency in Georgetown, Maine, for his sustaining writerly friendship. Linda and Bill Deetjen, for sharing their beautiful home.

Lauren Belski, Eliza Hornig, Bonnie Harris, Carl Schlachte, and Zachary Solomon, for reading drafts and offering astute feedback.

Anne Bard, Anthony Campuzano, Tommy DeNys, Audrey Fisher, Laura Fix, Janet Moser, Christine & Dietland Müller-Schwarze, and Michael Slaboch, for answering my questions and talking about ideas.

Jarvis Taveniere, James Toth, Jessica Bowen, and G. Lucas Crane, road dogs and constant poets.

Professor Daniel Wojcik of the University of Oregon, for discussing his knowledge of Eugene and his research on Steve Prefontaine.

Brigitte Blockhaus and the staff of the library and archives at the Kunstakademie Düsseldorf, for research assistance.

The following authors and books, which helped me imagine the world of this novel: Lucy Lippard's *From the Center: Feminist Essays on Women's Art*, Kevin Lynch's *The Image of the City*, and David Stubbs's *Future Days: Krautrock and the Building of Modern Germany.*

The MacDowell Colony, Marble House Project, the Saltonstall Foundation for the Arts, and the Vermont Studio Center, for the generous support and the time and space to work. My conversations with the writers and artists I met at these residencies were invaluable to my writing of this book.

The Funk family in Germany, in particular Leberecht and Maritta Funk, for their generous and generation-spanning friendship.

My family, with special thanks to my brother Carl Diehl, whose curiosity and imagination have given me a lifelong model of what it means to be an artist; my sister-in-law Rosy Boyer and her family in Oregon, who shared their stories; my aunt, Sigrid Meinel, for her interest and encouragement. My mother's connection to Germany, not to mention her boundless love and enthusiasm, made it possible for me to write this book. And though I wish that my father were here to read it, I'm grateful for his influence, which is on every page.

And Steve Gunn, my favorite musician, whose ways of seeing and hearing the world continually inspire my own.